# After The End

## G J Stevens

British Library Cataloguing-in-Publication Data
A catalogue record for this book is available from the British Library

Cover Illustration Copyright © 2020 by James Norbury  Cover design by James Norbury
www.JamesNorbury.com

ISBN: 9798698268024

Other Books by GJ Stevens

## IN THE END Series

IN THE END
BEFORE THE END


## Agent Carrie Harris Series

OPERATION DAWN WOLF
LESSON LEARNED


## James Fisher Series

FATE'S AMBITION

# DEDICATION

For Jayne. You make me.

For Sarah. My inspiration.

# ACKNOWLEDGMENTS

To my friends who inspire me every day and sometimes let me work on my passion, despite being on holiday!

To Laura Laakso, talented author and hard-nosed beta reader without whom this novel would be terrible!

Thanks to all those who helped me along the way, be it big or small, I am grateful.

# 1

## LOGAN

On the flat roof of the hospital, Cassie and I stood, mouths agape, both of us staring at the woman in the bright red trouser suit. We watched the elegant reporter turn away with a microphone still in hand as she followed her companion, moving from the camera pointed in our direction and stepping to the white van they stood beside.

With the ever-present stench catching in my throat, Cassie sagged, leaning heavy at my side. I shuffled her higher, my gaze moving beyond the corpses littering the hospital's road, beyond the remains of the boundary fence and to the sea of dead making their dogged way in our direction.

We were back to square one, fighting every moment for our lives, but despite her weakness, Cassie's grip tightened around my waist, reminding me I wasn't alone. She'd survived the worst.

Her grip loosened and I felt her sag. With such little strength remaining, I had to find somewhere safe for the medicine to take its full effect. With a smile rising, I reminded myself she'd come back from a death sentence.

It must have been the cure. There was hope for us all.

Standing on the edge of the roof, Shadow barked, my gaze fixing on the bald patch with stitches in a pink line across his stomach. Snarling, with his lips curled, the dog stared out to the woman in red.

"Hello," I called, waving my hand high in the air, shouting again as the first echo died.

The figures turned toward my voice.

Raising my arm higher still, I waved until a shrill call stilled my movement and sent me surveying the horizon.

The familiar piercing scream replied to its echo. Panic

gripped my chest. I knew no cure could bring anyone back from being torn to shreds. We had to get away from here.

As its own reply faded, I drew a deep breath, reasoning the call to be some way off and it would take them a while to cover the ground despite their unnatural speed we'd witnessed first-hand.

Fear spiked again, turning my view skyward to a heavy noise vibrating the air and a sound I'd known so well from standing in a crowd waiting in anticipation for the air show to start.

But today this could mean only one thing.

A grey jet roared into view above us, low enough that I saw the red tips of rockets slung under its wings. Tracing its journey to the right, I caught exhaust heat, real or imagined, on my face with its fierce anger rattling my chest. Turning away from the trail, I saw two dots looming high in the otherwise clear blue sky, under no doubt they too were zeroing in on our position.

About to raise the alarm for the approaching aircraft, glancing down I saw the reporter and her crewmate already in the moving van with the passenger's heads craned, peering up high through the windscreen.

I raised Cassie up despite her discomfort and guided her along the roof whilst shuffling under her weight, looking between the stairwell and the dots in the sky.

I barged open the door with my shoulder, the breath rushed from my chest as an explosion erupted somewhere close, heat blasting across my face as I grabbed at the doorframe. At the edge of my vision a fireball erupted, sending cars alarming a moment before their electronics were consumed by the chemical inferno.

Shadow moved past me and down the stairs with his claws tapping on the concrete. The building shook as another explosion hit, the pressure wave reverberating deep within my chest.

Daylight shrank away with every step. We were soon down one level, with Cassie's feet barely touching the ground as the building jolted to the right and a vast section of the concrete stairs shifted. I struggled further, heading to the ground floor and the place we thought yesterday had been our last stand.

Despite the ground shaking around us, I forced myself not to think of how it would have turned out if Lane hadn't gone off on his own. The children wouldn't be safely away in the helicopter, heading for where they could wake without fear and know where their next meal would come from.

The stale stench of death clung to the dry dust as it rained down, greeting our arrival at the sandbags staggered from the door leading to the hospital's main corridor.

Looking up, I watched as a great crack split the ceiling, sending a renewed shower of plaster and rubble over us.

Fighting against the movement of the building, I tried to visualise which route to take past the door and through the darkness on the other side. Which route would take us the furthest away from the bombs, but not into the arms of the creatures rushing to encircle us? I'd travelled both ways before, each time with Cassie by my side, but the journeys seemed so long ago now.

"Where now?" Cassie asked, her voice dry and forced.

"Left. I think," making my mind up to head the way we'd arrived yesterday in hope the crowds had yet to arrive that side of the building. We would retrace the journey we'd taken to seek out Doctor Lytham and what we had hoped would be the end to the nightmare.

With the structure vibrating as rubble fell all around, I leaned Cassie against the wall and opened the door, pushing as the wood scraped along its jamb.

"Wait there," I said, keeping my voice low and craning my neck. Peering both ways in search of Shadow, the darkness gave no clue as to which way he'd gone, even if he could have opened the door and closed it behind him.

In desperation, I turned around, and despite the dust raining down to sparkle in the last of the light, I saw a door to the left of the stairs. My feet fixed with fear, knowing that any decision risked leaving Shadow alone.

"Here boy," I called out, but another thud rocked the building. Instinct dropped us to the ground, sending my arms cradling around Cassie as I bent to shield her from the heat surging down the stairwell.

The building complained, deep groans vibrating as concrete scraped; at that moment I couldn't imagine any future other than the structure tumbling down around us.

A high bark cut through my thoughts and I looked up, peering around until I saw the glint of Shadow's eyes low from the door ajar to the left of the staircase. A great creak of metal came from above with dust falling as the building gave a shrug. With the concrete ceiling sagging, I spread myself wide over Cassie's body, tensing for the inevitable.

When after two breaths the ceiling hadn't fallen, I knew our only chance would be to follow Shadow through the door into the unknown.

Rising with my feet slipping on the rubble, Cassie's legs wheeled in slow motion as I dragged her under the armpits.

"I can walk," she said, and although she took her own weight, I felt her falling as I loosened my hold around her.

With my arm back around her shoulders, I pushed at the door but it held firm, sticking open just enough for Shadow to have fit through. I shoved with my shoulder, but it still wouldn't release its hold against the frame.

Time ran out when an explosion shook the building under our feet, sending large chunks of concrete bouncing down the steps.

With a heavy pressure at my back, I lost my grip on Cassie and collapsed into the darkness.

# 2

Blinking through the haze, my focus flashed to my empty arms and the incessant pounding in my head. Shadow's bark forced me to sit, pushing up with my palms against the sharp debris. Coughing through the dry dust, I stared at his eyes at the gap in the doorway.

The jagged remains moved to my side and with a painful twist, I caught Cassie's outline spread across the rubble. An overwhelming urge gripped my stomach and I fought the uneven ground, pushing away lumps of crumbled concrete as I clambered to get my footing, knowing this would be our last moment together if I didn't fight against my aching bones and help her to safety.

The building shuddered a reminder I had no time to think as concrete crashed down the steps, falling from the ceiling and scattering as it landed.

Remembering the jammed door, I turned, cursing the speed of my movement and locking eyes with Shadow panting from the gap. It was then I saw the twisted door frame had moved when the structure around us distorted.

The building creaked as if readying for collapse.

Pulling Cassie to her feet, I pushed away any thought of what her dead weight could mean and shoved against the door with our combined weight, closing my eyes against the dry heat.

It gave way with a crack, closing up then pushing what remained of the wooden jamb either side and falling open in a direction never intended. Our momentum carried us forward, our gratitude short-lived as after a few short paces my feet were unable to find the floor.

With nothing I could do to stop our tumble down the steps, I did my best to tuck Cassie's head against my breastbone, folding around her whilst stumbling to get purchase on any step as rubble raced down the staircase at our backs.

Landing on my side, a surge of pressure smashed at my shoulder; rubble jabbed into my arm as the chaotic fall ended in a splash of icy water, sharp stones showering down and peppering my back.

Tremors rose through the hard floor, pushing me to ignore the pain and shove aside the growing despair for our new situation.

Relaxing my grip from around Cassie, I slid to my back, feeling a warmth against my hand as a grip tugged at my sleeve, a pull urging me along in the pitch black. I reached out to swat away in panic, but when I touched at the fur of Shadow's snout, my fear eased.

Gently pulling my arm from under Cassie, I rose with care, gritting my teeth against the ache as my hand went out into the darkness, searching our surroundings.

Finding nothing but space at my fingertips, I bent down, feeling at my feet. With my hand touching her warm skin, my muscles complained as I edged further and took Cassie by the arm. The rubble continued to fall as the building above complained and with no time to check her condition, I heaved her to her feet, delighted when she held her weight.

"Are you hurt?" I asked, leaning in close and listening to her breath until she spoke.

"I'm okay. I think."

With my arm around her shoulder, together we took tentative steps through the shallow water, heading slowly deeper into the darkness with the ever-present fear the building could crumble down at any moment.

A great rumble radiated up through our feet, sounding as if chunks of concrete fell through the storeys above. The heavy bass of an explosion lit every nerve as if it had gone off directly above and sent us stumbling forward with the pressure wave.

When the ceiling hadn't fallen within a few speeding breaths, I stared into the pitch black, blinking at the hot, heavy dust. Cassie coughed at my side.

Racked with indecision what to do next, I kept my feet

planted, listening to the ringing in my ears and the low vibration of the building, hoping it would settle in its new position and not trap us underground.

A caustic stench stung my nostrils, and along with a thick taste of burnt flesh, the pervasive odour of sewerage made the damp, dusty air seem solid with each breath.

Water dripped from above our heads, its frequency at the right pitch to cut through the feeling of cotton wool stuffed in my ears and the high, piercing tone inside my head.

The ringing subsided, and I heard an unfamiliar noise, soon realising it was Shadow's bark calling me from the darkness.

"It's okay boy," I said, but I barely heard my soft words, feeling a layer of grit coating my mouth, made worse as I wiped my lips on my sleeve.

The surrounding vibrations had slowed; about to reach low to make sure Shadow stayed close, Cassie's panting made me stop. Pulling my arms from under her shoulder, I clamped my hands around her upper arms in fear she might fall at any point.

"Are you okay?" I asked, my voice alien and barely heard despite the volume I'd attempted.

"Yes," she whispered. "What is this place?"

I looked around, searching in vain for any light to break the darkness.

"I don't know. A basement maybe," I said, leaning forward whilst taking care not to let go of her.

"It smells like a sewer."

Water splashed from what I hoped were Shadow's paws as he stopped barking.

I found Cassie's left hand with my right and she gripped as I clasped. Pushing out my other hand, I touched at a rough, damp wall, feeling the lines of mortar between each course of bricks.

With my hand at the wall and with Shadow's footsteps still echoing in the water ahead, I took comfort in the guide at my fingertips until my left knee cracked against something solid.

Pulling up with the pain, Cassie tensed, Shadow's footsteps stopping as I shook with the intensity whilst trying to stifle a scream.

"What's wrong?" Cassie asked, but I couldn't speak.

After a few moments the pain receded, leaving me to concentrate on my breath. Feeling cautiously at my knee, I sought what I'd hit and found a cool metal bracket rising from the ground. Its surface felt like a treat to touch, a momentary relief from the heat building around us.

"Smashed… my knee… against something," I said, releasing a held breath.

"What is it?" Cassie asked, her voice still dry and pained, but rather than relaxing, I nodded in the darkness and extended my touch to feel the rounded material at ankle height.

"It's a pipe. A big one," I said, standing up straight and stretching out my leg as I realised where we could be. "I think we're in a duct. I can feel a pipe. Heating, maybe."

"Is that good?" she said after a moment.

"This tunnel probably runs between the buildings. Maybe to a boiler house and somewhere we can get out. If only we could see where it leads."

I stepped forward, using my sleeve to wipe the sweat from my forehead, and along with the sound of my steps, I heard Shadow's gentle padding in the water. The structure of the tunnel seemed to creak as I edged us away from the side, leading the way with tentative steps as my free hand swept out in front.

A chorus of great thunder clattered above our heads, freezing us where we stood. The last of the buildings falling, I thought, visualising the desolate scene until light flashed ahead with what sounded like a door slamming shut soon after.

With the momentary break in the darkness hurting my eyes, I tried to linger on the image now only in my mind.

I'd seen Shadow peer forward with his head low and pipes running along both sides of the brick tunnel whose damp, stained bricks curved over our heads.

The light seemed to have come from a bend to the right a little way off, but disappeared before I could take in any more detail.

A heavy thud echoed from along the tunnel, followed by the high noise of breaking glass. For a moment I thought I heard voices cursing in the air, but immediately questioned the sound.

"Hello," I called, and its echo came back dull to my ears as if a muffled grumble had run across my parched throat.

I held back from running, from dragging Cassie at my side, not wanting to speed and dash the hope of other survivors. Putting a tentative foot forward whilst still gripping Cassie's hand, I listened to the echo of my steps.

The voices had quietened.

"Hello," I called again. With no reply, I questioned why they weren't calling back, whilst still overjoyed someone else had survived.

"Sssh," came the distinct sound from the other end of the tunnel.

If there had been light, Cassie would have seen the delight in my face when the noise told me I'd been right, then my expression dropped as I thought of what else might make a similar sound.

Maybe those ahead were not as alive as I hoped them to be.

Despite the fear of being shut in with the foul creatures, I took hope that if something could get in, there must be a way of getting out.

Shadow barked, his call rattling through me like a blast of wind. Stumbling forward with Cassie still in hand, I tried to reach out to the darkness to settle him before he frightened anyone away or drew something else towards us.

I found the warmth of his back, feeling the vibration of his call through my touch. As he twisted around, he calmed.

I listened to the continual drip coming from behind, along with the grumble of rubble settling somewhere along the corridor. There were no footsteps. No slow plod of feet other than ours.

As each moment passed, my hearing seemed to sharpen. With each moment gone I could sense the clarity in Shadow's low rumbling growl.

"It's Shadow," I said, squeezing Cassie's hand, trying to reassure us both, but her trembling didn't slow as we stepped forward.

I swept my hand out in front in anticipation of the wall ahead and the right turn I'd seen in the flash of light.

A flurry of footsteps echoed down the corridor. A confusion of feet scraped against the concrete floor and the sound of something brushing against the littered rubble.

I stopped and gripped Cassie's hand tight, but the noise receded again.

Leaning forward and reaching out, I felt the cold, damp brickwork just ahead and followed its coarse surface as we turned. I stopped again, holding my breath at the sound of hushed voices so clear.

Feet landed heavily to the floor, their breath no longer held back.

About to speed forward, my foot bumped against something soft, Shadow letting out a whimper as I touched at his stitched wound. Pulling away as I realised, his growl turned to a bark as voices called out.

Light burst ahead to silhouette a figure floating in the centre of my vision. Its arms swept around in circles and I couldn't do anything but stagger back as a gunshot electrified the air.

# 3

## JESSICA

I couldn't help but stare as the couple peered down from the roof, my gaze lingering on the woman with her shoulders stooped, leaning against the guy holding her up.

Was she another not long for this world? Another victim of Toni and her mother?

The guy waved, his face full of optimism as he stood tall with his arm tight around her.

How could he not know what he faced? How could he not know the end of the world had come?

My focus switched to the sound at our backs and the crowd still following in our tracks; the crowd we'd led to these people who, by the destruction all around, had already been through so much and probably more if Toni and her mother were involved.

What next for these people on the roof? Heartache and pain were inevitable.

I turned to Alex, still at my side, her gaze intent on the pair.

What next for us? The same fate, no doubt.

Alex looked to me with a rising smile.

Who smiles at the end of the world? These two, apparently.

A warm glow rose inside me and I turned back to the roof where the guy continued to wave.

I tried to put myself in his shoes. What would my goal be if I were in their position?

To survive. The same as us.

Although my survival was so I could get to Toni and end her plan, then find out what she'd meant for me and if I could live this new life without the need to eat human flesh.

Perhaps to find out if I'd meant anything when she'd made that call, bringing me across the country.

Did that matter anymore?

I couldn't answer, but I knew the pair staring back had survived; were surviving, for now at least.

Like everyone else, they would want the chance at safety. For them. For their families. Hope.

But they'd just witnessed their children being led away. They couldn't have known of Toni's plans, or they wouldn't have let them go so easily.

For Alex there was genuine hope. She'd been unaffected; her body at least. I should have sent Alex on her way to join the pair on the roof. Unless the woman held up by the guy had been bitten, then I needed to get Alex as far away as I could.

Despite barely knowing her, I knew Alex wouldn't give up on me so easily.

The dog's bark echoed through the silence, the sound seeming to draw out, holding in the air until I realised, or had I known all along, the low hum of the creatures heading our way had taken over.

The guy called out.

Once. Twice, and I willed his silence for their sake. My wish came true, but only because of the reply following; the call into the air reminding me of the previous night. Reminding me of what I'd done.

No.

It reminded me of what Toni had made me do. She'd given me no instructions. She'd not told me how I could control it.

We had to get away. I owed Alex that much. I had to get her away from here. I had to get her somewhere safe so she could have her chance of normality. I didn't owe those on the roof anything, but I wouldn't put them in harm's way either. The list of people who'd died because of me was too long already. Helping these strangers out would do nothing to clear my conscience.

I could do no more for them.

Heavy engines roared in the air, the sound rising so quick I knew these were the real deal.

The pair heard it too. The look on his face across the distance told me he knew what was coming.

"We have to go," I said, watching as Alex pulled out of her daze, losing her train of thought which I could only guess would be the opposite side of where mine led.

I watched the motion of her head tracking the jet as it raced across the view. We had no chance to react as it flew low.

"Grab the camera and let's get you somewhere safe," I said, lifting the camera body as Alex unlocked the catch at the top of the tripod.

I looked around. Alex did too, both of us hoping for an empty path back the way we'd brought the van. Bodies ambled towards us in every direction apart from where the building blocked the view.

"There," Alex said, pointing past the building and to the left, where only a short section of the temporary fencing still stood like a tall island in the decimation.

With none of the creatures in that direction, I looked up to the roof, nodding to see the pair still fixed to the spot.

"We can meet them at the corner of the building," she said.

"No," I replied as I climbed into the back of the van, glancing up one last time before I slammed the doors from the inside.

"What? We can't just leave them here," Alex said, as she joined at my side, getting to the driver's seat before I could and revving the engine to life as she peered up at the roof. The people were already gone.

"They're better off on their own," I said. "Let's go. Just go. Quick."

Alex stared back, tilting her head to the side; her concentration focusing on me.

This was the moment we would set our future. Stay or

go. Me or them.

I didn't want to find out. I saw her decide, then we looked up to the growing dots in the sky.

# 4

Alex remained calm as the first explosion hit. The pressure wave through the glass didn't weigh down her foot and I marvelled at her calm as she kept a consistent pace across the debris of bodies.

A jet burst through the air, much higher than the one which had just buzzed past. I guessed its bombs would be for this place, with the pilots on orders to target the evidence left behind by the experiments. They were part of the coverup. Part of the travesty I had to reveal to the world.

Despite the turmoil of the jet's call and the ripple of energy from the explosion, I could still hear alarms shrieking all around. For a split-second, my thoughts flashed to what the creatures would feel. The chaos of the sound, each noise rousing them to investigate its source and calling them to action.

I followed Alex's gaze fixed to the side of the building; with my hand gripping at the door handle, the other to the seat at my side, we lumbered over the fleshy mess covering our pathway.

We were halfway to our goal, still rising and falling as we covered ground, when the second explosion hit, the strike landing just beyond the building. The concrete of the hospital shielded us from the worst, but the glass shooting out from the windows peppered shards across the van's thin metal, sending a blanket of dust over us.

The windscreen wipers worked at full speed, scratching debris across the glass as Alex leaned forward to gauge our slow progress.

I looked out through the smear to the roof, seeking the pair whilst telling myself they were never my concern and were just more nameless victims of someone I'd once shared a bed with.

But the thoughts didn't sit right. They were another reminder I'd failed. Every death resulted from my delay in finishing the job I'd started.

Why had I waited until the morning when I could have been here last night? I could have got here, put the news out and given them a chance to live. Or perhaps I would never know.

Jolting forward, the thoughts disappeared as the van slammed to a stop, sending me into the dashboard and Alex into the steering wheel.

With no point searching through the smeared mess to see what we'd hit, Alex pulled open her door, filling the cab with thick smoke laced with toxic dust and the perpetual stench of rotten, cooked flesh.

They'd already responded to the dinner bell.

I watched Alex through the driver's window as she disappeared around the door. She returned so soon, her head shaking as she peered through the opening.

"It's not going anywhere," she said, turning away before I could speak, her eyebrows raising as she peered out along the length of the van. I could guess what she saw.

We'd passed them on the way here. We'd mown so many down, but it hadn't been enough to stop those spurred on by the falling bombs.

"We need to go," Alex said, but I was already out of my seat, climbing into the back and turning to see her wide-eyed as I held out the camera.

She shook her head, but I thrust it again, leaning forward and she took its weight.

Popping open the rear doors, I found I'd been wrong; there were so many more than I'd thought and coming from all directions. A sea of undead creatures called to this place greeted me as I jumped to the ground, each turning their heads to the sky as another jet roared by and climbed out of sight.

"Is it on?" I said, moving around to the side of the van, pausing at the great chunk of concrete we'd smashed into and the long metal rebar in the side of the tyre.

Alex stared back, holding the camera at her side.

"Quickly. We've got very little time."

"No. We can't do this here," she said, with her brow relaxing from a frown as I clambered over the great block of concrete which had been part of the hospital.

Arriving beside her, she looked at me wide-eyed as I guided the camera to her shoulder and pulled the microphone from its slot, switching on the rectangular light hovering above the lens in the hope it would help cut my image through the dust.

"You'll get us killed," she said, but after glancing behind, she pushed her eye to the viewfinder. As the red light brightened, and I drew in a breath, a third explosion pushed us off our feet.

Coughing in acrid dust, I wafted at the air as best I could whilst peering back in hope Alex would rise. And there she was, my heart rate spiking when I saw the cut on her forehead, a slow drip of red from her hairline.

"Shit. Are you okay?" I shouted into the microphone still in my hands. The words came out muffled with my ears feeling as if they were stuffed full of expanding foam.

Alex nodded, shaking off dust as she clambered backwards to get her footing. With surprise, she settled the camera on her shoulder as the red light continued to shine.

"No. You're right. Let's go," I said, climbing slowly over the debris and stuffing down my guilt at the danger I was putting us both in. My foot slipped as I rose and I reached out to take Alex's outstretched arm despite her burden. I turned, looking to the crowds heading our way as they stumbled over those floored by the latest explosion.

A hundred bombs wouldn't stop that many creatures.

I turned, about to speak again when I saw a clearing in the rubble ahead. A square of tarmac edging a small, brick outbuilding like a beacon of safety in the middle of the destruction. With the rest of the hospital nearly flat, just a corner remained unaffected.

"Devastation," I said, holding up the microphone and staring to the building whilst trying to concentrate on making it across the rubble to get to its promise of safety. I tried not to look too hard at what was under my feet, knowing there were at least two people, and a dog, who would have been right in the firing line when the first bombs had fallen.

"So many dead," I said under my breath.

Without further words, I pointed across the view, but pushed away the need to tell Alex to angle the camera and get pictures of the bodies strewn at the outskirts of the rubble.

Grabbing a battered pistol discarded to the fallen concrete as we scrambled over the rubble, I returned my gaze to the outbuilding the size of a garden shed, small and square with a door facing towards us. Its bricks were potted with shrapnel and the sloping tiled roof dusted with crushed concrete. A thick metal chimney too large for the size of the building rose out high, jutting at a steep angle I guessed wasn't in the original design. A bright yellow warning sign on the door told me there was more than met the eye inside.

I hoped there would be, and we had little choice but to find out.

I turned to see Alex looking in the same direction.

"This way," I shouted, my eyes widening as I chanced a backward glance, wishing I could unsee the hoard of foul creatures still making their dogged way towards us.

The roar of engines took up again and moments later the blast pushed me off my feet with a wave of caustic heat, feeling as if it seared off my skin. As the rocky shrapnel stopped falling, I rose, helping Alex up at my side and readied to see the building we'd rushed to flattened.

As the dust settled, I peered in its direction, the air still vibrating with the thunder of aircraft engines. A sudden clarity fell across the view and with Alex pushing me along, I saw our sanctuary standing proud.

Arriving at the unlocked door first, I pulled it towards me. My gaze fell into the darkness and the descending steps. Alex raised the camera above my head, using its light to penetrate further, but all I could see were more concrete steps.

A roar rose in the air again, and the blast sent me tumbling forward, falling down as I watched as if disconnected, the darkness punctuated by flashes of light, rolling left and right until I closed my eyes, coming to a sudden stop with the sound of breaking glass ringing in my ears.

# 5

Alex cursed, but the sound seemed so far away until searching hands found my shoulder and her touch sparked a sensation rushing from her fingertips. Impulses fired across my body, waking every nerve as if she'd hit me with a welcome bolt of electricity.

Rising to my feet, her touch withdrew as an animalistic call echoed in the distance. I pushed my finger to my mouth, but realised despite my eyes stretching wide, I couldn't see anything in the darkness.

Alex moved at my side, her feet scraping on the rough ground.

"Sssh," I said, and her movement stopped as the wild sound in the background took up again. "We're not alone," I said, hoping she'd heard the words I'd barely formed.

The noise came again, an animalistic beat; with it followed a stench and a vision in my head of a creature hunched over with its nose high as it caught our scent. Or could they see in the dark? I tried to recall if I'd been able to, but shook away the pain of the memory.

Gritting my teeth against my body's ache as I twisted, I laid my hands flat to the hard ground and swept the dust and damp debris either side. Our hands touched, offering a fleeting warmth. My fingers jabbed the clean edge of glass, but I pulled back just before it could embed. Metal scratched against the hard ground and Alex's sharp breath told me she'd found something.

Just before my words formed, my fingers touched at the soft wind cover of the microphone. Taking it in my grip and about to put it to my mouth, I stopped when I realised the idiocy of the moment. Instead, my hand went to my jacket pocket, my heart sinking with the realisation.

"The gun's gone," I said, my words breaking through the low growl of what sought us out in the darkness. "The light. Can you get it working?"

Without waiting for a reply, my hands returned to the ground. Rising to my knees, I sucked up the pain of the rubble digging into my skin as I swept my hands in circles again.

"Can you hear that?" Alex asked, her head close to mine, but I didn't need to pause and listen; I hadn't stopped hearing the low rumble which had been close at hand these past few days. "The camera's a mess," she added, but I'd already guessed as much from the shattered glass covering the ground.

"We need to find a way out," I said when I heard her fingers fumbling with the camera. "Let's go. Leave it," I added, as my hand found her warmth.

Letting me pull her up as I stood, I kept my hand tight in hers and she followed. Leading her to the right and away from the noise, I pushed my other hand out in search of some part of the structure to use as a guide. I didn't want to go back up the stairs knowing the many more creatures waiting above, or the jets ready to rain down their destruction. I had to hope we could find another way out before the creature with us caught up. Before it found Alex.

A breeze washed across my face, carrying with it the stench of sewers laden with a heavy growl growing nearer.

We weren't done for yet. We had time, according to the sound at least. Still my feet hurried when I couldn't feel anything as I reached out, racing away from the animal noise.

Alex didn't speak, but with my hand still in hers and to the sound of her steps in time with mine, I pushed us quicker for fear of whatever followed would catch us; for fear of it sinking its teeth into her flesh. The fear much greater than of running into a wall, or the desperation of our blindness in this terrible place.

I pulled my hand back, slowing to a stop when I felt the first touch at my fingertips. With Alex clattering into me at my side, the flat of my free hand pressed against the uneven surface of wood with flecks of paint scratching at my skin.

"A door," I said, groping around.

"Is there a handle?" she replied between heavy breaths.

I said nothing. Instead, I ignored the sense of loss when I let go of her hand and swept both of my palms across the dark surface.

With Alex by my side, her fingers joining the race, our search sent paint flecks stinging under our nails, jabbing at our skin as our hands collided. When neither of us found what we sought, my hands balled to fists and I hammered against the wood, sending the echo outward.

Alex grabbed around my shoulders, pulling me back and wrapping her arms around me as she held tight until I relaxed, unclenching my fists. Loosening her grip, she stepped back and her hands found my cheeks to send sparks racing across my skin.

She pulled me in close.

"We have to go back," she whispered. Releasing her grip, she grabbed my hand and led me the way we'd come to the renewed echo from the other end of the tunnel. As Alex pulled me along, I felt an overwhelming need to take the lead.

Fighting to control my breath, I knew our best bet now would be to climb the concrete steps we'd fallen down. We had to trust from the quiet that the bombs had stopped so we could take our chances with whatever still lingered the other side.

Alex didn't complain as I rushed past her to take the lead whilst doing my best to block out the growing noise ahead.

She gave a huff of air and pulled out of my grip as she squealed to the sound of a heavy thump at the ground, followed by the scrape of metal. My first thought was of my worst fear coming true and they'd found her. With adrenaline surging, I forced my eyes wide in hope I could make out where the attack had come from.

Before I could get my bearings in the darkness, the tunnel lit bright and in front of me I saw Alex in shadow, hunched over the camera body and the light blaring out at its front.

I saw the pistol right at my feet, with light refracting to

rainbows in the scattered glass. With a sharp breath I grabbed at the gun just as movement caught in the corner of my eye and I swung around, holding the gun gripped with both hands.

A shout called out, the volume so loud but the word indistinct as the echo died. The potent stench had grown so strong as I turned and instinct took control, exploding the shot out when I saw the creature in the centre of the curving tunnel.

The bullet smashed into its skull, sending it spinning in a circle. Before I could shoot again, I watched as it slumped but remained in the centre of the space. Shaking my head, I followed the line from its neck to a rope tied to the ceiling. Peering down, its feet dangled from the floor with another two pairs just behind.

Flexing my finger back to the trigger, I zeroed in on the new target.

# 6

## LOGAN

"Noooo," I called, feeling Cassie draw back from the sound. With the sudden light and boom of the gunshot, rancid blood sprayed from the body hanging with a cord around its neck.

Ducking for fear of another bullet, I pulled Cassie down as Shadow continued to bark. Panicked voices rang out ahead, and I realised another bullet hadn't launched from the ominous figures standing on the other side of the strung-up creature.

The light dimmed, turning to the wall to reveal dark, patchy brickwork as the limp body hung between us, slowly twisting on the cord tied with a rough knot to a bunch of cables at the ceiling.

Despite seeing it from behind, by the cut of its short, grey hair and the breadth of its shoulders under the blue overalls, I could tell he had been a man. A hole gaped out of the back of his head and I wiped my face, releasing Cassie's hands to rid myself of the foul mess which had sprayed our way.

With Shadow still barking, my gaze settled below the hanging man's feet and a short stool laying on its side. He'd made a choice to kill himself before he turned into one of those things. Time would tell if it had been the right one.

The body's turn slowed to a stop, then spun in the opposite direction. I had no interest in seeing his face and looked past him to the two figures staring wide-eyed in our direction.

With the light bouncing from the dull walls, I saw the red pant suit of the reporter we'd seen from the roof and beside her stood the cameraman holding the camera with its light tilted to the side. My focus snapped to the gun the reporter held two-handed, its barrel drifting downward as she peered low to Shadow, then around the body to Cassie.

None of us moved. As Shadow wouldn't relent with his noise, my gaze fixed on the reporter's face, trying to imagine her thoughts as she kept looking at Cassie.

"Are you okay?" the figure with the camera said in a soft voice which made me question if they were a man or a woman. Reaching out to the reporter, they guided the barrel of the gun further downward.

Feeling the tension ebb, I turned to Cassie, taking her hand as she stared back wide-eyed and spoke with a croak in her voice.

"You almost killed us."

Turning to Shadow, I bent down and stroked his back to reassure him.

Relieved when he stopped barking, I wrapped my arm around Cassie to take her weight. "I'm okay," she said, fighting against my touch.

"I'm sorry," the reporter said softly. Her well-spoken accent sounded so familiar. "I thought..." she added, but cut herself off.

Her words had been enough. She was Jessica Carmichael. The tall, attractive ball-buster from the television news.

"I get it," I replied. "We understand," I said, keeping my voice flat as I used my sleeve to wipe my face but looked away when I saw the dark, clotted blood which came away. "Can we get out that way?"

I waited for either of them to speak, still with the creature slowly rotating between us. I watched as Jessica's companion with their short hair, checked shirt and dark trousers, looked to her with an uncertainty on their face, as if neither had understood my voice.

"It's okay," I said, watching Cassie manoeuvre around the body.

I rushed forward as she stumbled, my shoulder touching the dead man's arm to send him in a slow spin in the opposite direction. I kept the gun in view as I took Cassie's weight. She didn't complain this time.

Jessica hadn't raised the pistol; instead she stepped back to give us space.

"I'm Logan," I said, raising my hand in a shallow wave, but pulled back to wipe my palm across my trousers when I saw the dirt.

She held her gaze for a long moment before eventually turning up to look me in the eye and nod.

"And this is Cassie," I said, twisting around and watching as Cassie glared back.

"I'm Alex," the person at Jessica's side said, pointing to their chest. "That's Jess." In the darkness I still couldn't quite confirm if they were a guy or not.

"And Shadow," I added, turning to stroke his head, but rather than drawing forward to my side, he remained planted to the spot with his lips pulled back in a snarl.

It was the first time I'd seen him like this with anyone, but then again, like Cassie, I hadn't known him that long. "He's saved my life countless times," I said when he wouldn't move.

The pair nodded, raising weak smiles as they looked at him with caution.

"Do you think the bombing's stopped?" I asked, looking up whilst trying to ignore the short white stalactites hanging from the concrete and the long black crack running through the centre of the brickwork above our heads.

Looking back to the pair, both had turned to the ceiling, but none gave an answer. I broke the silence.

"How did you get in?"

Alex turned, the light following to edge away the darkness at their backs. For a moment, the turning light highlighted Jessica in its full brightness and despite her ashen features and pale skin, her features stood out, vivid and pronounced. The only part of her missing from her TV image was the crisp confidence in her expression.

I peered along the tunnel as the light from the camera

filled the void. Broken glass glinted across the stained concrete floor, mixed with scattered rubble and debris brushed to the side of the dingy space.

At the far end, the tunnel headed right, but directly ahead a set of concrete steps rose high.

"That's where we came in, but it's blocked with rubble now," Alex said.

"It's the same the way we came," I added, twisting around despite the darkness.

"We should try a door we found further down," Alex added, their voice almost juvenile in depth as they pointed along the tunnel. "We couldn't get it open in the dark."

"Yes," I said, clutching Cassie tight at my side. Not looking back, the pair moved off.

We followed behind, keeping with their pace, but when my foot hit something loose on the floor, sending it clattering to the wall, the light span around, forcing my hand to shield my eyes.

After a brief pause to stare at Cassie, Alex spoke.

"Are you okay?"

"She's fine," I said in quick reply, lowering my hand.

"She's bitten." It was Jessica who spoke.

Twisting around to Cassie, I turned to put myself between her and the pair as Shadow's low growl returned.

# 7

## JESSICA

Alex turned the light towards the pair as my words came out. The guy, Logan, drew himself in front of his companion, twisting in anticipation of what he thought might happen next. With his lips curling, he squinted, seeking us out behind the brightness.

I glimpsed the woman before he'd shielded all but her knotted blonde hair from our view and even if I couldn't smell how different she was to everyone else, her drawn, gaunt features made it obvious enough something wasn't right.

These days it could mean little else.

She'd been bitten, but there was something different compared to those I'd seen. If she'd been with Toni then there could well be more to her story.

The guy, Logan, stood tall, tensing to show his determination to protect her; the effort stretching out tired creases worrying his face, the rest hidden by a few days of growth around his chin.

At their side, the dog growled, drawing back to his hindquarters as if to pounce.

I hadn't seen such a picture of love for a long time.

"It's okay," I said, pushing the gun into my pocket and holding my palms out. "I understand."

Without waiting, I turned back down the tunnel, heading to the door we'd been banging on only moments before. With the light casting my long shadow as I walked, it wasn't until I arrived at the door, moving to the side to the let the light fall to the right, that I saw the tarnished brass handle we'd missed in our panic.

Putting my ear to the wood, at first I didn't pay attention to what I might have heard the other side; instead, I couldn't help but listen for the pair heading my way.

I pulled away from the wood, turning back to see Logan with his arm under the woman's shoulders. Despite her stoop, I saw the fight still inside her.

"Did they give her anything?" I asked. I had to know if they'd met with the doctors.

Alex turned the light back to the wall.

"Give me a moment," she said, and darkness fell around us to the snap and click of plastic.

No one spoke. The dog, Shadow, had calmed, but I felt him on the edge of launching another noisy assault. It wasn't until the light came back, revealing Alex holding just the square of the light with a cable coiling to a battery pack in her other hand, that Logan spoke.

"Yes," he said. I sensed a mix of worry in his voice, but with the rise of his head I felt his hope.

"She'll be okay then," I said.

Logan nodded. If he believed me or not, his expression relaxed and he turned away to check on Cassie before twisting back. Beyond his smile, I saw the desperation to ask so many questions.

He was about to speak, his lips parting in the bare light, when a noise came from behind us, the low bass tumble of something heavy above our heads percolating through the rock above.

"Try the handle," Logan said as the sound settled.

I wanted to reassure him that Toni knew what she was doing. I was, after all, the proof. But then again, how did I know what they'd given Cassie? My questions sat heavy and unasked. Which came first for her, the bite or the medicine? When did she get the dose? Did she have to take more? Would she feel the extreme side-effects I had? Did he know what he was in for?

I turned back before the words came out and Alex met my look, nodding as if understanding.

"She'll be fine," I said, forcing a smile.

Looking back to the door, I placed my hand on the

brass, surprised when it turned as I twisted my grip.

Backing away from the door, I glanced to see the others shuffling away along the dusty floor out of its arc.

Logan looked behind him, peering into the darkness as he helped Cassie move. Alex leaned to the side, angling the light for maximum effect, ready for when I opened the door. I pulled the pistol from my pocket and with my left hand I gripped the handle again, twisted and counted to three in my head before pulling the door wide.

Shadow barked and I peered forward, trying to penetrate the darkness, but only as Alex stepped alongside with the light could I see a tunnel much like where we stood. Pipes ran along the ceiling, insulation sagging with its failing grip. Spurs ran off and rose through tight holes in the ceiling, the rest darting away at ground level before disappearing into the darkness.

Despite Shadow's worry, his call turning to a long low growl, we saw no one hanging from their necks. No bodies littered the floor. The only concern was the confusion of footprints in the dust.

A fine powder filled the stale air, sparkling in the bright light. Logan tried to calm the dog, but he wouldn't be stilled.

Taking a step forward with Alex at my side, I pushed the gun forward. Shadow called out, the echo of the bark resounding through my head. I tried to stop the flinch each time his explosive noise sent dust swirling into the light.

With each step, my gaze traced the pipe, whilst Shadow's bark grew more intense until Logan's voice cut through, a deep but sharp tone to stop the high call. The relief felt instant as Shadow replaced the cutting sound with a low growl.

Still with the pistol taking the lead, I concentrated my view at the horizon of light as it pushed through the darkness, but I saw nothing else other than the slow right-hand curve of the tunnel.

I had to find a way out. I couldn't stay much longer in this place. For my sake. For theirs. When my hunger came again, I wanted to be as far away from these people as possible.

Shadow's growl slowed, and I turned back, the light following to the dog and his snout high in the air. We watched as he raced forward, stopping with his nose at a gap between the lowest pipe and the ground, eager to get at what lay beneath.

Logan stepped to Shadow's side, gently ushering him away. As he reluctantly moved, Alex angled the light and each of us lowered to a crouch, only drawing back when we saw the picked-clean rodent's remains.

"Keep going," Alex said, as the light turned away.

With a slow pace, I held the pistol tighter, taking time to examine every feature, distracting myself from thoughts of what could have stripped the meat from the bones and piled them so neatly under the pipe.

With reluctance, Shadow took his attention from the pile and drew up beside me, more eager than ever to test every part of the ground.

After a few more steps, I took a deep breath when a familiar scent caught in the stale air; the smell that for a week had been an early warning sign. The stench of waste. Of rot.

I turned to Alex, the light bright in my face, her eyebrows raising in a question before I twisted back around to step slowly forward again.

Shadow's growl grew with every moment, but still he wouldn't venture any further forward, not racing away to see what waited in the darkness.

I continued on, looking left and right, glancing behind each pipe as it cast its shadow, lingering every few steps whilst keeping the gun fixed forward, ready to move in an instant.

Catching an impressive bulk blocking half of the tunnel, I stepped closer to the large pipe with one end disappearing through a hole in the wall, the other dropping below the tunnel floor. There was something else there too. Something in the bend's radius tight against the wall.

Pointing, I tried wordlessly to direct Alex to move the

light and improve the view. When the shadows peeled away, my arm relaxed, letting the gun point to the ground as I took a moment to stare at the familiar blue pattern on the fabric contrasting to the dusty silver of the pipe insulation.

My gaze rose along the pronounced line of bumps on the curve of the material to the lank, greasy hair at the top. It wasn't until Alex moved the light further to the side that I jumped back, almost falling against the wall as the high, tearful voice cried out.

"Go away, please."

# 8

## LOGAN

"Go," the trembling voice said again as it peaked to a new volume.

Cassie flinched against my arm and I took a step back, gripping tighter around her waist whilst Jess stooped closer to the bend in the pipe, angling herself so not to block the light.

"It's okay," Jess said, her voice quiet. "You must be frozen." She looked as if she were about to remove her scarlet jacket when the childish voice spoke again.

"Go away, please."

I watched a wide smile grow on Jess's face, her profile rising to reassure and hide the uncertainty of what she saw. At some point, Shadow had stopped his bark, instead switching to a low growl again.

His snarl faltered, and for a moment silence hung in the tunnel. No one moved, and I stared at what I now realised was a girl in a tatty denim dress with knotted brown hair flowing down to her shoulder as she folded over to squeeze under the curve of the pipe.

Jess moved closer to the girl and reached out.

"Leave me alone," the voice sobbed when Jess made contact, as the girl tried to push herself further into the tangle of insulation.

A low rumble of falling rock echoed through the tunnel and pulled my gaze from the girl. The light followed as I twisted around to the dust raining down in front of the door we'd come through moments earlier. The indistinct sound filled me with a new dread that our tiny space had shrunken even further.

"How did you get down here?" I called out, returning my gaze back to the child. When she didn't reply, I walked with Cassie closer to Jess's side. "Just take her with us. We've got to get the hell out of here before it's too late."

"No," the high call came back from below the pipe. "You need to go."

I stopped, turning back at Jess's side, just able to see the tangle of hair before it disappeared behind the pipe.

"She must have been down here a long time," I said, looking back in the darkness towards where we'd found the tiny bones. "We need to get out of here. Now."

Alex turned the light to point down the tunnel as we moved past, before swinging it back around when a gasp of air caught everyone's attention. The girl stood to three quarters of Jess's height but it was the black veins like tree roots lining her face and the beard of dried blood around her chin which sent us recoiling back.

Cassie stumbled as I lurched. Shadow barked. The child stood staring at Jess as we recovered our footing. The moment seemed to span an age, a voice in my head screaming out for Jess to raise the gun.

This girl had the hunger. She needed to feed, but she was talking. What the fuck was going on?

Rather than blowing the creature away, Jess pushed the pistol into her waistband and stepped forward.

"What the fuck are you doing?" I shouted, sending Shadow's pitch even higher.

"Let's go," Cassie said, her voice barely heard.

"Go," Jess said in a calm call, not turning my way, instead opening her arms to entice the girl into an embrace. "Go," she repeated when we hadn't moved, twisting around to catch my eye and glaring in my direction.

I should have done as she said right then. I should have dragged Cassie away and Shadow as the echo of his bark rang through the narrow tunnel.

But I didn't. I waited there with my feet fixed firm, watching the creature struggle as Jess enveloped her in the embrace.

I watched as the young creature's mouth flashed to a

hungry snarl pointed in my direction, seeming to ignore Jess altogether. Blood-stained teeth bared instinctively; her red-raw gaze shifted to Cassie, the snarl faltering for a moment before looking past the light to Alex.

But Jess didn't react other than to clamp the girl tight, not pulling out the gun and putting the creature out of her misery. Jess would die because she couldn't get past the childish features and high voice.

# 9

"Let's go," I said in a quiet voice as I turned away. Holding Cassie tight, I helped her into the darkness, walking forward whilst trying to remember the layout of the tunnel I'd seen moments earlier.

With his claws clicking on the concrete floor, Shadow followed and behind him Jess alternated between pleading for Alex to go then switching to a gentle tone as if to talk the child from a tantrum.

When I'd seen Jess from the roof standing amongst the death, destruction and the foul twist of nature, I thought she understood the new world we lived in; I'd been wrong, and she would pay the price. Despite the confidence in her eyes when she told us to leave, she'd have no chance of talking down a frenzied animal from its need to feed. It would rip Jess apart before it moved to us to sate its appetite.

Light shone at our backs as footsteps ran from the rising commotion.

Jess must have realised her peril.

Despite my desperation to turn and leap to her defence, I picked up the pace when the light cast our shadows to the curve of the tunnel ahead. My first duty had to be to Cassie and I couldn't sacrifice her safety, even knowing the girl-creature had flipped, her hunger becoming too great.

It was already too late if the pained calls were anything to go by.

As we sped, I felt Cassie's effort increasing despite the obvious toll it took. We were running for our lives, knowing once again we had an unnatural beast at our backs.

"Run," I heard from behind, Jess's call taking me by surprise when I realised she'd survived. But still she'd come to the choice too late and her high call told me she knew she'd be a victim of the new species occupying the earth.

As we ran, already going as fast as we could, the commotion behind stopped but the racing footsteps hadn't.

"Run," her high shout came again, but we needed no encouragement in the strobing light when we saw a wooden door ahead.

Shadow took the lead, barking as if to point out the brass handle. A confusion of heavy footsteps landed at our backs and my heart pounded as I raced, staring at the handle and willing the door to be unlocked.

"Please open. Please open," I said, not able to keep the voice just inside my head.

"Quickly," the voice called at my back again.

I let go of Cassie, tentative at first, pausing just enough to make sure she could take her own weight. With my shoulder leaning into the wood, I gripped the cold metal and gave it a heavy turn.

Falling through the doorway, I only just caught my fall when the metal twisted and the door opened away from me. I took Cassie's outstretched hand, with Shadow stepping past me into the darkness, his claws skittered on the concrete floor.

Alex caught up with the light, twisting around and plunging us into darkness. My gaze flickered in the direction we'd come, but I couldn't see anything other than the slow curve of the corridor.

With the light through the doorway from behind, I saw concrete steps rising a few paces ahead. Without pause, I took Cassie's arm and led her upwards, soon finding another door at the top and frantically searching for signs it would lead us back outside.

"Hurry." The high words came from beyond the light at my back; someone, Alex perhaps, but the voice was so high, helped to heave Cassie's weak frame.

The door held firm as I twisted at the handle. Over our heavy breath, a rush of feet came from far back, a scuffle, but Shadow's renewed barks drew me away and my concentration fixed on the door without answering the question screaming inside my head.

Was the creature still chasing behind Jess or had Jess succumbed to her end?

At my feet light spilled under the crack where the door met the floor as cold, fresh air surged from underneath. Trying the handle once again, rattling left and right, the light soon shined on the door and I saw Alex's silhouette taking Cassie's weight, their bodies swaying up and down as they fought for their breath.

I didn't linger for long, instead slapping my shoulder to the door, hoping to feel the crack as I hit against the wood.

The door didn't bow or split, its stout structure designed to slow a fire for hours.

Shadow's bark rang through my head. I felt the overwhelming need to bend down and comfort him to stop, but we had no time. Once the creature had finished with Jess, we would be next.

Slamming hard against the wood a second time, I knew the futility of the task. Sinking to my knees, the impossibility of the situation slapped me to the ground.

A voice called in the background; short words, but Shadow's bark blocked their meaning. The time had come. The end close. With Jess gone, it was our turn.

About to take Alex's place, I rose then halted, hearing the urgent words between Shadow's calls.

"The key."

Cassie had spoken at my side and I twisted back to the door, shaking my head, but then I saw the thin metal protruding from the lock below the handle.

Whoever hung from the ceiling must have locked himself inside.

Fumbling at the metal, I felt it twist and turned the lock left, then right when it wouldn't open. Chilling air and bright light blasted through the opening as I pushed and stumbled out to the grass, staring to the space and the rubble piled where the hospital had once stood.

I turned around, grabbed Cassie by the hand as she stepped through, collecting her in my arms as I stared at the chaos all around.

The rubble moved in so many places; rock and concrete

still crumbling and settling to its resting place. Small fires burned everywhere.

Alex rushed to my side, before turning back to the doorway. In that moment I saw her as if for the first time and realised she was a woman.

"Jess," she said in the same high, hurried call I'd heard in the corridor; that same voice I'd thought had been the reporter's.

Panic had pitched her voice higher, the call so full of affection and despair I couldn't help but feel a deep sorrow toward her. I saw Alex's smooth, pale skin, but my fascination lifted as my gaze followed her rush back to the door still open wide. If those calls hadn't been the reporter's, it must have been the childish creature who'd won the battle.

Leaving Cassie to take in the view, I took long steps to the door and slammed it shut. Regretting the bellowing noise, I planted my back against the wood and fixed my feet firm. I had to stop the creature from getting out. We had to make the most of the chance they'd gifted us.

"Move," Alex said, stepping to my side, but I didn't meet her look; instead I searched the horizon for our next escape route.

A thud of hands slapped to the door from the other side and a low visceral scream rattled the wood. With Alex's eyes widening at the call, her mouth opening, I couldn't watch the heartbreak.

"Let her out," she said, her voice calming.

I couldn't let the creature out. Despite her age, she had as much of a killer instinct as those who'd already killed so many of my friends.

# 10

## JESSICA

I couldn't think with the dog's incessant bark. I could only watch the hunger in the child's eyes. Despite trying to hide her face from the light, I saw the battle in her tensed features. I pictured the terrible memories racing through her mind.

Something pricked her interest, and she pulled her gaze from the hiding place to peer at each of us. The corners of her mouth rose as her gaze settled. I twisted around, following the deep sense of longing as she stared at Alex and stood up.

For a fleeting moment I wanted the memory of Alex's scent, feeling robbed I couldn't taste the sweet smell in the air, but knowing I couldn't compare her nectar to that of Toni's. Horror pulled me back when I realised what the girl wanted to do to my newfound friend.

"Go," I said, before turning back to the child, whilst pushing the pistol into my waistband. Wrapping the child in an embrace, her eyes went wide as I held her tight, her lips curling at my touch.

The girl's muscles tensed and relaxed as she tested my grip around her shoulders, a hiss of complaint rising by my ear. Tightening my hold, I saw her looking back to Alex. When her breath faltered, I released my grip just a little, and I remembered the girl's voice.

She was like me and it could mean she too could live without eating human flesh; without having to kill with her bare hands. Once I found out what Toni had intended, all of us could live alongside each other in this changed world.

"Go," I repeated, louder this time. The guy, Logan, hurried them on. I could hear their steps heading away, but the light lingered at my side.

"Go," I repeated in a soft voice. It took the girl to buck

against my hold, hissing with her teeth bared at Alex, for the light to go altogether.

The barking returned in the distance, still stunning my ears with each call and sending shivers through the girl.

"What's your name?" I said, whilst trying to catch a look at her face. With just enough remaining light from the tunnel, I watched lank strands of inky hair as she tried to twist her view to follow those already so far away.

She didn't reply; instead each of the muscles in her upper body went tight at the same time. Not letting my grip falter, I pulled her closer.

Tightening further, I remembered how I'd felt as I stepped from the van in the pale dusk. I remembered the blank emotion as I led the soldier, Jordain, to his death. I closed my eyes, but could barely tell the difference. I tightened my grip a little more.

I couldn't help but wonder if she felt the same as I did when the hunger came, and she could talk, a little girl still somewhere behind those eyes. Toni wouldn't have left me like this. She wouldn't have left me to live out the rest of my life like an animal; a predator on humanity. The very fact I had these thoughts gave testament to my hope.

But this wasn't about me; the dark, bulging lines on the girl's face told me she could be different.

Did she have the same hopes? Could I take the risk to find out? The price for being wrong wouldn't just be my life.

Her breathing slowed and her muscles stayed limp as if she'd given up, accepting the decision I hadn't voiced.

Her chest went in further as she expelled air and I tightened a little more. It would be best for Alex. Best for the others. Best for the girl.

It would be over in a moment and if only the dog would stop barking, this would be a beautiful ending to her pain.

"Emily." The small breathless voice came from below. I no longer wanted to know her name.

Without thought, I relaxed my arms to the deep pull of breath rushing into her lungs.

Why did she have to speak again? Why did she have to remind me she was a girl first? Human, in some part. A tragedy afflicted by the same designers of my cross.

A terrible thought ran through my mind. Had her experiment happened before or after mine? Was she meant to be a better version of what I had become? Or just another failed guinea pig?

"How long have you been down here?" I asked, keeping my voice quiet.

My grip loosened, but still wrapped her tight. She didn't reply and all I could think of was how scared she must have been to wake alone with animal thoughts in her head she could do nothing about, other than to seek satisfaction.

"Did you escape?" I said, but she didn't react. I couldn't bring myself to open my eyes, even though I knew there would be no light. The last thing I wanted to see was the affliction spidering across her face. "How long have you been down here? You must be so hungry."

Regretting the words just as they came, her shoulders flexed, her power too great for my hold and my arms burst wide. Light speckled with tiny white stars as a heavy blow landed to my chest.

She was out of my arms and at my side, running, racing down the corridor to the noise of the dog. Racing towards Alex.

Lunging out low, I caught a leg in the darkness, gripping for a moment but I couldn't keep hold. With my fingers scratching at her skin, I heard her fall.

Over-balanced, I tumbled forward, the gun clattering to the floor. I heard her scrabble to her feet as I swept my hands across the dusty ground until I retook the gun in my grip and jumped up to give chase, my finger twitching on the trigger as I sped through the darkness.

A door slammed ahead and by instinct alone I launched myself forward, somehow catching at her ankles and bringing her to the floor again.

Scrabbling to my feet, I heard her in front and before I

hoped she could rise, I jumped forward, landing on top of her compact frame, but with such strength in her movement, she tried to throw me off.

I dropped the gun and grabbed at her hands as she struggled. Fighting against her thrashing body, thrown left and right as she pulled from my grip, she rolled to her back with a soft, quivering voice; the voice of a victim. Her voice like mine had been.

Yes, I'd killed a man for his meat. I'd done the deed, but I'd woken from that moment still human. Why shouldn't this girl have the same chance too?

"Say something," I said through gritted teeth as I struggled, willing her to calm as she bucked with my hands at her wrists.

With a surge of strength, she slammed me left and right like a rodeo bronco but without the stadium of hollering fans. Perhaps she was past the point of no return.

Did we share a fate?

Letting go with one hand, I reached out to my right and where I hoped I'd dropped the pistol. Before I could search, she twisted me over and sent me spilling to the wall with a ring of pain resonating across my head.

Blinking away the sparkling dots across the black view, I sensed her stare; in my mind, she leaned over, snarling in my direction.

I rose tall, steadying with my hand out to the wall, having decided; I wouldn't kill her if I could help it, but I couldn't let her loose on Alex either.

Lunging where I heard her snarl, my foot touched at the gun and I dropped to scoop it up as I lurched forward, connecting with what I hoped was her head as I slammed into her.

Her body went limp and her animal snarl stopped. Now was my chance.

Keeping the gun in my grip, I ran, following the curve of the wall with my left hand as I listened for the others ahead and for any sign of her rousing at my back.

A door slammed in the distance, the noise cushioned by something blocking the way.

Feet scraped on the dusty floor behind me and I heard footsteps, slow at first but they soon rose in volume.

Somehow, I'd slowed before hitting against the door barring my way and I searched for the handle, handicapped by holding the pistol. I found its curve, gripped hard and twisted until I felt her force at my back, sending me through the door to clatter against the concrete steps on the other side.

Blindly kicking out, I didn't know where my attacker stood, but not waiting for her to come again, I scrabbled up the steps toward the door at the top. Frigid air circled where a sliver of light met my eye-line. Banging hard at the door, I screamed for release, but heard nothing other than her teeth snapping as she rose behind me.

Turning in a swift move, I could just about make out her shape from the line of light under the door. I pushed my left hand out and heard the scrape of the concrete as she lurched toward me.

Still, I couldn't kill her. Still, I couldn't put her out of her misery. I couldn't take away her chance, my chance, of salvation. It would be as if there was no hope for either of us.

But I wouldn't let her through the door. I wouldn't let her feed on Alex. I couldn't let her pass the pain to others.

The door showed no sign of opening at my back. Had Alex decided there was no hope for me either? Or would it open at any moment and release the beast?

Remembering the weight of the pistol in my hand, I kicked out against her attack and raised it high.

"Goodbye," I said out loud as the gun's mechanism slid together.

# 11

## LOGAN

Hearing Jess's voice, then the gunshot just the other side of the door, sent me staggering backwards as I turned. I looked to Alex open-mouthed, reeling from the gravity of what had just happened as we heard something heavy slumping down the steps beyond.

I should have called for her to see some sense and not release the creature with childish features from the other side. Instead, I watched as she yanked the door wide and stared expectant into the darkness.

Shadow's bark pulled me from the view and to the edge of the rubble, but I turned back when I heard faint footsteps.

Shadow called again and I ran to where he stood, kneeling and stroking his back to calm him as I peered out to the horizon and the unnatural figures heading our way in every place I looked.

When Alex didn't scream in pain, I chanced a glance and saw Jess walking into the light before stepping up to Alex. Alex grabbed the gun from Jess's grip, throwing it to the tarmac before she pulled her tight in an embrace.

It was Jess who had been trying to get out and not the girlish creature.

Still holding Alex, Jess looked at me, her face pale and blank of emotion.

As I raised my eyebrows, the only outward show of my surprise, she gave a shallow nod in my direction.

The foul odour on the breeze reminded me that just because we weren't being ripped apart this moment, the need to be somewhere else was ever-present.

I rushed to Cassie, helping her up as she fell to her knees and wrapped my arm under her. Tensing as I held on, she barely acknowledged my presence.

The pitch of Shadow's bark rose, and I slowly twisted us around, looking for the news van and our best chance of escape. Everywhere I looked, steaming rubble lay in a disordered mess as if the great concrete hospital had never existed.

With the two-storey building no longer standing, the horizon was so different. The constant slow approach of the creatures almost everywhere meant I couldn't linger on the view, instead shifting my gaze to the next place in hope of a gap or at least somewhere for us to run.

My mood sank to a new low when in amongst the smoking destruction I picked out the misshapen remains of a satellite dish.

Somewhere close, rubble scattered, and I turned towards the sound, twisting Cassie around to face the end of the hospital where we'd last entered. Examining the rocky debris for the source, a gust of hot dust flashed across my face and a figure rose from the remains, its head covered in white dust contrasting against the darkness of its snapping mouth.

Chancing a glance to Jess and Alex, they stared at the creature. I looked to the sky, searching for black dots between the rising columns of grey.

"There," Alex called, and I turned, expecting to see her outstretched arm high and pointing to the next aircraft in line to attack, but her arm held level and I followed her pointed finger to the tall spire of a church on the horizon.

I shook my head at the sight, knowing the last place we wanted to be was anywhere where a horde of the creatures could follow and trap us until they could get past any defences we could raise. A low moan from Cassie at my side reminded me she had to rest and perhaps a church, with its solid doors and stone walls, could be the place to wait it out.

There'd be no food, but it could give us a reprieve and the spire would have a great view so we could find a better place of safety. Could we last long enough for the horde to find something else of interest and disperse?

No. We needed to find a car and race away; we needed to get somewhere not littered with the creatures and where the military weren't targeting their bombs.

A high screech at our backs helped to push us into action.

Shadow led the way towards the rising spire and what I hoped would be a car park full of options.

For a moment I watched him with his snout high in the air, twisting left and right to find a path through the mess of broken concrete and mangled flesh.

Concentrating on our footsteps, I guided us in the same direction, whilst trying to ignore the rising sounds coming from all around.

With the rubble thinning, I peered in the direction we headed and the buildings congregating around the tall spire. Squat houses stood in two disordered rows either side of a road too narrow for a white line to divide.

Either side of the village, low hills rolled out of view and where herds of sheep, or cows, or horses, should have been scattered, something else filled their space, spreading the stench brushing across us with every breath of wind.

With the sight, my spirits took a further dive, knowing there would be little chance of finding the village clear of the creatures.

We'd seen the village before but from the back of the Land Rover. The small settlement seemed mostly intact, but as if in a war zone, the only cars left lay strewn to the side of the narrow road or crashed through houses. Craters dug deep into the black tarmac. Barely any glass remained in window frames and limp bodies scattered each place I looked. I'd yet to see any sign of movement in that direction.

As if not noticing the chaos, Shadow kept the lead, following a path around the bodies, not once touching their flesh. Heading past the hospital compound's battered chain link, his pace quickened as I scanned the view, unable to stop glancing to movement in my peripheral vision.

"They can smell us," Jess said, and I turned, startled as

she answered the question I'd kept in my head.

"How...?" I said, quickening, then remembering how the cooking meat yesterday had drawn them in, but before I could speak again, she cut me off.

"I've been following the story," she said, turning away from catching Alex's eye.

"How do you know this?" I said, glancing forward as my foot caught on a small boulder.

"Stands to reason," she replied, not looking my way.

"Do you know what's going on?" I said, slowing in anticipation of her answer. When she didn't reply, I turned to see her nod, and an excitement rose into my chest. I had so many questions, but a feral call in the distance pulled away my enthusiasm for anything but getting to safety.

Cassie tripped and I almost couldn't hold back her fall, but Alex came around her other side, taking some of her weight so we could pick up the pace.

"Thank you," I said, looking across Cassie, but Alex didn't turn my way.

Peering up, I saw the first building; a hall, its walls no higher than the houses along the road. The church spire rose just beyond.

With the litter of bodies thinning, to the right stood a detached post office with a compact car amongst the shelves, leaving jagged fingers of glass hanging from the window frame.

My thoughts turned to the last village I'd visited with Cassie as we hid from the looters, bringing with it the fear we'd had for our lives; for our friend's, too. But we'd made it then, we'd survived, and I was more determined than ever we wouldn't join the number that hadn't.

Steeling myself for whatever would come next, I peered in through the windows of each stone house, thankful the structures blocked the fields either side.

Watching my footing, my gaze landed on the open cavity of a soldier's stomach just in time to avoid falling into the foul mess.

I watched for signs of life. I watched for signs of death; my nerves on edge, knowing we were always only moments from the next event.

A high-pitched scream called out from somewhere in the distance, but I didn't look back; instead, I peered to the small crowd lumbering their way towards us from the far side of the village.

Despairing when I didn't see lines of vehicles neatly parked up, I took in the height of the spire, but turned away in search of another sanctuary, a place to go if the church was no good. To my left there were no windows in the St Buryan village hall, the white sign splashed with dark blood streaking down to the announcement of the Saturday Farmer's Market.

What day was it?

I shook away the inexplicable thought. What did it matter anymore? Survival was our only goal.

I laughed, feeling Cassie move, her head turning my way with Alex on the other side, peering around with a raised brow.

I shook my head, dismissing their looks, but my smile didn't drop as I looked along the road, watching as Shadow broke into a run and disappeared around the corner of a house.

A shrill call repeated, but I couldn't judge the distance or the time it would take for the worst of the creatures to be on us.

Rounding the corner, peering left and right, the view filled with bodies piled high. The piles dotted around the cobblestone square surrounding an ornate fountain filled with stagnant scarlet water.

It appeared as if someone had been tidying up, but the thought evaporated when I couldn't see Shadow anywhere.

The slam of heavy doors and his muffled bark pointed me in the church's direction.

Lifting our speed, another shrill scream lit the air, sounding as if behind us.

Hurrying to the door, excitement grew at how solid the

dark brown doors seemed and how they would soon keep us safe for as long as we needed. The stained-glass windows were still intact, the stone solid and the roof covered every part as it should. The impressive tower would give us a superb view, allowing careful surveillance for a safe route for the rest of the journey.

If only the door hadn't slammed shut before we were inside, the vibration of the wood hitting home and sending the echo through our chests.

Shadow's muffled barks filled the air, bringing with it the inevitable shrill reply coming from what seemed like everywhere around us.

# 12

## JESSICA

Why didn't I pick the gun back up? Alex was afraid of what she thought I might have done, I got that. But why hadn't I picked it up as we left?

Why had I stepped over so many bodies holding pistols, or those with rifles still slung over their shoulders?

Running towards the church, so much weaponry lay scattered to the ground. But now everywhere I looked the dead were civilians, armed only with bloodied fists or the occasional long kitchen knife.

The shrill call electrified my nerves as the church doors slammed after Shadow passed through. I'd seen the terror in the whites of someone's eyes, looking past us from between the gap in the great doors as if we weren't there.

Still rushing forward, I turned my back to the church, barely slowing my pace. I expected to see their fear aimed at the woman held between Alex and Logan. I expected her ashen face to be their reason for shutting us out, but before I could complete the turn, I realised what I would see glaring at our backs.

Slowing, I backed up to the doors whilst trying to keep my expression calm, but by the fear projecting my way I could tell the three knew I stared at a terrifying figure who hadn't been behind them moments earlier.

Each of us knew what the sound had meant and as my back hit against the heavy wood, I felt the dog's bark from the other side, catching hurried words as I banged with my knuckles hard against the solid doors.

"Let us in," I called, my knuckles stinging with the assault as I kept my back to the door and my gaze fixed on a young man with his teeth bared in my direction. I didn't want to join his ranks; I wanted to stay alive to be human for as long as I could.

I heard a soft feminine voice beyond the thick wood.

The others arrived at the door, but I kept staring to the young man's face as he crouched back on his heels, knowing what would come next. Looking down from the sharp line of his crewcut, his face was covered in a mask of blood; the lens of his eyes were crystal clear, not white. The ragged remains of the hospital gown did little to cover up his lean torso and couldn't hide the ripple of his leg muscles as he tensed for the jump with his dog tags settling around his neck.

It still hadn't jumped as Alex called out, her fist joining mine to hammer at the door.

I stopped hitting at the wood, my mind racing in search of what I could do to save Alex from this fate.

I stared, my thoughts turning to question why it still hadn't leapt. Was it lethargic from a feed or was time passing so slowly in my mind alone? But no, the drum at the door told me nothing had slowed. The dog still barked at our backs, and muffled voices called out an argument raging the other side.

A chill breeze sent a wave of stench across my face and I saw the first of the crowd coming around the houses.

Logan moved at my side, heaving Cassie too so I could share her hold with Alex. Her warmth distracted me, but I daren't look from the creature who had yet to make a move.

Shuffling her weight, I watched as Logan stepped forward with his fists balled. Was he insane?

It was then I caught sight of the body in green, discarded in the tumble of flesh we'd seen piled up as we rounded the corner. From this angle, I saw the black and green of a rifle.

"Logan," I snapped, trying to keep my voice even in hope I wouldn't startle the wrong response. The raised voices at our backs quietened.

Although Logan hadn't replied to my call, he turned to look as I raised my hand to point out the weapon.

The creature settled further back on his haunches, his

chest bulging. The coiled spring was about to pop and it issued a squeal so loud I wanted to fall to the floor with my hands at my ears.

Logan pounced, rushing with great strides, but before he'd covered a quarter of the distance to the gun and our only hope, the creature leapt to the air.

# 13

## LOGAN

With the decision made somewhere deep inside, my gaze set to the long black barrel pointing skyward. I ran towards the pile, ignoring the creature's speed as it rose to the air and out of my vision.

I expected time to slow or my strides to falter. Instead, staring at the weapon, I just hoped it was loaded, primed and ready to go.

Screams called out, but not just from the abomination; the sounds echoing from high inside the church and all around me. I stayed my course, staring to the pile, keeping my gaze away from the crowd of creatures which had followed us here, knowing even if the magazine were full, there wouldn't be enough ammunition to deal with them all.

Four more steps were all I needed and with my arm outstretched, fingers ready, I raced ahead. Surprised when I felt the cold of the metal, my fingers were too eager and pushed the barrel away. As it slapped to the slick of blood, it broke through a thin crust drying on the surface.

In awe I'd covered the distance with my life intact, my fingernails scraped to the tarmac as they dived into the cold, thick blood to pull up the rifle. Spinning around with its slippery weight in my hands, I stared, mouth wide as I watched the creature land on top of Jess, who collapsed under its weight.

I'd known her for such a brief time. An icon from the TV, who early in her career had uncovered a massive child abuse ring in a series of kids home. They'd named the public enquiry after her, with a raft of laws following.

Not content to settle back, a few months later with the country still reeling from the level of the abuse, she discovered an MP taking money to help a rogue pharmaceutical company get government contracts. The MP went to prison. A competitor took over the company when its share price fell through the floor.

The next we saw her covering war zones, reporting border skirmishes between Israel and Palestine. For someone so young, she'd achieved so much, but with her status, neither the public nor the producers had the appetite to watch rockets raining down around her. She moved to a new domain. She took on heads of state, interviewing leaders of terrorist organisations. Company heads. She questioned the worst regimes and those who'd made the biggest of mistakes; those that wouldn't give anyone else the answers.

Glamorous to the point of a movie star, the audience loved her. She never appeared on panel shows. Never sat next to a comedian to make light of the world.

And now here she was, her life ending during the biggest news story ever to be told, under the weight of a crazed new being tearing at her flesh.

But no.

With Cassie at her back, hitting out as best as she could, and Alex beating at the creature's shoulder, its bared teeth hovered above Jess's face as she stared back with a fear I'd seen for the first time.

The world seemed to have stopped.

I don't know if its pause was real or imagined, but it passed, the former soldier pulling back from the bite, lifting its head and turning up to Alex.

By this time I had the sight to my eye, the tip of the thin metal at the centre of its forehead; I'd pulled the trigger and watched the creature spill to the side as a great spray of red burst from its head.

Three faces turned in my direction, their mouths wide. Only then did I realise the risk I'd just taken; if the shot had only been a little less lucky, I could have killed any one of them.

With the rifle shaking in my grip, I locked eyes with Jess

until her fists were back at the door and I raced from the footsteps getting ever closer.

Without warning, the voices from behind the wood were crisp and clear as the heavy doors opened, a crack at first, then pulled wider when dirty rough hands shot out, yanking Cassie into the darkness.

# 14

Panic erupted as Cassie disappeared, wrenched into the next hell. Before I could act, the hands were back, finding Alex and pulling her from my view, despite her protests. As she slid between the gap, Alex reached towards Jess still on the floor.

Jumping forward, I peered into the darkness then rushed to Jess, dragging her from her daze, helping her to her feet as she struggled to get purchase. As she rose, I felt hands through the crack, pushing me away. The sun behind me lit up two pale figures, but then they were gone, taking Jess with them.

I thought the door would close and I would have to turn to face the crowd gathering over my shoulder, but the sun glinted low to the horizon and Shadow barked as the pair of large, dirt-covered hands grabbed at my coat, pulling me forward between the doors before the wood slammed closed.

Metal slid across metal as the hands released their grip. The thud of bodies drummed at the wood and I paused, my panic only subsiding when the barrier held firm.

With my vision settling, growing accustomed to the flickering candles dotted around, I turned with my fists balled, searching for Cassie in the faint orange glow.

Figures gathered in a circle, their shadows moving against the wall. To the slow hammering of movement on the other side of the doors, each figure stood still, feet fixed to the floor, as faces I knew and others I didn't, stared on wide-eyed in silence.

Stalemate.

Again, time felt as if it slowed; only the pounding rhythm of bodies slapping against the door kept me in the moment.

I watched the faces, their forms coming into focus as my fists relaxed. I found Shadow, or he found me with excited breath as he arrived at my side. I saw Jess standing beside me, her expression as unsure as mine. The corner of her mouth rose as she found Alex opposite her.

I glanced over the four strangers; two men and two women, each of their stares uncertain. Then I saw her, Cassie kneeling at the side of the door, peering to the stone floor as she fought to catch her breath.

The strangers stared at the rifle gripped tight to my side. I ran the short few steps to Cassie, pulled her from her knees and cupped her hot cheeks. She shook away my touch as if in pain, but grabbed at my hands to steady herself. She was burning up.

Alex joined at my side, helping take her weight and we turned, fixing our attention back on the eyes gawking in our direction.

To our left, and closest by far, stood a silver-haired man about my height. With aged-weathered skin and wrinkles accentuated by the flickering light, his mouth stretched out a warm smile. With tired, red eyes, he wore a blue overcoat, the type technology teachers wore over a shirt and tie.

Next to him stood a younger woman, my age I guessed. In jeans and a fleece, she held her palm flat to her cheek. Although her eyes were wide, they seemed small as they darted between us and the scuffle beyond the door. She looked to the guy beside her when he turned and ran out of the vestibule, leaving only the echo of feet slapping on metal stairs rising up the tower.

Each pair of eyes roved around the grand space, flitting from one noise to another, imagined or not. No one seemed to know the next move, and we stood in the darkness, drawing in the dry dust and scents of oil, grease and warm candle wax as the clatter from the steps above faded to nothing.

Next to the woman with the hand at her cheek stood another, much older and with a stern expression looking my way. With her face covered in wrinkles and a head full of fine light hair, I could just make out she wore a tweed skirt and white blouse, looking as if she was there for Sunday service.

Beside her stood the other guy; he'd been stroking Shadow's back before the dog ran to my side and I pinned the soft voice we'd heard on him, even though he'd not said a word since. His age was somewhere between the other two and with a slight frame, he wore large round glasses he kept pushing up his nose.

We each listened, appearing to share a hope the noise beyond the doors would soon fade.

I expected words, but no one spoke. Only the building sound of feet on the steps from above forced any reaction. The women gave a collective gasp as the feet above missed a step, only to land with a clatter on the next.

"Those stairs are a death trap," the guy with round glasses said, his voice high and head shaking in the dull light. Heads turned to where the steps started when the grey-haired guy reappeared with his deep voice slightly out of breath.

"Too many. Hundreds."

No one needed to ask what he'd tried to count.

"What about...?" the guy with the round glasses said.

"It's dead," the larger guy replied, his forehead damp with perspiration. "Excellent job, son," he added. Turning to me, he raised his dirty hand, but held himself back from patting me on the shoulder.

I nodded, unsure how to take the praise as the memory of being shut out flooded back.

"Which one of you wouldn't let us in?" Only just able to keep my voice level, I watched the guy glance at the one with round glasses, but then turned away as if he'd realised what he'd done.

"They're scared. We're scared," he said in a deep voice, his hands opening out towards me as he took a step forward. "You can understand that. Can't you?"

"Those monsters..." The woman who held her hand to her cheek spoke in a high voice, wrapping her free arm around herself when she couldn't bear to finish.

I looked past the guy without glasses, scowling as I checked out each of the strangers, tensing my grip on the rifle between my arm and side. No one moved; only the guy with the glasses looked my way with his chin raised in defiance.

I looked to Jess, squeezed Cassie at my side and my anger faded. These people were a sorry sight and didn't look as if they could take a cold-blooded decision to let us die.

A distant shrill scream cut through the air, breaking through the drum of limbs against the wood.

"But you're here now," the grey-haired guy said. "Right?" he added as he took a white handkerchief from his pocket and wiped his brow.

Turning my head, I saw the shadow of another figure at the edge of the room to the left. A woman with long ebony hair and a slim figure stepped into the soft light where she stared from a doorway.

Eventually she pulled matches from her pocket and lit more candles on a table opposite the entrance.

"Sorry," the grey-haired guy said with a sudden great enthusiasm. "How rude of me. We haven't introduced ourselves."

Stepping back, he turned the handkerchief on his hands and began rubbing at the black marks smearing his skin as I connected the smell of grease, sawdust and something else I couldn't quite put my finger on.

"Paul," he said, extending his dirty hand in my direction.

About to hold out my free hand, I peered down to the drying blood caking my skin. The same blood which covered the rifle. The blood of so many victims.

Looking back to Paul, I watched him slowly pull away as if embarrassed we couldn't shake like civilised society required us too.

"Logan," I said. "This is Cassie," I added, then looked across her as Alex spoke.

"Alex." She raised her palm and gave a shallow wave. "And this is Jess," she said, pointing two fingers in her direction.

I watched Paul linger on each of our faces, nodding with such enthusiasm he reminded me of an excitable dog who just wanted to make his owner happy. His look returned to Cassie, lingering just long enough for me to notice.

I expected him to speak, to voice concern, but he turned away, offering his hand out to my side and the lady with the long dark hair who'd just lit the candle.

"Amanda," he said. We each exchanged polite nods, our heads settling when she fixed a squint to Cassie.

"Is she okay?" Amanda said. "And it's Mandy, please."

Drawing my head up and down in a slow nod, I tightened my grip around Cassie's shoulders.

"She's fine," Jess butted in as she stepped forward.

"Beth and Harry," Paul added, gesturing to the older woman and then to the guy whose glasses continued to fall down his nose. "And this is Stacey," he said, turning to the younger woman who seemed as if her palm was glued to her cheek.

Paul peered down to my side. "And who might this be?" he asked in a childish voice.

"Shadow," I said, keeping my voice flat.

Paul stepped forward, knelt beside Shadow and ruffled the hair around his neck with great enthusiasm.

"What happened to you boy?" he said when his hand traced the wide circle of shaven hair along Shadow's abdomen.

I didn't reply. No one did. Instead, we exchanged nods without voice to the occasional rattle of the heavy doors.

Jess's voice cut through the silence first. "How long have you been here?"

Paul stood, glancing to Beth at his left before turning back to Jess. "A few days."

"Why weren't you evacuated?"

"By the time we realised they were evacuating it was too late. They were drawn to church," he said with a corner-mouth smile, as he pressed his palms together and pushed the edge of his hands to his lips.

"Do you have supplies?" I asked.

"Some. Yes." I watched his gaze catch on Mandy's as she stepped closer into the circle. "We got a little of what we need by scavenging the houses." He nodded towards the door. "There used to be more of us. We had people out there when the bombs came. I don't think..." His words tailed off, and I heard one of the women sniff. "Do you know what's going on?"

I looked to Jess, but although she'd seen me, she didn't look my way, instead speaking to the group. "Do you have a TV?"

They each shook their heads.

"The power's been out for a few days now. Even if someone could carry a TV over, it's not worth the risk."

Cassie sagged at my side, then tensing, she pulled herself upright, but her look remained vacant.

"Is there somewhere Cassie can rest?" I asked, turning to Paul.

"Oh, sorry. Yes. Come in, come in."

Paul rushed away, beckoning me to the right and through a wide doorway to the main hall of the church.

Glancing to Jess and then to Alex, each nodded a reply, seeming to agree this place would be safe enough, for now at least.

I was the first to follow, supporting Cassie with Alex on the other side as I tried to soften my steps, desperate to keep the echo from resounding across the wide chamber.

The space where the rear rows of pews should have stood in the main hall was empty. The tang of sawn wood and chemicals grew stronger as we crossed the threshold. Shadow followed at my side, but after a few steps he stopped, turned and barked.

I twisted, watching as he pointed his long snout back towards Jess following.

With all eyes turning to the dog, the echo of the bark died. I could almost sense each breath pause in the room, not listening for the call but the surrounding effect.

Paul rushed back, kneeling beside Shadow and ruffling the fur around his neck.

"It's all right boy, you're safe in here. No one's getting

in."

I watched as Shadow kept looking at Jess whilst rolling his head in time with the guy's enthusiastic rubs.

Turning away, I did my best to ignore the whispers at the back of the room and I tried not to note the fragments of hushed conversation I caught. Instead, I took in the room's detail.

Wood covered each of the lower level windows, held in place with metal bars, the wide hall lit with candles around the perimeter flickering in the swirling draft. To the side were the leftovers of the task. A pair of tall, dark gas canisters with pipes snaking from the top and two plastic sawhorses standing to their side supporting the remains of a pew, the top scattered with tools.

After a moment, Paul stood and followed my gaze.

"Are you good with your hands?" he said, with a wide, optimistic grin.

I shrugged a reply. "It looks like you've got everything under control."

"I was an engineer, before I found my true calling. It's good to have a project. I live..." He paused and corrected himself. "I lived over the road and just about got some of my tools," he said, laughing, but the joy in his voice seemed to slow as he looked to each of us not sharing his enthusiasm.

"Nearly killing himself," Beth said, stepping beside him.

Paul gave a wry smile before turning to the floor like he'd been a naughty boy.

"Anyway, sorry," he said, and strode forward to the front of the church as we followed, pausing only when I heard a raised voice from behind us.

"No. I won't," she said, the voice rising further.

I turned to see Mandy striding past Jess, stopping an arms' length from me and pointing to Cassie with her face pinched. "I demand you tell us what's wrong with her. Now."

# 15

## JESSICA

The dog knew.

He knew the monster I'd become.

I couldn't stay there long. They should have barred the doors with me outside.

"Follow me," the man with the oily hands had said, his voice as if already in another room.

I paused, checking for the hunger, pleased when I couldn't feel the sensation rising from my gut. I felt nothing, no emotion for them or myself.

The dog followed as the guy moved away. I was sure he glanced back, the shine of his eyes glinting in the candlelight telling me he knew. Telling me he was keeping a close eye.

I stayed towards the back of the group, but pleased to get away from the slap of flesh against the door and the low hum vibrating through the wood that I wondered if I was the only one to hear.

As the room opened out into the nave, my anxiety lowered in the glow of candlelight and upturned benches, relaxing more when I smelt the freshly cut wood and the deep, almost fruity scent of ancient timber mixed with the dust and warm candle wax.

Paul made some comment to Logan, but I didn't catch the words and when he looked to each of us to join in his laughter, I didn't reply, only nodding to hide my distraction.

I watched as Paul led Logan and Cassie forward, turning as the panicked call came from behind.

"I demand you tell us what's wrong with her. Now," Mandy said with her voice on the edge of hysteria.

No one replied. Logan turned away, Paul following as

I stayed to the spot, watching them walk away from the woman who looked on in disbelief as they ignored her call.

I held back, looking on at the end of the impressive hall as Paul fashioned a makeshift bed from kneeling cushions, heading back only when they'd laid Cassie down to rest.

"Am I invisible?" Mandy said, shaking her head as she looked between Paul and the others we'd found in this place. "You need to get a backbone, Paul, or are you going to let these people walk all over us?"

He turned, glaring with a withering look, his deep voice booming in the wide space. "These people are our guests. Just wait."

Mandy muttered to herself as if Paul's words had taken her by surprise.

No one else spoke as Logan waited, sitting by Cassie's side, touching her forehead and shaking his head. We waited as if the tension would explode as soon as Cassie settled.

After a minute, maybe a little more, Logan stood, catching those in the room by surprise as he spoke.

"I'm going up the tower. I have to see what's out there, then I'll come back and explain everything. I promise."

He strode out of the grand hall with Paul following. Shadow sat at Cassie's side and Logan didn't look back to check, as if he knew the dog would watch over her without instruction. I had to marvel at the trust he'd placed in the dog, enough to leave Cassie in amongst the people he'd only just met.

I didn't look to see if the dog stared my way.

Striding down between the remaining pews, Logan didn't speak and Paul held his hands open as he walked behind as if in apology to their slowly shaking heads. I felt a little sorry for Mandy, agreeing that Paul's obvious need to please people was sooner or later going to get him killed.

I expected the raised voices to start moments later, but instead I heard feet on the metal steps and found Paul with the others in a semi-circle around the entrance to the staircase and the sound of Logan's feet rising up the tower.

"Is she bitten?" came Mandy's dry voice again.

They each turned to face me. Mandy gripped a hammer, pointed out by Paul's widening eyes as he caught the sight in his peripheral vision, double taking to make sure he'd seen right.

# 16

## LOGAN

In darkness and with my feet slipping on the worn steps, the rifle pinned at my side, I rubbed my hands with the rag grabbed from the side cabinet just before I rose up the tower. At least the clatter of the metal shut out the rattle from the big wooden doors.

Sucking air, I jabbed my shin on another riser, but felt thankful as I looked up to see light from above growing more intense as I rose. I pulled back from the thoughts of what I'd see when I summited, instead concentrating my effort on placing my feet.

I heard steps join the chorus from below, their feet adding to the rattle. I had to do this quick. I had to get a look and form my plan. The way that woman looked at Cassie, I had to get back to her side. At least Shadow would bark if I had to race back down.

The smooth stone walls lightened as I climbed, seeing old metal candle holders protruding empty from the wall and a long rope hanging in the central space, running through holes in each wooden floor I passed.

My lungs felt as if I'd been climbing the Empire State, not the four or five storeys I'd already lost track of. The length of my back ached from the fall down the steps into the tunnel.

The dull brass of the great bell came into view, and I readied myself for what I knew would be an abominable sight. It would be much worse than we'd already glimpsed. Steeling myself for the scale, I placed a foot on the wooden floor.

Now here I was, and I glanced to my hand, still blotched red despite the stains covering the dark mottled cloth.

Each face of the square room had a small window set

in the centre of a much larger stone wall. Taking slow steps, I looked to the wall, not wanting to see anything until I was ready to process.

I chose the window furthest away, hoping it would face from the hospital despite the climb disorienting my sense of direction.

I'd chosen right. The remains of the hospital were not in the view; instead, I was greeted by familiar columns of rising smoke in the distance which varied in thickness and colour, spewing into the air. Trees spread across the ground with the dark green of those that didn't change with the season.

With a slow clatter of feet on the metal steps rising, about to move, I saw a crater of what I could only guess used to be a house. In the garden, a trampoline sat covered with rubble and brick scattered across its black surface.

I shouldn't have focused on that space. I shouldn't have looked around its perimeter. I shouldn't have stared at the bodies. The remaining parts, at least.

Movement caught my eye, and I peered closer, seeking detail, but I should have known the regret I would feel when what remained of the small body moved. I closed my eyes before my brain could tell me if they were still alive.

Footsteps climbed the stairs, and I turned, knowing these days I couldn't trust those we'd just met.

# 17

## JESSICA

Logan turned from the window as I arrived.

"How bad is it?" I asked.

He closed his eyes, shaking his head as he moved to the next window. He still hadn't spoken, instead turning his head from side to side as he peered across the view.

"What are you looking for?"

"A vehicle. Something big enough for us all," he replied without looking back, his gaze intent on the horizon. "I didn't see anything drivable on the way here. Did you?"

"No," I said as I stepped to the nearest window, the columns of smoke more numerous than when I'd filmed this morning.

Looking out, I couldn't help but think of the people in their homes in hope by now they were watching my message. In hope they were taking note.

I tried to ignore the occasional body on the floor and didn't care to peer over the edge of the sill to see the crowd I could hear still surrounding the building.

My gaze ran across the horizon and caught on bright colours painted on the washed-out grey of the tarmac. The playground empty of kids. Neither alive or dead, or anywhere in between. I was thankful of the timing. Thankful it had happened in the holidays when families would have been together and evacuated as one unit.

Those that made it, at least.

"Did you get left behind?" I said without thought. The words seemed to echo in the compact room.

After a moment he huffed a distracted reply.

"Why didn't you evacuate?"

In the pause, I heard him turn as new footsteps rose

from below. Logan stood beside me, but with his focus still beyond the window.

"We missed the evacuation. We were out in the sticks." He scanned the horizon. "Even more isolated than here."

I nodded, but he wouldn't have seen. He pulled in a sharp breath and I knew he'd found what he'd been looking for.

"There," he said, pushing the window wide on the creaking hinges to let the smoke-filled air in as if he needed to check he wasn't seeing an image projected to the glass. I followed his finger to the back third of a white minibus just visible as it protruded out from a stone building. The School.

He thought we were going with him.

Logan rushed out of sight as I lingered on the view, only turning around when I heard his steps falling with a great weight as if he were taking two at a time.

He wasn't my problem. No one was. I'd done my bit.

I only owed Alex safety. Perhaps she should go with them.

I turned back to stare through the window, peering to the minibus. It was one of the few vehicles around and seemed undamaged, from the part I could see at least, protected by the canopy above. All others sat on their roofs or otherwise abandoned.

I couldn't fault his plan, other than he had to leave the safety of the church to get it.

I had a decision to make.

When the crowd died back, they could run to the school and hopefully find the keys, or maybe hot-wire it.

I looked again to see if I could make out the registration plate and therefore the age, but I couldn't.

Stepping closer, I peered over the edge and saw enough to know the creatures weren't going anywhere in a hurry.

I listened to the mis-step as Logan lost his footing, catching himself before regaining a rhythm a little slower than before.

I'd decided.

I'd get Alex to the minibus, then when she was safe, I'd slip away to make sure I could no longer be a danger to anyone and start my search for Toni.

It must have been a good few minutes later when the raised voices downstairs pulled me back from my gaze.

A woman. A deep voice, too, and I thought of the hammer in Mandy's hand.

I waited for Shadow to join in, the crowd outside taking note with the beat at the door punctuated by a shrill call in the distance which made me pull the window up tight.

# 18

## LOGAN

The raised voices lowered as I slowed to drift down the tower and hush my pace, knowing with every quiet moment one of those things outside would lose interest until they were all gone and I could get the minibus to continue our journey to safety.

With each step down I tried to turn away from scenes which had become all too familiar. The destruction. The death spread across the sleepy village and beyond.

I tried not to think about the places we'd travelled on our journey so far. I tried not to imagine the villages we hadn't seen, or the towns, the cities. All those people affected. How far did this reach?

A short flurry of footsteps rose from below, bringing with them an orange glow and the odour of grease and sweat until they stopped and I laid eyes on the figure waiting in the stairwell's curve.

Paul smiled up toward me, unable to meet my gaze as he held a candle. He moved back down, but stopped when I hadn't followed.

"They have questions," he said.

I nodded. I would too in their situation.

"They're scared. I'm sure you can understand."

I nodded again.

"Is she bitten?"

Taking the last few steps, the lobby seemed so dark now I'd witnessed the sun again, but I still made out each of the four gathered around the foot of the stairs with Alex nowhere to be seen.

"Let's go somewhere we can talk," I said, making eye contact with each of the group, then looking across to the doors rattling in reply to the slightest sound.

Paul nodded, leaning toward me as he held his hand open to the main hall.

Moving to the wide space, our footsteps echoed as the procession followed past the pews. Shadow raised his head, lying at Cassie's side as we passed. Alex sat on the pew a few rows back, then stood, heading the opposite way to where we headed.

Eventually we gathered in a compact room at the back, lined with white, black and purple robes hanging from hooks buried deep in the stone.

"She's cured," I said, moving to the wall, my gaze catching Jess as she joined the back of the huddle.

A collective gasp ran through the room. Stacey's hand flashed back to her cheek, Harry kept his finger on the bridge of his glasses to hold them in place as the other two swapped looks. Paul raised a single brow, but otherwise didn't react, and I noticed Alex hadn't followed us into the room.

Mandy met my gaze as Beth to her left said something under her breath.

"She's fine now," I said. "They were working on a cure. In the hospital."

"She's bitten?" Beth asked, glancing back as if she could see Cassie through the stone walls.

I nodded. "But she's cured," I said, looking to each of them.

They swapped looks as if trying to come to a consensus about how they should feel. Paul's expression dropped as Mandy spoke again.

"She doesn't look fine. How do you know she's cured?"

I took a hard swallow, my gaze flitting to each again. Fixing on Jess's raised brow, I spoke. "She's tired. That's all. Maybe a little fever. But we've been through a lot."

"Did you meet her?" Jess cut in. Everyone in the room turned and for the first time, I saw an interest in Jess's expression.

"Who?" I asked, shaking my head as they looked back

in my direction.

"My height and build. Brunette. Wore lots of makeup. She left in the helicopter."

I stared for a moment, pushing down the annoyance of the question until the image of the woman she'd described became clear. I nodded, forcing away the memories of the glass cell and the purple liquid.

"Briefly."

Jess's face lit up as if she'd woken for the first time.

"How did she seem?"

Mandy stepped forward, holding her palm in the air.

"Hang on. Never mind that. How do you know that woman?" she said, almost spitting the words as she pointed past the closed door at her back. "Isn't she putting us in danger?"

I turned away from Jess and looked Mandy in the eye, trying to remind myself I would be the same in her situation. I would want to know. I would want to be sure.

Taking a deep breath, I told them everything.

I told them about New Year's Eve. The party. The lights going out. The music stopping.

I told them how we didn't leave until the next day. I told them about the roadblocks, watching Jess nod as I spoke. I saw their eyes widen, and hands cover their mouths. I told them of the first sighting in the dark. How Chloe had been bitten, remembering each of my friend's faces.

With a smile rising, I spoke of finding Cassie and her sister, my lips faltering as I re-lived how I'd almost killed them both.

Fixing my gaze on Jess, my smile fell away as I spoke of the fire and the moment Chloe turned, taking two more of my friends.

I told of the helicopter. How we'd thought they'd saved us. How we waved our arms not to be missed. I told them of the gunfire. The utter destruction.

My voice broke as I spoke of Andrew saving the day with fireworks.

I told them of Commander Lane. How he turned out to be an exceptional friend.

I told them of Shadow and then Toby and his sister. I told them how Toby was bitten the day before, or one before that. I was no longer sure.

I watched Jess's reaction as I spoke the boy's name. A rise of her brow as she turned away, then back to me. She was looking for Alex.

Wiping my forehead on my sleeve, I told them about Naomi laying in the bed, then going with Cassie to the next village. I spoke of hiding away, the fear of looters and then finding the hospital. I told them of Doctor Lytham, Jess not able to hide the flicker of her eyelids as I spoke.

My voice caught when I talked of the doctor's interest in the boy and how I wasn't sure if telling them was the right thing, but now I knew I'd made the right decision.

I told them of the group of soldiers who tried to protect us. I told of how they hadn't known about the powerful creatures we all came to fear so much. By the wide-eyed looks between them, the once-human I'd shot outside was the only one they'd seen.

I spoke of how the fast creatures overwhelmed us, forcing us from the Land Rovers. I told them how we got back to the village, only able to find my friends because of Shadow.

Fighting to keep my voice level, I told them all but the children were now dead.

Paul stepped to my side, gripping my arm as I patted the top of his hand, not able to thank him with my cracking voice whilst I marvelled at the kindness of someone I'd only just met.

I told them how McCole turned in the back of the Land Rover as we escaped. I told them how I had to put down one of my oldest friends. And then to find Andrew bitten. And Cassie. Shadow with the wound to his side and how he'd saved the day for the second time.

I spoke of the hospital, finding the place overwhelmed. I spoke about surviving against the odds to find the doctor still alive. Gritting my teeth, I told of how she'd killed Andrew.

Jess kept her gaze fixed my way and I turned back to the group to find each looking back, slowly nodding.

Then I spoke of waking in the glass room, Shadow stitched up, lucky the wound was only superficial, then Cassie arriving back to sleep at my side.

"That woman was there," I said directly to Jess. "They offered medicine."

I laughed gently as I told them how Cassie wouldn't take it unless I had some too. My words slowed as I spoke of waking in the morning. This morning. Waking to the sound of the helicopter on the roof, then finding everyone piling in. Of seeing the children being led into the helicopter and off to safety.

I spoke of the joy of knowing the children were safe. I watched Jess's reaction as I spoke of the kids, but my mind was on not telling them about how they'd shot Lane.

I told them how we would move on as soon as Cassie was well enough; as soon as the creatures outside had moved away. We would find where they'd taken the children so we could reunite.

"So, yes," I said. "Cassie will be fine."

We stood in silence for a long moment.

"How do you know it's worked?" Mandy said in a quiet voice, the other four turned to glare at her as I cursed the run of feet echoing and the clatter of metal beyond the main hall.

"Because she just has to," I said, and took a seat, closing my eyes to slow the welling of emotion rising to my voice. It felt such a relief to share what we'd been through. I'd been strong for so long, knowing I had to lead the way.

"I don't think we should take the chance," Mandy said, looking between each of the people who were in the church when we'd arrived.

I tried not to let the disappointment tell in my voice.

"What are you going to do?" I said in a slow voice. "Kick us out there?"

Paul stepped forward and pushed his arms out. "No

one's getting kicked out. Let's take a breath."

I looked up to see Mandy shooting a venomous glance in my direction as she turned to Paul.

It was Jess's voice that broke the silence, stepping toward me.

"I'm afraid the children are not as safe as you think."

I lifted my head, my vision swaying with the rush of blood.

"What?" I said, the only word I could get out. I felt the anger flushing away with her words, but before she could speak, the door flung open and Alex stood with wide-eyed alarm as she fought to calm her breath enough to speak.

"Helicopters. And lots of them."

# 19

## JESSICA

Alex's appearance at the door jarred my thoughts, shaking away the questions building up at Logan's extraordinary account. If the tale hadn't been so much like my own, I don't know how I could have believed him. But could the helicopters mean she'd come back? Had Toni seen my transmission and turned around now she knew I was still alive?

Alex disappeared and to the pounding of rotor blades, they each ran. Logan and I followed in procession to the hallway whilst ignoring their flurry of questions about what their appearance could mean.

I looked to Logan, both of us turning to watch with disbelief as they headed to the door as if to lift the great metal bar and let the creatures in. They'd not listened to a word he'd said.

Logan raised his voice. "What are you doing?" he called, running past them then turning to stop their flow to the main doors as the thumping rhythm of the helicopter grew near. He let the rifle dangle by the strap over his shoulder. He slapped his hands to the top of the heavy bar spread across the door, then pushed his back against the wood, holding his hands out to keep Mandy away. A flurry of feet clattered up the steps to the insistent shouts for Logan to get out of her way.

"They're still the other side," he pleaded with his eyebrows low, not hiding his confusion at their need to die horribly. "Haven't you heard what I said back there? Those helicopters are not here to save us."

Paul stepped to Logan's side, his eyes widening as if he'd woken from a trance. Turning, he pushed his hands out to match Logan's gesture.

"No," he said in his gruff voice. "He's right." But only Beth seemed to take notice. "No," he snapped, raising his volume.

Out of the corner of my eye, a renewed surge from the other side of the door jolted both the men forward.

With the boom of Paul's voice, the three slowed their frenzy, standing still to look up as if seeing Logan and Paul for the first time. None of them could look my way as their breath settled.

"They're not here to save us," Logan said. The wood at his back rattled with a renewed vigour as he took a slow step from the door.

I turned away in the lull, listening to the heavy sound above our heads. The helicopters hovered close by and I shared an unsure look with Logan.

"I've got to see," I said. He nodded back and we split from the group to race up the steps, trusting Paul could handle them on his own.

With Logan out of breath, we found Alex staring out of the window facing the hospital, her gaze fixed on the two Apache gunships I recognised from my time in Afghanistan as they swarmed low over its remains. A third helicopter came into view from the right, thumping at the air with its twin blades, the Chinook circling down from a great height.

"It's coming in to land," I mumbled.

We leaned forward as if to get a better view, shoulder to shoulder, watching as the gunships widened their circles until one rose high in the spiral.

Alex turned, bending over to catch her breath and swallowing hard. She looked up, holding my gaze, only standing and turning back as my eyes went wide to the sight of ropes uncoiling from the Chinook's rear and four ominous figures rappelling to the rubble.

It wasn't what I had hoped for.

The blacked-out figures spread across the ground, their heads down-turned as they picked their way across the rubble.

I heard the first call go out. Had they just found the van, or what remained? Or it was my imagination?

Alex looked to the ground below and I leaned forward, peering to what had taken her attention. The creatures were moving away from the entrance in a steady stream with their heads upturned, fixing on the buzz of the aircraft swarming around the hospital.

As they walked, they turned to follow, their legs correcting the direction, causing the crowd to seem as if it swayed left and right as they made their journey to the noise.

Rapid gunfire in the distance drew my attention and sped the creatures on. I saw fire erupting from the backdoor of the Chinook directed to the ground as the gunships swooped in from both directions, their long nose-mounted guns popping with smoke in quick succession.

The ground burst with explosions and raised dust to haze our view, rockets firing from the short wings slung with ordnance. I glanced back to see the crowd nearly gone from below us, dispersed on their journey away.

I looked for the dark soldiers in the rising dust at the hospital, trying to make out the snap of their guns. Only as the Chinook went low, its guns silencing, flanked by the gunships, did I see the group of four picking their way through the destruction in a rush to get to safety.

Then I saw it. A fifth figure behind. Gripping at Alex's upper arm, I stared at the race to the back of the wide helicopter.

As if someone had fast-forwarded the scene, the last figure was no longer in view. I refocused at Alex's intake of breath and caught a dark blur arcing through the air to the renewed call of gunfire before it slammed into the rotors, leaving only a cloud of blood and gore. The engine changed pitch, and the helicopter rocked with the hit, but lifted, unsteady into the air.

The guns took up again, rockets exploding where the Chinook had been as if in a last show of who was in charge. With an Apache taking a place at its front and back, they led the Chinook away.

Logan's voice took me by surprise, breaking the serenity of the icy winter's morning left behind.

"Look," he said, and we turned to see him raised up on his hands to balance on the sill of the next window along, nodding down to the village square and the fountain in the centre where only the truly dead, the unmoving, lay in the space which moments before had been thick with the bodies on their feet.

Dropping down, he moved to the next window and rose again. He turned with a brilliant smile and a glint in his eye.

"Now's our chance."

# 20

## LOGAN

Taking care not to call the creatures back with the clatter at my feet, I raced down the steps, knowing if they came back we had no idea if we'd ever get such an opportunity again. I hadn't dared to think about how long we could last in this place.

Despite everything that had happened since, I couldn't get what she'd said about the kids out of my mind. I was desperate to question what she'd meant, but for now I had to concentrate on getting to the minibus so we could stand a hope of finding where they'd taken the children.

Jumping from the last step, I realised I hadn't formed a plan. Who would keep Cassie safe whilst I wasn't here? Who would take care of her if I didn't make it back?

Jess landed a step behind, followed by Alex. Jess pointed to the door, raising her finger to her mouth for all to see.

Paul looked up wide-eyed as he stood with the others surrounding him in a semi-circle as if in some great debate.

"I found a minibus," I whispered. "It's big enough so we can all get away."

I watched eyes widen and mouths hang low.

"What about them the other side?" Paul said, stepping closer whilst keeping his voice low.

"They're gone for now, but they'll be back," I replied, matching his volume.

"I'll come with you," he said. "I've got something that might help."

Before we could debate, Paul stepped to the door, then heaved the metal bar from across the wood. Looking as if he was about to speak, Jess again raised her finger to her lips in silence, then turned to Alex.

"Stay here please," Jess said.

"Can you watch after Cass?" I added.

Screwing up her face, I saw Alex's brief protest, but as she relaxed her shoulders, she gave a shallow nod, helping Paul lay the heavy metal bar to the side of the entrance. Alex would be the one to protect Cassie.

As we rushed the short distance to the doors, Paul's eyes went wide and he dashed off to the main part of the church.

Dropping the rifle from my shoulder, I glanced to the huddle of the other four who looked on in disbelief as we headed to the door to do the very thing we'd stopped them from doing moments earlier.

Jess heaved the right-hand door with her shoulder and I took the left. Each side swung wide, letting in the chill of the bright morning as I gripped the rifle, arcing it in a semi-circle, thankful the village square was just as empty as we'd seen from above.

"Be ready when we come back. We'll get you guys somewhere safer," I said, turning.

Not waiting for their response, I ran from the church, looking to the road opposite the way we'd arrived, whilst trying to visualise where the school sat in relation to what we'd seen from the high view.

Turning to heavy breath behind, Paul followed with a long metal pry-bar, held two-handed like a spear as I cringed at the bass sound of the doors slamming closed.

Twisting back around, scanning left and right as I ran with the gun tracing my view, swinging its weight either side at my hip, still not able to forget McCole's few seconds of training on the rifle. He'd told me never to do this if I wanted to hit anything.

Jess ran alongside with Paul's heavy footsteps not far behind. I tried to ignore the scattered piles of bodies whilst wondering for a fleeting moment who put them there.

My gaze switched to the smashed windows in the

houses we passed, glancing to their dark interiors, hoping I wouldn't see movement and turning away as the sight got too much for my nerves.

At the other side of the square, a house on the corner marked the start of the road leaving the village. I didn't pause at the thought of what could be around the corner, instead surging on past the fear of what we could run into.

As the distance grew between us and the church, the thought of leaving Cassie behind weighed heavy with each step.

A gentle wind rustled through the trees and I marvelled at the near silence broken only by our footsteps. I should have been grateful, but I just couldn't help thinking it was yet another lull before the storm.

The road ahead snapped back into focus and, clenching my teeth, I realised I hadn't been paying attention.

Thankful the coast was still clear, the road ahead merged to a narrow lane as the houses on either side thinned. Bound by tall hedgerows, trees climbed at the edge of the road to form a canopy shielding us from the winter sun. The surface of the road had survived the bombing with no scars, leaving just a sheen of thin rubble scattered across the tarmac.

Still running, a gap in the hedge came into view to our right as the road veered to a single lane pointed out with a faded white sign, the lettering grey and washed out; St Edmund's Primary School.

Glancing to Jess, I walked forward in a wide arc, peering through the gap to the road which, although heavily worn, had been protected from debris by the dense hedgerow either side and the canopy curving above. I nodded to Jess who replied with a tip of her head and I repeated the gesture to Paul, puffing hard as he held the metal bar high.

With each long pace the road swept to the right, taking us back in the church's direction. Bright-green gates came into view, each side held to the other with a heavy padlock as they sat in the centre of the tall metal fence wrapping around the school.

Not far beyond the gates were three buildings, each so different from how they had looked from the tower. The thought pulled my gaze high in the church's direction, but I couldn't see it for the knot of trees.

A two-storey building stood in the middle, looking much like an over-sized cottage but with a row of roof windows and bright-red double doors in the centre, the school's name emblazoned above.

I scanned the posters in the downstairs windows, peering at the faded alphabet, times tables and childish works of art, lingering on a large picture with five tall figures growing in height from right to left. A family.

A vision of my parents came to life as they stared wide-eyed at me stood on the roof of the hospital with Cassie, watching the bombs fall amongst the carpet of bodies. I wondered if they would realise it was their son in such danger.

I closed my eyes at the thought of how they would react when they saw Jess's broadcast.

Swallowing hard, I looked to the right and a building much like a tall box with a flat roof. With thin windows high up the wall, I guessed it was a gym or a sports hall. The building to the left was much smaller and could have been a gatehouse or another classroom perhaps. None of the buildings appeared to have any damage, as if in a bubble protected from the chaos all around.

Between the two leftmost buildings was a thin road, and I turned my focus back to the gate, watching as Paul strode forward to push the pointed tip of the long bar into the centre of the shackle. Heaving on the other end of the bar, the long lever made light work of the clasp, sending the scrapped parts clattering to the road.

With a beaming smile, I nodded in Paul's direction then glanced around to make sure our sound hadn't drawn out creatures hiding in the bushes. I paused at the thought. Had I seen them hide before? The thought dissipated as the gates groaned wide against Jess's push.

Nothing ambushed us as we stepped through.

I looked to Paul and our wide-eyed expressions matched. "Stick together," I said, and he nodded.

We headed side by side down the narrow lane along the largest building, each looking left and right as we took slow steps in the eerie quiet. A sheen of pale dust covered the playground's bright-coloured markings, but otherwise we would never have known what had gone on outside its boundary.

I saw the side of the minibus half under a plastic canopy, its paint covered in the same thin layer. Finding it locked, as I let go of the handle I caught sight of a half-glass door to the main school building on the other side of the van.

Turning back toward the gates, I stared at the smaller building we'd passed, greeted with a view of the roof caved in at one corner.

Stepping to the main building's door and finding it locked, I twisted the handle a second time to make sure, then moved to the side as Paul hefted the iron bar high and hit at the glass.

Despite the force, it held with great cracks spidering out from the point of impact. Two more heavy thumps made me cringe at the volume, but the sheet fell through the other side to the single chirp of a siren, lighting up my senses for the briefest of moments until the battery died.

My thoughts turned to the gate again, and I tried to remember if we'd pulled each side closed behind us.

I shook away the question, watching as Paul reached through the opening to unlock the door, but turning away as I caught movement from the other side of the playground, swinging the rifle around. Movement flared again, but with relief I saw the creatures were on the other side of the metal fence.

With a nod to Jess to share what I'd seen, I stepped over the threshold to follow Paul, pushing the broken glass panel to the side with his feet.

Dust and dried paint pulled at a long-forgotten memory as we entered. The sight of small chairs in the classroom to the right raised a smile, reinforced by the view of the cloakroom just ahead with wooden coat-stands forming a line in the square room with laminated name tags above each. I took confidence in the stale air and shouldered the rifle, splitting from the others to begin the search.

There were two classrooms and judging by the improving skill of the drawings in each, I guessed the rough ages of the children.

I moved to a compact kitchen with two fridges, but found them both empty for the holidays. The cupboards held tea and coffee, mugs and brightly-coloured plastic cups.

My interest grew when I saw a small office with computers on three desks, plus a small chair in the corner. I imagined a boy in shorts with a grazed knee, waiting red-faced for his tears to calm.

As I rifled through the cabinets and drawers, Jess and Paul soon joined me with the shake of their heads, telling me all I needed.

Whilst trying to be as quiet as we could in our search, we each looked up to the ceiling when we heard the creaking of the floorboards above.

# 21

The sound from the floor over our heads stopped, and keeping still I sought out every clue as to the source of the noise.

Eventually I turned, looking through the office window and across the playground, peering out to see if the noise could somehow have been from the creatures I'd seen the other side of the fence.

When nothing stood beyond the green slats and realising the notion made no sense, my thoughts flashed again to the double gates as I tried to remember if we'd pushed them closed.

Turning back to Paul and Jess, I raised my hands in the air, shaking my head to confirm I hadn't found what we'd sought. Each replied in the same way, and together we looked back to the ceiling as the scuffle on the floorboards came again.

Nodding to Jess, we followed Paul's lead out of the office and to the short corridor, waiting beside the only door we'd yet to open.

Paul stood to my side and I raised the rifle, gripping hard with the butt tight in my shoulder as he dropped the handle, pulling in one swift moment to reveal a tiled corridor leading to the front double doors and a stairway rising to my left.

Sniffing the air, I breathed out with relief when it came back with the same dull, dusty odour as the rest of the ground floor.

They followed behind as I slowly walked across the tiles, pausing when I reached the bottom of the staircase and peered up, straining to listen.

With no sound coming from above, I rose up the narrow steps, looking high to another short corridor and three closed doors.

Edging the first door wide whilst keeping the muzzle

high, it didn't take me long to back out of the storeroom filled with office equipment and stationery, but I paused for a moment to take a second look for keys hanging down from hooks.

When we found nothing of use, the pair moved from my back, giving me room to step to the next door, an office with a single desk and chair. About to step backward, I paused as the scuffle of movement came again.

Nodding toward the next door, I listened to the sound, so much crisper than before, but it was so light I felt myself relaxing, doubting it could be from the dead.

For a moment I lowered the rifle, but raised it high again when I thought of the size of the children who would have attended the school.

A vision of the girl in the tunnel flashed into my head, the dark veins like tree roots across her face; I tightened my grip as I moved toward the far door, hovering my hand over the brass handle whilst I collected myself.

Shaking my head, I shuffled a little to the left, nodding for Paul to do the deed. Raising the bar one-handed like a spear, he gripped the brass with the other.

Jess leaned in as he twisted the handle, waiting for my command.

I nodded, reluctant for any more delay. The door swung wide and I clenched my teeth at the shards of glass covering the floor of a classroom. Looking up to the skylight, I saw the remaining fragments, then turned to the desks pushed up against the walls with chairs piled in stacks alongside.

Faded drawings filled the walls, but movement drew me to a black cat in the centre of a great dark pool of blood. As I looked on, my focus fixing, it still stood on its back legs, but its front had collapsed either side with its only remaining fore-leg just white bone and stringy connective tissue.

A faint waft of sewerage called on the breeze from the high window and Jess pushed gently past me, kneeling to the mess.

"Wait," I said, as Paul went to step from my side. "It could be infected."

Jess didn't flinch, but Paul stopped, stepping back until the mass twitched and it looked up, prompting Paul to move forward with the bar still held high.

I looked away.

To the sound of a heavy thud and a crack of bone, I focused on searching the drawers of what must have been the teacher's desk in the corner.

Coming up empty-handed, I avoided looking to where Paul and Jess crouched as I headed back to the corridor.

With Paul wiping the end of the pole, they soon joined me downstairs and in silence we headed back outside as I tried to figure if the familiar stench had grown stronger since we'd last been outside. The pair followed around to the front of the school until, with relief, I saw the gates were closed with none of the creatures waiting on the other side.

I couldn't help but think this place would have been an excellent location to hold up and wait, but then I thought of the children. Of Cassie's sister, Ellie. Sweet Tish and Jack, the hope of humanity.

I pushed away the thought of how we would find them, with my mind instead drifting to thoughts of Cassie and a sudden need to be by her side.

As if coming out of a daydream, I stood at the glass door of the bungalow, but instead of reaching for the handle, my attention drew to a rattle of the gates as a figure bumped into the metal. Where its face should have been, dark contours of muscle stared back with long clotted blood drying across the front of a thick white top.

I turned to Jess and Paul, watching as they stared the same way, then looked to me, steeling themselves for the challenge ahead.

A distant scream cut through the background noise and I couldn't help but imagine it came from the church, lighting up every sense and telling me to run back.

I glanced to Jess and her expression held firm. I turned,

gripping the long brass handle of the glass door and pushed down. The door held in place.

Peering to the window beside the door, I looked past wilting potted plants to the compact kitchen and without being asked, I stepped to the side as Paul moved forward with his bar raised.

The single sheet of glass collapsed to the floor with a jab in the near corner; the high flurry of glass sent a rush of activity through those at the gate but I didn't dare turn to see how many more had joined their number.

With the worst shards smashed from the edge of the frame with the butt of the rifle, I slung it over my shoulder and boosted up to the sill, climbing through only to gag and heave as I landed on the floor the other side.

With the stench nothing like the foul sewerage we encountered each day, I forced myself to hold back a wretch as I tasted the rotting meat in the air and attempted to breathe just through my mouth.

Grimacing, I turned back to the window, hoping for relief from a gust of fresh air, but I held myself still whilst my fingers worked to unlock the door before rushing out to pull air deep into my lungs.

"There's something dead in there," I said between breaths.

"Dead, dead? Or, you know...?" Jess said before she stopped herself. I half expected her to raise her hands, but she just repeated herself.

I shook my head.

"I don't know, but it smells fucking bad," I said, before tipping my head towards the massing numbers at the gate raising their hands out towards us between the slats.

Holding back, I watched Paul lean forward through the doorway, pausing for a moment before he took a step, crunching glass under his feet. The muscles in his neck strained through his tanned skin as if holding back desperation for a breath.

Stepping backward, he took a moment before he spoke.

"Whatever it is, it's been dead a while," he said, dropping the tip of the bar on the ground and leaning against.

"We've got no choice," Jess said, as she stepped through the doorway and out of view as if she couldn't smell the horror.

She was right, and filling my lungs, I followed.

# 22

## JESSICA

Although the stench of the day's-old meat hung heavy in the air, with the rot soaking into my taste buds, I didn't gag or wretch as I circled the kitchen in search of the key.

Logan had followed with Paul at his back.

Paul, lifting the bar high and with his red eyelids blinking without control, moved away and headed down the corridor, leaving Logan with me in the kitchen to look across the counters.

By Logan's contorted brow, burying his mouth in the crook of his elbow had done nothing to lessen the smell as he searched through the drawers.

I took after Paul, following to the source of the smell.

Passing a bookcase in the short hallway, Paul called out, urging me around the corner.

"Shit," he repeated as I looked to where he stood next to a wide section of missing roof with loose tiles and torn felt hanging from the edges.

A jagged concrete boulder the size of a shopping trolley sat in the centre of the room with a pair of legs projecting out from under its weight. Despite the carpet littered with shattered roof tiles, the scene reminded me of the Wicked Witch's legs, the only part of her not under Dorothy's house.

Plaster dust paled the wrinkled ankles, the rest of the legs covered with tartan pyjamas. Between the debris I could just about see the curl of grey hair beside dried blood, long soaked into the carpet. By the smell, she'd been here long before the bombing of the hospital, dispelling any danger she'd rise again.

Glancing to Paul, he hadn't moved from the middle of the room, fixed to the spot, but the shake of his head told me he was okay.

A chill made me look to the great void above and the remains of felt flapping gently in the breeze, the blue sky beyond. Remembering our reason for being in this place, I peered around the room in search of the keys.

The rest of the living space seemed untouched. With Christmas cards strewn around the fireplace, a tree in the corner stood tall, its branches brightened with a dusting of plaster.

Movement scraping from behind a closed door at the opposite end to where we'd entered drew my attention.

Paul turned in the same direction, raising his head as a vision of the dying cat's scratch jumped into my head. I couldn't help but wince at the thought of another injured pet left to fend for itself.

Paul stayed firm, staring to the destruction at his feet as I stepped between the debris. Pulling at the door handle, it opened with ease. The rot of meat still prevailed as I moved toward another two doors beyond the short corridor.

Glancing through the open door to a toilet to the right, I listened to the sound as it came again, much stronger this time.

Pushing down the handle of the door directly ahead, I heard Logan's excitement as he called out. He'd found the keys, but as I turned, his voice cut off and he stared past Paul to the dusty legs in the middle of the room.

The handle ripped from my grip and I twisted back, eyes wide, to a tall figure blocking the light from the window behind. Before I reacted, it stepped forward into my path, sending me stumbling backwards as if it hadn't seen me.

Fighting to regain my balance, I watched as if in a silent movie, but a few moments behind the action. Pushing against the wall to steady myself, the towering figure stood with the top of his grey hair reaching just below the architrave around the door. Pale skin around his neck wobbled with his stilted walk and wearing the same tartan patterned pyjamas as the woman, he reached forward, revealing a blood-soaked bandage wrapped at his wrist.

Regaining my footing, I staggered forward, turning to Paul as he looked away from Logan's hand and the keys he held high.

Logan dropped the keys, fumbling the rifle from his shoulder, but instead of looking at the creature heading toward them, Logan's eyes locked with mine.

Ignoring his furrowed brow, I felt rage building within me, growing exponentially from deep in my gut. As I lingered on Logan's stare, the rising strength wilted when for a moment it was Jordain standing with a lifeless expression. The anger soon smothered with guilt and with all my remaining energy, I pushed back the feelings, clamping down with all my might.

We both turned to Paul as he tripped backwards over the rubble, attempting to bring the metal bar up from rest on the carpet.

Logan lifted the rifle horizontal, but it was too late.

I watched, holding back from the rage that wanted to explode as the creature toppled to Paul with its clawed fingers outstretched and teeth bared.

# 23

## LOGAN

Looking below the pale, wrinkled face, my gaze fixed on the figure's bandaged wrist as he stepped past Jess. Still, I expected him to shout and call, asking why the hell we were in his house. Instead, as if she were invisible, he walked straight past her with a stilted stride I knew too well.

Looking again, for a moment I stared to the bandaged wrist spread with dark blood, before catching his blank expression, wide, milky-white eyes and lips drawn back to bared yellowed teeth.

My gaze swung around to Jess, despite the obvious danger coming our way; I just couldn't understand how it could stroll past her like she wasn't there.

Shaking off the stare, I almost fell back when I saw how close it had got in that split second. Instinct took control and with the keys we'd searched so hard for falling from my hand, I brought the rifle up to bear.

Firing from the hip, I watched the lead thud uselessly into its stomach, not knocking the creature from its lunge at Paul heaving the bar over his head.

Lifting the rifle higher, Paul's anguished call wrenched at my gut as I pulled the trigger, knowing that nothing I could do would save him as the creature's teeth embedded in his cheek. Not the burst of red from the back of its head as the shot echoed in the small space; not the hit of the rifle's butt as I slammed it into the creature's eye socket, sending its lifeless form backward to be with his wife once more. Nothing I could do would change the inevitable if we didn't have the cure.

I looked away from Paul's ashen face as his hand went to the wound on his cheek.

Jess stared back open-mouthed, shaking her head.

The bar clattered to the smashed tiles and I forced myself to turn back as Paul whimpered. Blood seeped between his fingers as he pushed against the wound and fell to his knees.

"Get towels from the bathroom. We have to stop the bleeding," I shouted, only turning part way to Jess, instead looking to the ever-increasing darkness flowing down Paul's neck.

He tried to stand. I couldn't bring myself to hold him down.

"Towels," I called, as I guided him to his feet then turned to see Jess standing in the same spot, staring at the man's body lying on the carpet.

I called again and somehow it got through as she rushed from the room, coming back within a few seconds carrying a haphazard pile of white towels.

I covered Paul's hand and the side of his face as I held him steady.

"Oh no," Paul called, his voice low and breathy. "Oh no. Don't let it end like this." Fighting for breath, he pulled his hand from his face, sending a fresh wave of blood pouring down his neck before I pushed the towels to the wound.

"Can you make it to the minibus?" I blurted out, but I couldn't understand Paul's slurred reply as his legs gave way.

Jess hurried to his side, helping him to the floor as he let out a pained moan.

"No," he called out in a moment of clarity. "Not like this."

I knew what I needed to do and Jess turned away, her face pale as she nodded at the question I didn't need to ask.

***

"Are you okay?" I asked with the gunshot still ringing in my ears. But it wasn't the question I wanted to voice as I sat in the driver's seat of the minibus.

Jess stared through the windscreen in the seat at my side, her gaze fixed into the distance and not the brick of the building we faced.

I hadn't turned the key. I hadn't checked to make sure the engine worked and there was enough fuel to get us away from this place.

"Are you okay?"

Still I didn't ask about the girl in the tunnel. I didn't ask why Jess seemed to know all about her. I didn't ask about the creature at the doors of the church and why it hadn't attacked straight away. Or why the creature we'd just killed walked right past her, attacking Paul instead.

I caught the slightest nod in the corner of my eye.

"I've seen worse. I'm fine," she replied, but her vacant expression told me otherwise.

"We've got to get out of this place."

She nodded again, but still I didn't turn the key for the questions running through my head. What if she was like Jack? What if she was immune to the creature's bite? What if she too held the key to the cure?

"Has it happened before?" I said, unable to construct the sentence I wanted.

"What?" she replied, still looking to the wall.

About to speak, I stopped myself to correct the words. "It was like you weren't there. It just ignored you."

"We should go," she said, nodding toward the steering wheel.

I took a moment before turning the key, not paying attention until I realised the engine rumbled in front of me. How had she not noticed they'd ignored her?

My distracted gaze fell to the dashboard, the gauges telling me the minibus was half full of fuel with no orange lights warning the engine could cut out at any moment and it had all been a waste of time. A waste of a life.

We rolled backward at my command and the front wheels turned as I twisted the steering to get us moving along the narrow lane. The brakes halted our course when I saw the crowd deep at the gates, clawing out towards us.

As we came to a stop, I made the mistake of staring at the detail of their faces, thinking of the villagers in their sleepy state as I wondered how their last moments had played out.

When we left the hospital for the first time, the creatures were already gathering together as if they knew about the pocket of survivors. The tall fences hadn't been tall enough. The village had no fences, leaving the residents only with their wits to defend themselves. But they wouldn't have known the new rules.

Dead people come back to life.

They didn't stand a chance and now there they were on the other side of the gates. Parents in pyjamas. People who had been enjoying the season. Would there ever be a time when we could sit back and relax again?

My gaze settled on a short figure at the far edge of the fence. A child in the tatters of Spiderman pyjamas. His face still intact. A blessing, I guessed, but for who?

My thoughts flashed back to Jess's words at the church.

The children are not as safe as you think.

I turned to Jess, anger rising that she hadn't answered the questions I had yet to voice. As I turned, I saw she'd been watching me with a raised brow.

"What did you mean about the children?" I said, but she stared back, then turned to the kid in the superhero pyjamas covered in an apron of blood. "Cassie's sister, Ellie. Jack and Tish." I said their names, hoping to stir her to speak again.

Jess fidgeted in her seat, hesitating as if about to look my way, then didn't.

Guilt rose when we hadn't made our way back to the church, or at least figured out how we could get through the massed crowd at the gate and back to the people we'd each left behind.

Still, I didn't move, instead staring back to Jess.

"She said they would be safe. Jack's blood is the miracle we need. Was she telling the truth?"

"Do you believe in miracles?" Jess asked, her tone flat and devoid of emotion.

"I believe what I see," I said, raising my brow to the crowd.

"They're not looking for a cure."

I guessed that despite Jess's look to the gates, it wasn't what she saw in her head.

"But Cassie?" I said, and she nodded, serving only to build my frustration and I hurried to speak. "She's not dead. She should be dead by now. Everyone who I've seen bitten is dead. The doctor gave her the cure."

Jess shrugged, but before I could raise my voice, she turned to look my way. "How do you know she's cured?"

I held back the reply I wanted to blurt out and considered the words. "She's not dead. She's not going to die."

"Okay," Jess replied, turning back to the gate and letting her shoulders relax. "But the cure is only a side effect."

"What do you mean? Please be straight with me."

"I think they're using this virus to make superhumans. Hybrids with exceptional strength. Is that straight enough?" she said, still with a calm voice.

"What...?" My word spat as I twisted in my seat towards her. "What the hell? This isn't a fucking movie, and that's not funny."

Feeling my heart beating hard in my chest, I watched as the glimmer of a smirk appeared on her lips and her eyebrows raised as she stared to the baying crowd.

Following her gaze, I took hold of the steering wheel and looked at the crowd. I peered at the dead people walking on two feet. The dead moving around in a relentless need to feed and I realised I had no idea what could have caused this unreality. This new reality.

"It's always the military," she said, seeing my grip relaxing on the steering wheel.

I let the silence hang, listening to my breath over the low hum from the crowd and rattle at the gates.

"I don't get it. Why the children?" I said when the quiet grew too much.

"I can't be sure."

"I don't believe you."

She turned toward me scowling. Pulling back, Jess fixed me with her furrowed brow, anger flashing across her face. For a moment she seemed to ripple with energy, muscles tightening as if about to attack.

With adrenaline rising, I held my ground, fighting the urge to jump from the minibus. "You know more than I do." I let my voice soften as I continued. "You know more than most. You must," I said, whilst trying to keep the aggression from my tone.

I watched as she relaxed, trying to gauge what she'd do next.

"Experiments," she said, still looking my way.

"To make soldiers?"

Jess nodded.

"How...? What...?" I blurted out, the words coming before I formed coherence. "They'll infect them with the virus?"

Jess gave a weak nod, but I couldn't tell if it meant she knew for sure or if she was reluctant to tell me the truth.

"What have I done?" I asked, but not to Jess as I replayed the events of the last few days in my mind and turned towards the gates, gripping both hands to the steering wheel. "I delivered them to her."

"You also saved Cassie."

I glanced around as she spoke. "I don't think she'll see it that way."

"You didn't know what they'd do."

"But I always knew it was a risk," I said, tightening the grip on the steering wheel.

"What would have happened if you did nothing?"

I didn't reply straight away, instead trying to remember. "I don't know. Do you think it's too late?"

"For what?" Jess looked up with her eyebrows raised.

"To rescue them."

"I don't know," she said, shaking her head. "Are you willing to risk your life even if there's only a slim chance?"

I knew I should have had the answer ready. Would I give my life for Cassie, someone I'd only just met?

Yes. That answer came without thought. Would I do the same for her sister? For the two innocents, Jack and Tish?

Without reply and leaving the rifle in the footwell, I pulled the driver's door open, jumped to the tarmac and strode towards the gates.

# 24

## JESSICA

I watched as he headed from the minibus with the length between his strides announcing his answer.

He didn't know what he'd committed to, but he knew something was up with me. He knew to be scared of being so close, but I couldn't bring myself to give him the straight answers; these people could be the ones to help Alex when I no longer could.

I didn't think he saw my building rage as I was about to let myself go and stop the creature from taking Paul's life, with no thought to whether I could hold back and not carry forward the destruction, felling them both before I calmed. But the moment passed. His look made me force the feeling away. His look forced me to control myself.

The scrape of metal pulled me from the questions I was about to ask; instead, I looked to the creatures going crazy with desire as Logan slid the bolt across the gates and pulled each open just in time to miss the fingers clawing out. I couldn't help thinking he'd given up, or how he had lasted this long by taking such stupid risks.

With the driver's door still wide, he slowed to a jog half way on his journey back to the van, his concentration on the floor, not wanting to trip and never get back up again.

I pictured his fall, but he was back through the door before I finished thinking about how I would react.

Would I have rushed out and scooped him up whilst fending off the pack? Or would I have slid over to the driver's seat, slamming the door and putting him out of his misery under the wheels?

I shuddered at the thought, revelling in the relief I got from my revulsion.

My thoughts caught, and I looked to Logan.

He heard the high voice too and stopped, our gaze locking.

I pointed to his side and he hurried to slam the door closed, sealing us from the crowd about to engulf us.

"You heard that?" he said, as his foot landed heavily on the accelerator before the minibus surged forward.

I nodded, not wanting to voice my reply; not wanting to say I'd heard the call and the dog barking not so far away.

Something had to have happened at the church and thoughts sprung of Alex running with Shadow taking the lead, calling out for his master.

Logan stared ahead. With his brow furrowed, I guessed his thoughts were much the same. If they were running, then what had happened to Cassie? Had that woman been right all along?

Had Cassie turned to rage around the church in search of her first feed?

# 25

## LOGAN

Cassie was my only thought as the dead slammed against the metalwork, their bodies disappearing, crushed underneath the tyres. Despite the slap of limbs against the panels, I didn't let the barrage slow our course for fear Cassie had turned without the chance to say goodbye.

Glancing to the mirror with the junction just ahead, what remained of the crowd followed along the tree-lined lane. I sped, leaning into the corner and joined the wider road toward the village.

With the tyres silencing their squeal as I straightened the wheel, I saw the village square and Shadow racing around the corner. My search fixed on those following, leaning forward to get a better view of who they used to be and what they had since become.

To the blur of movement, I slammed on the brakes, throwing us forward as I yanked the steering wheel to the left to avoid the dog racing in our direction.

We ground to a halt with the bonnet in the hedge and a camouflage of greens through the windscreen.

Dazed by the pace of events and not sure if I'd diverted the turn in time, for a split second I couldn't bring myself to twist to the right and look down the road.

Shadow's bark forced me to look, his claws scratching at the door as he rose to his back legs, steaming the window of the sliding door with his breath.

Leaping out of my seat, I jumped in the back and slid the door wide, watching as he bounded in, jumping up in greeting before turning back to the figures following to bark in their direction.

Beth led the chase our way, the oldest winning the race,

but I couldn't quite tell who or what came from behind.

Glancing to the driver's seat and the rifle in the footwell, I hesitated, unsure if I should grab the gun or rush out to help those still alive. Clutching at the barrel as the pause passed, I swung it around and searched through the scope pointed down the road.

The view settled on Alex with her arm around someone. Cassie.

The barrel drifted toward the road as I jumped from the minibus, the sky seeming to brighten.

Beth rushed past, her breath racing as she clambered up the rise to take a seat. Another of the women, as far as I could tell, lagged by quite a way.

I caught the effort on Cassie's face; she seemed barely awake.

Swinging the rifle back up, I centred the crosshair on the woman running at their backs, but despite steadying my aim, I struggled to make out her features for the blood covering her face. But I could at least see her slack-jawed expression.

Her name wouldn't fix in my head, but as she neared, I could tell she was the woman who'd been so against our stay. So against Cassie laying up to give her time to recuperate.

Further movement caught my attention at the bloodied woman's back and distracted my growing anger. I didn't know the people following her. I didn't know their names, but their slow, dogged walk and wound-covered bodies told me the chance to get to know them had gone.

Dropping the rifle to point out from my hip, I looked to Alex.

"Are you okay?" I said, hurrying the words out.

She nodded. "We're fine. We're both fine," she said, and I raised the rifle's sight back to my eye as those already in the minibus helped Cassie up the step.

Mandy. Her name popped into my head with just a few strides remaining until she reached us, but to the frantic call of my name, I backed up the step and inside whilst looking to

Mandy's blood-smeared expression as she reached out to the door, which someone shoved closed in front of my face.

The crowd continued in its dogged path towards us.

With the smeared blood contrasting against Mandy's pallid skin, her balled fists blotched scarlet to the glass and to a screamed call from close at my back, I twisted around, catching sight of the group from the school nearly on us.

Leaping into the driver's seat, I noticed Jess had moved to the back and I revved the engine hard, slamming the gear into reverse, but before I could let the clutch out, Mandy's pleading voice cut through the adrenaline.

"I'm not bitten. Fucking let me in."

# 26

Mandy's shrill voice pulled me back to the church and the moment she had looked me in the eye and told me Cassie had to leave.

With my foot heavy on the accelerator and the engine racing, I kept my hand hovering over the gearstick. But I couldn't move away; instead, I turned, looking to her wide-eyed terror with the creatures growing near.

Pulling up her sleeves, she bared her arms, holding them up to the smeared windows.

"I'm not bitten. Let me in."

No one moved to open the side door as the raised voices continued to call. I heard Paul's name and its panicked repeat as I turned to see Beth looking around the seats to see if she'd missed him at first glance.

"What happened?" I shouted, cutting through the calls.

Beth silenced her shout, but Mandy continued to bang her fists at the glass and as I turned toward her, she moved to the passenger door, trying the handle.

"Don't let her in," Beth called with high-pitched venom in her voice, as Mandy rushed back to the sliding door.

Glancing to Mandy's back, I watched as she turned around, following my look to the masses only two car lengths away.

Twisting back, Mandy ripped open her blouse, sending the buttons pinging against the metal body and pulling the material high to expose her pale skin and the sturdy white bra streaked with blood. "I'm not fucking bitten."

"Do you see a bite?" I shouted, rushing the words into the jumble of voices in the back.

Alex called to let her in, only for Beth to shout her down whilst snapping for us to move.

Although I couldn't see a wound, the blood must have come from somewhere. I'd made the wrong choice before and I vowed not to do the same again.

"What happened?" I shouted again, louder than any of the two women, but I knew there was no time left to find out. We had to let her in or leave her to die.

"Let her in," I called to the back and watched as Beth jumped from her seat, pushing her hand to the black handle, but the door didn't open.

"Let her in," I shouted again, but Beth didn't flinch. I twisted to Jess in the back, but she didn't offer any help.

Hitting the clutch and pushing the gearstick into reverse, I leaned over to the front passenger door and pushed my hand to my handle just as Beth called.

"What the hell are you doing?"

Mandy's blood-caked face lit as the door opened, and she thrust herself forward, leaping through the doorway and over the front seats into the back, leaving the door wide.

Just as the first of the creatures arrived, I hammered the accelerator with my foot and let the clutch out. As we jolted backwards, shouts called from behind at the sight of hands at the edge of the open door and the creature dragged with us.

Slamming on the brakes just before we hit the trees on the other side of the road, the minibus stopped and the chaos paused. But the door still hung wide open, and the creature had somehow kept its grip.

I stared for a moment, locking eyes with its thick, cloudy whites, and watched the woman in her later years in a pale blue nightdress as she bared her teeth.

The calls from the back pulled me out from my daze and I looked beyond, where tens, if not hundreds more walked doggedly, ready to trample over her to get to us.

Pushing the gearstick into first, I hammered the accelerator a second time, listening to the roar of the engine as I twisted the wheel to the right.

The door came away from her grip and for the first time I looked through the windscreen and recognised faces, features at least, from the school gates as they slipped beneath the bonnet, rocking the minibus from side to side with their weight pushing the door shut.

Past the worst of the crowds, I kept our speed as we headed along the clear, narrow road under the dark canopy.

With my breath running hard, I tuned out the cacophony of calls behind me, focusing instead on the road and taking only the quickest of glances in the mirrors to make sure we'd left the crowd behind and Mandy hadn't turned into the monster we feared.

"Is she bitten?" I called, but when no coherent reply came and with a long view of the single-track road ahead and hedgerows either side like walls of protection, I slowed the minibus.

Leaving the engine running, I jumped to the tarmac and took a slow walk around the van whilst trying not to take any notice of the sorry sight of the white paintwork.

Beth unlocked the side door as I arrived to slide it wide and all eyes turned to Mandy on the first row of seats, her arms wrapping the remains of her shirt around her torso as if shielding herself from the cold.

A flush of panic rose when I couldn't immediately see Cassie, but the space next to Alex brought reassurance enough that she was okay.

Glancing the way we'd come, I waited, listening to the calm air whilst taking reassurance I could only smell the slightest of odours calling on the chill breeze. For a moment I wondered if we were doomed to the stench for the rest of our days.

Refocusing, I stared at Mandy, forcing myself to look past the gory mask across her face and raised my foot to the step before offering my hand out with a gesture for her to come forward.

"Step out a moment," I said, keeping my gaze fixed. "We need to check you over properly."

Shaking her head, she glanced to Beth's scowl.

"Get out," Beth shouted, cutting through the calm.

Mandy didn't flinch at the words; instead, she tightened her arms around herself and sunk further to the opposite side of the minibus.

Beth's face flared with anger, but as I pushed my palm out toward her, she relaxed back in her seat, giving a slow shallow nod. I turned back to Mandy and stood back to the road with my hand offered out again before speaking in a calm voice.

"If you're bitten," I said, watching as she shook her head before I'd finished. "If," I repeated, slower this time. "If you're bitten, then you can still come with us for a bit. If not, we can all calm down and we'll get you some clothes. Okay?"

Catching a strong waft of sewerage in the air, I hesitated as I examined Mandy's clear eyes. With a slow breath, I pushed down the urge of my racing adrenaline.

"Please."

After a brief pause, Mandy dropped her grip from around herself to show her blood-soaked shirt.

Forcing myself to keep calm, she stepped forward as she glared my way. I leaned toward her outstretched hand, but as we touched, I felt a grip around my leg and I looked to the road and a bloodied, clawed hand grabbing my leg with a battered head pulling from under the van, snapping its teeth toward my ankle.

# 27

When the creature hadn't already sunk its rancid teeth, I focused on its slow crawl, realising it must have tangled underneath the minibus. With my heart racing, I leaned back, tugging my leg to pull as far away from the mouth as possible, whilst trying not to fall back and give it the opportunity to doom me to the same fate as Paul.

Confused calls came from inside the minibus. A scream rose from Beth as she stared at Mandy, looking as if she'd attacked me. I heard Cassie's weak call, asking what had happened, and watched as Alex and Jess followed my wide-eyed glare down to my feet as they realised something else was going on.

I wanted to kick out with my other foot, but it would have meant standing still and giving it a chance to pull my other to its mouth.

Unable to break from its powerful grip, it gave a sudden jolt, dragging my foot closer. Bracing for pain, instead the pressure eased, and I opened my eyes to the sight of Jess's trainer stamping down on its head for a second time.

When the grip didn't completely release, I watched Jess hold the minibus door as she dropped to the road before taking aim and refocusing her attack.

With flayed flesh slapping to the paint and to the gut-wrenching crack of its skull, the grip finally relaxed.

"Where...?" is all Jess said between breaths as she turned to me and then back down to my leg. "Are you bitten?"

Stepping back and pulling up the leg of my jeans, I took a long look at my leg from every angle. "No," I said, before repeating twice more, then lowered myself to the road to check nothing more lurked underneath.

Stepping back to the side door, I watched as Mandy held firm in her seat with her bloodied arms wrapped around her chest.

Jess spoke before I could. "She's not bitten," she said,

and climbed past me to take her spot the other side of Alex.

Slowly nodding, I held my gaze on Mandy from a distance, but despite not being able to see every detail, somehow I knew Jess had been right.

Keen to get away from this place, I jumped back in the minibus, sliding the passenger door shut before speeding us along the road.

After a short distance, the wheels rolled over the corpse as it released from the underside and I called out to no one in particular. "I'm heading north."

When nothing but nods came from behind, I let the speed build.

"What happened back at the church?"

No one replied.

"Is Cassie okay?"

"I'm fine," came her weak voice, and Alex nodded without delay; I remembered the conversation with Jess. She'd been wrong. I was sure they cured Cassie.

Alex's voice cut through my thoughts. "I was checking on Cassie. I didn't know where the others were, but I heard their whispers."

I looked between Beth and Mandy in the mirror as Alex spoke.

"There was an almighty scream. I'm surprised you didn't hear it from where you were."

I glanced to Jess, but she didn't acknowledge the look.

"Then we heard someone falling down the metal steps."

"They're a death trap," Beth cut in. "I said all along. Harry. He fell. He was up the tower with Stacey. By the time I'd arrived, I found him at the bottom of the steps. He'd bent both his arms the wrong way, and I shouted for Stacey to get away from him. It was obvious he was dead. We all knew what could happen next, but Stacey was so distraught and kept apologising like she'd made him fall."

"Harry turned?" I said and looked at the rear-view mirror.

"No. He wasn't moving. There was no way he could have been bitten," Beth said.

"When Mandy saw Harry's blood on Stacey's arm, she started shouting that she'd been bitten," Alex said, her voice soft as she turned down to where Cassie slumped.

Beth closed her eyes as I flashed her a look in the mirror.

"This one," Beth said, raising her hand to point at Mandy, "panics, screaming the place down and throws stuff at Stacey. Mandy went crazy."

I looked to Mandy as she scowled back at Beth.

"She attacked Stacey, and Stacey defended herself, but slipped on a candle Mandy threw. She hit her head, knocking her out cold. We're all staring in disbelief, but at least the commotion was over. Mandy's all for killing her there and then, but we don't agree."

Beth looked to Alex, who nodded back.

"So she runs off and brings back a metal bar from Paul's work area and before we can stop her, she's going at Stacey. But Stacey's not dead. She wakes up. She's alive. Not one of those things. We tried to stop Mandy but by now Stacey is lying motionless on the floor, covered in blood. Mandy's killed her. There's so much screaming, most of it from Mandy and then Stacey soon wakes up and her eyes are different. Like those creatures."

"So she had been bitten?" I added.

"Yes," Mandy said, raising her brow.

"Yes, but we don't know how," Alex said, glancing to Mandy.

"And you ran?" I said, looking the way we were headed.

Nods replied from Alex and Beth when I turned back.

"Still, she's not safe to be around. She has to go," Beth added, looking to the deepening anger on Mandy's face.

Snatching a glance to Jess and then to Alex, both shrugged their shoulders as Alex spoke. "I don't know."

"We can't have someone like that with us," Beth added to fill the silence whilst glaring at Mandy.

Letting the words hang, I turned back toward the road, but was soon distracted by a building, tensing at the thought of another village like the last. I slowed the minibus with a hope I'd chosen the right speed to react to whatever happened next.

Passing the first house, I realised I'd held my breath and there was silence in the back as everyone seemed to have done the same.

"Mandy," I said, causing her to flinch, "just sit there and be cool. This is under control. No one's going to throw you out if you remain calm. Do you understand?"

Beth didn't hide her murmur of protest.

"Do you understand?"

To her shallow nod, I glanced at Beth as a warning before I turned back to concentrate on the road.

We passed four brick houses either side, each wrapped with sizeable gardens and other than the wide-open doors, there was nothing to say the hell behind us had affected them.

With relief, the last of the buildings went past the window and, taking the corners slowly, weary of what could be the other side of the stone walls, the road eventually straightened out to give a welcoming long view into the distance.

Cracking the window to let in the chilly breeze, the air smelt fresh as we each scoured every angle outside.

I let a smile creep across my lips as miles of normality headed by the window and we joined a wider road whose surface was so much smoother than the narrow lanes from the village and, bound by short hedgerows with fields either side, I felt relief, optimistic we were through the worst of the nightmare.

My mood faltered at the sight of cars ahead stopped five abreast, blocking the road with boots wide open.

The missing windows brought back visions of that first day; the day we didn't understand the mess we were getting into.

With no choice, I slowed, eventually coming to a stop

a little way back and peering to the fuel gauge, but barely noticing it hadn't dropped, when a screech called through the air to send a chill of icy fear through my body.

# 28

## JESSICA

I had wondered how long it would be before we hit the first of the roadblocks.

After seeing so many on our way over, the first of which where I'd lost my crew, I'd hoped it would have taken more time before we reached the first obstacle. We'd travelled maybe two miles and hadn't seen the fences anywhere. The fences reminded me of the two soldiers and I pushed away the image of Sheppard falling to the ground in his own blood and the other soldier, Jordain, whose name I forced to the front of my thoughts.

No one said a word when the call filled the air just as we stopped. Logan's only reaction was to look to the fuel gauge.

For a long moment no one moved, until Logan twisted in his seat to catch my eye, then did the same with each of the others, even lingering on Shadow's optimistic wide eyes before his expression turned to surprise as Cassie rose from where she'd lain.

He smiled on seeing her face, but he turned away when she looked out of the windows instead of his way.

"The whole area is jammed with roadblocks," he said and I nodded, turning back to Mandy and Beth, swapping looks between us. "We need to keep on the move," he said, and as if to punctuate his point a distant screech echoed through the air.

Each of the faces flickered to the windows before turning back to Logan.

"I suggest we take our chances going around in the field. I don't think we should waste fuel going the long way only to find it blocked."

"But..." Beth said, and Logan nodded in her direction.

"I know. If we can't get out the other side, or we get bogged down, then we'll have no choice but to walk. Do you all understand?"

"What do you think we should do?" Beth asked.

Logan turned his gaze to me and then to each person in the back before looking to Cassie.

"Cassie and I need to find where they've taken the children. I think the best opportunity is if we head to Exeter. If there's a chance we can get through, we have to take it."

I followed his look to Cassie and watched her nod as she held the back of the seats at her front to help her stay sat up.

"Why Exeter?" Alex said at my side.

Logan seemed to think for a moment before speaking. "It's the nearest city. I think it makes sense. If there's power and people then we can ring around. Maybe contact the media," he said.

"And if it's like back there?" Alex replied.

He thought again. "Then there's still more resources than out in the middle of nowhere, don't you think?"

Alex nodded.

"Let's go around," Beth said, nodding as she held his gaze. I couldn't help thinking how quickly Logan had become a leader, despite his obvious reluctance.

"Is it safe?" Mandy blurted out.

"If you're not with us," Beth quickly replied.

"Let's do it," I said. I had my own priorities and for now, what Logan said made sense, it worked for me and for getting Alex somewhere safer in the longer term. I pushed away thoughts of Toni, of finding her and taking her to task, putting her on camera so I could destroy her in front of the public. With the anger building, I took a slow deep breath.

Logan turned, pulling on his seatbelt, then pushed the gear into first as he revved the engine.

# 29

# LOGAN

Tensing with the scratch and scrape against the thin metal panels, I forced the minibus through the hedge line in hope it wouldn't get any thicker. With the claw of the wooden fingers dying back, I kept the speed low over the undulating grass, whilst trying to concentrate on the view ahead and avoid the distraction of the high-pitched calls which sounded as if they were stalking us from beyond our view.

Voices in the back stayed silent, and with a rare glance in the rear-view mirror, I watched the others look at the view as all but Cassie sat up high, peering over the hedge line as we rolled parallel to the blocked road.

My thoughts turned to when I'd seen the first of the roadblocks and the impossible number of cars jammed in the narrow lane, each facing the same direction.

At first the line had seemed so orderly. A queue for the promise of transport, of safety at the other end. Maybe this time it hadn't just been a promise. Maybe this time there had been enough coaches for everyone.

As we bounced high from a bump in the field, I pulled my thoughts back to the view and the spread of flat scrubland rolling ahead. A few moments more and we'd be at a second hedge line, which I scoured beyond, checking for any reason to divert.

All too quickly I'd committed, and we thrust through the dense foliage, the suspension cushioning the clatter from the uneven ground.

Beyond the hedge, the field of dry brush fell away from the horizon. The hill rolled down into a valley so steep I couldn't see where we headed. To the right, I watched as the lengthy line of cars mirrored our downward journey in parallel.

A thump slammed from underneath, sending a shock through the structure, feeling as if the tyres were made of stone.

Wincing to the collective intake of breath, I snapped the steering to the left, hoping whatever I'd hit would miss the back wheel.

"Sorry," I called out, slowing our speed whilst scouring the undulating ground at our front.

A short, shrill call came from behind, sending out a surge of indecision. Should I slow to miss an unseen obstacle, or race ahead so what sounded as if it chased us couldn't catch up?

I made no reaction, instead searching the view to catch anything I hadn't yet noticed, but my survey found nothing of concern.

Ahead in the valley's basin we rolled toward, a road crossed our course. To the right stood a junction where the line of cars ended, held back by the all too familiar concrete blocks. A single white coach waited at the head on the otherwise empty road.

For a moment I hadn't seen the figures, the undead crowded around the door, but when I saw something move, each of the figures snapped into view; as did the smashed windows and the red-stained tarnish to the paintwork.

Figures continued to reveal themselves as I slowed to a stop, watching them bent over, bobbing their heads as they fed.

"Why are we stopping?" Mandy said, her voice rising with each word.

"Look," I said, pointing to the coaches.

"Shit," came Alex's reaction.

"We should go," Beth added.

"Wait. Let me think," I said.

Holding back my breath, I counted twenty in the pack, then tearing my gaze from the terrible sight, I looked at the hedge line between us and the empty road.

Nodding to myself at the plan I'd formed, I knew it wouldn't be pleasant, but we'd soon be on the smooth tarmac and able to race out of sight.

Mandy was the first to see where I looked. "The road's empty," she said, then my name called from behind, causing me to turn back to the coach and the creature turning its face skyward as if catching our noise on the breeze.

Gripping the steering wheel tight, I had no breath to give my thoughts voice as the illusion shattered that these were just a slow pack of the dead risen who at this distance were no threat. The feral chorus sent Jess's words into my head.

Every time we came into contact with these hybrids, someone died; Naomi in the field as we raced from the woods. McCole in the country lane in an ambush. Zoe by McCole's hand, or what he'd turned into. Andrew. I couldn't bear to think what led to his ending.

For a moment I thought I'd voiced the words when Jess spoke in almost a whisper.

"They're still human," she said.

I heard the twist of bodies in their seats. I turned to glance back, but only for a moment, forcing myself to look to the danger.

"They're infected with a bio-engineered form of the virus."

Holding my breath, I waited for the others to react whilst hoping none would make enough sound to call the creatures towards us.

"What?" came Beth's voice, repeated by Mandy.

"What do you mean still human?" Cassie asked in a breathy voice as she sat up.

"They're experiments," Jess said, keeping her gaze towards the coach. "Each given different versions of the treatment, if you can call it that."

"Some are barely human, much like those who die and come back to life after a bite," Alex added.

Jess nodded and took over. "We've seen those that

appear untouched with injury, despite what it looks like they've gone through and we've seen those that we just can't understand how they can still walk, they're so badly injured."

No one spoke for a few seconds.

"Do they deteriorate?" I said, turning around. My gaze fell on Cassie, leaning her head on the headrest in front of her with her eyes closed. "Do they become more like the other creatures as time goes on?" I looked to Jess and she held my look, but before she could reply, Alex spoke.

"We don't know."

"I think they're designed as weapons," Jess said.

"Soldiers," I added, staring to the figure still with his head turned up in the air as if listening to the conversation.

"So someone did this? Someone is behind all this?" Beth called out with indignation in her tone.

"Keep your voice down," I said in a whisper, leaning forward to check if the creature's stance had changed.

Just the low rumble of the engine filled the air until Beth spoke. "You seem to know a lot. What on earth is going on?"

I turned to Jess and nodded.

"They're different," Jess said. "Have you seen that?"

Beth glanced at Mandy, then turned back to Jess with disdain.

"We saw something in the distance. Are they the ones that make that terrible noise?"

Jess nodded. "And they're so much faster and can jump so high."

"They really can jump," I said, nodding.

Jess tipped her head towards the windscreen. "They're an attempt to make something superhuman. Each one is different though because the scientists gave them different versions of their creation."

"Like the girl in the tunnel?" I asked.

Jess nodded without pause as I ignored the question on Beth's face.

"She could talk."

Jess continued to nod, and I turned to the coach, but my thoughts kept coming back to the foul liquid they'd given Cassie.

"What girl?" Beth said when no one replied to her searching look. "How do you know all this?" Her voice tailed off as I turned to glare at her volume. She repeated the question quietly as she leaned forward.

"I know..." Jess said, pausing as if the words caught in her throat. "I thought I knew one of the scientists."

"You thought you knew?" I mumbled, already seeing the pain in her eyes.

"Her name is Toni. The younger of the two doctors."

"How did you know her?" I said.

"Does it matter?" she replied, and by her downcast look, I knew it at least mattered to Jess.

Mandy raised an eyebrow.

"And she told you all this?" I replied, lowering my voice whilst still twisted around in the seat.

"Some of it, but I figured out the rest."

"How many are there?" I said, looking to Jess.

As she turned with her mouth opening, Mandy cut in before she could answer.

"Hey."

Looking to Mandy, she looked past me and through the window, her eyes wide as the dried blood highlighted her concern.

"What?" I asked, already turning back and knowing what I'd see.

I found the answer despite her silence. The figure I'd been staring at looked up as if sampling the air, but to his side another now stood. A tall man with his head skyward.

My instincts told me to move would be the wrong decision, figuring if we kept quiet and still, they wouldn't be able to see us, like crocodiles, despite not understanding how I'd come to this conclusion.

Another stood from its feed, pointing its head to the sky and letting out a scream to rattle our glass. My theory failed when each of their heads turned as one in our direction.

They'd started running our way before I could put the stick back into gear and feel the wheels slipping beneath us.

# 30

Mandy shouted for us to move, despite my obvious effort to do so; I lifted my foot to slow the spin of the wheels.

"Come on," she called, as we rolled forward whilst I stared to the pack, watching wide-eyed as they ran toward us.

With our speed building, I turned the wheel, glancing to the wing mirrors and listening to the chorus of screams, which despite sounding much like a series of calls and replies, I dismissed the chance they could communicate, no matter how it sounded. Then I reminded myself of what Jess had said.

They were at least part human.

Tearing my stare from the rear as we rose and fell, the ground undulated in waves, my foot to the floor whilst I battled with the steering to avoid rocky outcrops that would end our journey and lives moments after. With each of the hits jarring my spine, I cringed, waiting in the lull for fear the bodywork would dig into the ground and bring us to an abrupt halt.

From the mirror, it seemed as if my efforts were in vain as the creatures reduced the gap, running in great strides with their fingers curled and arms at their sides. I took no solace when I saw only five or six of the total were still chasing, the rest no longer in sight. There were still too many for any chance of survival should they catch up. Our only chance would be to keep them at bay until we could get to the smooth tarmac and race away across the horizon.

With a great thud tearing my view from the mirror, it felt as if the front right wheel ripped from the axle, but when we didn't drop and slow, I looked ahead, desperate to find some way to the road.

The road ran parallel to the direction we headed, but now we'd travelled further along, a dry-stone wall clung on our side of the tall hedgerow, its foliage climbing too high for me to see if the tarmac the other side was clogged with abandoned cars.

Ahead, the fields seemed to stretch out forever. Another heavy thump from underneath pulled my foot from the accelerator and I looked dead ahead as we bounced, pushing my hope over the brow of the next hill.

Leaning forward and holding the steering wheel tight, the hill seemed to keep rising with the divots becoming deeper and more pronounced.

"They're getting closer. Speed up," came Beth's high shout and glancing in the mirror, I saw all but Cassie had turned to stare out of the rear windows.

The creatures hadn't tired and two raced ahead of the pack and were now less than two car lengths from the rear doors. With an impressive leap they would be on the roof.

Pushing the pedal as deep as I dared, I winced as the suspension slapped and squealed; the tyres slipping for a moment until we were finally at the top of the hill with the brow falling away.

My wide-eyed gaze snapped to the right where the hedgerow still stood tall and dense, but with a hole gaping wide as if driven through by a great truck.

This would be our way out, if we could make it before they caught us.

Craning forward, I saw discarded stone and greenery, but otherwise the road looked clear and with a sense of relief rising, I knew the gap could be our saviour.

With a backward glance, my optimism rose even more when I saw the pack had reformed. They were slowing.

To add to my delight, as I turned ahead the grass looked so flat and already the suspension had ceased its complaint.

We would make it.

Aiming for the centre of the gap, I concentrated on the ground ahead, hoping an errant pothole wouldn't trash our growing chance. Peering forward, I watched as two pairs of bloodied trainers pulled up, pushing me back into the seat as I took in the full height of the two tall men, their faces draped with blood, racing towards us through the gap with countless more following as they took the sharp turn from the road.

My stomach sank, realising they'd caught us in a trap I should have seen coming. To do so meant they were so much more than I had ever wanted to admit possible; engineered superhumans who could cooperate with each other. How could we ever defend ourselves from that?

To the squeals and calls from behind my seat, I had no time to weigh up my options. The split-second for thinking had gone, and I'd wasted it scaring the shit out of myself.

Following my gut, gritting my teeth, I jammed my foot hard to the accelerator.

"Down on the floor," Jess called, as she moved to the passenger seat and grabbed the rifle laid down to my side, twisting it in her hands, ready to club whatever came through the windows.

With my hands clamped tight, I fought the steering wheel as it pulled left, then right, before ripping from my grip as the speed built, sending pressure jolting up from the snap of the wheels. Despite being convinced we'd lose a tyre at any moment, I held our course locked on the centre of the gap whilst I tried to focus beyond the blood-streaked bare chest of the lanky creatures leading the group.

"Hold tight," I said, then forced my eyes closed as the figure loomed so large in the windscreen.

As it hit the bumper and slapped the bonnet, screams shrieked high inside and out, but the pained calls cut short with each slam of pressure and the bass drum of flesh to the thin metal above our heads. Although desperate not to see the gory detail, I opened my eyes just as a youthful woman, her skin stained dark, slipped below the view.

Beyond the great cracks and spider-web lines in the windscreen, the last of the shadows leapt out of our path, jumping high as we shot through the opening. The tyres clashed hard with the joint, but still in one piece, I corrected our path along the smooth tarmac.

We were through, but my elation was short-lived when I couldn't see any detail through the wrecked glass. Holding the wheel straight and peering through the windscreen, I tried to make out any shape to give me an idea where the road headed, but movement pulled my attention to my left and the dark hands gripping at the wing mirror.

The call of the feral creatures hadn't lessened as we'd joined the road; instead, the sound stayed so near I thought the high-pitched chorus would shatter every remaining window.

Jess moved at my side, raising the butt of the rifle high, but I couldn't see what she was doing. Instead, I searched out through the rear-view mirror as the creatures continued to keep pace on the road behind.

The only thing we could do now was to keep going until they eventually tired, or we hit something unseen through the wrecked glass. A heavy thump came at the glass to my left, punctuated by gasps from those in the back.

Glancing past Jess, still holding the butt high, I watched a red-raw fist retreat below the window line as the other hand gripped at the wing mirror.

Swapping glances uselessly between the vague colours passing the trashed glass and to the mirror in the centre, hope renewed as the creatures behind us shrunk in the view. The feeling dissolved when I turned ahead for fear the road, bound by dry-stone either side, would narrow or take a sharp turn which I had no chance of anticipating at the speed we were going.

Not able to keep up the gamble with our lives, I wound down my window. Catching only fresh, unsullied air, I pushed my head out, taking delight at the unobstructed view of the road ahead.

Its course took us to the right, and I twisted the wheel just in time to make the long turn, letting the steering wheel pull itself straight so I could stare at the long stretch of dry-stone wall ahead.

"Jess," I called out as the idea came, and with my head still out of the window, I let the minibus drift towards the left-hand wall. Feeling the light debris at the side of the road through the tyres, I glanced back to Jess as she nodded in understanding.

Drifting closer still, I didn't need to wait long for her to tell me I'd scraped the creature from its hold and I centred us back in the middle of the road.

About to revel in our new situation, a scream called out from behind my seat as a great force grabbed sharply at my hair. With the sting of pain in my scalp, an upward pressure forced my left hand from the wheel just as I caught sight of a steep left turn in the road ahead.

# 31

## JESSICA

Revelling as the gap decreased, the wall closed in as I watched the creature's fist pull up for another attempt to break the glass. With a scrape of flesh which should have turned me away, the body clattered against the stone before dropping to the ground and rushing out of sight. I couldn't help but imagine its impassive look with its teeth bared as it raised itself back up to give chase.

Lowering the rifle to my lap as the minibus centred, we lurched to the right to an agonising call from Logan. Twisting in my seat, I saw his head far out of the window, his torso almost following but for the belt across his chest and his right-handed grip on the steering wheel pulling us toward the other wall and the same fate he'd just inflicted.

The minibus jumped, riding out of some unseen pothole as Logan's head dipped to a squeal of pain and I saw for the first time the tense, dark fingers from the roof, hooked into his hair.

Lurching across the seats, I grabbed the wheel, pulling to the left, but Logan's grip in his life or death battle was too strong. His right foot somehow kept clamped down on the accelerator and I knew despite the obvious danger, we shouldn't slow for those behind to catch up.

"Help," I shouted, but Alex had already jumped through the back seats and, to Shadow's bark, she slid the side door open.

Air forced through the open doorway and with the huge stones blurring past, Alex leaned out, standing on the doorsill. With the wall close at her back, she peered up, eyes widening as she looked along the roof to the sound of a terrifying screech calling above.

"Rifle," she shouted in competition to the rush of air and, leaning back in, she held out a hand, grasping into the cabin while I kept both my hands pulling the steering wheel as hard as I was able.

Beth lurched into my view, over the seats from the back, to grab the long gun at my side.

Taking the rifle one-handed, the other hand gripping the edge of the roof, Alex would have one shot, with no hope to contain the recoil from ripping the gun from her grip.

To Shadow's barks, Logan's desperate calls and Mandy's angry screams to do something cutting through the rush of air, I stared to Alex as she pushed the gun high, her features contorting with the strain of raising the metal against the pressure of the rushing wind.

With the gun nearly high enough, Alex lurched forward, tensing as her back kissed the wall.

From somewhere, I found more strength, wrenching the wheel a little more to jerk us to the left just as the round exploded above our heads.

Twisting around to the sound of the rifle clattering to the road behind and desperate to see Alex still holding on, she climbed back in through the side door, grabbing Beth's offered grip as a body flashed past the back windows.

The pressure at the steering wheel relented, and I corrected us to the right for fear I'd lurch us too far the other way.

Our speed slowed as Logan took stock, rubbing his head and I turned to Alex, watching her grimace as she slid the side door, shutting out the raging wind.

She looked up, but instead of catching my eye, her eyes shot wide at the windscreen. I turned just in time to see the darkness at the same time Logan slammed on the brakes.

A haze draped over my thoughts as a soft voice called from the distance.

We'd come to an abrupt stop, not soon enough to miss whatever blocked the way, but enough that the impact was so much less than it could have been.

An ache ran across my back. I'd held the wheel as we collided and I dared not think about how it could have been if Logan hadn't spotted the darkening view through the wrecked windscreen.

We had no time for the dazed expression on each face to melt away; the creatures were still running to catch up.

Mandy pulled the seatbelt from her chest, her eyes wide as she stared, scowling as if it had been my fault.

Cassie sat up, blinking, her face bright red as if she'd been holding her breath.

Shadow whimpered from somewhere I couldn't see as Alex turned to look out of the back windows, Beth reaching down to comfort Shadow.

I followed Alex's look and saw the rifle laying on the road in the distance with the body beside it. My gaze couldn't linger, instead looking to the crowd heading towards us at speed.

"Close the window," I called, keeping my voice low. "Close the window," I repeated when no response came.

Gasps called from inside the minibus as I opened the passenger door, dropped to the tarmac and ran off with my sights set on the gun.

# 32

# LOGAN

Jess spoke before she'd left through the door. She'd repeated words, but the constant high pitch in my ears wouldn't let me hear. Pain seared on the top of my head as I reached up to touch my scalp. Chilly wind blew across my face and she vanished to the sound gathering in the back of the minibus.

Close the window, were the words relayed as my brain caught up. Close the window.

I listened to the whispered sounds, but it was the low, unnatural moans which piqued my interest.

Turning to my right, my fingers found the winder and leaning forward to do as Jess had insisted, after one revolution I stopped to stare at the vision in the wing mirror.

Jess ran with an impressive speed from the minibus. My instinct feared she'd lost her mind and was leaving us to our own devices. Cutting us loose. Freeing herself for her own ends.

But she was running the wrong way. The dark figures were heading towards her at a speed that seemed to match, but in opposite directions.

Twisting in my seat, I turned to look back in the cabin, my gaze flitting to each of the faces as they peered back, unsure what was going on; Mandy wide-eyed and in a daze. Shadow looking up expectantly as if waiting for a command. And Cassie. Confusion covered her reddened features.

Tearing my gaze away, I glanced through the back windows to a dark shadow of a creature passing by Jess as she crouched to scoop something from the ground.

Someone asked if everyone was okay and all I could think of was what could have been if I hadn't slammed on the brakes.

A gunshot exploded in the air and I peered back through the windows, but I couldn't see Jess anywhere. My look fell on the creature who was so close I could make out its dishevelled clothes and the side of its face shaven of skin.

A second shot boomed out, and the figure lurched forward, bowing down, but it still ran, tangling itself in its legs before regaining balance and continuing its race.

"Down," I shouted, as a round shattered the back window; an errant shot missing its target, I hoped. "Down," I screamed, as I pushed myself into the footwell, but I couldn't stay there; we had to get moving.

Not waiting for the next shot, I jumped up, wincing at the pain as I leapt over the seat to Cassie, barely looking through the remaining rear glass panel and the dark figure the other side.

Movement and that smell greeted me as I stumbled between the seats. I span around and looked to Alex, her face contorted as she moved with blood running in a slow drip from above her left eye.

Another shot rang out, quieter this time and a dull thud came from behind me, rocking the minibus on its suspension.

"Keep down," I shouted, as a hand gripped tight to my leg from below. Snatching my foot from the grip, I looked up to see Mandy, her eyes wide and so white against the contrast of her face still caked in dried blood. She pointed, opening her mouth as if unable to get words out, towards where Alex grabbed at the side door handle.

"She's fine," I said. "It's just a little blood." I turned Alex's way as the door slid open and she nodded back as she touched the tips of her fingers on the trail on her forehead.

"Move," Jess called through the front passenger door, but she'd gone when I turned toward her voice.

Before I could seek her out, the side door slid wide, filling the cabin with sunlight as Jess guided Alex out to the road.

With Cassie's legs quivering and my arm around her holding her up, I helped her to the road with her heat surging through my clothes as I peered at the estate car we'd hit, the last in a line snaking out of sight.

"Is everyone okay?" Cassie asked in a weak voice.

"I think so," Beth said, getting out of the seat to follow.

I didn't need to look along the road to know what caused the stench drifting on the breeze as Jess held Alex by the hand to guide her between the cars with the rifle slung over her shoulder.

Beth jogged past, joining Mandy walking between us with Shadow close, his nose to the air as we followed. With every step, Alex seemed to recover from the bang to her head. I wished the same would have been true for Cassie.

I followed Jess's look, sweeping left and right as she hurried forward, releasing Alex's hand when we found the white coach abandoned with its door wide at the head of the roadblock.

Alex turned, stopping to glare for a moment, not the only one of us fearing our current situation repeating. Her backwards glance looked beyond me, but I dared not follow; her widened eyes told me all I needed to know.

Alex let us catch up before tucking herself into the other side of Cassie so we could build our speed.

Setting off with a quickening pace, Mandy tripped, falling behind and forcing me to look back when Beth carried on forward, regardless.

Slipping hold of Cassie to clutch at Mandy's wrist as she regained her footing, I looked away from the three ragged figures in the distance as they bounded towards us, quickly bridging the distance.

"Run," I shouted, tugging at Mandy, but ready to let go if she remained stubborn.

"The camper," Alex shouted.

I let go of Mandy's wrist as she pulled back.

"Your choice," I said, not slowing as I caught up with Alex and wrapped my arm back around Cassie to hurry her between the cars.

I didn't glance back but I could hear Mandy's steps and

we were soon within touching distance of a VW minibus; a California with its side door wide and the driver's door held open by Jess, but my alarm rose as instead of an empty road ahead, another car blocked the way to whatever held the cars back.

With hope Jess had a plan, I watched as she diverted around the wide-open door and out of view whilst we bundled Cassie into the back. Beth followed to sit by the window. Alex jumped through the centre of the front seats and into the driver's position.

The engine started just as I dropped backwards to the road and I turned to Mandy as she stumbled forward to Shadow guarding the door as he panted.

With her breath pumping hard, Mandy came within reach and I grabbed at her outstretched hand, but my look fixed on a figure blackened and burnt to a crisp. Scorched from head to foot, it was unrecognisable as anything that should stand, let alone run with such a pace, almost skipping with the other two who looked human in comparison. Catching their stares switching my way, I turned, shivering at the sight.

Shooing Shadow past his reluctance to get in the van, I slid the door shut from the outside and ran to the next car, a BMW, to search for Jess and her plan. She stood at the block beyond the car with the rifle pointed down.

A shot went off, and I flinched away, slowing my run in horror of what she could be attacking. Another shot rang out, but I continued to walk toward her with a mix of intrigue and fear that she'd lost her mind. Then I saw it.

Instead of a giant cube of concrete, the road was blocked with huge square containers of water and the one beside Jess had holes spraying the clear contents out to blacken the road.

Jess turned with a glint in her eye as she let the rifle down, her gaze looking past me to bring the fear back. I turned, hopeful she'd considered all options in her plan, but looking through the window I saw the ignition of the BMW empty.

Shrill calls rose in the air and Jess raced around the passenger side of the VW, jumping into the seat as Alex revved its engine to push against the back of the BMW. It barely moved.

The VW's engine note rose higher, and I glanced back as something high in my peripheral vision caught my attention.

There was no time to get to the VW before those things would land. The screams raced closer, reverberated through my head. To the sound of gunshots, I pulled open the BMW's door, falling to the seat, just able to grab the door closed before the blackened creature slapped to the metal with a great call, its fists thumping at the window with such a force I couldn't quite believe the window hadn't given with the first hit.

Looking behind at the VW under attack, two beasts scratched and scraped at the doors and windows with its bumper pushing harmlessly against the car I sat in. Then I saw the gear stick in first and the handbrake pulled up. Pushing the button on the end of the brake, I grabbed the long handle to let it down and yanked the gearstick into neutral.

The car jumped forward, but the relief vanished under a shower of glass and a cloud of burnt flesh bursting from outside. Gagging at the new stench, I hit out toward the window with my hand balled, punching it square on the cheek. Its flesh felt supple, the black char coming away as it lurched forward, snapping its teeth when I withdrew my knuckles.

Knowing it outmatched me, I scrabbled over the centre console, glimpsing back as it fell through the missing window.

With no other choice but to get out, I cursed our speed building along the straight road.

Pushing the passenger door open, I paused, glaring at the tarmac rolling past, getting faster every moment I looked, but the fear dissolved when I felt a slap at my foot and I jumped out, hoping I wouldn't land in the path of the VW still rushing us forward.

A shot rang out as I hit the road, glass shattering as I tumbled with no way to control my direction, only with hope I was rolling out of danger.

When nothing hit me, and I came to rest on my back with my legs tucked up to my chest, I unfolded hearing the VW's engine so loud and pushed myself flat to the road.

The VW passed by, basking me in its heat and spray of exhaust.

Blinking, I sat up, trying to make sense of what had just happened, then saw the back of the camper racing away along the road with the BMW still at its front.

Climbing to my feet and with a sudden realisation, I looked back the way we'd come, but with relief I saw no creatures chased. The reassurance didn't last when a blast of a horn drew me back to the VW heading off into the distance, swerving from side to side as if Alex were trying to dislodge the creature gripping the roof rails with the other bent over the side, its arms swinging down to hit at the windows.

I ran, watching as the VW grew smaller with the BMW veering to the right and disappearing through the hedge, down into what I could only imagine as a river when a great crash of water spewed into the air.

With the VW surging away, its movement became more erratic as it veered left then right and back again until someone, or something, launched out from the side of the campervan, landing in a heap to lay, unmoving on the road.

I sped, despite the ache pounding down the side of my body.

As the distance grew too great I slowed, gripped by despair at who the body could be as I watched the camper take a sharp turn to the right, flipping to its side, then rolling over and down the incline and out of sight with debris flying into the air.

I pushed myself forward to run again.

# 33

The world had fallen silent, other than the sound of my breath.

With pain screaming from my legs, I ran on, concentrating on the white vapour rising from where I'd seen the VW roll out of sight and the lifeless figure on the road.

Closing the gap, the column of smoke turned black, billowing to great clouds as I searched for any sign of life in the distance. I forged forward, gritting my teeth against the pain whilst dreading an explosion from beyond the ragged remains of the hedge.

Racing past the gap made by the BMW, I chanced a glance too late to see anything but the steep incline.

Still with no sign of movement from the slumped body or survivors where the van had crashed, I ran faster still.

With every second it soon became clear Beth lay on the road with bloody marks along her arm and her neck at a sharp angle; an angle incompatible with life, in the sense of what the word used to mean.

Pushing down the guilt of not getting close and checking for a pulse, I kept up my pace as I took a route wide of her body.

I didn't have time to linger on the grief, arriving at the hedge line moments later and the great gash in the foliage where the VW had busted through sideways, rolling to splinter branches, crashing through what had grown unhindered for so many years. Leaves scattered the route gouged in the soft ground, leaving behind plastic and glass shrapnel littering its path.

Before I followed the trail of smoke, I saw the unmistakable chrome bumper, twisted and mangled as it had been shed to the side to settle next to the remains of a pale arm.

I felt immediate relief when I saw an armless creature, a once human being, lying mangled in the churned earth.

From his crushed skull I could just about tell he'd been a man, with thick eyebrows below an opening in his head where grey tissue leached to the ground.

Slowing to a jog, I peered down the bank. Picking my way through the metal debris, I saw the rifle with its barrel bent in the middle amongst flesh and foliage. My heart rate rose again at the sight of the remains of the camper at the end of the great track of mud down the bank.

The body of the VW sat upside down in the bed of a low river, the exposed underside billowing with smoke from the engine as its bulk partially dammed the slow flow of the water which refused to let the tragedy impede its journey.

With my fear not abating, I caught sight of Shadow paddling in the river as if in a daze, then shaking away the water before he scrabbled up the bank towards me.

I rushed forward, seeing the glass missing from each window, the white of the primer showing through the metal body in great swathes.

Movement caught my eye, pushing away the question of whether anyone could have survived. I gripped at the side door, unsurprised when it didn't slide. Peering in, Cassie lay on the upturned roof in amongst the contents of spilt suitcases and bags from the previous passengers. Water pooled by her foot as it searched for a route around her unmoving body.

Rushing to the driver's side, I stared to Alex, crumpled face down, but she was at least raising slowly to her hands and knees. With the door wide and with no other choice, no emergency services on the way with cutting equipment and spinal boards, I ducked low, grabbing at Cassie's foot, relieved at her pained calls as I dragged her outside to settle on the grass at what I hoped would be a safe distance from any explosion.

Stopping to grab a small green first aid box half buried in the mess, I did the same with Alex, only needing to guide her in the right direction.

Bounding back to the minibus for a third time, I peered

in, pausing when I couldn't see Jess, my gaze instead latching on another body shivering and struggling for breath. It took me a moment to realise it was Mandy as the rush of water had cleared away the worst of the scarlet from her face.

With a gust of wind, the van filled with choking smoke.

Gritting my teeth, I grabbed her by the legs, pulling her to safety. As I let her feet down to the grass, a blast of heat shot across my back, followed by the boom of pressure knocking me down as the fuel tank released its energy in a great fireball.

Alex was the first to rise after the blast, calling out Jess's name as I wracked my brain trying to figure out if I could have missed her as I searched inside.

# 34

## JESSICA

I never lost consciousness. I just couldn't move. With my eyes wide and fixed on the sea of unending branches and leaves, I lay facing upward.

Hearing the great rush of water, I settled back with the fading memory of my flesh tearing and bones breaking as I fell through the thorns.

I never closed my eyes for more than a moment, despite the pain. Despite the fear for Alex. And the others, of course.

I tried to turn, twisting to my side, but when my shoulder burst with feeling I couldn't hold back the vicious call.

As the pain died, I looked along the length of my arm and just before the wrist, a bone pressed, tight against the skin.

I heard my name called close by. The gentleness of the voice took me by surprise despite the panic rising in her tone.

Rolling to the opposite side, and fighting to regain breath stolen at the effort, light greeted me as hot knives seared in and out of my shoulder and I knew the scrape and jab of thorns had been nothing in comparison as I rolled from the bush's clutches, tumbling down the bank.

Footsteps raced in my direction as I slowed. Someone called my name with excitement, then again with more care, as if remembering the danger all around.

Her visage came into view as I lay on my back, settling in an unknown place. I glanced to the busted bone and with surprise I saw the roll had straightened out the limb and I could barely make out the damage. The pain, as I tried to lift, made it clear it hadn't been a vision.

Alex grasped me by the shoulders, hurrying me to my

feet as she checked I was okay.

"My arm," I said through heavy breath, and she looked back with a thin smile as if trying to hide her own pain from the bruises to her face.

Logan stepped to my side, reached out to help me steady as I gritted my teeth.

"Beth?" I said, remembering how she'd been plucked out through the window with such ease as the campervan swung left and right in Alex's attempts to shake the creatures off the roof.

He shook his head and with a furrowed brow, he spoke. "We have to get away," he said, already looking back along the trail of destruction from the road.

The surroundings were a mess. Great gouges in the muddy bank. The VW billowing black smoke with flames engulfing what hadn't already fallen off.

After checking I could hold myself up, Logan rushed to where Cassie still lay on the grass and helped her to her feet as Alex snapped open a first aid kit, rifling through its contents to pull out a fabric sling.

The pain eased with my arm held up, wrapped in bandages and splinted with a broken branch. Mandy climbed the steep incline, her movement slow and cautious, followed by Logan, Cassie and Shadow.

Alex guided me by the arm, with each step jarring through my broken bone.

Soon back to the road and with glances all around, we continued along the road we'd planned to take away from the roadblocks, but with footsteps instead, and in silence.

Hope rose as after a while we came to a cottage nestled to the side of the road. In the driveway, a four by four BMW rested with its passenger window open, but moving closer we saw the clear cubes on the road and that no glass remained in the car or cottage's ground-floor windows.

"It's no good," Logan said.

Leaving the car and the cottage behind, and with the pain in my arm easing with each step, the emptiness of my stomach soon became the pressing need.

Within a scant distance, a dirt side road split off where we walked, marked out by a sign showing the way to 'Home Farm'. With barely a glance in each other's direction, we diverted on the new route.

After a five-minute walk and with the pain in my arm barely there, I felt the need to release it from the bandages to test if it was just a trick or if it had really healed in the short time since the slightest of movement put me on the verge of passing out.

But did I dare do anything to raise Logan's suspicions?

# 35

## LOGAN

Five minutes after passing the sign, a ramshackle patchwork of corrugated roofs came into view with a treasure trove of useful supplies promised behind their battered doors. The ache in my joints seemed to ease and Cassie's weight at my shoulder reduced when, between us and the first of the weathered agricultural sheds, I saw a stout cottage with its front door shut.

Letting Cassie down to sit on a vast stone marking the fork to the cottage and the farm, then checking she hadn't worsened, I turned to the others only a few steps behind as Shadow trotted off towards the farm buildings. Some colour had returned to Jess's cheeks and gone was the effort I'd seen in her face as her injured arm caught with each step.

Alex held close by her side and Mandy walked with Alex's coat zipped up to her neck, her face highlighted with a darkness the water hadn't washed away.

"How's the arm?" I said to Jess as they caught up. She barely acknowledged the question, instead taking more interest in the cottage and the buildings beyond. "Can you watch Cass while I check out over there?"

"I'm okay," Cassie said with her head bowed.

Jess nodded anyway.

"Alex. Can you take the house?" I said, and she glanced at her side, looking to Jess's arm in the sling. When Jess waved away her concern, Alex turned back, already stepping towards the front door.

"Look for shotguns. Car keys, or any other keys in case the sheds are locked. Food." I paused, collecting my thoughts as I took the first steps in the opposite direction of the fork. "Mandy. Go with her. Find some clothes for everyone."

"Yes. All right. We're not children," she said, then she followed after Alex.

"Grab painkillers or something to bring down Cassie's fever. Get as much of everything as you can carry," I added, before turning and striding after Shadow as I ignored Mandy's sarcastic reply.

"Yes, daddy."

Speeding to a jog, I turned back as I heard breaking glass, but when the distance between us was already so great, I thought again about calling out my advice, convinced they should already be well aware they might not be alone.

With his nose buried deep in the gap between two double doors, Shadow waited at the first of the tall sheds on the right of the hard-packed dirt road. As he sniffed at the edge with his tail raised, I peered along the shed's window-less corrugated skin.

Stepping to his side, I went to usher him away when I caught the first hint, quickly turning to a stench coming from beyond the door.

It wasn't the same foul odour I'd grown to expect. It was more like the decay hanging in the air at the school's bungalow. It told of true death; of rot and decomposition. Not the danger of the dead risen.

I looked along and over the road to the next tall building, much the same height but with a wide double sliding door and wheel ruts leading away. A noise from where I'd come made me look backwards to Cassie still sitting on the large stone, staring at the ground. Jess looked to the cottage out of view.

I knew I shouldn't open the doors. The smell alone told me I should have left the building alone, instead stepping across the road to where the evidence showed my search would be more fruitful.

Despite my common sense, I pulled the doors open, twisting away as the wall of thick stench and a warmth that took me by surprise lodged in my throat as I took a step forward into the cattle shed.

Shadow stayed at the threshold as I looked high, not finding anyone hanging from the rafters. Holding back a deep breath of relief, I gazed through the bars to the rotting flesh of the herd of cattle laying the other side.

Through emaciated flesh, thin skin contoured the great round of cow's ribs as I looked to each. How long had it taken for these animals we'd bred to depend on us so wholly to lose their battle for life?

It must have only been three or four days since we'd left the holiday home and we'd found the world changed, but these poor animals had been left alone for a lot longer, casting doubt on when the world had started to go wrong.

Desperation hit when I caught a movement in the corner of my vision, the flicker of a great lid and its sullen eyes staring right at me.

Racked with guilt, I turned away whilst trying not to think of how many of the beasts were on the edge of death, knowing there was little I could do to ease their situation without inflicting further cruelty. Instead, I hung all hope on Alex finding a shotgun and a bountiful supply of shells so we wouldn't miss just a few.

Feeling such a coward as I sealed the doors, I took no relief from the cold air so much fresher than it had seemed for such a while.

I travelled without thought to slide the door of the opposite shed, taking less delight than I should have when I saw the pickup truck, a Ford of some sort.

With a double-cab and a short bed at the back, it would be perfect as long as Alex could find the keys. I tried the handle, then turned away, not able to glance to the shed opposite.

As I headed outside, the pickup's lights flashed at my back and I saw Alex with a set of keys in her hand, her head swinging from side to side as she searched me out. Cupping my hands, I caught the keys mid-air.

To the bass sound of the engine, I drove to the front of the cottage, watching as Jess loaded supplies into the back.

My despair at the lack of a shotgun faded when I saw Jess's sling hanging loose around her neck as she used the bandaged arm.

***

Despite the cold, Shadow kept his nose to the crack in the window as Alex directed each of my turns of the wheel with her finger tracing the map taken from the cottage. They'd found no shotgun, but plenty of supplies. As I drove, most of us ate from tins, Cassie only accepting the painkillers and a blanket as she sat between Jess and Mandy. Jess turned down any offers.

To my surprise, a stern look in Mandy's direction was enough to stop her kicking off when she saw she had to sit next to Cassie. Even after washing her face at the house, blood lingered in her creases, but with fresh clothes, Mandy looked less like one of those creatures.

I didn't tell them what I'd found. I didn't tell them what I'd left behind in the barn. Too eager to get moving, I didn't raise a question when Jess nodded, catching me staring at her use of both hands to load the back of the pickup as if the pain we'd all witnessed had been a false memory.

It was Mandy who raised the subject after a few short miles.

"So your arm is okay now?" she asked, keeping her voice even.

I looked to Jess in the rear-view mirror as she glanced Mandy's way, giving a shallow tip of her head.

"It sounded like it was broken back there," she said.

Jess didn't reply for a moment, still looking in her direction as Mandy stared out of the window, stroking down Shadow's back.

"I guess I'm lucky. It's just bruised," Jess said. I saw Alex looking to Jess when she spoke.

Dismissing the conversation, I was too eager to enjoy the sensation of putting distance between us and the challenges we'd left behind, soaking up every minute on the journey towards the A30 and the wide sweeping road we'd travelled down a few days before New Year's Eve.

We were heading out of the South West and it would take a great deal to crush my optimism.

Despite my elation, I remembered the signs for the Foot and Mouth outbreak, having forgotten them until our journey. I remembered the fun we'd had in the car. The games in the convoy of three, calling out at every yellow car across the phone lines, and the childish names we gave to the towed caravans.

For the first time since the world had turned upside down, I wondered what could have happened to Leo and the others we'd last seen when we hit the first roadblock. Frustration had taken them off and out of our lives ever since.

Could they still have been alive? Could they have found the lucky route out of the madness? Were they at home watching the TV open-mouthed?

Despite setting our aim via the quickest course, it surprised no one when we had to divert, racing along the single-track roads we feared the most, enclosed by tree canopies hanging over our heads with stone walls either side. Passing open fields with gates left wide and empty of life.

Houses loomed in the distance, a picture postcard scene if it wasn't for the terror we knew could stalk our every move, or the columns of smoke ruining every angle of the view.

We passed the occasional vehicle abandoned to the road, usually with its engine exposed, or its blackened remains still smoking.

The road twisted and turned, tracked either side by thick hedges or tall, solid walls blocking our view, forcing me to monitor our speed, ready to brake at a moment's notice, mindful of what could wait unseen.

Arriving at a village, Sheffield according to the sign, I couldn't help but think of its namesake in the north. The great industrial city.

Had the worst got that far?

I thought of Manchester, Birmingham, London. My home in the capital was only five hours away. We had to hope we were getting close to where normality waited with soldiers, guns and rockets to fight for our survival. We had to hope we were getting close to where humans were winning the battle and were on our side.

The city of Exeter would tell us so much.

As a handful of buildings shrank in the mirror, I slowed, catching sight of a lone white van facing us on the road ahead. For a moment I thought I saw a flash of colour, but concentrating as I slowed, I couldn't make out any more of what I thought I'd seen.

Fighting the urge to surge past, I slowed to a crawl, ready for something to leap. Before we would pass, the road widened to two lanes and edging forward, the double doors at the back were closed and no one sat in either of the front seats, but I caught the low rumble of the engine running and I cracked the window further, much to Mandy's complaint.

Her surprised call rose high behind me when, coming alongside, a plump figure walked from around the other side of the van with his fingers at his trouser's fly.

# 36

The smile spanning the width of the stranger's round face caused me to ignore Mandy's command and I pushed my foot at the brakes and not the accelerator. Tensing against the seatbelt as we lurched to a stop, I peered his way with my interest piqued at the great rucksack on his back, laden with equipment hanging on the outside.

The red bobble on top of his woollen hat rocked back and forth as he nodded and raised his palm to wave.

"Hey," I said, pushing open the door much to Mandy's continued complaint, but I paused half-way through the arc when I saw what looked like a small pick with a bright yellow handle tucked in his belt.

"Howdy," he replied in a classic English accent, either Kent or somewhere similar, with no hint of an American twang, despite the greeting.

Keeping my gaze fixed in his direction and to the sound of the van's stuttering engine, I pushed the door the rest of the way open and stepped to the road.

The guy's smile faltered for a moment, but as Shadow pushed past me through the opening and raced off to explore, his eyes lit again.

The van's engine stuttered and didn't recover, leaving just the low rumble of the pickup.

"Car trouble?" I said, nodding to the van.

The guy nodded back with his smile so wide as if pulled with hooks. Looking past him to the sound of running water, Shadow cocked his leg against the front wheel.

"Sorry," I said, shaking my head, but the guy turned, laughing when he saw the dog finishing up and rushing to explore the side of the road.

Copying my gesture, he turned around as I spoke again. "Where you headed?"

Instead of replying, the guy's smile dropped as he peered through the pickup's windows. Following his look, I watched as all, even Cassie, leaned toward the glass, staring at the stranger.

"Is that...?" the stranger said; looking back I saw it was Jess he stared at. "Jessica Carmichael. You're alive!"

Hefting his bag from his shoulders, he settled it to the road as Jess opened her door, looking across the horizon as she stepped out. Alex came around from the other side.

Wiping his chubby hands on his combat trousers, he licked his lips and stood to his tiptoes.

I turned to Jess, raising an eyebrow, watching as she nodded in his direction, seemingly used to this kind of reaction.

"Have we met?" she said, but he spoke before she'd finished, shaking his head.

"No, but I'm your biggest fan. Well, since the broadcast. But they said..."

Glancing between Jess and the guy, I shook my head.

"I saw the news this morning," he said, then his gaze stopped on my face. He took half a step back as he studied me. He then looked to Cassie in the car and then found Shadow with his nose in the grass and looked back. "Are you the guys from the roof?"

But before I could answer, he peered past Jess to the back seats of the pickup, looking to Mandy and then Cassie with her eyes closed.

He nodded and looked back to Jess. "You broke the story. You broke the story of my life. I've been preparing for this forever."

"Wait," I said, holding my palms out and glancing between Jess gazing at the stranger. "Where've you come from? How far have you travelled? What's it like out there?" I stopped myself as he nodded at each question.

He took a deep breath as I leaned forward, eager for the answers.

"Chertsey, in Surrey," he said with a wide smile.

I held back the questions continuing to form in my head, like how he'd got here in such a brief time.

"Everything's fine until you hit Somerset."

"Fine? What do you mean fine?" Jess cut in before I could.

"Other than some Foot and Mouth epidemic in the South West, you'd have no idea any of this was going on."

"What?" Jess said, her brow lowering as she turned to Alex then back to him. "But you saw my broadcast? There's no Foot and Mouth."

The bobble on his hat nodded as he replied. "I know. That's why I'm here."

The questions kept coming as he spoke, but I held myself back.

"They didn't show everything. The footage was so disjointed, badly edited, and the feed cut before it seemed like it had finished. We saw you on the roof, but they blurred out most of the rest."

"What happened after they showed it?" Alex cut in with the same question on my lips.

"The government discredited the report, calling it an act of domestic terrorism to spread mass panic. They said the BBC had been hacked, and they arrested some editor."

Jess pulled in a sharp breath, her brow bunching with anger at the edge of my vision.

"No one believed me?" she said after a moment.

"Some people did. I did."

"Why didn't they believe me?" Jess said, stepping back to let the pickup take her weight.

"They pixilated most of the footage and said you weren't well. You'd had a breakdown. But the energy, the emotion in your words, it was obvious you believed what you were saying."

"A breakdown," Jess said, looking to Alex with a furrowed brow.

"I don't get why they're trying to completely cover this up," Alex said, turning to the guy.

"It's obvious, isn't it?" he said, glancing to Alex then Jess when she shook her head. "Over the last ten years the government has been slowly taken over by the Chinese and now they're deliberately being slow to react. Yes they've cut the power along with the Internet and phone services, and yes they've made passing comments about a big outbreak of Foot and Mouth, but other than that…"

"Wait," I said, stepping in. "I find this very difficult to believe. What would they hope to achieve?"

"Annihilation of our country," he said, his tone matter of fact.

I turned to Jess, hoping she wasn't going to back up his theory and was pleased to see her shaking her head with her eyes narrowed.

"Or it could be that they don't know their arse from their elbow and are just fucking this whole thing up," she added.

"Or anywhere in between the two," I added. Alex and Jess nodded as the guy looked back with his eyebrows raised in disbelief.

"The point is," Jess said, "the people don't know. They didn't believe me and they're going to die." It was my turn to agree.

I looked to the guy who still had his brow raised.

"Why did you believe the story?" I added.

"I found the full version."

I watched as Jess's expression lifted, and she stood up from leaning against the metal.

"I found it on the Internet."

"Stan," Jess breathed.

"It was so intense. It looked like CGI, like some film promo. In fact, it was so real looking, I thought for a moment you made it up and I checked the listings to see if you had a film coming out."

"But surely mine hasn't been the only report coming out. There must be others telling this story now? There must be millions of people displaced. Thousands missing. Hundreds dead?"

The guy shook his head. "Nothing. Have you seen the

roadblocks? They go all the way back to Somerset."

Jess, Alex and I swapped glances.

"When the commentary started, people questioned what you said and the government's response. The authorities started talking about something going on, bigging up the Foot and Mouth thing and talking about putting the area in quarantine, using that as a reason why the power had been lost, because essential supplies can't get in. They've been very vague. The news is so sparse and no radio since Yeovil."

"But they're telling people to get away at least? To stay indoors? Please tell me that's what they're saying? Are they telling people what to do if they come across the... the creatures…?"

"No. Nothing like that," he said, slowly shaking his head.

Jess turned back to Alex with her mouth slack and gaze unfocused.

"All for nothing," she said in barely a whisper.

"No. Not for nothing," the guy said, stepping forward. "There are people that get this. There are people that understand and took notice. They know what's going on."

"But not enough people," Alex said, turning away to look at the horizon.

The guy slowed his nod for the first time.

"I think you might be right."

Taking a step forward and tilting my head to the side, I spoke again. "So what do you think is happening here?"

He didn't pause. "It's the end of civilisation as we know it. It's the fucking zombie apocalypse."

Dumbfounded at his words, I stared back. He'd got it. Simple. He knew the truth we'd experienced for the last week, or however long it had been. But why the hell was he grinning from ear to ear?

"The funny thing is," he said, as he moved to look back to Jess. "If they hadn't tried to discredit you, fewer people would have believed you. Then when they said you'd died…"

"Died?" Jess stepped back, her mouth wide.

"They said you'd died in an accident. That you were reckless."

I turned to Jess, watching as the blood seemed to drain from her face.

"Now that was a big mistake," she said, with the first hint of a smile rising in the corner of her mouth. "They've just made it easy to prove they're lying. But Stan..."

"Stan Fraser?" the guy said, and Jess nodded, her eyes widening. "They arrested him."

Jess turned as a thought seemed to come to mind. She stared with a great intent, first to me and then to Alex. "The helicopters over the ruins of the hospital."

My eyes widened when I realised what she was thinking. The guy spoke before I could give my thoughts voice.

"They showed the wreckage of the hospital. They showed a destroyed and burnt out news van."

"How did they explain that?" I said.

"The whole thing was filmed in a demolition site and she got crushed when a building collapsed."

"No. That's not right," Alex added, shaking her head. "They bombed that place to get rid of the evidence of the tests."

I watched Jess's eyes narrow and teeth grit together.

"They wanted to make sure I'd died and I think we all know what they'd do if they found me alive."

# 37

"We've got to do this," Jess shouted, the words echoing out to send each of us scouring the horizon.

"What?" I said, seeing her eyes wide with the excitement.

"I need to get in front of the camera again. I need to show them I'm not dead. I need to show the country I'm alive and more of what we've seen. Then they'll have to believe what's going on."

Alex turned to face Jess, putting her hand on her shoulder.

"Even if somehow we can get more footage, if Stan's not there to show it..." Alex said. "And won't they come looking for you if they find out you're alive?"

We all turned to Mandy coming around the side of the car.

"Filming? Are you mad? We need to find somewhere safe. We need to get out of here and find the authorities," she said, looking at each of us in turn as her voice rose.

We turned away from her, much to her annoyance.

"They'll probably figure out where you are from the footage," I added.

Jess nodded, her excitement still rising as she spoke.

"So we need to get to Exeter. We have an office there with all the kit I need. Cameras and generators and batteries," she said, turning to the guy. "I don't care who knows where I am. They have to see I'm still alive, then the people will have no choice but to believe and it won't matter what the government says. They can protect themselves by keeping their doors locked."

I swapped a glance with Alex who hadn't reacted in the same way, her brow fixed low.

"We can't stay here," she said, breaking the look.

I turned away, peering through the window to Cassie, watching her sitting up but with her head tilted back and mouth open as if asleep.

I nodded. "Alex is right. We have to get going. Jump in the back," I said, turning to the guy. "No room up front."

He shook his head as I was about to pull open the pickup door.

"No thanks," he said with his smile fixed.

I looked at the van again, reminding myself it faced the opposite way to where we headed.

"Where are you going?" I asked, furrowing my brow. "Why did you come here?" I added, when at first all I got was a widening of his smile.

Pulling the pick from his belt, I took a step back as he did the same, raising it over his head with the pointed end in my general direction. "I'm going hunting."

"Have you seen any of these things?" I said, dumbfounded and flashing a look at Alex and then Jess still at my side.

Nodding, somehow his smile had grown even wider. "There were loads heading the way you're going. It's like they're lining up for dinner. The slow ones and the crazy motherfuckers, too. My guess is going south will be the best place to wait this thing out. Once I clear out the last of them, I get to do my own I am Legend thing on the Lizard Peninsula. Cool or what?"

I ignored the question and the flash of his eyebrows, forcing down the feelings of anger at the flippancy of the words, but the anger soon drained as I realised he didn't know who we'd lost since this started. Instead, raising an eyebrow, I shook my head.

About to turn away and wish him luck, I stopped.

"How did you get in? Isn't there a front line?"

Alex leaned forward.

The guy nodded as he pulled his pack from the road, shuffling his shoulders to settle its weight on his back.

"There're loads of soldiers moving around, but no real restrictions, until you get to Salisbury. But it's only the roads that are closed."

"How did you get through?"

"I just moved the cones to the side and drove in. It wasn't until a few miles out of Yeovil that I had to leave the car. I couldn't have gone much further even if it wasn't for the blocks of concrete. I've done a bit of walking. This thing's only got me twenty miles," he said, tapping the roof of the van, then thinking better of the bass report.

"So you've walked most of the way from Yeovil?"

He laughed, and I remembered Jess only made the broadcast this morning. How early had it been when we'd seen her from the roof of the hospital?

"No. I borrowed cars from the back of the roadblocks. Most still had keys in the ignition."

"You should head north," Jess said. As she spoke, I heard less of an edge to her voice. "Get as far away as possible."

"Many people in the community did just that, but no. I'm true to my convictions. The others were full of shit. Posting memes on Facebook from their comfy armchairs, telling everyone how great they'd be when the shit hit the fan. But when it came to it, they just ran away like little children."

"There's a community?" I said, unable to turn myself away, despite knowing we should run too.

He grinned.

"Hell yeah. All over the world there are people who love this shit. Or say they do, at least."

I looked at Jess, raising my brow, but she shrugged back, showing no surprise.

"Sorry. I can't stand around gassing all day," the guy said. Raising his hand to his forehead, he nodded then walked in the opposite direction.

I looked back to Jess and then to Alex. Maybe he was right. If those things were going north to the population centres, perhaps the safest place to go would be back down south. But we couldn't do that. I had to get Cassie to her sister. To Jack and Tish before that woman could do anything to them.

And I agreed with Jess. She had to make it known she was alive to stop the lies that would get people killed.

Tapping my thigh, Shadow came to heel. Pride rushed through me, taking me by surprise when he jumped through the open passenger door as everyone settled back into their places.

No. I couldn't take the painless way out and hide away. We had to head on, no matter the danger. No matter how much the thought scared me shitless.

Without looking back, we drove in the opposite direction of the stranger.

As the miles passed the window, we watched the settlements gradually lose their picture postcard appeal, with the outskirts of a town called Newlyn coming into view and its spread of buildings marked by smoke rising high to a great cloud.

Slowing, despite the deserted roads, I took care, checking along each empty driveway to the wide-open front doors for any sign of what might linger.

When nothing made itself known, I let the pickup stop at the crest of a hill and took in the town, with its buildings bunched together to fill the view right to the edge of the expanse of blue water.

With Jess and Mandy leaning between the seats, and Alex alongside peering down, we stared to the harbour in the distance with its water empty of boats and a lengthy line of cars jamming the approaching roads. The excitement of escaping by sea drained before taking root.

As we sat back in our seats, I let the pickup freewheel down the hill, only slipping into gear when I first saw the litter of belongings discarded across the road and I guided the wheels to slalom around the open suitcases, their contents spread amongst the pools of dried blood.

On seeing a spray of scarlet against a white wall to the side and the centre of the mess potted with what I guessed to be a bullet hole, I sped us away.

Concentrating back on the road, we descended further

into the town, passing guest houses and B&Bs blocking the view of the sea as we reached the centre. A darkened chip shop marked the corner of a T junction where the road widened to the right with white signs and black letters pointing along a disorderly line of abandoned cars toward the seafront and harbour.

I built speed in the opposite direction, blinkering myself from the buildings on either side; the pubs, the shops, the restaurants and trinket store with smashed windows whose glass covered the paths and bodies at rest.

Relenting, I looked to each door standing ajar and the flames rising from the roofs from what seemed like every other. The wind must have changed, filling the cab with smoke and covering our path as we fiddled with the air vents. Hacking at the fumes, we wound down our windows to find the smoke across the road gone with a gust, leaving the sight of a pub ablaze to the left and a school with flames climbing high and black smoke billowing from every window opposite. An explosion sent glass across the road.

I stomped on the accelerator and charged through the heat radiating from both sides. Cassie moaned from the back until we were out the other side as cool air flooded in, leaving just the stench of smoke.

We raced through darkened traffic lights with the buildings thinning. Without talking, I slowed, searching out the road signs for our direction, but the adrenaline faded when I saw our route ahead clogged with abandoned cars right through it.

# 38

Not slowing, I tensed to the sound of the body panels squealing with branches scratching down our right and metal scraping away the paint on the other side. Pushing us on despite the pickup's complaint, we squeezed between the cars and the hedgerow at the side of the roundabout with a hope I could keep this up all the way beyond the horizon and to the main road.

I remembered travelling from the other direction with the road clear a few days before. It had seemed so much wider when were excited to head to the secluded destination near the sea.

Squeezing through the corner, the road stretched out ahead filled with three jumbled lanes of cars, vans, minibuses and so much more; each had jostled for position before they'd had to give up, leaving doors wide and possessions littering the gaps. To the right I steered us along a short grass verge lined with thick bushes before trees took over to block the view of what could be on the other side.

"Where are all the people?" I said, watching as everyone in the back shook their heads.

Cassie opened her eyes. "There's not even any bodies," she added.

"Let's hope they all made it away," Alex added and all but Mandy nodded.

"At least it looks like the creatures have moved on," I said, but no one replied as if afraid to tempt fate.

I pushed us on and after a few seconds more, the left-wing mirror ripped clean off and disappeared below the view with an impact against a plumber's van. Moving us as far to the right as I dared, I'd take the scrape of wooden fingers over the scratch of metal any day.

Searching ahead, I peered at a lamppost sat tall in the middle of the space we needed to get through. I thought of ramming it down, but I ignored the temptation as visions of head wounds and steam rising from the engine sprung to mind.

Instead, I trusted the ground didn't fall away beyond the thick foliage of the hedge to the right so we wouldn't slide and roll to a more terrifying end.

Despite the violent clawing at our thin metal skin, I edged us further into the undergrowth as the lamppost grew closer. By the time we'd reached the tall pole, we hadn't rolled away and out of sight.

Back on the verge and past the post, we drove on like that for a little while longer, having to divert from the safety of the grass every so often, each time fearing a fall into the unknown. But still we hadn't disappeared, and I tried to ignore the chaos of cars, the debris and the dark patchwork of dried blood sprayed to the paintwork. The white cars were the worst.

As we passed car after car, I tried not to imagine the time when panic came, sending everyone running, chased in fear of their lives or at the thought of missing their last hope.

I remembered back to the dark hospital corridor when we'd interrupted the creature dragging the bodies away and tried not to think of a pile of rotting flesh beyond where we could see.

We were making excellent progress; roundabouts came and went with the same scene to our left. Not able to judge how far we'd travelled, I eventually spotted the road clear ahead. Each of the vehicles stopped in a neat line up against one of the six concrete blocks across the entire width of the road, including on the verge.

I didn't pause. As soon as I knew there was no chance of getting through, I pulled open the door, jumping down and squeezing into the bush to scrape down the side, followed by Shadow. The others were out too, Cassie helped by Alex.

I rushed around the side to catch her when her step faltered. With my arm around her waist, I guided Cassie back up straight as we shuffled sideways between the cars, crunching cubes of glass under our shoes.

I worried for Shadow's feet as he snaked between the cars, but nothing seemed to hinder his pace.

As we approached the head of the roadblock in the distance, a sudden thought turned me around to see none of the others had thought to pick up any of the supplies.

"Shit," I said. "Fuck." Cassie stiffened under my arm. "No one's brought any of the food."

The others turned back, looking at each other before settling on Mandy at the back of our trail.

"Don't look at me. I'm not your mother," she said.

Stuffing down the anger, I thought about telling her to head back as we waited, then wondered if I would wait at all. Then at least she'd realise how grateful she should have been for coming along for the ride.

Cassie's soft voice drew away my anger.

"Leave it," she said. "It's not her fault. None of us can think straight."

She was right of course. None of this was like anything we were used to. Each of us were having so many first experiences, how could we react right every time? Our punishment would be hunger and thirst if we couldn't find anything to replace it, but I took solace that it had been so long since we'd seen any undead.

Without further word, we walked along the open road. I tried to ignore the thought of being so exposed, whilst listening out into the silence broken only by our steps. I heard no hum of traffic, no scurry of animals in the hedgerow. No call from the birds.

We walked at a slow pace for what I guessed could have been an hour and with the sight of the sea and a roundabout, we'd found civilisation again, just without the people.

At a petrol station we came across a queue of cars lined up at the pumps, maybe ten at each. The numbers on the tall sign were dark, and I guessed the cars were out of fuel when the pumps ran dry or the electricity went out.

"Will you guys wait here?" I said, looking to their faces.

"Yes. Go," Cassie said, and untucked herself from my

hold.

Just before I turned away, I looked to Alex who nodded back.

Jogging to the petrol station, I glanced in through the glass door at the shop and turned away at the sight of blood splashed across the floor just inside, instead peering at each of the vehicles. Some still had the nozzles plugged in. Each had their doors wide. Who shuts up their door when they have to run for their lives?

Checking the first, the keys were still in, the orange light coming on as I turned the ignition, with the needle sat under the lowest line.

I moved to the next, looking past the blood sprayed across the four by four's white side and the pump strewn to the road with the scent of fuel. With no keys, I moved to the next.

Glancing back to the road, each of the five still stood staring in my direction. Mandy watched with hope and I drew a smile as I saw Cassie standing with Alex near and her head raised, peering in my direction.

The next car, a Ford Focus, had keys. The tank was three quarters full and the engine started on the first attempt. I tried not to wonder why the owner hadn't raced away when they had the opportunity.

***

I revelled at the speed, driving a hundred miles an hour down the empty roads potted only with the occasional car abandoned to the side. No one had the will to check them out; instead, we stared at the impact damage or the burning embers as we passed in the widest possible arcs.

With the town behind us, I slowed at junctions only to make sure we headed in the right direction. The road became a dual carriageway separated by a barrier and with our speed growing, so did the hope we were on the last leg of the journey and the next roadblock would be the last. On the other side would be a friendly army and their trucks to take us away; their guns and great numbers set to keep us safe.

I tried not to think what would happen if they recognised Jess, or if they had the same orders that had been given to Commander Lane and his crew.

The roadblocks continued to come and go and we skirted around the haphazard cars in lines and through walls smashed through with big trucks, bumping our way into fields to see vast lorries abandoned to the side with massive front-end damage.

Arriving in the town of Hayle and with the call of hunger, we stopped at a small trading estate and a bunch of shops; clothes and a coffeehouse. A pharmacy and supermarket. The carpark deserted, save for a battered old Ford Escort with its bonnet up.

I drove slowly into the expanse of tarmac and across the front of the shops with each of us peering in, stopping only when no one gave voice or warning of something seen.

Leaving the engine running and the door wide, Jess joined me, both of us looking to the horizon as we turned on the spot.

Shadow jumped out, peering around, but he waited by the car as if protecting the others when we walked away.

Jess opened the shop door, and I half expected a bell to sound. The place stank, but not of sewers and I hoped it to be the stench of food no longer so fresh.

A few people had been there before and they'd taken what they could carry and left, leaving a trail of tins and groceries. Grabbing wire baskets, I piled up cans, bags of crisps and bottles of water. Pulling open the boot, I was surprised to find someone's belongings inside. The owner of the car.

Moving past the guilt, I dropped the suitcases to the road and filled it after five trips, along with the baskets, dropping the excess to Alex's lap before jumping in the front seat.

Jess stayed outside of the car.

"Eat, close the door," she said, as she continued to look across the horizon.

# 39

## JESSICA

I couldn't stand the smell of their food. Ever since I'd eaten human flesh, the thought of anything else in my mouth tightened a grip on my insides and that need for more was always there in the back of my mind. Only when Logan called for us to leave could I force myself into the car, leaning at the crack in the window like Shadow as the wind sprayed in.

The confinement did nothing for the stomach cramps, nor did Logan's glances as if he knew what I felt. Still, better to be on the road eating up the miles. Two more hours, Logan had said, if there were no more roadblocks.

Or soldiers, I added in my head. Or Toni's failed experiments. Or the dead massing in our path.

Hope built as we sped, but each time he braked, I feared I would need to find my food, something to keep away the total loss of control, of feeling, or sympathy for the race I'd once belonged to. The feelings I hoped wouldn't only ever be a memory.

I watched each time the road narrowed. We all did. At bridges. Junctions. Wide trees at the side of the road, or anything danger could hide behind. Relief bloomed as we passed, then dashed as the next appeared on the horizon.

We were making good progress, not dropping from over a hundred for a long while, but as I blinked, I felt us slow. Without having to ask, I saw the articulated lorry in the distance, the trailer jack-knifed and diagonal, blocking each of the four lanes. But that wasn't all.

Bunched either side were cars strewn, stacked as if placed there by a crane in a breaker's yard. Logan had to brake; the view looming too soon and with debris under the tyres, each head peered around the view.

"What now?" Cassie said, unable to hide the tiredness in her voice.

There had been a roadblock. The lorry hadn't stopped. I couldn't tell if it had been a deliberate act to break through the mess of cars, or an accident. The result of an attack, perhaps.

I looked for bodies as we drew closer. For blood marking the roads.

I saw none. No signs. Perhaps it happened when everyone but the truck driver had gone.

As we coasted to a stop, Mandy spoke, rushing her words. "What are you doing?"

"We have to walk," Logan said, still letting the car slow.

"Are you mad? Go around," she said, raising her voice.

I watched as he drew a deep breath, as if to hold back a verbal assault, then spoke.

"We won't get up those banks. This thing's two-wheel drive. It's nowhere near as tough as the pickup."

"Go back then," she said. "Find another way."

"No," Logan replied as we stopped. "Listen. We don't need this car anymore. Feel free to take it and find another way around. But if you're coming with us, bring some food." Without further pause, he stepped from the car, going around to the boot and hooking out a basket.

I pulled out of the car, taking a basket held out by Alex and kept an eye on Mandy still sat in the back seat with her arms crossed. Turning away, I scanned for threats, scouring the view as we stepped away from the car.

The truck wedged either side of the road, both ends buried in metal wreckage, crushed to the rising banks.

Shadow found a route. Disappearing at first through a gap under the trailer only he could fit, but reappearing further down at a place we could follow. And we did, crawling on our hands and knees, we helped Cassie between us before rising to the lengthy line of concertinaed cars on the other side. Mandy followed a few moments behind.

We had to climb the metal, although Shadow found his

own way. As we helped Cassie forward, it felt like hours before we saw the end ahead, partly hidden by the brow of the hill.

Cresting, we saw a roundabout in the distance. The warning signs must have been long flattened. At least by now the effect of the truck at the back had lessened and we could walk through the thin spaces between the cars, towards the concrete blocks.

I turned to the sky. It would get dark soon. We had to find a car and race through the miles before the hunger grew.

Movement ahead pulled me back to the moment. Logan followed my gaze as he saw me turn toward a Toyota dealership and the figure who'd disappeared below the roofline.

My stomach tightened. Saliva flowed; my eyes narrowing as the need came like a switch flicked and for the first time I couldn't help but wonder why Logan and the rest hadn't triggered the same reaction.

# 40

## LOGAN

Jess saw him first, then Shadow; their silent stare to the horizon guiding me to the figure standing on the flat roof of the car dealership. Shadow's silence didn't last for long, but he quietened down as I leaned down to stroke along his nose.

The others turned as I did, seeing the last of the dark clothing lowering through the middle of the roof.

Standing on the exit of the dual carriageway, I couldn't see much else of the building for the hedgerow. I turned to Jess and despite the faraway look in her eye, she glanced my way.

"What now?" I asked, but no one replied. "Shall we go say hello? Maybe they can spare a car?"

Jess and Alex shared a private look, a nod between them and seemed to make some unvoiced agreement.

"What?" I said, but they both just nodded in reply.

"Let's go," Alex said, and I turned to Mandy who'd caught up.

Out of courtesy, I asked. "What do you think?" I got nothing back other than her scorn radiating when she refused to look me in the eye. Still, she followed as we left the road.

Walking with a slow, considered pace, we kept the hedgerow between us and the building as it receded to reveal the tall glass walls of the dealership. A sign stood at the front rising to just below the roof with a round logo sat on top of bright red writing.

My eyes widened when beside the dealership's car-crammed lot was a petrol station. With our pace increasing, I kept focused on the detail, careful to guide Cassie over the central barrier between the lanes.

Despite the distance remaining, I squinted through the

large glass front, but couldn't see any sign we should avoid the place.

The foliage ended as the hedgerow was replaced with a low brick wall.

"Everyone wait here," I said, still peering to the glass as I settled Cassie to rest on the grass verge. "I'll get a car," I added, as I knelt to Cassie who looked up. I felt a sudden flash of guilt that I hadn't yet told her what I knew of the danger the kids could be in.

Reasoning that now wasn't the time or the place, I put my hand to her forehead. The second lot of painkillers were doing their job to keep her temperature down, but she was still so weak.

"I should go." Jess's voice took me by surprise and Alex too by her wide eyes as I peered up towards her. "You stay and look after Cassie," she said, but I lingered on Alex's face, wondering what the concern in her furrowed brow could mean.

"Alex. Can you?" I asked.

"I don't need watching over," Cassie added in a weak voice, not looking up from the grass.

Alex nodded and looked to Cassie.

"It's fine," Jess eventually said. "We can both go."

I turned, scanning over the cars and pickups neatly lined up, but not pristine, each covered with a thin layer of dust, or perhaps ash. I glanced back to see Shadow had stayed behind to prowl up and down the wall.

Jess sped, hopping over the wall with ease.

"Slow down. We don't want to scare them," I said when her walk became a jog. She slowed without glancing back.

The front half of the showroom consisted mostly of glass, the back half formed of tall white walls surrounded by a slatted metal fence to create a compound. As we got closer, there were no lights on, but the wide inside space gleamed with sun shining through skylights to glance off the car's paintwork.

Jess tried the glass front doors, but when they didn't move, she headed around the side and out of sight as I leaned up against them, shielding each side of my face to get a better look. Old food containers, tins and packets littered around the desks at the back, but I couldn't make out any movement and no sign of any disturbance.

To the sound of a door slapping closed where Jess had walked, I headed around the corner to an open door in the white metal siding with Jess out of sight.

Glancing around, nothing but the road ran this side of the building; beyond, fields headed off to the horizon lined with distant columns of smoke.

Mindful someone could lie in wait, I pushed past the fear and headed through the door, half expecting someone in a suit to call out, 'Welcome to Parklands Toyota. Can I get you a coffee?'

No one stood on the other side. There was no sign of Jess and nothing but stale air greeted me.

Jogging forward, looking left and right, I called out, "Jess," I said in a stage whisper, but only my echo replied until a muffled scream called out to my right and I ran.

Without thought, I grabbed the metal handle of the first door, pushing it wide, ready to pounce on whoever had taken Jess.

# 41

## JESSICA

The door burst open at my back and I sensed Logan rushing through before he spoke. I stopped whatever I was about to do, biting at my bottom lip as I pulled back away from the three cowering in the corner.

"Shit," Logan exclaimed, his words muffled despite the volume I'd expected. "What's going on?"

He peered around, searching for threats in the office, not hiding his lowered brow when all he could see were the man, woman and kid.

"You're bleeding," he said as I flashed a look his way. I could already taste the copper, wiping my lip across the back of my hand.

"Are these it?" I asked, the first words coming to mind.

"Are what?" Logan hurried out.

"All the people here?" I added, shaking my head. He spoke, but I didn't understand what he was saying. Something about the door.

He didn't wait for an answer, instead turning to face the family. "Are you okay?" he said, holding his palms up. "We just need a car."

"Or a place to stay the night?" I said, wiping at my mouth a second time.

Logan turned back my way, his gaze lingering as his brow furrowed.

"Let's keep on the road," he said slowly, his voice clearer as the pounding in my ears seemed to slow.

He was right. We had to keep towards Exeter and no one should leave me alone with these people. Or anyone. There was enough of me left to understand.

When I'd seen the person on the roof, the surge of

hunger had taken me by surprise. A blood lust. The only way I could describe it, growing with every step towards the building, blinkering me from anything else but finding them. My senses enhanced. I could smell where they hid, and I knew what I would have done if Logan hadn't burst in.

I had no idea why, but with his arrival it had been like the hunger shattered, or someone had pulled the plug and it washed away. I soon felt as if I was nearly back to myself, or the parts of myself I could at least get back to.

Could it be that I had some level of control over my new feelings?

"There's a safe where I think they keep the keys. But it's locked." The guy spoke with a quiver in his voice as he ran his hand over his tight wavy hair.

His words stirred me from my contemplation. I couldn't look him in the eye. He wouldn't look in my direction.

"In the office next door," he added, when neither of us had moved.

Rushing out faster than Logan could follow, I used the last of my draining energy to pull the thin metal cabinet open, the lock popping as if made of plastic.

Handing bunches of keys to Logan, I led him outside and away from the damage and his questions.

Back in the frigid air, I thought of staying behind, but as I saw Alex walking down from the road with her arm around Cassie and carrying the baskets, the thought vanished and I took a seat in the white pickup as the engine came to life.

# 42

## LOGAN

With a tank full of syphoned fuel and the light not yet fading, we made steady progress along the A30, despite having to make our way around roadblocks, or back-tracking to find another route. Cassie slept, alternating her lean between Alex and Mandy's shoulders whilst they stared, searching out of the windows.

Jess sat quietly in the passenger seat as if asleep, with her face to the steady stream of wind from the gap in the lowered window. Shadow sat next to Alex with his nose at the same crack.

Jess moved for the first time, shuffling in her seat as we passed the sign for Bodmin, growing more animated as we diverted from the A30 to pass The Jamaica Inn, a famous smuggler's museum my friends had pointed out as we made the drive down here. A growing guilt nagged at my thoughts when I couldn't remember who had said the words. Was I already forgetting my friends?

Jess dropped the window further, leaning closer to the gap as her hand went to her face, nodding when I asked if she was okay.

Soon after, the roadblocks were shorter and easier to skirt around with walls and hedges already badly damaged.

On the journey, my mind would drift back to the day the New Year's celebrations had ended. The last day the whole group were together and we'd tried to sleep on the supermarket floor before we had to run again; the group growing smaller so quickly. I thought of how Andrew, his name catching, had saved us later that day.

As the fuel gauge dropped, I expected to see fewer signs of the chaos, but each mile continued to mirror the debris of before, the rising columns of smoke, the decay and destruction wrought across the land. But the one thing we didn't see, at least up close, were people, those who were still human and those who were arguably not any more.

I felt the tension in the car lower when we saw the first signs for the M5 motorway ahead and the road to the left leading to Exeter.

"Exeter," Jess said, pointing to the sign, speaking for the first time since we'd left the car lot.

"Do you think it's safe?" Alex asked from the back.

I listened out for a reply because I was in no place to make any guesses.

Jess didn't reply either. Our silence must have been enough of an answer because no one repeated the question; it was only when we saw the first of a long line of cars blocking the road to the motorway that we knew we might have little choice in the direction we took.

I made the turn to Exeter at speed, aiming alongside the cars facing our way filling the slip road, when without warning Jess turned to me.

"Stop," she said, and I slammed on the brakes, staring forward, scouring to see what I'd missed in our path.

"What is it?" I asked when I couldn't see any reason for the call, but she didn't speak, letting the heavy thump of the twin rotor blades over the idling engine do the talking.

Twisting the ignition off, I looked to the dashboard to make sure the headlights were off.

"Oh my god," Mandy called out, and wide-eyed I turned to the passenger door behind me before slamming my hand to the central locking. The locks clicked at each door just in time for her to pull at the lever.

"Are you nuts?" I said, raising my voice. "They're not here to save us." By now I was shouting, fighting with the din of the rotors so close.

Cassie woke, lurching forward with her eyes wide and bloodshot as if shocked with a defibrillator. She turned, stopping as she stared at Mandy pulling the handle back and forward.

"Let me out," Mandy said, her voice rising.

"They're not here to save us," I called out. "You heard what I said back in the church. Did you see the roads? It was soldiers in helicopters like this one that tried to kill us. They don't care if we're not infected."

"And if they know it's me, then we're done for," Jess said, her voice flat, but her words seemed to have the opposite of the intended effect. Mandy's eyes grew wider as she pumped the handle back and forth.

"I need to get out. Let me," she shouted, so loud I worried they'd be able to hear her above the din of the helicopter whose pressure felt as if it would dent the metal and crack the glass at any minute.

"I'll smash the window," said Mandy, her fist thumping to the glass.

I looked across to Jess, then behind her to Alex with Cassie staring at Mandy, still in a daze.

I turned away as the light from the sun blotted out, seeing the underbelly of the long Chinook with its back door sealed up. Along each side, an Apache gunship flew, all three helicopters so impossibly close to the ground.

Mandy's fists at the window added to the shake, and I snapped around, pulling my handle to release the locks. Her door opened, and she gave no time to pause on its movement, rushing out through the gaps in the cars toward the helicopters as they headed to the horizon.

Checking to make sure Shadow had stayed put and sliding down the window, I leaned out wide, closing the door she'd left open and joined the others as we watched her run. The helicopters were soon dots in the sky and Mandy had slowed as her breath seemed to let go and she bent over with her hands on her knees.

Starting the engine, I expected at any moment for a horde to rush out at her sides; the group consuming her in more than one way. I expected to have to jam the gear into reverse and race away.

I took comfort when they didn't materialise and rolled along the road, squeezing down the line of traffic and the grass verge as she stood bent over, looking to where she'd last seen what she thought were her saviours.

Pulling alongside her, I stopped and waited, but she wouldn't get in. Only as I pulled away did she move, and I stopped to let her in.

None of us spoke as we rolled away, scraping between the cars as the bustle of Exeter's buildings came in to focus.

"So where are we heading?" I said into the silence.

# 43

## JESSICA

"Edmund Street," I said, watching Logan wince with the pickup's bodywork scratching against the Armco barrier and to the thump of the wing mirror as regular as a pendulum. By now, the light had almost gone and it was plain to see from the skyline there was no power in the city.

Logan leaned forward, squinting in the night as he guided us as best as he could with ours the only lights, aside for the orange glow pocketing the horizon. I had to look away and out to the view, staring to the smoke and dust hanging in the air to distract every other scent growing the want in my stomach.

As buildings rose on the horizon, the volume of cars squeezed into our path thinned, but our speed slowed with the road cursed with rubble spat from buildings reduced from their former glory. Still, I took comfort in those that remained, those the bombs had missed as I pulled in air through the wide-open window, searching for faint pockets of flavour.

Logan's voice startled me from my concentration.

"Are you sure we should stay here?" he asked, looking across the view. "There's no power and what if they start bombing again?"

"We shouldn't travel at night. That way. The building looks intact," I said, and pointed over to a bridge on the right over the fast-flowing River Exe.

He didn't move off straight away, instead his gaze lingered my way. "Are you okay?"

"I'm fine," I said, hurrying out the words.

I forced my lips closed, my senses near overwhelmed with flavour of survivors.

Lit only by the eerie moonlight, an army truck stood on

the wide bridge with the engine cover raised up. As we turned to give it more light, we saw the bridge split in sections with row after row of sandbags across each half of the road. Stacks to the right had collapsed, with darkness splashed over the coverings. But with no bodies lying to the road, Logan twisted us left and right through the checkpoints. It looked as if it had been the last stand when the jets roared close to bomb the city.

I pointed towards the tall building ahead, one of only a few left intact over the river and standing beside a hotel of the same height. He didn't need any further direction when the headlights illuminated the tall white letters high to its front.

Itching to leave the confines, we were nearly across the bridge when on the last turn the pickup fell forward, lurching to a stop with the floor scraping the road as if the wheels had fallen off. Logan stared back wide-eyed as if he hadn't seen the great crater I'd only just spotted but too late to shout out and stop the front wheels vanishing into it.

I couldn't wait any longer, pulling my door wide, each of the others doing the same and staring down at the great section of missing road.

Shadow skirted around the hole and I waited unseen as the rest guided each other around the debris, staying put as they ushered Cassie and Mandy through the revolving glass doors of the hotel.

Looking on, Alex turned, the last to go through, and seemingly with no surprise that I hadn't followed, she gave a nod before pushing through as my thoughts turned to the prey I tasted on the air.

# 44

## LOGAN

With curled bread and dried vegetables sat on plates and crockery smashed to the kitchen floor, it was like seeing into the past; the moment frozen when the staff dropped everything to run for their lives.

Following Shadow with his nose high in the air, then to the floor and back up again, I stepped with caution through the rooms on the ground floor, reassuring myself with every lungful of stale air.

Anxiety rose as Shadow raced away, only to calm as his feet padded against the tiles to return to my view. Back in the wide reception, Mandy stood to the tall glass, staring out across the darkened ruined city whilst Cassie lay on the sofa where we'd left her. I guessed Alex and Jess must have been on their own exploration.

After pushing the reception chairs between the revolving glass doors, checking twice they would no longer move and the single glass door to its left remained locked, we made ourselves comfortable in the kitchen, digging out the last of the fresh ingredients at the back of the cupboards and the cuts of meat not too warm in the silent fridge.

It hadn't been long since they'd run from this place. Two days, I could only guess.

We ate in the restaurant amongst tables littered with half-eaten meals, glasses smeared with lipstick and wine to hint at the timing. Even Cassie perked up enough to take a few mouthfuls between sips of water.

With the meal complete, I stared out of the wide windows and into the darkness of the night, whose glow seemed alive.

Alex appeared once we'd eaten, a frown hanging heavy

on her face. Following her to the kitchen, I left Cassie and Mandy with their feet up in the lounge and Shadow sleeping off his meal. Finding Alex raiding the cupboards, she pulled what she could from the stores, but most were catering packs too large for the road.

"Is she okay?" I asked. Alex knew who I meant, peering back, not able to hide her concern.

"She's gone next door. To the offices."

"Alone?" I replied. "We need to stick together."

"I didn't get a say. We'll make another broadcast at first light," she said, turning back to her search.

"She won't be able to get back in. I've blocked the front door."

"I've got a feeling she won't be back until the morning."

She held my gaze, her hand twisting the black watch on her wrist as she rearranged the giant tins at her feet. I left the conversation there, knowing her reluctance to say anymore, and that's when I knew she'd seen the same signs I had.

My thoughts turned to finding a place for us to sleep, knowing it would be a busy day tomorrow, not least of which would be to figure out where we were going.

We didn't have the pick of the rooms. With no power, the electronic locks held closed, but as I arrived at the top floor, the signs of panic were everywhere. Cleaners had abandoned their carts, wedging doors open; others stood wide, blocked from closing by abandoned luggage.

Choosing the furthest down the corridor, I settled Cassie down, pulling the covers over her clothes.

Leaving only for a moment, I told the others of the rooms, returning with Shadow at my heel, pausing as I watched Cassie's breath already settled into a rhythm.

\*\*\*

Peering through the great windows, I watched as first light crept up the horizon, its glow broken only by the rising dark lines of smoke across the view.

After laying Cassie on the bed last night, I'd torn down the net curtains and pushed the upholstered chair to the window. Wrapping a blanket around my shoulders, I'd intended to watch over her, but had fallen asleep in an instant with the relief I didn't have to tell her about the children until the morning.

Twisting in the seat, I watched the mound on the bed stir. Shadow laid at her feet with his paws in the air.

Stretching out a stiffness in my neck, I wrapped myself tighter from the cold and turned to the windows. As darkness melted away, I stared to the pickup with its front wheels in the great crater I'd only seen after it was too late. Looking along the rest of the road littered with so many holes, I knew the way would be impossible for anything but a tank to navigate.

My mind turned to where we should head and with no clue as to where the children were being held, our only option would be to go north and see how far we could get.

My slow gaze caught on the buildings missing from the skyline and the rubble in their place with smoke rising from the remains. The scene reminded me of black and white images of the blitz, minus the people rallying to help.

I turned to the sound of movement at my back, smiling toward Cassie who sat up in bed, rubbing her eyes as Shadow righted himself. She peered around the room as if unsure of where we she was, before looking to see she still wore the clothes she'd had on since we'd met.

Her frown bloomed to a glorious smile, sending joy surging through my body, but about to rise and walk to the bed and take her in my arms, I knew this was the time.

"The children aren't safe," I said, regretting the words as they came out.

Cassie squinted in my direction as her smile fell away.

"How do you know?" she said in a dry voice.

"Jess knows the doctors. They're not looking for a cure. I know how it sounds. I know you're alive because of what they gave you, but they're not safe and we have to find them."

"How are they not safe?" she said.

"They're going to be experimented on," I said, knowing there was no easy way to put the words across.

I watched as her breath raced, her chest pumping hard as if in the first stage of a panic attack. Before I could move to ask if she was okay, she scrambled from the bed, jumping up with such energy, then rushed to the bathroom and pulled the door behind her.

Still nothing could push away my elation that she seemed so much better.

Light from the fresh day had all but filled the room when the bathroom door opened and without words, Cassie moved to the dresser where I'd piled food gathered from the night before. Without looking my way, she pushed stale bread to her mouth as I marvelled, but taking a bite, she reared back at the taste and spat the contents to the bin at the side.

"How are you feeling?" I asked, pulling myself from the blanket as she frowned in my direction.

After taking a moment, she replied with a flat, dry voice, "Tired," she said, shaking her head, turning away as if she couldn't look at me.

I stood, watching her lean against the wooden dresser as I picked up a large bottle of water from the floor and poured her a glass.

"The bread's a little dry."

"It's not that," she said as she gulped at the water, still staring my way.

I turned, self-conscious of her stare.

"When did you find out?" she said.

"After I left the church. I wanted to tell you, but you've been so unwell."

Cassie looked away from me and I followed her stare, turning around to see the outside had brightened to a fresh dewy morning. I looked along at the bridge we'd crossed last night. The river rode high and fast, water lapping at its span because of the buildings fallen from the banks.

About to turn back to Cassie, I saw a figure walking in

the distance, but when I tried to focus on the detail, they disappeared behind a building and out of view, leaving me with the memory of her red outfit and the outline of someone I thought I knew.

"We should go soon. Keep heading north. Take a minute if you need," I said, not turning from the view.

"I'm ready."

When I turned around, Shadow jumped from the bed and stared at me as if he had something to tell.

Cassie walked by my side down the corridor, bearing no sign that yesterday she'd had to be carried and I couldn't wipe the smile from my face when all she'd needed had been rest. They had cured her.

Alex opened her door as we arrived at her room. "Are you ready?" she said, as if she'd been waiting to hear our steps. She looked to Cassie as I nodded, still beaming. "Did you see Jess?" she added, turning to me.

I paused for a moment, thinking back to the woman in red, but shook my head.

At Mandy's door, Alex gave a gentle knock. Knocking harder a second time.

As Alex stopped, I was about to lean into the door to listen when it opened to Mandy standing on the other side, pushing her long hair from her face.

"Be ready in five minutes, please," Alex said, and we left down the corridor.

I hadn't expected Jess to greet us in the reception downstairs. Dressed in a black jacket, white blouse and black skirt, I double-took to make sure it was her; she looked as if she'd been at a spa retreat; refreshed and rested. But how could that be?

Turning to the revolving doors, I stared at the chairs neatly stacked on the other side of the glass; the chairs I'd used last night to jam them closed. I remembered checking I couldn't make the doors move, no matter how hard I pushed.

I turned to Alex, but she didn't seem phased; instead she wore a grin and looked to the two bulky black cases at

Jess's feet.

Jess stared at Cassie with her eyes pinched and Cassie looked back at her with almost the same expression. Jess was the first to turn away, glancing to Alex before peering to the cases.

"I got batteries. There should be enough," she said, and Alex nodded as if continuing a conversation involving no one else.

"The roof?" Alex asked, and Jess replied the same, grabbing the handle of a case in each of their hands. "Are you coming?" she said, turning to me.

I paused for a moment, but Alex didn't wait for my response before following Jess to the staircase.

The winter's chill hung in the air and the sting of acrid smoke gusted across us as we walked to the edge of the roof.

I turned to check for Shadow and found him waiting at the head of the stairs as they rose through the roof in the middle of the building. He wasn't moving from that spot until we headed back down.

Standing by Cassie, I tried not to stare as I hoped for her to talk and tell me how she felt. Instead, to her silence, I watched as Alex opened the cases, pulling out the camera equipment and what appeared to be an upturned umbrella from the second case as Jess pointed to the buttons at its base.

I watched with fascination as Jess switched to the professional we all knew from the TV; staring down the lens of the camera with her posture perfect and the microphone in hand as she described our journey with such eloquence.

The bombing of the hospital. The helicopters. The creatures we'd run from but that were no longer around. As she continued to speak, Alex panned the camera on its tripod to take in the destruction across the horizon.

I watched as the camera's red-light darkened and Jess's shoulders relaxed. Sharing a nod and a smile, they turned down to the satellite transmitter and Alex began pressing buttons at Jess's instructions.

Shadow's bark echoed across the city and as I turned

from the stairwell, I stared at Cassie stood at the edge of the roof. She'd climbed up the three bricks forming the lip of the roof and stared out in the direction where the camera pointed, her expression blank.

About to call her name in a soft voice, hoping not to startle her, she turned around and jumped down from the wall; her look not connecting with mine as if I wasn't there. She headed to the stairwell, apparently overtaken by a sudden need.

I followed, rushing behind her, leaving Jess and Alex to their growing frustration at the equipment.

I couldn't catch up with her on the stairs. Only as she reached the glass doors of the reception did she stop, but rather than speaking, she looked out of the windows.

"Cassie," I said, coming to her side, following her gaze into the distance. "Did you see something?" All I could see was the chaos and distraction of the view, the gaps between the buildings, and those that seemed so badly damaged they would soon follow their neighbours to the ground.

I turned, and she shook her head. Instead, she leant forward to open the single glass door.

"We should wait for the others," I added, and she let go of the handle. Her singular response.

Mandy arrived down the steps just as Jess and Alex did, both carrying the heavy black cases.

"They can't fail to believe you now," I said as I nodded to the camera equipment.

Their sunken expressions and furrowed brows didn't follow the joy they should have held.

"What's wrong?"

Jess shook her head as she rested the case at her feet.

"It wouldn't go through. I think the satellite is refusing to lock. I don't know how these things work, but whenever that kind of thing happens, I just speak with the tech at the station and within minutes it's back up and running again."

"Do they know it's your transmission?" I asked, looking between them.

Jess nodded. "It's my credentials."

"Could they have locked you out?"

Jess turned to Alex with a frown. "Remember what the conspiracy nut told us," Alex said.

We each nodded.

"Stan's in custody," Jess replied, and I spoke again.

"Do you know anyone else in the newsroom, or wherever you need to get the footage to?"

I watched as she squinted with the thought.

"Sure, but I can't exactly just make a call."

"Do they have satellite phones next door?" Alex said, looking toward the BBC building.

Jess's eyebrows flashed high, and she turned as if able to see through the walls. "I'll go look."

We took it in turns through the revolving door back out to the icy air, but on the other side, Jess didn't wait, veering off to the building as we followed, stopping only as she paused at the door.

"You wait here," she said. "I know where to look."

I glanced at Cassie, but she hadn't come to the building; instead, she stayed outside the hotel doors and stared in the direction she'd been watching all this time.

"I'll come with you," I said.

"Me, too," added Mandy, as she looked across the horizon wide-eyed.

Jess held her ground, looking at Alex before turning back and heading through the door.

"Cassie," I called softly, but she didn't turn and I followed them into the building.

Jess strode off across the wide foyer, not flinching as Mandy gasped.

I bumped into her back when she stopped dead in my path, Alex knocking into me.

I stepped to the side, following Mandy's wide gaze to a headless man, naked from the waist up in the centre of the foyer.

# 45

The contents of my stomach rose as I stared at a skull so white and clean as though left out in the sun to bleach for years, or painstakingly licked clean.

Not able to linger on the smooth, stripped-bare bone of an arm detached from the body, I moved my focus to a haphazard string of intestines leading out from the chest ripped wide open. My thoughts turned to how this person had lost their life, but by the lack of odour, the remains had no chance to decay.

I guided Mandy around to face the door, not able to turn my gaze until a sudden fear rose that Cassie had left. Leading Mandy by her shaking form back into the frigid air, I breathed a sigh of relief to see Cassie standing where I'd left her in the same place, with Shadow still by her side.

Alex followed, but only a slight furrow to her brow gave any sign of what we'd just witnessed and what it could mean.

Watching Mandy walk toward Cassie with her mouth hanging open and her hands at her face, I thought about grabbing Cassie by the shoulders and running off into the distance for fear that Jess had cleaned those bones of their flesh and harvested the organs.

Something held me back. Something stopped the fear from multiplying. Could it have been because she'd shown no sign of this instinct to us? Or could it be that I'd already realised what she might be capable of? She'd said herself, the creatures were each different; some more human than others.

Alex stood by my side. When I turned from the ground she was already staring back, her brow raised and eyes wide as if to reassure my unvoiced questions.

We both knew how the body had got there, but before I could speak to voice my lingering fear, Jess strode through the door with a rucksack weighing down her shoulder and in her hand she held to her ear what looked to be a large mobile phone but with a thick antenna the size of my index finger.

Turning to Alex, she let the phone down, looking thoughtful and wearing a grave expression as she moved her way.

"You spoke to someone?" Alex said, the words doing nothing to temper Jess's expression.

"Stan. He's out of custody but it's worse than we thought," she said, but without explaining she pulled the rucksack from her back and handed it over to Alex. "We'll need this. It's a smaller camera."

Without looking to the cases still resting where she'd left them at the front door of the hotel, Alex pulled on the rucksack whilst Jess peered over my shoulder, raising her brow.

"Where are they going?" Mandy asked.

Looking over my shoulder, my questions disappeared when I saw Cassie and Shadow striding off down the road with more energy than I'd seen even before she'd been bitten.

"We're heading north," I said. "It seems as good a route as any. We'll follow the motorway and hope we can find the front line or whatever's there."

"What about the doctors and the children?" Alex said, looking to Jess and back to me again.

"Do you know where they are? I don't. North is our best chance." I looked around to Cassie, already with a long head start and when neither Jess or Alex gave an answer, I jogged to catch up.

"She's feeling better then," Alex said, arriving at my side with an eyebrow raised and head tilted.

"What is it?" I asked, but Alex just shook her head, looking to Jess coming alongside with Mandy shuffling a few paces behind.

Walking in the middle of the road, now clear of debris, the two lanes of the one-way street joined up with another double lane heading the opposite direction. With no cars in the way or parked along the side, to our right were half-height metal railings and to our left were small shops, still with their tall windows intact.

About to ask Alex once more, I looked up as she peered to the sky, listening with a rising dread to the faint buffeting we'd last heard just before arriving in the city.

"Cassie," I called ahead in a stage whisper, despite knowing the helicopter crew wouldn't be able to hear my call even if they hovered directly above us.

Cassie turned, her expression pinched and I raised my palm. She paused, then gave a shallow nod, cocking her head when she caught the sound of the helicopters.

"Perhaps they'd take you to her," Mandy said.

I turned around, glaring her way. "Or they could shoot us where we stand," I said as I turned back to look along the road.

We had no way of telling where the noise came from and so quickened our pace in our original direction.

To our left, a grassy bank rose from the road to a cluster of three-storey flats.

"This way," Cassie said, changing course and climbing. Without complaint, we followed up the bank and down the other side as I scoured the sky between gaps in the buildings for the source of the rising bass.

In amongst the small development of flats, the monotonous thump of the rotors echoed, flashing across the brick in a disorienting amphitheatre of sound.

Cassie rushed to the wide front door of the first flat, but it didn't give as she pushed. Alex jogged past her, trying the next, but found the same.

By now no one could deny the helicopters were close, so near I thought I could feel their downdraft.

Not diverting to try any door handles, I led the way out of the cul-de-sac, through the car park whilst sticking close to the buildings and twisting to peer to any hiding place, searching for what could leap out.

With the others following, I ran through a street lined with shops and run-down retail units either side, but when none of the doors gave way to our attempts, I continued rushing along the road empty of cars parked to the curb.

The pounding in the air remained ever present, but still searching high above the buildings, all I could make out were the rising columns of smoke everywhere I looked. As the road divided, I lurched down a side street, with Cassie and the others catching up before stopping and staring at the looming shape of an Apache gunship flashing across the air space ahead.

Out of view no sooner than it appeared, we could only hope those on board hadn't seen us as they glanced between the buildings.

Picking up the pace when the sky became clear, we dived left to a narrow road between two tall concrete buildings. Relieved as everyone followed, I beckoned them further between the high concrete either side as I leaned to a handleless steel door whilst looking to where the space opened out and the sun shone on a private space empty of cars.

Dismissing the option of somehow getting through the bulky fire exit and into the building, I listened to the receding sound of the rotors, trying to decide if they were turning around.

"Is it coming back?" I said, staring wide at Cassie who wouldn't turn my way. She'd already recovered from the rush and instead of replying, she edged out from the safety of the building's shadow to look to the sky with the dog panting at her side.

Alex doubled over to catch her breath and Mandy looked at me red faced and with her hand to her chest. Jess appeared as if she'd just stepped from a cab.

Cassie walked past, looking to the air in the direction we'd arrived and when I thought she'd stepped too far from the cover, I rested my hand on her shoulder and went to draw her in, but she shrugged my hand away as if my touch was acid. Without catching my eye, she moved back to the opposite opening.

A cloud of guilt came over me as I reminded myself

she'd almost died and was separated from her only living relative who she'd just found out wasn't as safe as she'd thought. Maybe that was it; maybe she regretted letting me decide. Perhaps she thought she was in no fit state to have agreed with my decision and she blamed me for all that could happen to her sister now.

The pound of the rotors were back as if amplified and I had no choice but to accept they were looking for us. Perhaps Jess's failed transmission had singled us out without getting the story to the masses. By their expressions glaring in my direction, it seemed as if Jess and Alex agreed with me.

Still listening to the rise and fall of the beating blades in the air, Jess and Alex came over. Cassie stayed staring out to the car park with Shadow by her side. Mandy sat on the cold tarmac with her hands over her ears, leaning to the concrete wall.

As Jess stepped close, my first thought was to step back, but I somehow rallied against my instinct and held my ground.

"We should leave," she said, and looking to Alex I knew she was right, but before we could take the first move, I turned to footsteps and Cassie, with Shadow, running from under the cover in the direction opposite to where we'd entered.

What else could we do but follow?

We were out into the car park with the sound of the helicopters seemingly further away, or perhaps it was the echo caused by the concrete walls which had made them seem closer. Taking a tentative look up to the sky, I followed Cassie's lead again.

As I ran, my gaze turned to a dot in the sky. It could have been a helicopter, but the sound of another, higher pitched this time, rose to obscure each of my senses. I froze to the spot as the others kept up their pace, rushing past.

Relieved with the helicopter disappearing from view, I sprinted, catching up to Alex dragging Mandy as Cassie jumped, side by side with Shadow, over a low metal fence at the end of the car park.

Taking Mandy's arm, Alex guided her over and I took the other hand, ignoring her complaint, pulling her toward the others already back to the main road. I expected at any moment the helicopters would appear to strafe us with its guns and end the cat and mouse. And our misery, perhaps.

Seeing a short path to the right, I called out, pointing the way with my free hand.

"This way."

Jess and Cassie turned in unison, their late decision allowing us to catch up as they doubled back. Together, now with me in the lead, we ran between tall blocks of flats as I looked to the doors, running on when none were open.

An old Victorian-looking building, a Salvation Army hall, looked so inviting with its thick walls and solid front door, but as I bounded up, using all my weight and turning the handle, the door held firm.

I carried on past as each of us slowed, looking left and right to the locked-up buildings. Panic rose until I caught a stench mixing with the drone of the helicopters and I forced down any thoughts of giving up.

Still running, I turned away from the noise, heading past a sign pointing out a dead end. It was then I saw what I'd sought; a door wide open at the base of another set of tall flats and I changed direction towards it.

"No," came a call, and another unfamiliar voice added to the volume.

"This way," Alex said, but I carried on, ignoring the disgusting but familiar smell. I was more interested in getting away from the guns I expected to spray bullets in our direction.

Running, my gaze held firm to the horizon and across the river, watching black ropes dangling below the body of the Chinook hovering in the air with soldier after soldier rappelling to the ground as if they had no grip.

Shadow barked and at the same time I spotted movement through the building's open door ahead; a new instinct took over and pulled me to slow. Then came the scream. Not a terrifying call of the monsters, but an animalistic determination of someone still living; someone who wanted to stay that way.

A woman in a flowing orange patterned dress ran from a dark corner beyond the door, wielding a blood-stained kitchen knife the length of her arm. I paused at the sight of a child's doll in her other hand, stopping in my tracks with my gaze fixed on her alarm, as if I'd caught her by surprise.

New movement, this time at her back, made me look beyond and, only a few arm lengths away, the ragged, black and blue face of a figure locking its milky white eyes my way. And another at its back. Then so many more I had no time to count.

# 46

## JESSICA

I saw it in her expression. I could taste in the air as we ran, clear as day that something new hung behind Cassie's eyes.

I wondered if I smelt the same way to the others. She didn't smell human, but not disgusting like the creatures I felt all around us.

The guy with the backpack, the apocalypse junky, he'd said they were all gone from here. He said they were massing towards the border. It would make sense; like any creature, they would head to an abundant food source. But from the smell in the background, I knew it was only partly true.

With Shadow's bark, I looked up to Alex shouting to Logan with such an urgency as he ran toward an open door.

He looked up just in time, pushing his arms out and stopping at the doorway.

I felt as if removed from the action, a little dazed, perhaps on a high from the last night. Did I feel the same way yesterday morning?

Reality rushed back, forced by the chaos of calls and Shadow's bark, and I watched as a woman ran towards Logan from the doorway with a knife raised high, but the real danger lay behind her.

The woman stopped running, seeming to realise where the true enemy lay, and turned toward the creatures. But Logan grabbed her around the shoulders, pulling her away, nearly getting stabbed in the arm for his efforts.

Alex joined, grabbing at the woman, and suddenly fearful at what might happen, I added my weight to the pull, stepping between those living and those not; the new order of things to come.

I called for them to run as I turned, pushing at the

creature to send it stumbling back, then another as it rounded the corner. Then another as I stepped into the house.

"Go," I shouted again, but they'd already taken heed, the knife clattering to the path as they did.

I ran after, watching the woman so much slower than the others, my companions, and it wasn't just because she kept looking over her shoulder to see when she would get caught.

"Just run," I called again.

Logan, Alex and Shadow were making good their escape, heading to the squat building where Mandy and Cassie were already, but this unknown woman was running too slow. She had an injury easy to see, blood coming through a bandage at the hem of her billowing dress.

Bitten. Perhaps. I couldn't take the chance of her being around Alex. Or the others.

I grabbed around her waist, diverting her left as the rest ran ahead. She took my direction, slow with her injury, but turned, then peering back with a question, asking why the creatures were running at my side and not attacking me.

Pushing on harder as they launched to feed on her, I knocked each of them to the side, paying no attention as they stumbled. Pulling her up by the shoulder from where she tripped, I dragged her to her feet, heading the way we'd come whilst watching the other three pursued towards the building by the river, hoping at least one door would let them past as creatures seemed to come out of everywhere as if drawn by the helicopters noise.

# 47

## LOGAN

"Quick," I called, catching up with Mandy as she leaned to the dark varnish of the first of many doors, her hands tangled in the handle. About to kick out to the lower of the long panes of glass, I pushed her away, dragging her by the arm until she joined my rush to catch up with Cassie running to the next.

When the second door didn't move at Cassie's shove, I ran with Shadow at my side, not needing to glance back to know what still raced from behind.

Reaching the third of seven doors, my heart sank, finding it locked, the door not moving despite my grip twisting with as much force as I could muster. Regretting a look back, Cassie rushed to the next door to tell us if we'd have to take our chances in the rushing river. Despite the urgency of Cassie's task, I couldn't draw my attention from the surging crowd of undead closing on us from so many directions as I wondered where they'd all come from.

Alex shoved me with her shoulder, dragging Mandy along, her hit distracting my search along the brickwork as Cassie disappeared into the building.

With a rush of energy and hope, I pushed Mandy's back, hurrying them along and watching Shadow head in through the opening and barking as if calling us to join. As I reached the threshold, I couldn't help but check for Jess or that woman I hadn't seen since the block of flats.

Pushing the door closed and leaning my weight to hold it shut, I saw another door just along the darkness of the short corridor as Shadow's excited bark electrified the small space.

Turning back and scanning up and down the wood for a lock, something to keep us safe, I tried to ignore the bloodied mess of creatures through the glass, almost at the other side. Looking down to the small metal lever, the lock turned as I pinched it between my fingers, but it hadn't slid across before bodies the other side pushed the door open enough so it wouldn't catch.

Blocking the light, blood smeared across the glass as hit after hit added weight to force the door open. Alex landed at my side, straining her shoulder at the wood enough to stop it flying wider.

Regaining my footing, somehow we stopped their advance as thud after thud from the other side added to the assault. Only as Cassie lurched in at Alex's side did the door move the way to keep us safe. It was like she alone forced them back, but the metal of the lock's bolt hit against the jamb, holding the door open.

I scrabbled for the small lever, twisting it left, then right when the wood hit the jamb.

Wary of the lock's ability to hold the door in place against the massing creatures, we each released our pressure, testing one by one as we stepped away, but ready to pounce back at the first sign of movement. When it held, we stepped to the darkness, looking up to the light coming from the top of the door's upper window.

Alex turned my way and we shared a glance at Cassie, perhaps with the same question in mind, but I gave voice to another.

"Did you see the soldiers?"

No one replied; instead, we all looked to the other door with Shadow's call reverberating in the small space.

Taking tentative steps, I looked through the side glass. Peering to the darkness, I could just about make out a pair of fire extinguishers beyond. Pushing against the wood, I braced, ready to pull back, but I couldn't see any sign of danger in the small anti-room. Just four more doors.

Sniffing the air, I couldn't tell if the stench was stronger than at the door, but what choice did I have but to hope for safety deeper in the building? Stepping forward, movement at my leg jolted me from my concentration, but breathing a sigh of relief, I saw Shadow rushing past with heavy breath only to lose him to the darkness.

Turning back, I ignored the slathering, squashed features at the glass and ushered the others in as I wedged the inner door wide with a fire extinguisher to keep what little light remained.

"Did you see the soldiers?" I whispered the question again, but when no one replied I carried on my exploration.

There were six doors, not four, as I stepped in. Three toilets, based on the round signs on each, and another marked staff only. The two remaining doors, one to the left and one to the right, were solid with no glass to show what waited on the other side.

"Yes," Alex whispered at my back. "That fucking helicopter must have drawn the creatures from everywhere. Do you think the soldiers saw us?"

I shrugged an answer, listening to what I hoped wasn't something moving behind the door to the left whilst wishing I had a weapon.

Alex must have heard it too and didn't press the question. With Cassie joining at my side, the three of us moved to the left-hand door.

Light spilled out as Cassie pushed the door wide. We followed Shadow squeezing past our line to the chaos of a narrow restaurant with its tables and chairs scattered to their sides as if caught in a whirlwind. A short bar stood to the right as we entered.

Feeling a chill in the air, I looked up to the ceiling; scanning the skylights, I soon found one in the centre of the room with its glass missing.

"No," I snapped as I looked down, calling Shadow back from one of three bodies lying amongst the broken furniture and scattered glass. He pulled back at my voice, changing course as I took in the rest of the view, hoping any movement, any threat would be easy to catch in the disorder.

Nothing showed itself and I scanned the room again, taking more time for the detail.

Glass walls overlooked the rushing river to the right and the empty car park to the left, but as I looked across the scene, the left-hand view filled with the creatures moving along, but rather than break the glass with their slaps, they merely smeared sticky decay across its surface.

I couldn't help but imagine the place in better times and how the view would have looked when the water was calm, the city wasn't in ruins and the bridge wasn't crumbling into the river.

Glass crunched under my feet as I turned. Peering over my shoulder to Alex, I saw they weren't bodies on the floor but husks, the remains of a meal with skin, jewellery and glasses discarded to the side. We'd seen this before and I couldn't help but think how much time it would have taken to separate out the meal. Whatever had done this must have felt safe. Whatever had done this must have been shut in with their feast.

And could still be somewhere in the building.

Taking a step closer, my foot knocked against a lump of wood, one side varnished, the other side raw and jagged. As it landed close to the remains, a swarm of flies took to the air and I pushed my mouth to the crook of my elbow at the wave of decay rising after.

Stepping back, I tried to hold my gag with Alex mirroring my motion as I stumbled to the door. My gaze caught on Cassie, who seemed content to ignore the mess as she walked to the bar and rifled through its contents out of sight.

Retracing her route out from behind the wooden bar, she held a long knife tight in her grip. Alex and I moved out of her way as she strode past us, heading back to the anti-room.

We followed with slow steps into the darkness, watching as Cassie's pace picked up, not able to grasp why she charged through to the opposite door, sending a flash of light as she jumped forward.

The realisation hit and I rushed to catch up. She'd had

the same thought, and I watched helpless to the sight of a figure crouching in a dining room so similar to the one we'd left.

Glass crunched under Cassie's feet and the figure lifted its head, its eyes not glazed white and mouth turning to a sneer as it stood, issuing a piercing scream.

# 48

I wanted to turn, to run and hide and slam a heavy locked door in its path and push my hands against my ears to stop the penetrating scream. I knew I couldn't just stare, transfixed on Cassie's back as she rushed without flinching away from the figure standing at the other end of the room. With the knife high in her fist, she charged, her battle cry barely heard from under the figure's unnatural shriek.

Glancing left and right, Mandy stayed fixed to the spot in the anti-room and was half in a turn to the main door, frozen between leaving our side and rushing away alone. Alex stood poised at my side, her head turning left and right in what I could only imagine was a desperate search for a weapon.

Shadow's leap forward with bared teeth spurred me on, and I grabbed a discarded chair, with Alex mirroring my movement. Rushing at Cassie's back with the legs of the chairs facing out, I watched Cassie closing up, adding my feral call to the cacophony.

Thrusting the knife down as she arrived, the high-pitched squeal of the creature halted as its arm rose and fell, sweeping Cassie off her feet to clatter sideways into tables and chairs, sending crockery and glass into the air.

The room darkened and at the edge of my vision I caught dark shapes filling the window with the weight of their gaze and their hunger upon us.

With Cassie crumpled to the side, I got my first look at the naked woman, its skin covered in a multi-hued red blanket from head to foot. The depth of the blood covering its body created false shadows to hide the detail of the breasts, but accentuated the slight curve of its belly ridden with deep claw marks. For a fleeting moment I imagined it before. Her beauty when she was alive. Her dreams and aspirations for the future. But they were all gone now, reduced to an animal we had no choice but to put out of its misery before it did the same to us.

Other than the scratches across its front, it had no visible injuries, but its long blonde hair was the only part untouched with blood.

My thoughts took little time, two steps of our charge with Alex still by my side and Shadow in the lead. He stopped as if he knew what we were about to do and instead barked out a call, whilst Alex and I lunged at the same moment with the chair legs jabbing against its torso, our strength holding it from its leap. Our force sent it backwards with its mouth snapping and hands clawing out.

Cassie jumped to her feet, her face set in a snarl with the knife in her hand rising high above her head as we kept on pushing it backwards. Cassie let out a great call, releasing her rage as the blade slipped in through the skull and she pulled back, the knife coming out dark, matted red. The creature's movements slowed as Cassie jabbed again from high to its shoulder.

Still holding the chairs at our front, we jumped back, and the figure fell to the floor in a heap, its mouth half open as its head hit the floor.

With the knife back high above her head, Cassie dropped to her knees and forced the knife down, arcing with such force I heard bone cracking as the metal slipped into its chest. With her eyes closed, Cassie pulled back again, before plunging the blade back in.

"It's gone," I called, quietly at first, but still Cassie drove the knife, thick blood flying out as she jabbed. "It's gone," I said, louder this time as I stepped toward her, then mindful of the blade, held back.

The knife snapped, the blade separating from the handle with a great crunch and I stepped away, watching Cassie drop what remained with her teeth gritted as she rested her arms at her side, left only with the frantic rise and fall of her chest.

Alex turned away to look out at the creatures lining the windows, but I closed my eyes, not wanting to take in the horrific scene.

"There's another one," Mandy called out, and we turned to see her pointing to the floor.

# 49

I didn't rush to Mandy's side; instead, snaking through the fallen tables and chairs, I followed Shadow leaping the debris whilst staring at a body in a dinner jacket laid on the floor. Leaning as I ran, I tried to peer around a fallen table but saw nothing more than the figure's white shirt mottled with red.

Slowing from the initial scare, no longer in a hurry to see another dead body, I caught movement of his chest. Taking long strides over the debris, I glanced back to Alex as she caught my eye.

Alex arrived by Mandy only moments before I came around the table and stopped beside Shadow, stroking his head, more as a reflex than for his sake when I saw the mask of blood, the open mouth and scarlet-stained clothes detracting from what could have otherwise been any viewing in a funeral home.

Plus his shallow breath.

Middle-aged, perhaps in his fifties with weathered, dark skin and grey hair, for a fleeting moment I imagined grandchildren on his knees as he sat in a comfy armchair passing around the hard candies.

"He's alive," I said under my breath, whilst not moving my gaze from his chest, concentrating on its rise and fall to the sound of Alex rushing over.

"Shit," Alex said at my side, taking in the horror of the bloodied mask which before the clotting agents had taken hold, had dripped down his face to make a great blot in the dark carpet. "We've seen this before."

Her words were enough to grab my attention, but she wouldn't take hers from the guy laid out so neatly at our feet.

"What do you mean?"

"Jess saw it. He's alive, but it's one of those creatures," Alex said, looking in the abomination's direction. "It made him."

"Made him?" I said, standing straight.

"The ones that are still alive," she said. "They can reproduce."

I pulled back, unable to process her words and my foot knocked against a fallen table.

"We have to kill it," Alex said, and before I could think, I felt a shove to the side and a table leg dived between us and into the man's torso, his eyes flashing open before his chest fell.

Rearing back, I stared at Cassie standing tall between us with blood splashed across her front, resembling the blonde we'd just killed.

With my mouth hanging wide, I checked my footing, stumbling away from the body, from Cassie, to look around the room, trying my best to look between the debris and searching out any more unwelcome surprises. I soon realised the space was a mirror image of the other end of the building, including the bar beside the door.

We each stayed still for what felt like such a long time; Mandy moved first, walking to lean against the bar and mumbling to herself.

"It just gets worse," I heard her say.

Cassie stared at the body as the blood running down her front stopped its journey.

I stepped back as she turned my way, her face devoid of emotion and clutching the chair leg dripping with blood I hadn't noticed her pull from the fatal wound.

"Are you okay?" I asked. Her vacant nod sent a chill along my spine and I couldn't help but question what the hell had happened to her since she'd woken this morning. I'd only known her for a few days, but still we'd gone through so much in such a brief time. We'd grown so close, but now she seemed like a different person.

Mandy stood, moving to the furthest corner of the room and, sliding her back down the glass, she sat on the carpet.

"Take a breath," I said to Cassie as she gazed at the creatures staring from the other side of the windows, clawing at the glass, their hands smearing blood and who knows what else over its surface.

"We need to move the bodies," Cassie said, her tone flat. I nodded in agreement.

Somehow keeping the contents of my stomach in place, I took one arm of the blonde as Cassie took the other and with Alex holding the doors open, together we dragged it along the carpet whilst I looked anywhere but its skin, or the dark blood oozing from the wounds to mark out our route. After doing the same with the guy in the tuxedo, I hoped I wasn't getting used to a new normal.

I couldn't stop my mind wandering to the moment the creature burst through the skylight. Had it smashed the glass or had something else sealed their fate? Was the dining room full when the creature jumped from the roof and were the remains those that hadn't got away?

With no way to know the answers and back in the other dining room, now clear of anything dead, I pulled a fallen chair upright and sat with Shadow resting his head on my knee.

Stroking along the length of his back, I felt as if I could calm if it weren't for Cassie not able to keep still, continually walking the perimeter of the room with the chair leg she'd at least wiped of blood. I couldn't watch her any longer and I moved around to behind the bar, finding Alex sitting up against the wall with the rucksack still on her back. Shadow didn't follow.

No one spoke for what seemed like an age as if we each took the time to process what had just happened.

After a while, the quiet, punctuated with Cassie's steps and the slow drum of hands at the windows, became too oppressive.

Cassie's steps. The crunch of glass. The percussion at the glass in an irregular beat.

"Where did Jess go last night?" Despite my whisper, I felt Alex pull herself up straight and pause her breath.

"To the offices. Like I said. She brought back the cameras." She couldn't hide her high, defensive tone, and I paused to diffuse the moment.

"I thought I saw her early this morning." When Alex didn't reply I spoke again. "But the light was bad."

I held my breath at the sound of the door opening, but relaxed at the thought of Cassie extending her patrol.

"What happened to Cassie?" Alex asked, and it was my turn to be surprised at the question, jolting me back to what seemed like a lifetime ago. About to remind her I'd already told them everything in the church, I remembered she was the only one not in the small room when I'd poured my heart out.

"We were in a car heading back to that hospital. There was a soldier with us. He'd been bitten, but we stopped the bleeding. We thought he'd be okay. That's what she said we had to do. But..." I held my breath as I tried to force away from the direction my mind was taking. "But he wasn't."

"Who told you about the bleeding?"

"Doctor Lytham. He turned as I drove. I lost so many." A dull thud banged at the glass in my pause.

"I'm sorry," Alex said, her voice low.

"Everyone's lost someone now. I'm sorry for everyone." I stared at the row of glasses behind the bar, reminding me of a time long ago when the world had been straightforward.

"My people were already dead," Alex said.

I nodded. "I'm sorry for that too."

"I'm not. They didn't have to go through this."

"I guess," I replied, and shook my head as my thoughts veered towards my parents and the image of them watching the TV cuddled up on the sofa.

"So this doctor fixed her up?" Alex asked, catching my look.

"There were seven of us left, and Shadow. He saved our lives. Well, some of us."

"It helps to talk about it," she said, and I guessed she was right.

"Andrew was my best friend." I paused on the words. "Bitten, but he was too far gone." I stopped talking as I heard the gunshot in my head, biting down on my bottom lip. I still hadn't decided whether Doctor Lytham had been his saviour for putting him out before he turned or if she should have tried harder, tried anything to help him. "Lane. Commander Lane. A pilot from the helicopter."

Alex frowned back.

"A story for another time."

Her cheeks bunched and she raised an eyebrow. "Was he infected too?"

"No. But he's dead. They're all heroes. They've all done something selfless to get us where we are today."

She gave another slow nod.

"I don't know what that makes me," I said. I didn't need to turn to see her shaking her head.

"You've helped Cassie and us."

I tried to hold my thoughts from racing off. "They gave Cassie medicine. A drink. It stopped her from dying."

"What was it?"

I shrugged. "We had little choice and no time to ask. She was going downhill quickly. She drank it and fell asleep. She'd been drowsy ever since. You saw how she was. But today she's like..." I stopped myself from saying the words out loud.

"Like what?" Alex said, forcing her voice lower. "She's different, isn't she?"

I nodded, but didn't speak when I heard the door rest gently against its jamb. After listening to footsteps, Cassie appeared around the corner of the bar and stared at us, still covered in blood but I concentrated on the three tins of fruit in syrup in her hands.

"I found these," she said in a low voice. "There's a kitchen. You want them?"

I smiled back and nodded whilst taking the tins. "Thanks, Cass. You got some?"

She moved out of sight without reply and moments later the door settled back to the jamb again as I rested the tins on the floor.

"What was she like before?" Alex asked, and I turned to her as the memories flooded in. The time we'd spent scared for our lives in the wardrobe. When we'd walked alone to the village. When we'd almost kissed. The night she'd lain at my side.

"When did Cassie have the medicine?" Alex asked when the door swung closed, its hit against the jamb sending renewed slaps to the windows. "She's different now. Isn't she?"

"She's been through a lot. We all have."

Alex nodded.

"Yesterday. No, the evening before that. She drank it a little under two days ago," I said and watched as her expression hardened. "What is it?"

Alex swallowed as if trying to make a tough decision. Eventually she shook her head and spoke, "Jess was bitten, too."

I let the moment hang, my eyebrow raising as I spoke. "I think I knew," I said, nodding.

Alex turned her head to the side, eyeing me cautiously as she waited.

"What did they give her?"

"I only know what Jess told me. They gave her something, then infected her."

I reared back, sitting up straight, but didn't say a word as Alex spoke again.

"They infected her and then gave her more of the stuff. She was supposed to keep getting doses, but the place they were keeping her got overrun and she escaped."

"So many questions. Did it work?" I said, as Alex paused for breath.

"Only in part. She's not unscathed."

"What do you mean?" I added and then stopped as I heard the door opening. Before Alex could answer I spoke again. "Do you think they gave them the same thing?"

She shrugged, speaking in a whisper. "I think what they gave Cassie must have been better. A newer mix, perhaps?

Plus, they gave it to Cassie after she was infected. Is that right?"

Mandy came around the bar and she stared at the tins.

"Help yourself," I said and turned back to Alex as Mandy sat by her side and pulled the ring up to get at the fruit.

I wanted to ask so many questions. I had to know if we were safe around her. I had to know if it was Jess feeding on people. I had to know what she'd meant by not being unscathed. Would the same happen to Cassie? Was *she* safe to be around?

I stared at Mandy, willing her to finish slurping down the fruit and go back to where she'd been sitting on her own, but when I heard the door again, I gave up on answers for the moment; Jess had been fine around us, as had Cassie. So far, at least.

"What about you?" I asked, looking at Alex. "What's your story?"

Alex spoke after a moment, collecting her thoughts. "I was heading home from a job. I'm a locksmith," she said. "I saw those creatures in the road. Scared the life out of me. Then I literally bumped into Jess. I nearly ran her over."

"Oh," I said. "Funny that."

Alex replied with a frown. "How's that funny?"

"I almost shot Cassie when I first met her." For a moment a grin pulled at the corner of my mouth, until I remembered the depth of my fear for what might have been.

Alex raised her eyebrows and gave a shallow nod. "That's why you seemed so okay when Jess nearly shot you in the tunnel."

I nodded.

"I assumed you'd known each other for ages. I assumed you were..." I stopped myself as I saw Mandy leaning into the conversation, her features rising with alarm.

"No," Alex said. "I met her like the night after new year's night. I think. How long has it been? I..."

"It's just the way you are together..." I said, but stopped myself again. "Never mind," I added when I realised it was something she didn't want to talk about.

"And you and Cassie?" she said, turning the questioning back to me.

I paused, trying not to listen to the slap of hands against the glass.

"I don't know," I said, then turned, looking to the fast-flowing river rushing over the top of the bridge deck. "It was early days."

"It is early days," Alex corrected, and I twisted around with a smile.

A shot rang off somewhere in the distance, followed by the crack of glass. A second resounded in the air and Alex and I struggled up, rushing to our feet as a third shot came.

Coming over the top of the bar, we watched the creatures still on the other side, but they'd each turned away. I didn't follow to where they looked; instead, I peered to the two glass panels spidering with cracks as a plume of plaster flew from the adjacent wall.

Baring her teeth in our direction, Cassie stood in the opposite corner as the windows seemed to flex from the downdraft of a helicopter as if directly above us.

# 50

## JESSICA

"Jessica Carmichael," the woman in the orange dress said with her eyebrows raised and breath heavy as she sat opposite me in the baker's shop.

In her lap, a blonde-haired doll rested, its white dress spoilt with a splash of dried blood.

Giving a shallow nod, I leaned with my back to the glass door, watching her on the tall stool at a breakfast bar amongst the discarded plates and half-eaten remains of what looked like lunch.

With the buttery smell of stale pastries in the air, I couldn't help but think how Alex might like to visit this place, despite the food being a few days old.

"Your leg?" I said, narrowing my eyes as I looked below the hem of her dress and the end of a bandage on her right thigh. Tall and curvy and with perfect proportions, despite her scowl constantly questioning in my direction, she looked cute enough that in another life I would have taken note.

"Just a scratch," she replied with her knuckles white as they wrapped around the handle of a long knife angled down to the floor.

I knew if I moved, she'd walk right out of the door. I could see it in her eyes. She had a score to settle.

"What's your story?" I asked, nodding toward the doll.

She stared back, blinking each time I spoke, and rearranged the hair of the doll in her lap as if it were a child.

Still she didn't reply, looking to the window each time a shadow moved across. I didn't look. I knew what ambled down the street. With each shadow I watched her brow furrow and her eyes narrow as if unsure why the creatures didn't stand to the plate-glass windows, scratching to tear at my skin.

"You have kids?" I said, knowing the minefield the question presented.

She pulled her gaze from beyond the glass to meet mine. "A little girl. Five in May."

I nodded, watching as she stroked the fake hair and a smile beamed, but just for a moment, her cheeks bunching as she rushed out her words. "She's safe. With her gran." I nodded again. "You have kids?"

Normally at this point in the conversation I would laugh and shake my head, dismissing the idea before changing the subject. But for the first time I didn't reject the concept outright, and I felt like bursting with laughter, scared of the opposite emotion. You always want what you can't have. It was out of the question now.

I shook my head and raised my chin.

"There'll be a vaccine soon. Your daughter will probably be okay," I said.

"How do you know?" she asked, looking up from the doll.

"They gave it to me and one of the women you saw me with," I replied, nodding in the direction we'd arrived from. "And we're both doing just fine." I don't know why I misreported the facts.

"How can I get it?" she said, letting herself down from the high stool.

I shook my head. "It's not ready yet."

"But...?" she replied.

"We're the guinea pigs."

She stared wide-eyed, a smile rising, and I heard the thrum of rotor-blades from outside. I turned back from the glass to where she still stared.

"They're not interested in you. Are they?" she said.

I nodded just as the bass of the background sound rose in volume.

"But they are, aren't they?" she said, looking to the ceiling.

I nodded. "They want to see how I'm getting on."

"And to stop you telling people what's happening."

I raised my brow. "You've seen the broadcast?"

She nodded. "When will the cure be ready?"

I shrugged.

"Too late for me," she said, and I watched as she lifted her dress, showing off the red stain on the white bandage just above her knee.

"But not too late for your daughter."

She smiled, nodding as she took a step toward me.

"It's suicide."

"I'm already dead."

I stepped to the side of the door.

"Thank you, Jessica Carmichael."

"What's your name?" I asked, raising my head.

"It's Gemma," she replied, nodding.

"Nice to meet you, Gemma. Go kick some ass."

I pulled open the door and with the stench pouring from the street, she didn't flinch, gritting her teeth as she charged a group of ragged creatures ambling toward us. Raising both arms high, the knife in her right and the doll in her left, she jabbed out with a high cry.

As the pound of a high-powered rifle shot filled the air, I turned, running the way I'd led Gemma from earlier.

# 51

## LOGAN

It was as if the world woke when the shots came.

Rushing to our feet, we could do nothing but look on, switching my gaze between Cassie and the window with the crowd of creatures conflicted between those turning to the excitement at their backs and those who seemed intent on keeping the pressure on the windows.

Cassie's eyes stayed wide as she took slow, considered steps from the corner of the room, slapping fallen tables from her path with her teeth bared like an animal. Like one of them.

When the shots stopped, the crowd beyond the glass were in chaos. Each seemed to move its own way, either slapping to the glass to claw at the fractures or turning away toward some other call, only to knock into one of their neighbours. Beyond the movement, the crowd thinned with a blur of motion, sending bodies flying.

Before too long the glass darkened with thick, splattered blood rolling down the windows like lumpy treacle.

I didn't need to look behind to know it was Mandy's scream rising above Shadow's bark when a body slammed against the cracked window, sending the glass tumbling inwards to slap against the floor. The body stayed motionless, no matter how hard we stared.

Renewed light came through the space where the glass had been and with it the stench, so powerful it woke us from our collective trance, turning us to the movement beyond the gap.

Every figure lay motionless, spread across the car park.

At first I thought the helicopter must have sprayed the crowd with bullets as it came to our rescue, but I hadn't heard the whine of the weapons.

Cassie stopped halfway to the gap with a chair leg in her right hand hanging loose at her side as she peered forward, stepping sideways toward where I stood.

With footsteps at my back, Alex guided Mandy at her side. Shadow halted his bark. Coming alongside, I looked left then right, convinced we all had the same question in our minds, but before I could give it voice, the room darkened and we each turned to the bloodied figure at the space where the window had fallen in, standing motionless.

Jess.

I should have felt an overwhelming fear, and I did, but only that Cassie's fate would be the same as Jess standing in front of us. A fear she'd soon be drenched in the blood of her victims, her hair matted to her face and barely able to make out her features as she stared at a group of humans not knowing if they would be next. Could she control herself as Jess seemed to? Could she stop her unfamiliar urges from ripping those around her apart?

We stood for what seemed like an age, but when the deafening call from the helicopter blades came back into focus, I realised we had to do something.

Jess's voice cut through the turmoil. "They did this to me. So we have to get the children back before they can do the same, or worse."

Dropping the chair leg to the floor, Cassie stepped forward, working her way around the glass panel and stepping outside as if ready to take on the world.

Cassie said something, but I didn't catch the detail, instead looking to movement beyond the glass at the far end of the room. A piercing call cut through the air, but to the sound of a muffled gunshot, the shadow slumped to the ground.

"We've got to go," Jess said, turning back from the same direction.

Alex didn't wait, seeming unafraid as she walked to Jess, motioning for Mandy to follow.

I stayed fixed to the spot. "We can't run away from the

helicopters."

Jess turned back. "It's not the soldiers I'm worried about. Their noise is drawing more creatures from all around."

Picking a cloth napkin from one of the few tables still upright, I followed the others rushing through the gap and into the daylight which seemed so bright, bringing such vivid colour to the mess covering Jess.

As I stepped from the building, everywhere I looked the creatures who had lined the windows of our sanctuary lay torn, ripped beyond recognition and discarded all around, the ground slick with a sticky blood sucking at my trainers with every step.

I didn't have to avoid the putrid scene for long. As I looked around, I saw soldiers dressed in black, counting nine coming from where we'd run. Each turned, twisting around to look with their long rifles. I caught sight of a figure on a roof overlooking the carpark, beside him another crouched with the length of a long barrel aimed in our direction.

The helicopter buzzed over where we stood, then vanished after taking a steep turn away just as quickly as it arrived.

Glancing at Alex taking in the scene as I had, but with a hard-faced look as if ready to go down fighting, I turned back to the soldiers as a group of three in the centre separated from the others, walking ahead of the rest holding their positions.

Each of the three looked to my side, two through their weapon's sight, and I knew it was Jess they targeted. Who could blame them? I couldn't help but follow their look to the woman so far removed from the preened image we were used to from the TV.

I stepped in the path between the three and Jess with my heart pounding in my chest, not understanding why I did it, other than it felt like the right thing to do. I glared at the three, not adjusting their stride towards us.

Staring at the small group, I couldn't see any difference in their appearance, barely able to see anything apart from between the lip of the black ballistic helmets and dark scarves covering their mouths.

Within two car lengths, the soldier in the centre held his gloved hand to the air, and I flinched back as he swung his rifle from his grip, slinging it over his shoulder to rest on the strap.

I couldn't help but wonder why they hadn't gunned us down yet. If I had a gun and looked on at Jess for the first time, wouldn't I?

The middle soldier held his hands to the side, motioning to the ground. Without pause, each of those flanking him let their weapons down.

The centre man raised his hand to his mouth and pulled down the dark covering to reveal a clean-shaven face.

"I'm Major Thompson," he called out with a measured volume. He leaned to the side as if trying to get a better look at Jess. "We don't have time."

I stepped from her path, knowing they could have just shot me out of the way.

"Don't do anything," I said, and Thompson looked my way, his eyes narrowing but losing focus as if distracted.

"Hold position," he said, but not to us as he reached to a pocket at the front of his black jacket, pulling out a white envelope.

# 52

## JESSICA

I read the writing as he drew it out, pushing it towards me. It was from Toni.

Proof she was still alive.

It was her writing, unless her mother had the same beautiful curl to the letters I'd always marvelled at.

The middle soldier, Thompson, stepped forward and I licked my dry lips, regretting the dried covering of rancid blood. I couldn't wipe my mouth on my sleeve, there was no area of my body not covered in the same, or so much worse.

I turned to Logan in slow motion, my mind lethargic as if I was coming back from fainting. He held something out. A crisp white cloth. He raised a corner-mouth smile, and I took the napkin.

I saw the caution in the soldier's narrowed eyes. I saw in his expression how unnatural it felt to approach me when he'd spent the last week filling walking dead bodies with lead. He didn't want to show the apprehension to his men, his walk still strong and confident.

A major, I thought he said, but he wore no insignia or unit designation on the black uniform. He looked battle weary; fatigued by what he'd been through. I'd seen the look before, the tiredness behind the eyes, but I guessed most in the military would be the same by now.

I looked to the envelope, turning my head and staring at Alex. Raising my brow, I wanted to know what she thought I should do.

For a moment I marvelled at how I'd changed. I wanted her advice. I wanted to know if I should find out what the architect of all this pain wanted to say, or would doing so just make everything so much worse?

Alex's expression stayed blank as if she didn't want to influence my decision.

Thompson stepped back as I took the paper, but with surprise he didn't draw his weapon.

There was no doubt her hand had written it. My pounding heart told me so, or it could have been fear for what the letter would tell me.

Was she going to explain how I could stay alive and not be like this forever? Not need the taste of human flesh to be normal in between the hunger? Would I be able to control it? Could I switch it on and off when I needed? Maybe I'd already answered my question, and to those who'd been watching in the last five minutes.

I paused, breath halting for a moment as a thought flashed into my mind.

Were these soldiers here to observe what had just happened? Was this all just an orchestrated event? Had I passed or failed their test?

With anger growing, I looked up to the two figures on the roof. The long barrel of the high-powered rifle that alerted me to the peril turned away, moving as if I'd caught them looking where they shouldn't. Then I saw a camera pointed in my direction, held by the guy at his side.

She did this. All of this and I'd proven to her she'd succeeded, and I knew what this was all about. I knew I was the missing piece.

I could control the thing inside me, like I would have to if I were on a battlefield.

I couldn't read the note. To do so would be part of her plan and she'd somehow end up drawing me back.

It would all be lies to bend me to her will.

Turning the envelope on its side, I pinched two fingers to the edge, ready to rip it down the middle and throw it back in Thompson's face.

# 53

## LOGAN

"No."

Alex called out, lunging forward and snatching the envelope from Jess's hand. I watched as Jess's eyes went wide, her lips curling to a snarl as the soldiers at Thompson's flanks took a step back, bringing their rifles to bear, but Thompson held his footing, raising his palms at his side.

"Think of the children," Alex said, her voice sharp, then softening as she pushed the envelope back into Jess's hands. "They need to know if they're okay."

I looked to Alex, expecting her to shy back, but she held Jess's gaze with her brow furrowed. Almost without pause, Jess's snarl melted away, and the soldiers lowered their rifles.

A sorrowful smile settled on Jess's lips as she relaxed, drawing a deep breath.

"It will all be lies," she said, looking at Alex shaking her head.

"But it's all we have," Alex replied, taking a step closer and taking Jess's blood-caked hand.

I couldn't help but look away from what seemed like such a private moment. I turned to Cassie, staring on with a raised brow, gently biting her lip to show the first crack in her hard exterior since she'd woken this morning.

Turning back to Jess, I spoke almost under my breath. "Please."

Jess looked at me, but then away, not settling in my direction.

I watched as Thompson peered around, murmuring into his helmet microphone. The soldier to the right stepped close to Thompson's side and spoke, leaning to his ear.

"Five minutes to bingo fuel, Sir."

Thompson nodded, but didn't say a word as Jess looked to Cassie, then back to Alex before taking the envelope. Dried blood flaked to the ground as she slid her finger under the flap and pulled out a single sheet of paper, concentrating on the words we were desperate to hear.

My darling Jess,

To say I am sorry would not be enough, I know. By now you must have it clear in your mind. Your crazy, super-brain would have easily figured this out and I'm long overdue being honest with you.

I love you.

I know you loved me, but your other life took you away and I couldn't live without you. For that I am so, so sorry.

You were right all along. It is my medicine. My formula, but not everything I told you was a lie. We found something very special, and it was a gift I wanted to give to you.

I knew you would be a match. I knew you would be the first to overcome the complications.

If you're reading this, and there is no doubt in my mind that you have survived, then you are a very special person, but not just to me this time, to the world, because you have control over what you have become and, for that, humanity will be forever in your debt.

I need you to come back to me.

I need to show you how you can live like this without the bad parts. I know you understand.

Let these soldiers bring you to me on the Isle of Wight. You will be safe, and you can be by my side forever. Together we can live a new life.

We have much to talk about, much to work through, but I know you will do this for the greater good. That is what you do.

I'm sure you're angry right now. I know you so well.

I hope you can forgive me.

*Toni*

P.S. I'm really enjoying having these wonderful children around.

# 54

## LOGAN

Looking past the drying gore, I watched the pain on Jess's face, despite her obvious struggle to keep her features straight as she read the page for a second time.

Closing her eyes as she came to the end, the moment hung with just the sound of the helicopters in the distance and the tinny, far away voice I thought I could hear from the soldier's radios.

"I'm going with them," Jess said, keeping her eyes closed, but stepping toward her, Cassie gave her no time to explain.

"What about the children?" she said, leaning forward looking between Jess and Alex. "What does it say about them? About Ellie?"

Jess didn't reply; instead, opening her eyes, she glared to Thompson.

Cassie turned to the soldiers and repeated the question. The soldier to Thompson's left stared at Jess, whilst the one to the right turned his head to peer across the view.

"There's no real mention." Jess's words pulled Cassie to look back.

"What does it say?" I asked, looking to Jess.

"It says I have no choice," she replied, looking me in the eye.

"No choice but what?" Cassie butted in.

"To go with them." Jess barely finished the words before Cassie spoke again.

"Where?"

"To wherever Toni is. The woman who did all this."

"Doctor Lytham?" I said, my eyes bulging. "But that's where we're trying to go."

I couldn't understand why she didn't look so much happier and I turned back to Thompson, but with the shake of his head I knew the answer.

"Just Miss Carmichael."

"Fuck you. You haven't even asked. Why don't you get on the radio and find the fuck out," I said, taking a step to Thompson. As I moved, the soldier at his left dropped his rifle to its strap and drew his handgun, pointing it to my chest.

Feeling a gentle pressure at my shoulder, I held back from taking another step forward. "Doctor Lytham knows us. She gave Cassie here the cure," I said, glaring to Thompson, but he didn't react. I turned back, catching Jess's eye. "Don't go with them."

"You always have a choice," Alex added at my side.

Without saying a word, Jess reached out, handing over the letter with her red fingerprints still on the page.

Not even the gunshot echoing between the buildings could pull me from the words as an icy shiver ran down my spine when I read the final line.

"Go," I said, catching her eye as I looked up from the white page. "We'll find you." I turned to Thompson. His subordinate had stepped back but not holstered his pistol and stared with a blank expression. "Where exactly are you taking her?"

Thompson shook his head. I held my tongue for a moment then looked around, already trying to figure out which way we would start the journey. "We'll find you."

"Sir," the soldier to Thompson's right spoke, keen to move. As if they'd read my thoughts, the double boom of a Chinook's blades whipped up the air, sending dust in a swirling chaos around us.

Shadow barked as the left soldier motioned us back through the carpet of bodies and toward the building. When a burst of gunfire called from one of the other groups of soldiers, we ignored his instruction, instead watching as they headed our way, the sniper gone from the roof too.

I could guess the reason they were on the move, racing

to fly away and leave us on our own.

With no weapons, and Jess gone too, we'd have no chance.

"Give us a gun. Please," I shouted over the growing din of rotors and Shadow's bark, but none of the soldiers reacted to my words. Instead, crowding around Jess, they guided her away then turned their backs as she looked out from between their helmets.

With no choice, together we backed up as I coaxed Shadow with my hand on his neck, glancing at my feet to avoid the debris of bodies and slick chunks of decaying flesh.

It wasn't long before the sun blotted out with the bulk of the Chinook filling the view as it lowered to land beside the soldier's protective circle. A vision of the hospital roof sprang to mind, the memory so clear of when Lane fell backwards with the spray of blood. I held my arms wide to stop any of us making that same mistake.

Another shape, an Apache gunship, caught my eye to the side as it sliced through the air with its long round gun at the front following the gunners turn as he swept for targets. I couldn't help but wonder what his orders would be when Jess was safely spirited away.

I backed us up closer to the building, not caring for the mess down the face of the glass.

Alex saw it first. Then I caught the sight, too.

At the same time, Mandy's sharp intake of breath told me she was the next to see the spaces between the buildings filling with figures pouncing to the air and at their backs the slow amble of those without souls.

Cassie gave no sign, even as gunshots rattled from the soldiers walking backwards to empty their weapons as they closed up to the protective circle.

"Jess," Alex called, as the figures covered the distance in the blink of an eye.

Despite the Chinook so close, almost on the ground, sending the downwash of the rotor blades to batter us all, Jess replied.

"Go. Run. Quickly," she called through the turbulence, reminding me that as soon as they'd taken to the sky, they would leave us behind, unarmed and almost certain to die.

# 55

## JESSICA

I shook my head toward Alex, not able to battle against the fierce noise whilst trying to hide the desperation at being trapped by Toni once again. If she knew how I felt inside, Alex wouldn't willingly leave my side.

All I had left was to hope that I could make a difference when I got to where they were taking me, although I knew it was likely she would have planned for every eventuality.

Still, I had no choice but go with them for the sake of the children, for any hope of there being a future for me, forcing down any fear that I could make this entire thing so much worse if I gave Toni what she needed.

But I couldn't just ignore the fact that once the helicopter landed, it would be over. I would be hers.

Either way, someone else would take the pain and perhaps it wasn't my decision; maybe fate should have been the one to decide. Startling myself, I realised for the first time I was about to let someone else have control.

With the helicopter coming so close, holding steady in its descent, I spotted the soldiers coming towards us, knowing there were so few left of their number.

The helicopter pivoted around, turning, almost in touching distance so when the wheels hit the ground we could run inside, taking to the air and be gone from this place to safety and to hope I could stop the kids from going through what I had endured.

Toni would show me how to control myself, despite the progress I'd made. She would show me how to stop the hunger altogether and I would have time to think about what to do next. How to take back control. And find Alex again.

# 56

## LOGAN

With the building at our backs no longer able to protect us, I looked instead on the river to our right, remaking the choice I'd hoped we'd avoided. Glancing the other way and toward the pained calls and the wet, wrenching sound of a soldier being ripped apart, I turned away as another stumbled with a creature landing to drag yet more to the ground. There were so many everywhere I looked.

As the helicopter's wheels touched the ground, I grabbed out at hands either side and gripping tight I led everyone forward, along the building and toward the river.

Alex soon let go, pulling off the rucksack and holding it in her hands, jumping over the edge without hesitation and was quickly swept along by the torrent, her head under the brown water. I tried to let go of Mandy's hand but she gripped tight. As I looked her way, she called out through the whirl of turbulent air.

"I can't swim," she shouted, her eyes bulging as she shook her head.

Panic surged and I chanced a look to the rushing creatures at our backs and the last of the soldiers running to the helicopter, hoping I would see them take each of the creatures down before they flew away with Jess, and the pilot of the hovering gunship would forget any orders he might have to leave no witnesses.

Cassie flashed by at my side, followed by Shadow going under the murky water. I thought about his wound and the pain he must be in and the concentration needed to kick his legs under the surface.

"We've got no choice," I shouted to Mandy. "Hold my hand. I'll keep you safe."

She nodded, then we both turned to the fast flow, drawing a deep breath and holding tight to each other's hand as we jumped.

I listened to her squeal through the short fall, before we were engulfed, freezing water stealing my breath, but all I could think was keeping my grip. As the rush settled around me, the chill took hold; I tried to kick my heavy legs, willing myself up through the water and pulling against Mandy's weight as she seemed to sink lower, dragging me down. With my hand going numb, along with the rest of my body, I could just about feel my grip against hers as my lungs screamed for air.

The next moment, Mandy's grip wasn't there, her hold gone, the downward drag slowing and I pulled my heavy arm up. Her touch was gone.

Moving my arms around in a circle, I sought her out, but with my energy almost spent, my will draining as the cold penetrated, I could do nothing more than to save my own life.

With water rushing me along, somehow I broke the surface, gasping for air and spitting out the earthy water as I searched for her.

I couldn't catch my breath, unable to will my lungs to pull deep. I tried calling out, but the cold stole everything I had. I tried turning to search but it took all my energy to stop my trainers and clothes pulling back down into the water as I rushed along.

"Mandy," I tried again, but was rewarded with a mouth full of foul water I couldn't help but swallow. There was no sign of her.

With my breath still shallow and racing, I grew weaker with every moment, shivering as the rush of water seemed to settle, carrying me along as the last words I'd said to Mandy went around in my head.

The flow of water turned me facing back to where we'd jumped. Panic rose as I watched the remains of a figure hit the helicopter's blades, spreading chunks of red in a spray, before my foot caught on something under the surface and the dirty water filled my view again.

Fighting not to open my mouth under the water and twisting my leg, I rose to the surface to feel the chilly air on my face, batting away the water as I watched the helicopter crumple, disintegrating as it hit the tarmac and sent debris spraying to the water.

I tried to stay afloat; I tried to look for any survivors as bodies slapped into the water, but the thoughts dimmed as I circled my arms, fighting my heavy limbs so I wouldn't get dragged away with the current.

# 57

## JESSICA

The creatures were everywhere, our rescue no longer certain. Hundreds of them all around. But my only panic was for Alex, for my other companions. They stood no chance if they didn't leave now.

Relieved, I watched Logan holding Mandy's hand as they jumped into the turbulent, churning waters of the river.

I turned away, watching the air fill with wicked creatures pouncing, ripping through the last of the soldiers who had held back to guard the perimeter. Still flanked on three sides, I saw a figure in the air just in front of us and I knew before the creature bore down it would hit the rear rotor blades before it landed. The three soldiers saw it too, but none of us could turn away.

To the sound of flesh pulverised by the spinning blades above our heads, I pushed my arm out with a monumental feat of strength, knocking the three soldiers to the ground as the rotor blades caught against each other in the air and smashed into the metal body of the helicopter. For a moment, the aircraft rose but then fell to the sound of metal grating, grinding as if it consumed itself.

With the chopper tipping sideways, throwing up great clods of tarmac and metal to the air as the blades crashed into the ground, I raised to my feet, pushing each of the soldiers up, hurling them toward the river and running after them with the ground shaking beneath me and a fireball racing at my back.

# 58

## LOGAN

Cassie pulled herself from the water first, her skin almost blue as she landed a fair few buildings down from where we'd jumped. Turning, whilst still on all fours, she grabbed Shadow by the scruff of his neck, dragging him to the edge and wrapping her arms around his front quarters until his paws found purchase on the concrete ledge.

Kneeling on the slipway between the two buildings, I watched as Cassie searched out across the turbulent water. She soon fixed on another figure ahead, who fought with the current just as I did, arms pumping toward where Cassie beckoned.

Alex. She was high in the water using the rucksack as a floatation aid. As she bobbed around, the water rushed her wildly across the river. Despite her own search across the view and her pale, pained expression, she pounded the water with her legs, clearly knowing she'd be swept away and battered to a pulp by the sharp contents of the water.

Pulling her to the ledge, Cassie raised her up, Alex's clothes clinging tight as the water coursed to the ground. As soon as Alex had all four limbs on the ledge, she let go of the pack and twisted around, staring out, her look darting across the debris-laden surface to scan the water.

Still kicking my legs as hard as I could, despite their weight, I made progress to the bank and watched another figure between me and the two pale-faced women, with their arms extending my way. As I fought through the water, feeling disconnected with my body, I couldn't help but marvel at the energy of the figure floating by, reaching out towards the women.

On seeing it's stretch, they shuffled back from the edge,

staring on, but not grabbing hold as it floated past. Only then did I realise why.

If I had the energy, I would have turned around to check for more creatures in the water, but I was so numb and cold I wouldn't have noticed if one had already bitten through my leg.

As the creature floated by, Alex and Cassie shuffled forward on their hands and knees, shivering and shaking on the concrete. They watched, urging my effort as I forced my aching limbs through the pain, kicking my heavy trainers with all I could muster until I felt myself lifted up, my body numb to their hands on mine, pulling me from the cold and out of the turbulence.

"Mandy," I called out, still unable to make my voice loud as I scoured the surface, my search stopping on anything in the water. I dismissed the broken tree trunks, the dark-clothed bodies reaching out and snarling our way and lengths of wood and other debris.

There was no sign of her.

"She couldn't hold on," I said, keeping my view on the water despite knowing she would be long gone.

Feeling pressure on my shoulder, I turned around, disappointed to see Alex with her hand resting as she tried to reassure me. I stood, trembling as water coursed down to pool to the ground.

"It's not your fault," she stuttered, but then turned away, peering back to the water. "Jess."

I followed the way she stared with visions flashing into my head of what had happened after I'd jumped. As the images faded in my mind, Alex pushed her hand to my arm and we stared at the fire-ravaged fuselage of the helicopter rolling from the burning car park and into the water, sending spray high in the air. I gripped her sodden hand in hope she wouldn't do anything stupid.

To the grind of metal, we stood shivering, our attention moving from where we had jumped to the dark figures making their dogged journey in our direction, their stilted walk tracking around the edge of the car park, with no sign of any surviving soldiers.

"We've got to go," I said, looking the other way to avoid the anguish I knew would hang on Alex's face.

With her arms wrapped around herself, Cassie moved away with Shadow at her heel, both leaving a trail of wet prints along the slipway. Despite my gentle tug at her hand, Alex remained fixed to the spot.

"We've got to go," I said again, barely able to speak for my teeth chattering as I looked after Cassie, turning to Alex only when she tugged me around. "The creatures are coming," I said, before following her gaze and saw her squinting to the water.

"Cass…" I called backwards when I saw the four soldiers in a line, each sitting low in the water, two fighting to release their packs, the others having already done so. Despite their arms raising out of the water, they were losing their battle with the current and were about to be swept down the river.

Dropping to my knees and pushing through the ache, I reached out my trembling hand over the edge of the concrete, but I was nowhere close enough for them to take hold.

"Jess," Alex called and I looked up along the line, at first seeing a rucksack floating, but my gaze was drawn away to Jess, in her black jacket with her hair flat to her face, as she powered through the water with a breast stroke.

Reaching the back of the line of soldiers, she pushed against what looked to be a floating rucksack, shoving the weight towards the bank and the faster flow. As it moved to the edge, I realised there was a soldier underneath who hadn't made it.

Alex dropped to her knees at my side and together we grabbed the weight with numb hands and heaved it closer. Cassie joined, pulling the dead weight out of the water as Jess shoved each of the soldiers towards us, one after the other so we could grab hold to stop them being whisked away.

We each had a soldier's hand in our grip and I soon realised it was Thompson I held, but despite pulling as hard as I could, I didn't have enough strength to pull him out. The same true for the others. With each passing moment, my numbing grip seemed to weaken. I thought again of the moment Mandy had let go of my hand and I tried my best to keep my fingers firm, despite the pain.

Within a moment, out of the corner of my eye, I saw the soldier Alex had been holding dragged out of the water to the concrete as if she'd gained strength from nowhere. Thinking she'd summoned supernatural powers, I saw the same happen to the soldier Cass held, and then the weight at my hands became so much less when a pale pair of hands came from the side and hauled in the Major.

Collapsing to the ground as the soldiers leaned over on their hands and knees, rifles dangling down as the water flowed from their clothes, I twisted around to see Jess standing, sodden from head to foot, with barely a rush to her breathing and not quivering with the cold.

Two of the soldiers knelt to the body we'd pulled out first, the pair who'd flanked Thompson, unclipping his pack as they turned him over to his side and then his back before punching him square in the chest. The body coughed and they rushed him to his side as water spilled from his mouth and he gasped for air.

I watched them bring him back from the dead without fear they would be attacked. The shivers returned, along with a cold so deep. As I watched on, my reactions slow and senses numb, I followed as each head upturned to a sudden wind in the air from the Apache helicopter.

Cassie helped me to my feet; we knew we couldn't wait to dry off or take stock. Instead, we pulled up our heavy limbs and I watched in awe as the soldier's jogged up the slipway, one of them carrying the man they'd just brought back to life over his shoulders.

No one wasted their energy with words, but we all turned around as the gunship poured lead from its nose, and we looked to the car park and the disintegrating flesh of the creatures caught by the hot lead.

"Move," Thompson called out.

Alex and I tried our best to follow the soldier's lead up the slipway, Cassie and Jess helping as best they could with water still running from our clothes.

"So cold," I said, as I fought to put one foot in front of the other. My muscles were stiff and complained with every movement as if refusing to thaw. I couldn't bring myself to look again to where the bullets rained from the gunship or to seek it out when the noise of the gun and its rotor blades faded.

One of the soldiers called out with a backwards glance and I turned, catching sight of the great line of dark figures rushing along the banks towards us.

# 59

The three soldiers seemed to speed, despite the weight they carried with the two packs and their colleague and knowing they would be feeling the same whole-body pain I did, the feeling as if I could drop at any moment and not get up again.

Somehow I managed to keep going, following with Alex at my side as Jess and Cassie and Shadow overtook the soldiers. Panting for breath, I watched as Cassie slowed and without saying a word, she pointed to the right, veering off as the slipway met a road with buildings either side.

With a command from Thompson, the soldiers soon turned the corner to follow and were out of view. I grabbed at Alex's sodden shoulder as she put her palm to my back. We pushed each other on, following the wet trail.

At the junction, the last of the soldiers disappeared through an open door beside a tall, plate-glass window of a two-storey building. To the sound of orders issued and dragging each other through the pain, we followed.

Being the last through, I regretted the slam of the door when I couldn't keep a grip on the handle, my fingers so numb. Still, I fumbled with the lock in hope it might somehow slow the advance of what followed.

Inside, Thompson and one of the other soldiers dumped their packs and raising their rifles, surged forward in unison and along with Jess and Cassie, scanned the detail of the room as the third soldier settled his shaking colleague on the floor.

We were in a small commercial building. The first wide room was a reception area, separated from a large open plan office by glass partitions with a glass door in the middle. A set of stairs rose up the wall.

Alex and I watched on, shaking so violently I felt as if I would rattle apart.

Leaving the soldiers to search the building, one rushing up the wooden steps, the Major heading through to the main room, Jess sought out Alex and wrapped her arms around her. Cassie continued to look around.

Shadow stayed downstairs, moving around with his nose to the carpet. He seemed to have shaken off most the water, but the scar down his side appeared so much redder than I'd seen it before.

"Strip down," the soldier said, as he turned and watched me shaking. "We've got to get warm." The guy who he'd carried stood and fought with the zip of his jacket.

"I'm fine," he said as the other guy said something I couldn't quite hear, then opened a pack at his feet and started pulling out the contents.

A muted call soon came from upstairs, repeated by another on our floor. They each returned, all of the soldiers huddling together and stamping their feet at the bottom of the steps with their weapons resting at their sides. They didn't invite us to the discussion, but after a moment one of them grabbed one of the two packs and rushed up the stairs. The remaining three began stripping off their kit and wrung out the water.

"Please tell me there's a room full of dry clothes upstairs?" I said, motioning above my head through the shakes as I stamped my feet for warmth.

Thompson shook his head, his lips remaining flat. "Offices. Not much else. Get your clothes off and wring them out at the very least."

I started pulling of my jacket, then looked to the huddled women and back through the glass partition as I stripped.

The room filled with ten desks, computer monitors sitting on each beside office clutter and mugs likely filled with long cold liquids. Towards the far end of the room were three closed doors with small signs I couldn't read across the distance.

"Is that a toilet?" I asked, looking through the glass partition.

Thompson nodded. "Ladies. Why don't you get some

privacy in there?"

Alex looked up from pulling off her socks and before long the three of them moved toward the door in the glass partition.

Thompson stepped forward, about to follow, but Cassie stopped, looking down to Thompson's holstered pistol.

"We can look after ourselves," she said, reaching out for the weapon.

I stopped wringing out my socks, watching along with the others as Thompson's brow rose.

"She can handle it and much more," I said. "You can't imagine what we've been through these last few days."

Thompson hesitated before looking to one of the two soldiers half dressed in the corner, the one who hadn't been breathing only moments earlier. With his reluctance obvious in his scowl, he pulled the pistol from his holster he'd set aside and handed it to Thompson, barrel first.

Thompson checked the chamber, then passed it to Cassie with a slow nod, watching as she led the women towards the toilets.

After glancing to the window at our backs and seeing nothing but the blinds pulled across, I kicked off my trainers, slinging my jacket off and letting the water run down to the carpet.

Thompson was the older of the four men; I guessed he was somewhere around late thirties. As he pulled off his helmet, I saw his salt and pepper hair, his skin brown and weathered as if he'd been outside most of his life.

The soldier who handed over the pistol looked in his late twenties. Like the other three, he was well-built, muscled with a thick tree-trunk of a neck and his short mousey blond hair was so much longer at the top, the side of his head shaven.

I paused wringing out my T-shirt when Cassie pushed the toilet door open, only continuing when it closed at their backs and they didn't come out running to the sound of gunshots. Turning back, I saw the soldiers pulling on dry clothes from the pack.

"Have you got any spare?" I asked, looking on with such a longing. Each shook their heads and I turned away, barely flinching when the first thud came at the front door. Instead, dressing in the cold clothes I'd just finished wringing out, I looked to the soldiers to gauge their reaction.

# 60

## JESSICA

As Cassie and Alex stripped down, the water from their clothes running into the sinks, Alex shook so hard she seemed to be barely able to control herself.

I looked at myself in the mirror. There was so much to think about. Too much to deal with.

They'd all seen what I'd done to save them from the horde. The soldiers had been watching, filming so they could know the next step of their mission. Everyone had watched me switch from being Jessica Carmichael, the woman from the TV, to a hellish creature who could rip limbs from flesh, but had they noticed how I was back to me again? Would they ever see me as just Jess again? Would she?

"Dry off," Alex said, her voice trembling as she spoke.

I looked up to see both of them barely dressed, but neither of them seemed as if they feared for their lives. Alex reached out with a stack of paper towels shaking in her hand.

Was their trust that I could control myself around them valid?

How could they when I didn't know myself?

# 61

## LOGAN

Beyond the white blinds, black shapes moved with the muffled thud of flesh against the glass.

Despite the efforts we'd gone to to save their lives, each of the soldiers eyed me with caution, looking back with a weariness each time our gazes met. Although soon dressed, I couldn't help but shake.

Still with no sign of the women returning, I walked to the window, peering out at the edge of the blind whilst being careful not to touch or move the hanging material.

I could almost smell the stench and the charred flesh of those stood the other side, but despite all I'd seen, I had to look away for fear of losing the contents of my stomach from this morning.

I looked instead back into the room. The soldiers had dressed in dry kit and were searching through the remains of the rucksack.

The guy closest to me and the one who kept his pistol had deep red lesions running down his face and like the creatures outside, I guessed he must have been at the edge of the explosion. He nodded, and I wondered if the gesture was all the thanks I would be getting.

Each of them had the same weathered look; skin long exposed to the outdoors and harsh conditions of foreign climates throughout their careers.

"What now?" I asked, as I searched around the reception, spotting a large water bottle in the corner. Taking a cup from a stack in the holder, I watched the water slowly dribble in and then downed the contents in one go, returning it under the plastic tap.

"Our mission hasn't changed. We're taking Ms Carmichael to her destination." I turned to Thompson's voice and then the other two, not able to see any dissent at the instruction.

"Anyone else?" I asked, gesturing to the bottle as the bubbles gurgled through the water to collect at the top.

The soldier nearest to me nodded in reply and I took another cup as I spoke.

"We need to find a vehicle."

"We have this in hand," Thompson said. "Kit check you two."

I handed the nearest soldier the full cup. He nodded, and I turned to get another.

"The water screwed the radios," he said in a slow, northern accent I couldn't place. "Otherwise we're okay. The other bag, too."

"We're coming with you," I said.

The two subordinates looked to Thompson stone-faced as if they hadn't heard my words. I handed off the full cup to the other soldier, his hair shaven all over. He took the drink with a nod.

As I turned away, looking through the glass I saw the others emerging from the bathroom, each with damp hair and dirty, crumpled clothes. Alex still shivered.

"Has the other woman really had the cure?" Thompson asked, watching as the women approached, turning to me as I nodded.

"Cassie was at death's door." I looked away, swallowing hard in hope the rising feeling would dissolve before it showed.

Thompson stayed quiet for a long moment, watching as the women emerged. "I won't stop you following us, but other than that, no promises," he said, and then raised his brow to each of his men.

"Gibson. Like the guitar," he said, pointing to the guy with the lesions down his face. "Sherlock," he said, pointing to the northerner and the one who we'd pulled from the water not breathing. "Like the detective."

"Sir," Sherlock said, with his brow lowered and taking a step towards Thompson. "They're luggage and will get in the way, or worse."

"Ha," I scoffed. "Are you kidding me? We saved your lives."

Sherlock turned my way, his expression pointed and brow low. He looked as if he was about to take a step my way when Thompson raised his hand and spoke.

"Like I said, I'm not going to stop them following."

Sherlock looked away, moving to pull out a first aid kit from the rucksack at his feet before leaning to inspect Gibson's face.

"Upstairs is Carr," Thompson said.

"I'm Logan. Cassie is the one in the lead and Alex is at the back holding the rucksack." I turned down to Shadow at my side. "And this is Shadow."

"Nice dog," Gibson said in a soft cockney voice, only moving his gaze down to the dog as Sherlock probed his face with his fingertips.

"Where exactly are we heading then?" I asked, stroking Shadow's damp back.

Each of the soldiers glanced at each other, but no one answered before Cassie pulled open the glass partition door.

"Have you seen the children?" she said, stepping up to Thompson.

Gibson and Sherlock each raised an eyebrow.

"We haven't seen anything, or anyone," Thompson replied. "We only know our mission, ma'am." He turned away, delving through the pack at his feet.

"Where are you taking Jess?" Cassie asked, but Thompson continued to rifle without answering.

"The Isle of Wight," Jess said, then stepped to Cassie's side whilst talking to Thompson's back. "How long have we got?"

"Until what?" Cassie added, turning to face her.

"The letter…" Jess started to say, then stopped herself

and turned my way.

"The letter didn't say anything about the children. Well, not really," I said, shaking my head.

"You don't know her," Jess said, keeping her gaze on me as she spoke with her brow furrowing. "It's not what she said. It's more what she didn't say."

Thompson turned and held a fist full of energy bars, offering them out to each of the soldiers.

"I don't understand," Cassie said, waving away Thompson's offer of food as her voice rose.

I took an energy bar, as did Alex. Jess shook her head as he held out the food and looked to me with a raised brow.

"Will everyone stop looking at each other and answer some bloody questions," Cassie said, stepping between Jess. "Is Ellie okay? Do we know where they are?"

"She's fine as far as we can tell," I said and Jess cut in.

"For now. I think she's threatening if I don't go to her then they won't stay that way."

I watched as Cassie's eyes widened in alarm, but before she could press for more information, we turned up to the stairs and the hurried call from above, as a great brightness shined through the blinds just before the window imploded.

# 62

Tasting dust and with a punishing weight on my chest as I lay with my back to the floor, I couldn't see through the curtain of debris raining all around. Everything seemed still, until I felt a stirring at my side and I looked up from the floor to see a cascade of shadows moving everywhere. The sight forced back the memory of the charred, burnt creatures on the other side of the window which had just exploded.

To my relief, the weight fell to my side. Batting my eyelids in an attempt to clear the dust, I saw Alex in the sudden bright light staring at me as if she'd just woken.

Coughing up the thick air I took with each breath, I watched movement which seemed to be all around. Feet on the carpet, shadows on the walls and against the strewn glass and debris across the floor.

Then a call. Thompson's booming voice with his outline silhouetted by a pair of headlights where the glass wall had once been, bringing with it the memory of Carr's call from above and the roar of an engine as the wall burst in.

Turning around and looking up, I followed the sound of a deep voice and saw Carr pointing.

"Get in the fucking vehicle."

Only when I twisted back around did my brain make the connection that a minivan had smashed through the plate glass window and part of the wall, stopping with its front half in the building and only a few footsteps away from where I'd been standing.

Reaching out, I grabbed at Alex's shirt, twisting her around to see the minivan through the dust catching in the headlights as it rained down.

Glancing up past the battered front end of the minivan, the grill lay to the floor covered in dust and crushed brick. Peering around a long crack in the windscreen, I rubbed my eyes at the sight of a soldier in the driver's seat, furiously blinking, his hand raised, beckoning us from our daze.

Feeling a strong pull under my armpits, I stood, barely getting to my feet before whoever had picked me up launched me forward.

Staggering as I slowed, I stopped at the side door of the van in a daze, then froze to the spot when I looked along the side of the van to a dark inhuman figure at the gap where the last of the jagged wall remained.

A gunshot exploded at my back, then another, sending the dark figure backward and to the ground. To my left, Cassie stood with a smoking pistol pointed to where the figure had been. Sliding the battered side door open, I stumbled from air thick with dust into a haze of white powder, only just able to find the middle row of seats in the minivan as Alex landed beside me.

To the sound of gunshots from the soldiers shocking the air around us as more creatures took the place of those who fell, I watched the driver tear the white cloth of what remained of the airbag from the wheel.

Shadow jumped from the mess to squeeze in the space between the seats at my feet, then Jess bounded beside me. Round after round continued to slam against flesh as Cassie dragged herself to the rear row, followed by Gibson and Sherlock with the fire rate slowing.

Feeling relief as the gunfire stopped, I watched Carr slide in the front passenger door, pressing up beside the driver as Jess pulled the metal side door closed.

Thompson bundled in the front, throwing the heavy packs over the seats just as his ass hit the upholstery.

"Seat belts," I shouted, my mind flashing back to our recent success with vehicles.

I pulled on my belt as the remaining crowd slapped and clawed at the rear windows, moving to the sides as bodies filled the gap between us and the wall. With the engine revving high, we shot backwards, metal screeching against the brick as the wheels bounced over the figures knocked to the ground.

Out from the building, the sun poured in and we swung in a turn. Blood and mushy flesh sprayed out as a head burst, crushed between the van and the building in the right-angled turn just as clutter rushed from right to left across the dashboard, sending dog-eared catalogues, Styrofoam cups and a long-handled screwdriver from one side to the other. Braking hard, the van jolted, sending the screwdriver from the dashboard, caught by Carr and he'd thrown it back as all eyes darted across the view to look for the next threat.

"Where the fuck did you get this shit tip from?" Carr shouted, his booming voice turning to laughter. The driver gave a weak laugh as Carr turned the heating up to maximum.

Building our speed and with the air blowing hard and warm from the vents, we were soon going too fast for any remaining creatures to catch up.

I breathed a sigh of relief that none of the other kind survived the helicopter crash, despite the sounds we'd already heard.

"Is everyone okay?" I asked in the lull, as the shivering returned with the adrenaline fading. There was a moment when no one said a word, but soon the replies came, one by one, that there had been nothing more than a few cuts and bruises.

The van slowed as we entered a pedestrian lane between a long line of houses, but I recognised the lull that always came after the action and, despite our escape, I couldn't truly relax, waiting for the next jolt back to chaos, unable to stop searching out the next crisis in every point in the narrow space between the buildings as we passed.

Catching the sour odour of a dressing not changed in a long while, I took my first look at the driver. Despite his all-weather tan, my eyes were wide as I focused on his washed-out hue and the clammy sheen covering his neck.

With Thompson sitting in front of me in the passenger seat only looking up from a map to issue a command, left or right, trying to guide us out of the pedestrian maze, he hadn't once glanced to the driver.

I turned to Jess at my side and she nodded. She'd seen him, too. So had Alex.

"Nice one for finding us," Carr said. "But did you really have to smash through the wall?"

The driver let out a weak laugh.

"Yeah, sorry about that." His voice came out quiet and strained. "I hit a few of the fuckers as I drove in and couldn't stop in time."

"Thompson," I said, but he dismissed me with a shake of his head, keeping his concentration down to the map with his brow furrowed.

I turned around, pushing my back to the side door to get a better look across the inside of the minivan. Gibson held his pistol out, peering through the rear windows while Sherlock looked across the view with his rifle out of sight.

"Thompson," I said, louder this time.

He ignored my call, but Carr in the middle seat didn't. As he looked my way, I nodded toward the driver.

Carr followed my gaze, both of us watching as the driver's head dipped forward for a moment as if he were falling asleep.

Carr's face lost all its cheer as his gaze dropped to the soldier's leg, focusing on what I couldn't see.

"Shit," Carr said and turned to Thompson, glaring in his direction. "Sir," he said, his tone sharp.

Everyone's attention snapped to Carr. Even the driver.

Carr leaned back in his seat to give Thompson the best view possible across his front.

"Shit," Thompson replied, after looking the driver up and down. "How much time have we got?"

When no one replied, Thompson turned back to look ahead to where the path we were on seemed to end, but as the distance shortened, we soon saw a choice of a sharp turn left or right.

"Which way?" the driver asked, his voice lacklustre and dry.

I watched as he leaned forward with a pained expression, peering at Thompson as we slowed. When no one answered the second question, he looked to Carr who stared forward, then over his shoulder, locking eyes with me.

"Which way?"

With just the sound of the engine ticking over and my body shaking despite the rising temperature, I felt Shadow's panting in the footwell with steam forming on the inside of the windows obscuring the walls either side.

"Left," I said.

Slowly nodding, the driver pushed the selector back into gear and we edged forward.

Halfway through the slow turn, Thompson moved, rushing his pistol to the air, across Carr to point at the driver's chest.

Surprised when the driver didn't flinch, it was as if he hadn't seen the movement, but as he straightened up from the turn and the narrow alley stretching out ahead, he looked down the barrel of the gun.

"What?" he said. With the van rolling slowly forward, he glanced to his leg. "Oh, that." Screwing up his face, he looked back up to the road and our speed built.

Looking paler than ever, he spoke again. "It's not a bite. It's not, and I feel fine. Which way now?"

A silence filled the space as each of us looked between the driver and the narrowing lane ahead, littered with rubbish bins and scattered with what they had once contained. Blood on the walls drew my attention, but Thompson didn't let his view of the driver falter.

Only when we slowed to a stop did Thompson chance a look ahead, just as a Sherlock spoke from the back.

"Contact. Six o'clock."

# 63

Heads turned in the back seats, each of us squinting out through the moisture on the windows as Sherlock and Gibson continued to run their sleeves over the glass to clear the view.

"Which way?" the driver called, but Thompson kept the gun and his heavy-lidded glare fixed on him as he pushed the map over the back of the seat and to my lap.

"Get us out of this maze," he said.

"Right," I bellowed after turning the map up the correct way. We moved off again.

"Boss," came the low northern call from behind me, but looking to the smeared windows, they gave only a hint of movement beyond.

"How you feeling?" Thompson called out.

"You're okay, aren't you?" Carr added in a higher voice.

The driver gave an energetic nod, and I watched the sweat running down his neck as the steering wheel slipped from his hands with debris hitting the tyre, but he snatched back control, catching the wheel in time to avoid the wall. "I'm okay," he said, his voice breathy. "It's not a bite."

The scream called again, louder this time, and I felt the rumble of Shadow's growl between my legs. Stroking down his back, but being careful not to go near the wound, I watched as Thompson let his pistol drop before turning his attention back ahead.

"What are you seeing back there?" Thompson asked.

"Shapes, that's all, but they're moving on us fast," Sherlock replied.

With the bass bellow of an impact where the bumper should have been, I twisted back to the rubbish bins across the road and the remains of the plastic pushed to scrape against the rough tarmac. In the tight turn, the suspension cushioned much of our roll over the debris, but I couldn't help wincing at each crack of snapping plastic, imagining the shards perilously close to the fragile tyres.

The bumper kissed the brick, rocking us to the side; the rev of the engine kept us rolling, but at a pace I could easily out-walk.

With the smell of sour decay growing, the driver straightened up the wheel as the lane narrowed ahead to culminate in an archway with a wide-open road the other side. Despite the distance, it seemed far too small for our width to squeeze through. Hope rushed up through my chest when through the archway I saw a flash of a white vehicle across the view, and then another.

"Dead six. Single contact. Fast approaching from the rear," Gibson called from the back in an almost business-like tone.

They were the words we dreaded, despite having heard the shrill calls. Our speed built, even though the view gave us no hope we'd be able to make it out into the open to race at full speed from the danger at our backs. The rush of plastic we carried with us grew louder as more discarded flotsam added to the procession.

"Gibson?" Thompson called without turning, but he didn't reply, his face pushed to the rear glass with hands swiping left and right to clear the moisture. A heavy thud to the thin metal roof sent a shock wave across us in the cabin.

Glancing up, I called out over the scrape of the rubbish we pushed in our path. "Faster."

"Shit. Faster," another shouted to the sound of the roof deforming from the weight above.

Flinching at a loud bang, then to another much louder, the view through the left-hand rear window had cleared, and I realised the glass was missing, the shattered remains settling to the seats. My question as to what it could be was answered when a bloodied arm swung down from the roof, fingers grabbing at Gibson's outstretched arm with the pistol in hand, pulling his limb up to the missing glass.

Yanking off my seatbelt, Shadow yelped as I twisted around with knees to the seat, reaching out over the back to grab at Gibson's shoulders and anchor him down. Sherlock jabbed at the attacking arm with the butt of his rifle at our side and the bloodied hand pulled away, raking down the arm of Gibson's jacket and drawing blood as it whipped across his hand to send the gun clattering to the pavement.

Landing back in my seat, I barely heard the new call for more speed and through the surging adrenaline, I couldn't tell if we were getting any faster as I clicked my seatbelt into place.

Looking back, Gibson edged away from the rear window, holding his hand tight against the claw marks with Sherlock pointing his rifle's aim between the missing window and the metal deforming above our heads.

"Hold tight," came the words from the front, but gripping the sides of the seats, I didn't get a chance to take in the view before being forced forward against the strap across my chest.

***

An icy breeze sent dust-filled air across my face as I drew my head up slowly against the ache. Shadow's warm tongue greeted my hand, and I reached out, stroking his back, thankful he'd been safe in the footwell when we'd hit.

Stretching out a kink in my neck, I was about to search out his wound to check the stitches when movement through the windscreen sent my eyes wide. Searching past the great crack through the centre, the sight of the driver slumped over the steering wheel pulled me back to Thompson and Carr taking off their seatbelts.

Turning to my right, Jess helped Alex up from the footwell. Beyond, all I saw were bricks and lines of mortar up against the side windows with dark, treacle-like blood dripping down the glass. We were stuck, wedged in between the walls either side.

Cassie stared from the back row, her eyes wide, but she turned away, closing her mouth as I caught her staring.

Gibson, followed by Sherlock, rose from the space between the seats, quickly turning to search back through the rear windows, ignoring the slow drip of red from the roof.

"Is everyone okay?" I asked, my voice croaky. Drawing a deep breath, I felt a sharp sting in my chest. Listening for the murmured replies and coughed responses, only the driver hadn't answered, not moving since we'd stopped so suddenly. With relief, he raised his head as I took a second look, but watching him settle back into his seat my blood ran ice cold at the sight of the long handle of a screwdriver sticking from his chest and the vacant, white-eyed stare to Carr beside him.

A heavy thud to the rear called us away and ignoring the pain in my neck and chest, I turned to the snarling mouth snapping at the open window and the naked figures bounding along behind us.

Sherlock shoved Gibson to the side, raising his rifle to the space at the window and fired. The bald creature's blackened head exploded backwards before I saw anything more than fire-raged skin. Rather than feeling a sense of relief, my gaze fell to the brick wall through the glass windows with claustrophobia settling over me like a blanket as I sensed the incredible speed of the figures still racing toward us.

Turning back, I watched Jess's lips tense to a snarl as if she were about to join in our defence. She looked to Cassie at her side, her face an almost mirror image of rage.

A heavy thud pulled my gaze to the front row of seats and I watched with alarm as Thompson slouched, his heavy-booted feet kicking out at the windscreen. The sight filled me with such relief at the chance of escape from the confinement until from the front I watched the driver lunge at Carr.

Before I threw my fist out in hope of defence, a blur flashed across my front, pushing me backward and without knowing what was going on, Carr was launched over the seats into the back, with Jess in his place, her limbs a blur. I felt relief as I realised Cassie stayed where she'd been sitting and had not joined in the animalist attack.

Jess didn't stop her assault as a shot rang off by her side. With the gun still in Thompson's hand, he kicked at the windscreen, forcing it forward, then leapt through the space and on to the bonnet, kicking the sheet of glass to the ground, only to turn and stare at Jess as her motion slowed.

Bending her back, she snarled at the ragged mess in the driver's seat. With her face smeared with thick blood, she turned my way but didn't hold my gaze, instead looking to the three soldiers pointing their guns in her direction.

# 64

## JESSICA

It was dark as I came around, my thoughts flashing to the memory of the shot fired, feet smashing at my side and the frigid blast of air when the windscreen fell.

With the body of the driver limp in my arms, I felt the need for more and turned, searching, but something made me stop. A look to Alex, or to Logan perhaps, made the need to get away so much stronger. And that's what I did, launching through the window, running as if chasing prey.

I ran to an adjacent building on the corner of the road and up the stairs, the rage melting away with each step, the carnal need replaced by a nakedness, despite being fully dressed.

I felt so much fear, so much guilt at what I could only guess they would think.

I watched from the flat roof, looking to the van wedged in the archway and between the walls below as each slid down the bonnet, smearing the white paintwork with blood. I looked to my hands with the scarlet already drying and flaking to the roof as I flexed my fingers. Wiping my face on the dark sleeve, it didn't make me feel any better.

Thompson watched as Alex came out first, peering around and I knew it was me she searched for, but I stepped from the edge, leaving just the top of my head high enough so I could see.

"Don't look up," I murmured.

Then came Shadow with his nose high in the air, looking right at me, but he didn't signal to the others.

Then Cassie. Had I seen right? Was she about to take on the creatures at the window? Was she like me?

In that moment I felt the fear for Logan as I had for

Alex. A sorrow for what could have been. I knew of the heartbreak ahead. I could guess how Alex would feel if I never saw her again.

Logan came next, peering all around. Followed by the other three soldiers, one of them gripping his hand, the other two training their guns for cover.

I heard Thompson's voice. "Where is she?" All that came in reply were the shake of their heads.

"The children," Cassie said, seeming to realise what it meant if I was no longer going with the soldiers.

Shit. The children. A reminder to me, too.

Peering off into the distance, I looked over the tops of houses, of shops, across the horizon and between the columns of smoke catching in the wind and swaying with a beautiful rhythm.

"What happened back there?"

It was Logan's voice. The soldiers who had formed a protective circle glanced inwards, waiting for the answer.

Only Alex seemed to ignore the question, her gaze still searching. Stepping forward, I crouched to the edge of the building.

"Where is she?" Thompson repeated, his voice growing more urgent as he drew away.

"What happened back there?" the soldier with the damaged hand said and the voices merged into one.

"She's an animal."

"She's one of them. Isn't she?"

"Were you briefed on this shit?" His was the loudest. Sherlock.

They were speaking the truth, but the words still hurt.

"Can it." Thompson's command stopped the complaints and Shadow's bark pulled my look back to where they stood.

I expected him to be looking up, but he stared towards the van and I realised he saw the five new figures rushing towards them before they called with their chorus of screams reverberating every surface around us.

I couldn't help my high voice adding to the call as the rage came back in an instant.

# 65

## LOGAN

I paused, listening to the soldier's words, of which Sherlock's were the loudest. They made so much sense, especially when we looked up to the scream and saw Jess crouched on the edge of the building with narrowed eyes and covered head to toe in someone else's blood.

What else would anyone think after what we'd just witnessed? But she'd saved us, and not for the first time.

Alex's anger cut through my inner voice. "Don't fucking point those at her."

"Shit. Where's she fucking gone?" Thompson called out, dropping his gun and looking all around.

Turning away from the roof, I watched as Alex stepped in front of the remaining guns angled high, then one by one the soldiers moved, looking beyond the van and aiming their weapons though the interior to what I guessed was rushing towards us on the other side.

"Fall back. We need a gap, but hold your aim. We stop them here," Thompson called, already taking steps out into the open and widening the space between him and the front of the van, then stopping and crouching to the floor to reset his aim. The other soldiers moved to follow whilst keeping their sights fixed at the van.

Cassie, with Shadow at her heel, had already moved away and didn't stop as they walked along the road.

Jess had gone when I peered up and I couldn't shake the feeling we wouldn't see her again.

We had to go; the terrifying calls were so close. We had to at least get out from between the soldiers and those that would reach us at any minute.

As the screams called again, I gripped Alex by the

shoulder and ran past the soldiers and into the open, despite knowing if they got through the soldiers there would be no hope.

I stopped at what sounded like a fierce battle cry from the other side of the van and another, but in a distinct tone as if in reply.

The chorus of shouts cut off in their prime, turning to calls of effort and bodies slumping to the ground.

"What the fuck is going on?" I asked, but as I spoke, I realised there could be only one answer as to what had miraculously saved us a second time from the attack.

Jess.

Together we waited for a sign as if we all knew the danger had passed. We waited for some indication of what had happened the other side of the minivan. It hadn't come after a brief time and I went to pull Alex along when the door at the bottom of the building opened, each of our heads and the guns swinging its way.

Jess stood in the doorway, her hair matted to her head, wiping her mouth with the back of her sleeve but not able to clear the dripping red mess from her lips. She'd saved us, but could she stop herself from carrying on the frenzy?

Cassie hadn't stopped, but the rest of us just stared back.

Alex was the first to move, stepping toward Jess, nodding and I didn't need to see her face to know she wore a smile as she delved into her pockets as if searching for a handkerchief.

"Let's get you cleaned up," she said, guiding Jess back through the door.

"We have our orders," Thompson said, staring hard to the soldiers. None of them spoke, their brows low as if contemplating the consequences of their next move. "Have you got a problem with that?" he asked, staring back at his men. When no one replied, he moved off.

I looked on as he followed in Cassie's wake, the other soldier's stepping after, muttering under their breath.

No one talked as we slowly walked along the street which opened out from the alley, the road soon widening out to two lanes with the soldiers separating, each taking a flank with Thompson issuing commands to look out for suitable vehicles. The pace increased when Jess and Alex caught up at the back. Cassie stayed at the front with Shadow at her side as her lead opened up with every step.

I jogged to catch up.

"Are you okay?" I asked, the words sounding so lame, so weak, but it was all I thought to say. Was anyone okay in this mess?

Cassie nodded, and I tried to remember the last time we'd really spoken. I thought back to the village when some of my friends had still been alive and the morning when I'd woken to find everyone eating around the table. The calm before the storm. Then the night we'd laid in bed. The dream, but it wasn't a dream. Despite everything, I'd slept so well with her near.

I'd known her for only a few days. We had a connection, but now I was so damn scared I'd lose her, but to what I wasn't sure. Was it the bite or the cure that had made her this way? Or her worry for her sister and the rest of the children? Were they what had made her so focused? Or was her anger directed at me for delivering us, delivering them, to the doctor? Or was she turning, like Jess, into a version of those terrifying creatures?

And Jess. I'd had no time to process. I stopped, turning back, peering past the others. Thompson took the rear, a few steps behind Alex with Jess walking by her side. Her face at least resembled one of us, her jacket dark enough so the marks weren't so obvious. If someone had come along now, they wouldn't know what she'd done. Wouldn't know she'd flicked a switch in our moment of need and turned into a wild beast to save us.

The other three soldiers spread out amongst us, occasionally turning in circles to search for danger or transport to take us to the doctor.

Then realisation came so strong it felt like a weight on my chest, my breathing growing shallow.

She was a test subject. She'd become what the doctors had wanted all along and now they were returning her home. Jess had said as much; they'd made her in the hope she would have the power of the creatures but could control the urges. Was Jess, and people like her, our hope for the future? Would they and their kind be the ones who could save the country?

We needed Jess to make it to where they wanted her to go. The world needed her to get there, but did it mean Cassie would become the same and I would lose any hope of a life with her?

With Thompson in earshot, I spoke. "Where in the island are you taking her?"

He considered me for a moment as I started walking at his side, but kept silent.

"It's a large island," I added when he still hadn't spoken.

A map sprung into my head in his silence; we had to travel from the crook where the peninsula of Devon and Cornwall met the rest of England, a hundred and fifty miles away from the small island off the coast of Southampton.

A few weeks ago, the distance would have been three hours in rush hour to get to Southampton at least. An hour on the ferry across the Solent. We knew the military were all over this and I feared the ferries wouldn't be running and the Royal Navy would be in charge of a major quarantine operation. We didn't even have a car and when we did, we couldn't keep it on the road long enough to make much progress.

People had taken whatever transport they could to get away. We'd seen so few signs of any others making their escape. Apart from the Toyota garage and a few other lucky finds, anything left over had so far been junk and there were eight of us, including Shadow.

My thoughts paused at a low mechanical sound in the distance. Turning first to my left, I saw Gibson had also heard.

I followed his look back down the road, watching as Thompson huffed a command for each of us to stop at the sight of a tall dark car leaning heavy to the side and racing around a corner, heading towards us with its windscreen wipers rushing back and forth.

# 66

"Move," came Thompson's command and without question each of us separated, clearing the road to the left and right whist staring to the car over-correcting and lurching this way and that as it tried to straighten.

Racing closer in our view, I marvelled at the dent-covered four by four, the blue bonnet bent up in the middle. Glimpsing the driver behind the wheel, I focused on the whites of her wide eyes. For a moment I thought the impossible, until she blinked.

I looked at Thompson at my side, then to Jess, fearful of how she would react, but when she hadn't moved, I looked to the soldiers, each with their rifles pointed to the ground.

Ready to watch the car drive between us and off into the distance, it was easy to understand the compulsion to get away as fast as they could, so I waved. I raised my hand and gave the driver a signal as if we knew each other before the world ended.

Glancing over my shoulder, I saw Alex and Jess looking at each other, Alex saying something under her breath and the others in view took a further step back, despite the car slowing as it came closer, stopping only a few lengths past our group.

The tall BMW X5, according to the letters on the back, sat unmoving just along the road. With its side panels as dented as the front, but not covered in blood, guts or other gore, I wondered how long they'd been like that. The thought cut off as the driver's window lowered.

None of us moved until after a few seconds I stepped up, stooping with a wide, cautious smile to take my first proper look at the driver. A round-faced woman stared back, her light brown skin blotched with the red of effort, but with the start of a smile easy to catch. A bolt of silver pierced her left eyebrow and for a moment I thought of shrapnel until I spotted the silver stud in her nose. With dark hair pulled back in a bun, she wore a woollen dress and when she spoke I realised I hadn't said a word.

"Are you just going to stare at me all day?" she asked in a thick Scouse accent.

"Sorry," I said, then realised the stupidity of the apology, forcing myself not to look back to the group.

"You shouldn't really be standing around here," she said. "Have you seen what's happening?"

"Ah, yeah. Of course. We're trying to get away," I said, looking behind her to the empty back seats. "Where are you headed?"

She looked along the road, then turned her head, eyeing me with caution as she spoke. "Anywhere away from here."

I turned back to Thompson and watched his nod in my direction.

"Sir," Sherlock said, and Thompson turned around to look at him.

"We should stay outside where we can keep a better eye on it," he said in low voice.

"We need to get moving," Thompson replied, turning away before he could see the scowl on Sherlock's face.

The voice from the car pulled my attention back her way.

"So are you getting in or do you want to stand around in the open all day?"

I nodded, stunned by her words. "Thank you," I replied.

"Well, get in then. It's going to be a squeeze."

Flicking a control on the dashboard, she smiled as the windscreen wipers stopped scraping the glass.

Still dumbfounded by her directness, I turned to the others.

"Come on, guys. What are you waiting for?" I asked, then heard her snort as I pulled open the passenger rear door and motioned with my hands for the rest to come over.

Moving around the front and climbing in the passenger seat, I ushered Shadow to squeeze in the footwell and I twisted, looking to Cassie to make sure she'd moved towards the car.

With Thompson's nod of approval, the soldiers jogged at the sound of a distant howl, Carr running over and pulling the boot lid high, before yanking out the parcel shelf and frowning when he saw the size of the space but climbed in any way. The three women piled in the back seats as the other two soldiers squeezed in beside Carr to the sound of much huffing, somehow squeezing their rucksacks in too.

With no chance Thompson was fitting in the boot as well, and after he pushed down the boot lid, the women squeezed up closer together so he could sit behind the driver's seat.

The car rode low at the back as we drove off and I concentrated on deciphering the driver's words as she spoke again.

"Where are you headed?" she asked, as if we were hitchhikers out on a day trip.

Thompson coughed and I looked to the subtle shake of his head.

The driver glanced over her shoulder, smirking. "Never mind."

"Anywhere out of here," I replied. "I'm Logan," I added, holding out my hand.

"Mitch," she replied. Glancing over, the car wobbled as she took her hand from the steering wheel and squeezed my palm.

Turning forward, I watched the road as Mitch drove, still astounded at the emptiness of the wide road. We were yet to see any of the roadblocks we knew were further along and had seen on our travels. I could only guess it must have been a much more orderly evacuation. Perhaps they'd known in advance?

Checking each of the signs as we drove, I cracked the window just enough to give a breeze and to stop the window steaming. Seeing the first sign of concern in her expression, I powered the window up just a touch, making sure there wasn't enough space for even a persistent finger to get a grip.

"The roads are blocked as you get closer to the motorway," I said at first to Mitch and then twisted in my seat to repeat, forcing myself not to linger on Cassie's hardened expression. "Where shall we go?" I asked, locking eyes with Thompson.

"The coast. We're about ten mile out," Thompson eventually replied, and as I turned around we saw the last car in the long line clogging up the road in the distance.

"Shit. That's going to take forever to get through this," I said.

"Why the coast?" Mitch asked, turning to me as she slowed the car.

I twisted in my seat and back to Thompson in the sea of faces. "A boat?" I said, and watched as he lowered his brow, then glanced to his colleagues, seeming to regret the pause as each nodded back.

I wasn't sure how I felt about getting so close to the water again, still chilled from the last encounter.

Mitch gave a hearty laugh, distracting my concern. "If it's a boat you want..." she said, then without slowing she twisted the wheel, swinging the car around to the left and off the main road. "This is Exeter. Fortress on the Exe."

When she didn't slow, twisting and turning us through the side streets, I grabbed at the seatbelt to pull it across my chest. Eventually, Mitch took us through a gap in a hedge where the tarmac ended, turning into a packed mud track and I gripped the side of the seat as we bounced along the ground potted with holes.

To the groans and complaints from behind, it sounded as if, like me, the terrain highlighted the many bruises and aches caused by the events of the day. Letting go with one hand, I leaned forward, holding Shadow to steady him whilst I peered beyond another hedge line ahead which blocked much of the view, catching the very top of boat roofs moored up by the side of the river. I hoped one of these guys knew how to pilot such a thing.

Mitch slammed on the brakes just before the bonnet

touched the hedge line, jerking to a stop as if she'd only just realised we didn't want to take the car into the river.

I looked to a gap in the hedge ahead and a dirt path leading to the left and the white hull of a small vessel. Pulling the door open, a frigid breeze quickly found every spot that hadn't yet dried and I tested the air. At first smelling wet dog, I caught the background odour of sewerage.

Shadow jumped up from the footwell, busying himself sniffing the ground whilst taking a disorderly route towards the gap in the hedge with his nose switching between the air and the grass. Having found a scent of interest, he disappeared through the gap and out of sight along the path.

Rushing around the back of the car, I popped the boot, but didn't wait for the soldiers to unfold before I ran at the gap as everyone got out.

Glancing back, Thompson looked across the flat land with his hand on top of the holstered pistol as the other three soldiers pulled from the car. Mitch circled the BMW, pushing the doors closed and sniffing the air.

I stopped walking, following her back to the driver's side.

"Come with us," I said in a stage whisper, but she jumped back to the seat and closed the door, letting the window roll down whist shaking her head.

"No thanks. I don't like the look of this one bit," she said, then waved as her other hand pushed the stick into reverse.

I mouthed a thank you as she turned, heading away through the ruts to retrace the journey.

To the sound of Thompson's low-voice commands, a call for Carr to follow him whilst the other two waited, I turned as each slowly spread in different directions whilst keeping their backs to the hedge.

Hearing a splash of water from the other side of the hedge, panic rushed my thoughts to Shadow, but Sherlock's palm at my chest held me back with Thompson and Carr disappearing behind the gap.

Swapping a worried glance at Alex and then Cassie, I looked for Jess but couldn't see her anywhere. Forcing myself against Sherlock's hold, he took his hand away, stepping back and raising his pistol. Despite not pointing it at any of us, the movement conveyed the warning he'd intended.

A gunshot went off somewhere else, but before our nerves could settle and Sherlock could complete his turn to the noise, the great boom of an explosion instinctively made us duck as a chaotic sound of water compounded the dull echo, then a voice, a call for help vanishing as quickly as it came.

Pushing past Sherlock, I rushed toward the river as another explosion sent a jagged bright orange metal gas canister shooting into the air like a rocket.

# 67

First through the gap, I turned left along the river, glancing up the side of a narrowboat bobbing up and down as if nothing had happened. Looking to the faded paintwork, I peered through the nearest round window into the darkness, but turned away as the stench grew stronger.

Slowing when I couldn't see the danger I'd raced to, I looked along the line of three vessels, a white cruiser between two narrowboats. About to turn to continue my search, I followed movement in the water beyond the first and caught the dark soles of boots slipping under the surface.

Before I could jump in and grab on, I looked forward, seeing Shadow running my way from the last boat ahead. Rushing past the gleaming white hull of the middle craft, I half expected a silver-haired guy to be sitting in the covered canopy with a champagne flute in one hand and the other on the wheel.

But no. The only sign there had been any life was a dried bloody splatter across the hull and tow path.

Turning at the sound of footsteps behind, I saw Alex leading the way, rushing with Gibson and Sherlock running after, each searching for the danger.

Shaking my head at her raised brow, I turned back to the white boat bobbing in the water, twisting around at the sound of footsteps on wood. Passing the hull, I searched the gap between the next two, wincing at the sight of a bald head just below the water between floating splinters of wood. About to drop to my knees and push my arm out to help, I saw another at its side. Both heads turned up with their milky white eyes peering out of the dirty brown water, their hands raising and thrashing in my direction.

Staggering back, Alex helped me to my feet as I scoured the water. Hoping the shapes I'd seen beyond were just in my imagination, I turned my attention to the last boat.

Long and wide, each surface cracked and dried, it

looked like a museum piece dragged from the riverbed. It lurched from side to side and just beyond the cabin door at the nearest end, sharp, splintered wooden beams protruded out where more of the boat should have been.

Rushing forward, I caught muffled calls and a flurry of activity from inside. Jumping past the damage, I grabbed the roof as my feet slipped in the slick of blood I hadn't seen before I landed on the deck.

After steadying, I pushed open the door. Peering into the darkness, Jess's dark hands gripped at a figure's throat as they grappled just inside. Thompson fumbled on his backside, struggling to get traction on the slick floor as he tried to lean forward and grab at the double barrel of a shotgun at his feet.

Before I could react, a great shove pushed me to the side with Sherlock running past, his rifle raised at the tussling pair with his finger moving to the trigger.

Something in his look and how he'd acted before told me he wouldn't hesitate to use this moment to shoot Jess.

Recovering my footing, I launched sideways into Sherlock's shoulder, just as a single shot burst from the rifle. Dried splinters showered down as the wood erupted and Sherlock slipped in the blood with the force of my push and I followed, unable to stop myself from pinning the gun to his chest as I landed on top of him.

Pushing back, he lifted me up despite my weight and all the strength I could muster. Shoving me to the side, I landed heavily on the deck, and he loomed over me with the rifle aimed point blank at my face. For a moment I wondered what the nothingness would be like.

Closing my eyes, I thought of the calm that would follow. Not having to run or hide, or constantly be on guard.

When the sounds of the scuffle didn't vanish into nothingness, I opened my eyes, watching Sherlock pull away. I half expected Jess to rip out his throat.

Instead, Thompson gripped Sherlock's gun around the barrel.

With the sharp smell of the gunshot and metallic tang

of blood mixed with wet sewerage hanging in the air, I turned to the doorway and to Alex standing with Gibson looking over her shoulder.

Shaking with the cold, Alex leaned over to offer her hand. Getting to my feet, Jess stood staring our way, wiping blood on her sleeve. The guy she'd held lay at her feet in a heap.

Thompson spoke, but it took me a moment to understand the words. "The guy came at us with a shotgun. Carr set off a booby trap. The gas canister. She saved me," he said, moving his hand from Sherlock's chest and offering back his rifle.

"Again," I said, looking Jess in the eye. "She saved you again."

"Yes," came Thompson's reply as he nodded.

"Where's Carr?" I asked, but Thompson only lowered his head.

With the bloodied shotgun in my hand, no one spoke as we helped each other to dry land. It was then I realised there was no sign of Cassie and I turned to study our small group in case I'd missed her. I lingered on our sorry sight and Jess covered in blood again, wiping the drying mess from her face with a rag Alex handed her.

Turning around to the sound of an engine, white smoke puffed into the air from the back of the cruiser and I spotted Shadow on board. The note of the engine rose and out from the door below the cabin, Cassie stepped out, barely acknowledging our presence on the towpath.

The water around the white hull came alive, teeming with creatures just below the surface, their effort making it appear as if the water were boiling.

Rushing the few steps to climb aboard, I was last in the line and watched as her hand went to the throttle and for the first time I knew I'd lost her; she was not the Cassie I had grown close to.

But then, as if she changed her mind, her hand hovered over the control, turning her head just enough to see my foot land on the deck and we were off. Thompson grabbed me by the scruff of my coat before the sudden speed could send me backwards into the teeming water.

Crowding the small deck with the two rucksacks at our feet, I tried to ignore the sound of what brushed past the hull as we cut through the water. Still with the shotgun in my hand, Alex and Jess ducked under the wheel deck, heading through the door and into the cabin.

Sherlock stood on the other side of the deck with his palm on his holstered pistol and brow furrowed, glaring in my direction. To his side, Thompson leaned out from the hull whilst looking ahead with one hand shielding his eyes from the winter sun and the other gripping a handrail.

Sherlock dropped his stare, stepping beside Thompson, leaning in to talk low to his ear.

I looked away, not interested in what he said, instead turning to Gibson standing the other side of the boat and following his look to the figures just underneath the water, caught by the slow current and drifting the same way as us.

As Gibson looked up, I moved at the same time, peering out to the horizon and realised we were on a canal with a river a stone's throw over a short bank. If it weren't for the horizon lined with the tall columns of smoke of varying shades of darkness and the hint of stench mixed with the smell of the water, we could have been on a leisurely trip.

The weight of the shotgun turned me away from the fantasy as I stared to the bloody boot-prints on the deck, then to the shaven fur on Shadow's side, and then Cassie's cold, expressionless face.

No. We were definitely not on a pleasure cruise.

Thompson's raised voice dispelled the last of my thoughts, instead watching him with his face right up to Sherlock's as he tried to keep his voice low. Turning away when Gibson did the same, I knew Sherlock would argue about Jess and how they could travel with someone like her. I couldn't help but wonder if it was Thompson's orders or Jess saving his life that stopped him from throwing her overboard when she stepped from the cabin.

"Do that again and I'll take you down," Thompson said, unable to keep his volume low as he stepped away from Sherlock, instead staring at me before looking to the shotgun whilst walking my way. "Have you handled one of these before?"

Shaking my head as he held out his hand, I hesitated at the offer. But stepping forward, I didn't resist as he took the long gun with both hands and clicked the small safety switch into place. Nodding when he looked me in the eye to make sure I'd seen, he snapped the gun in the centre and an empty cartridge ejected from the barrel, flying out over the side and into the river with a splash.

A single brass-ended cylinder remained. "Did you find any more cartridges?"

Shaking my head, he snapped the gun closed, cradling it in the crook of his arm with the barrel pointing upward. I nodded to show I'd understood, and he handed it back so I could mirror the hold. Satisfied, he turned away, climbing the short steps to stand at Cassie's side.

All the time, Sherlock had been looking my way, glaring back when our eyes met.

A gust of wind washed across my face, the effluent stench drawing away my concern that any moment Sherlock might push me into the water. With heads angled skyward and peering across the view, I could tell the others smelt it too.

Seeing the sign on the left bank, I caught Gibson nodding in its direction as the others turned their heads to read the words and put themselves at ease. Each soon looked to the plumes of smoke rising above the trees which hid all but the tallest utilitarian buildings of the sewerage treatment plant nestled on an island bisecting the river and the canal.

The ring of green did nothing to hide the stench pushed high by the fires.

As we passed, I covered my mouth, trying to hold back the pervasive odour, and as it eventually faded, my attention went to a tall bridge across our path. Despite the distance, I saw the roofs of stationary cars and vans end to end across its length, forming the same scene we'd seen so many times before, but on a much bigger scale. Eventually I turned away, grateful the eight blocked lanes of motorway weren't in our way.

With the low drone of the boat's engine the only sound, no voices cutting over, I couldn't help but question if the others were thinking about the moment the cars ground to a halt. Like me, were they asking themselves what could have made the people leave their cars and walk away in the freezing cold? Or perhaps run for their lives?

Movement in my peripheral vision caught my eye, and I turned to the left, peering across the width of the river to settle on an animal at the far bank. Squinting for detail, I tried to figure if it was a dog or cat with its head down over a heap at its front. With nothing to give perspective to the size, it was as Thompson spoke the figure rose, standing tall to glare at us from across the water.

"Watch for contacts on the bridge."

I turned away as it walked into the water, then as it tripped over, falling headfirst when the water reached its knees.

Could a life on the water solve our predicament?

Thompson repeated his words and I followed his instructions, looking up toward the great concrete bridge looming in front of us.

I left the shotgun cradled in my arms as Thompson and the others pointed their weapons upward. The percussive hum of the engine magnified as we passed the concrete edge, giving a brief respite from the danger of the unwanted falling on top of us.

With the bridge soon at our backs as we continued downstream, a splash from behind called us to turn and scour the deck for who'd fallen overboard. Instead of finding someone missing, we turned up to the small crowd at the edge of the bridge who noiselessly called for our blood and proved Thompson had been right with his caution.

With the bridge shrinking from my view, I turned to a boatyard on the other side of the river standing empty as we passed. I imagined the river filled with tourists and pleasure seekers on a sunny day; the water teeming with traffic. In my daydream, families clustered on the banks with food laid out across their blankets.

Our course changed and the sweep of our journey heading to the left of the narrow channel drew my thoughts away. Taking the few steps, I climbed up to the small wheelhouse where Cassie didn't look from the water ahead.

About to question the turn, I caught sight of the white of an upturned hull in the centre of the canal, silencing my question.

With her right hand dropping the throttle, we slowed as Cassie leaned forward, concentrating ahead as if trying to look below the surface of the water. With a deft touch to the controls, adjusting the turn of the wheel and the throttle, she seemed as if she'd piloted a boat for much of her life.

Perhaps she had. I had, after all, only known her for such a brief time.

"Shit," she said, sending my eyes wide, the boat lurching to the left so violently as I rushed to grab at anything solid. A great boom reverberated from the hull as white water splashed high and we lurched to the side.

# 68

## JESSICA

Searching the small cabin with the door swinging closed at my back, I heard Alex's chattering teeth as I pulled up the tops of the bench seats, but found nothing warm to wrap her in, just space where the provisions should have been.

Shadow had followed us and sniffed around as I searched the cupboards on one side by the entrance and the other, a simple toilet, but they were empty too. Cursing the owners of the craft, I turned back to Alex with her arms wrapped around herself and took a chance.

Despite fearing how she would react, I took a long step toward her. When she didn't reel back in horror, I wrapped my arms around her and gripped her hard against her shakes. And there we held, the shivers slowing and we were at peace, despite the raised voices the other side of the door. Nothing could end that time where we were the only two people alive.

"The camera," Alex said, pulling away.

Still shaking, she pulled the rucksack from her shoulders and laid it to the seat, unclipping the clasps and pulling it open. She turned my way, smiling when inside she saw no water had got it and the camera sat safe and well, still nestled in the grey foam.

Clipping the case closed, she launched back into my arms, but the lurch of the boat to the side threw me backwards with Alex landing on top of me.

# 69

## LOGAN

As I slammed into Cassie's side, the motion sent the shotgun clattering to the deck, the boat groaning as the hull scraped over what lay just under the water. Trying to steady myself and grabbing for any handle, I paused beside Cassie with her warmth radiating through her clothes.

Reaching out with her right hand as the other held on to the boat, she pushed at my chest and I turned, gripping at the other side of the wheelhouse to pull away, despite the steep angle.

As quick as the change of direction came, we lurched the other way, violently coming upright with the motion sending us in the opposite direction. Cassie recovered before stumbling into my side and hit the throttle to hush the engine when the sound of a sudden splash in the water came from behind.

Turning to the sound, Cassie's eyes widened with concern over who had fallen. When I didn't see Alex or Jess, I tried to remember if they'd been on the deck moments before, just as Shadow bounded up from below where we stood, followed by the two women.

Looking back to the deck, I saw only two soldiers steadying themselves against the handrails.

"Man overboard," they called in a well-drilled unison. Gibson had vanished.

"What happened?" Alex shouted as she rushed to the soldier's side.

"We hit a sunken boat," I said, as I leapt down the steps to scour the water, joined by Thompson, Sherlock and Alex.

My search caught on the white of the upturned hull disappearing from view in the murky water as we drifted away.

"There," I called, pointing to a mop of long blonde hair near the edge of the canal, despite knowing the figure couldn't have been Gibson with his close crop. A sudden fresh fear gripped tight in my stomach when I realised there were creatures under the water, even though we'd travelled far from where we'd taken the boat.

"Eight o'clock," came the call, and heads turned just enough to see the dark hair of Gibson. The engine came to life and we jerked to a stop, watching as the pale figure burst from the water, but not splashing about in panic.

Despite the memory of the freezing water rushing back, I expected the soldiers to jump to his rescue. Neither did; instead, they stood to the edge and leaned over. Did they think he'd been bitten whilst under the water and turned already? Why else would they leave this man to fend for himself?

Stepping to the edge, questioning whether I should jump in instead, I looked to the water and saw movement a short distance the way we'd come.

I looked back to Gibson, watching with alarm as he dived under the surface again. Whatever he was doing it seemed he still had control, but not for long if the creatures spotted him.

With movement behind him rippling the water, short waves battered the sides of the hull as we sought any glimpse of other heads just below the surface.

"Gibson," I called, more voices adding to the volume. Someone had to do something or we'd lose him, but as if not afflicted by the icy temperature, he was still under the water, searching for something on the canal bed.

The rifle. He'd been carrying one of the two remaining rifles and must have dropped it as he fell.

"Gibson," the voices called again.

He'd been under so long, giving us no chance to tell him his life wasn't worth the length of metal.

Just then, Gibson broke through the surface to a chorus of voices calling his name, but he didn't seem to hear; instead, without a glance to the boat of people waving or the turbulent water whipped up by the dead walking below the surface, he dived back under.

A shot rang out loud from my side and I turned to see Thompson pointing his pistol toward the water, a wisp of smoke curling up from the end of the muzzle. Then another, this time to my right, Sherlock firing above Gibson's position at shapes moving in the water. Blinking as I turned back, I hoped they were certain they knew where he would rise again.

Just as another shot rang out, the soaked black metal of the rifle raised out of the water with fingers curled around its middle. Gibson's head rose soon after with his mouth wide, not waiting for the water to drain down his face as he pulled a quick breath. Glancing left and right before getting his bearings, he beamed as if he'd won a prize, but the elation fell away when he heard our muddle of voices screaming his name.

Rather than looking around, he lunged forward, paddling with the rifle in one hand as the other cut through the water. The engine tone rose, and we lurched back before coming to a stop close enough to lean down with Thompson by my side and reaching for a wrist each.

As I did, Sherlock knocked my hand out of the way and placed his grip on the cuff of Gibson's black jacket, heaving him back to the deck.

Glaring in my direction, Sherlock spoke, but not to me.

"You should have left the rifle, you stupid twat," he said, turning to the shivering soldier.

With water coursing down his face, Gibson glanced behind him to the murky brown, bristling with movement.

"Shit."

"Yeah," I said, and slapped him on the shoulder, ignoring Sherlock's returning glare. Thompson shook his head and took the rifle from Gibson's grip.

The engine note went high again and we moved off at an unhurried pace, much slower than we had before the crash. I watched as the water rippled under the surface.

Leaving Gibson to undress and wring out his clothes,

changing into whatever spares they had left, despite what they'd told me when I asked. I headed back up the steps, picking up the shotgun and resting it in the cradle of my arm.

Peering out across the water, Cassie kept her concentration fixed, scanning the width of the canal as we crept forward.

"Where d'you learn to drive a boat?" I asked once my nerves had settled. "Or do you pilot a boat? I'm never sure which it is." My voice sounded timid as if we were on a first date, or chatting to a stranger and scrambling to make small talk.

I didn't look around to catch Cassie's reaction but when I couldn't see her move in my peripheral vision, I felt a great weight over me.

The weight fell as she spoke, her words flat but at least she was engaging. "I don't think it matters."

When she spoke again, I had to push down the rising smile. "My dad taught me. We grew up with rivers and the sea all around us. He would take me out on a boat twice a year."

"You had a boat?" I replied, still reeling that we were having a conversation.

She shrugged. "We'd just hire one for the day." Glancing my way, I saw a hint of a smile before turning back to the water. In the brief moment, I caught a twinkle in her eye as if she was grateful for reliving a cherished childhood memory, but her smile soon dropped and she leaned forward again.

I turned ahead but couldn't see anything that could have pulled her from the memory.

Then I remembered her parents were probably dead; lost in the melee of roadblocks in the early days.

"Ellie hated the water." Cassie's voice held back my thoughts. "But she would still come along. She didn't have to, but she enjoyed the time with us. She'd take travel sickness tablets or be hanging over the edge for the entire day." Cassie stopped as if about to add something else, but after a few moments she kept it to herself.

Moving her hand to the throttle, she cut the power. Ahead I saw the low bridge blocking our path and we drifted, slowing to the speed of the current.

"How do we get…?" I said, but Cassie cut me off.

"It's a swing bridge," she said, as if listening to my thought before I'd given it voice. "Someone will have to get out to operate it."

I stared at the low metal bridge, tracing the painted white railings running along the top. Cassie turned to the deck below.

"Someone needs to get off and swing the bridge out of the way."

I turned, peering around the reluctant faces, catching only Alex nodding in reply.

"Alex and I will do it," I said.

Thompson paused for a moment before hurrying to push the last parts of the rifle back together.

"We'll cover," he said, and Sherlock glared up as Gibson nodded, shivering but still with a smile, slipping his arms back into a dry long-sleeved fleece.

"Hang on," Cassie said, turning away from looking to the bridge as we drew slowly closer. "It opens outwards. We might be able to push it out of the way without getting off the boat."

I turned, looking to the handrails coming into focus and the wooden deck only wide enough for two people to walk side by side. To the left the underside of the bridge was much larger than the right and I guessed it was the side where it hinged to the bank, the mechanism hidden by a stone surround.

Cassie lifted the throttle levers and we edged in close. Without being told, I braced myself as we slowed. Turning back, Thompson's pistol trained out across the horizon and the two rifles in the other soldier's grips covered the other two-thirds of the view, ready for whatever might lie in ambush.

I thought about jumping to the deck and glancing the

shotgun around the view when Cassie spoke.

"Get forward and push. I don't want to risk the hull." Her words were aimed at Alex, Jess and me. We climbed around the thin ledge, holding the metal rail as we shuffled to the front deck. Not able to take my gaze from the murky water, I stared, searching out what waited should we fall in.

Despite the boat travelling at barely a crawl, the bridge came at us too quickly. Cassie let the throttle out in reverse and we slowed, bringing our outstretched hands to the bridge's white handrail and we curled our grips to the cold metal. It was clear the hull of the boat could fit under the bridge, but anything above that level had no chance unless we drained the canal.

After checking we each had a hold, I nodded back to Cassie and the engine came to life. Taking a step back, surprised by the movement, I regained my stance and pushed. For a moment, its weight forced us back and it felt as if the bridge was stuck in place.

Just as I thought I would fall backwards, the bridge moved and I had to let it go when it swung out of reach, leaving only Alex to the far left to keep its momentum until it slammed into its stone home at the side of the bank.

It was only then I deciphered the hushed words between the soldiers as we'd pushed the metal. Had they seen something?

A sudden fear rushed through me when the heavy metal structure bounced against the stone, the bridge heading back our way, swinging into our path to send us into the murky water where more of those things could be waiting below the surface. Ready to rush back around the hull, the bridge halted, and we passed through, leaving the rise of adrenaline to drain away.

Back under the cover of the wheelhouse, I tried not to think of what would have happened if it had knocked us off our feet. Instead, I looked to the horizon.

The slow, continual motion forward helped to settle my fear as we travelled along the straight line of the man-made channel. The view from the wheelhouse filled me with confidence, with fields either side. A cluster of smoke columns rose to the sky, turning my thoughts to what could be a town, or perhaps a city ahead.

I had hoped as we headed further out of Exeter the towns might not have been a repeat of what we'd already witnessed and would offer safe transport out of the nightmare, or at least to where the children were. The rising smoke helped dispel the dream.

There was still hope, I reminded myself. Perhaps all was not lost. Perhaps the Royal Navy had a ship just off the coast, ready to pick us up and continue the soldier's mission. The thoughts dissolved when the waterway narrowed in front of us.

The muddy banks of the canal turned to concrete with a brick building, possibly a hotel or a pub, holding state at a set of lock gates we had no choice but to get out and operate.

## 70

The words I dreaded came from Cassie, pushing away any thought she could have another trick up her sleeve. "I can't push this one open." Her voice remained steady and she didn't look my way.

Turning to footsteps behind, I watched Thompson beside me, peering at the lock. After looking for just a moment, he jumped to the deck, raising his finger to Gibson.

"Stay on board and I'll over-watch canal-side." Gibson nodded through his shakes, moving to the back of the boat as Thompson pointed to Sherlock whilst reaching out for his rifle. "You and..." he said, pointing towards me as if searching for my name as he took the gun, "and you operate the lock. We'd help, but we need to keep watch."

I replied with a nod, then glanced to Sherlock, who held his expression steeled, a single brow raised.

"You," Thompson added, pointing to Alex as he handed the rifle to Gibson. "Take the shotgun as a last defence. Don't fire unless they directly attack the boat. Everyone understand?"

Only Jess's head remained static.

I watched as Thompson looked her way and raising his head, he spoke. "You do what you need to, if it comes to it."

None of us needed to ask what that might be; each of us had seen what she could do when our lives were in danger.

I don't know how I expected her to react, but she nodded with a frown, the thin creases in her skin still darkened with dried blood, despite the scrubbing. I was in no doubt she was clear what she had to do, whether or not she'd reconciled her new role.

Blowing out a breath, I'd resigned myself to the part I had to play. Despite the building looming beside the lock, at least I could get off the boat and away from the risk of falling in. I had no desire to end up in the freezing water again.

"How long?" I asked, turning to Cassie.

"Normally fifteen to twenty minutes," she said, still looking ahead as she nudged the throttle up. "You know what to do?"

I shook my head and waited for her to frown back, but keeping her voice level, she explained how to work the mechanism and let the water rise. She stopped talking, turning in tandem to stare at the brick building where anyone or anything could wait for someone to trap themselves in the lock and be a sitting duck.

At that moment, a dull thud resounded out from that direction.

I looked back to Cassie but she'd moved her concentration to the lock ahead.

Drifting forward past the empty wooden pontoons lining the entrance to the lock, I stared at the white letters coming into focus on the tall brick. The Turf Hotel stood three storeys high and seemed like it had once been a wonderful place to visit on a Sunday afternoon at the end of a stroll. I imagined the surrounding garden filled with tipsy day-trippers, some making their way over the thin lock to sit on the manicured lawn stretching out to meet a small copse of trees before fields and open land took over again.

Cassie's sigh pulled me away from the wide-open double doors leading out to white plastic chairs strewn across the garden. Following her gaze, I caught sight of the second set of lock gates pushed to the side as we drifted closer.

Nudging to the pontoon on the bank opposite the hotel, we didn't linger, our feet soon echoing on the wooden walkway.

"Wait in the middle," Thompson said.

I glanced back as Cassie gave the throttle a gentle touch and the boat drifted forward to settle in the middle of the canal. Shadow stood at the edge of the boat and peered out across the water with his snout raised high in the air.

Sherlock ran forward with his pistol unholstered, staring at the hotel as he crossed the water at the first set of gates. I couldn't help but wonder if he'd heard something other than the flurry of our footsteps.

Running along the concrete edge of the lock and with the echo of our feet against wood silenced, I listened, imagining the last boat heading through the channel and abandoning all etiquette of the waterway as they rushed to join the flotilla making haste down the estuary.

At the open gates I paused, noticing the desperately low water level in the lock and beyond, so far below the salted white line high up the concrete bank. Tracing the flow, I peered to the river and the stony bed through the clear water, not able to stop thinking how there could ever be enough for our boat to float.

Glancing back, Cassie stood on its bow, peering forward and down to the water, frowning and shaking her head, showing more concern than I thought possible, in recent times at least.

As I mirrored Sherlock's push against the heavy wood, she nodded, still staring to the water.

With the gates soon closed, locking into place with a thud, Sherlock rushed to grab the chunky metal key from the green cabinet standing proud canal-side. As the echo of closing gates died, I froze at the sound of a heavy thud from the direction of the hotel, the noise growing in volume as I stared on, not hidden as water flowed into the lock with Sherlock winding the mechanism.

Thompson had heard the noises too, as had Cassie. No one could have missed the sound and I felt my chest tightening, panic rising that whatever made the noise in the hotel would call creatures from all around and bring them to where we had to wait for the lock to fill. The water level had hardly risen as I glanced down.

Looking between the level and the open doors, I turned to Cassie who stood in the wheelhouse, then to Thompson with his rifle raised and taking steps towards the hotel. Was he mad?

Sherlock called out, his voice low. "Sir? Whatever's there, don't you think we should leave it alone?"

Thompson stopped, giving a curt nod, then stepped backwards towards the edge of the canal.

I imagined bodies rushing a blockage, banging bloodied fists against whatever had been used to keep them from piling out. With the sound of rushing water silencing and with renewed optimism, I glanced to the water, but it had only risen over the level of the inlet sluice with a long way to go before we could open the gates and the boat could glide in.

Waiting for what seemed like an age with the hollow boom from the hotel like the tick of a metronome, I realised the sky was empty of birdsong.

"Oi," Sherlock called, and I turned, expecting to see the undead racing my way. But I found him scowling whilst he waited for me to push the lock gate.

With my heartbeat pounding in my ears with the effort, it was only as the boat slipped through the opening that I caught the continued beat somewhere in the hotel.

Cassie brought the boat to a stop, pulling to the side as Sherlock and I worked the first gates to close. Cassie threw ropes to the edge, but rather than directing me to tie them off, she jumped from the boat, taking them from my hands before securing to the bollards either end of the craft.

Within a few moments Cassie stood beyond the far gates, looking down to the shallow river the other side.

"We need high tide," she said, but cut herself off, looking towards the hotel as the thumping stopped.

# 71

## JESSICA

Standing still was the worst. With the sound of the water rushing into the canal gone, there was nothing but the rhythmic drum from the hotel and it didn't help to keep my mind from what could happen at any moment.

I'd shown them and myself what I'd become. I'd shown them at times of need I could switch into something so terrible. I'd shown Thompson enough that he hadn't tried to put me in shackles and chains and drag me along; I could see in his eyes he was sure I could pull any metal bounds apart on a whim.

I hadn't told them I had no idea how I could turn into the monster. I hadn't told them the pain of my empty stomach or the need to bite down on flesh. I hadn't told them how I feared the next time could mean I wouldn't come back to who I really was. Or should that be who I had been before?

But still, here they were. We were all together and I hadn't ripped them to shreds. Perhaps there was hope. Or perhaps there was not.

When the sound ceased, I drew a deep breath and did the best I could to stop my heart rate rising.

# 72

## LOGAN

"Hold your fire," Thompson roared at the sight of a line of figures streaming through the double doors, their glassy, white-eyed stares fixed our way with their mouths hanging slack, stumbling in a stream that seemed to be never ending.

Thompson was the first person to move and rushed to the closed lock gate bridging the canal, with Sherlock following.

Although still shaking from the cold, on the boat Gibson held his aim to the pack, along with Alex, but neither pulled the trigger. Our only option would be to drift the boat to the middle of the canal and out of arm's reach.

I followed Cassie from the far gates and back to the boat, watching as she unwound the first rope from the bollard before jogging to the next to do the same.

"What do you mean we have to wait for the tide?" I called.

Cassie didn't reply straight away; instead, she kept one eye on the continual line emerging from the double doorway as she unwound the rope.

The first of the creatures were soon at the nearest lock gates and I followed Cassie back to the deck, looking to Thompson, then to Sherlock as their boots hit the hull.

"There's nowhere near enough water the other side. This lock only operates at high tide," she called out.

I looked past the end of the boat, remembering the tide mark I'd seen so far up the bank. "How long?"

Turning to Cassie, she'd disappeared from my side to push us from the bank with a long wooden pole.

"The tide's rising but I couldn't say," she replied.

"Can't we just open the gates and wait?" I asked,

twisting around to the creatures at the edge of the lock, their number spilling around and filing along, but somehow not falling to the water.

Cassie ran along the edge of the boat to the front, pushing the pole against the bank to keep us from turning.

"We'd ground out and topple on the keel," she said, moving to the other side of the boat, ready to push off as we drifted closer to the line of creatures clawing the air and mashing their mouths.

"The keel?"

"The fin-shaped thing underneath that keeps us steady."

I shook my head; it wasn't the time to learn these things.

"Shit," came Thompson's call, and I turned to see his rifle raised with his aim following a once-young man in a checked shirt, his legs bare, only in white boxer shorts stained with blood as he crossed the lock, edging sideways to grind his teeth in our direction.

"We have to wait until high tide," I repeated.

"Shit," he said again, glancing to Cassie for confirmation.

"We've got no choice but to wait it out," she replied, and I watched as a creature bent, reaching for the pole as Cassie pushed off the edge, whipping the long stick back before its gnarled hands could get a hold.

"That could be hours," I said, my voice desperate; for the first time in what seemed like an age, she looked me in the eye as she spoke.

"We have no fucking choice. Deal with it."

I stepped back, reeling from her words as I glanced at Alex. I didn't look as Cassie spoke in a softer voice.

"As I said, it's on its way in. Maybe an hour at a guess, but I don't know these waters," she said as she handed off the pole to Gibson once he'd shouldered his rifle.

I watched as she moved to the wheelhouse and killed the idling engine with the thin crowd slowly encircling us as more took the journey over the locks to bridge the canal whilst somehow not falling into the water.

They stood at the edge with their hands grasping out, bloodied mouths opening and snapping closed. Each time the boat strayed to one side, Gibson would crouch, pushing us gently off the bank with creatures swiping at the wood.

Without command, we formed a circle on the deck, each of us but Shadow, who stood proud at the back of the boat, peering at the unholy creatures who gaped back, almost drooling with hunger. Only Gibson moved when he had to push the pole to the edge.

For the first time since the disaster had begun, and with nothing else I could do, I studied the creatures, staring at their grotesque injuries and picking out their resemblance to who they had been before they had turned into something that, even after all this time, I had great trouble understanding how they could be real.

A chill breeze renewed the stench in my nostrils and I noticed the awful smell for the first time in a while.

I couldn't help but marvel at our ability to adapt, but once I'd taken notice of the putrid vapour, nothing could stop the waves of odour clawing at the back of my throat.

After five or ten minutes, or it could have been less, I found the stand-off so exhausting I felt my guard drop until one of the others moved, or took a step to steady themselves and a rush of adrenaline would surge through my body, fearing it could be our last moment.

A crash of water came from behind and our combined twist sent the boat rocking, forcing us to regain our balance. Relief came when I saw our number was still the same and it was a creature who had fallen into the water with its place on the bank already filled, leaving the blonde hair floating just below the surface as the only sign of what had happened.

I sat on the deck, holding my head in my hands.

"What happens when the water's high enough?" I asked, not lifting my head.

"What?" came Sherlock's heavy accent.

I looked to see him towering over me, but no one else had turned from the water.

"Get the fuck up, you little shit," he boomed.

"Give it a rest will you," I snapped back, turning away.

A foot came at me as if from nowhere and landed a blow to my back.

I jumped to my feet, full of rage, swinging my fist in his direction. He stepped back, then pulled his arm away, balling his fist, the boat rocking as he jabbed, but before he could swing out, Thompson was behind him, pinning his arms at his back.

"Fucking stop it," Thompson bellowed, his voice booming so loud it seemed even the creatures paused their clawing to take note.

Shouts rose from others, arms wrapping around me to take hold.

Realising Alex held me tight, I didn't struggle, but glared to Sherlock as Thompson released him.

"One more, Sherlock, and you'll be up on a charge."

A splash in the water caused us to turn, and Alex released her grip so she could look. Another splash came, the noise from all around and we watched as one after the other all of the creatures stepped into the water, plunging down with their expressions unchanging as if they hadn't noticed the fall.

Soon the water teemed with movement as a mass of hair waved in the water with bubbles rising to the surface. I looked around the now unimpeded view on the bank as if night had turned to day.

With all of the creatures in the water, it made everything so much better again. Turning around with a smile I couldn't suppress, I looked to Sherlock and although he didn't nod or show any apology, he at least didn't launch into another attack.

"It must have been the noise," I said.

"Guess so," Alex replied, along with a few murmurs from the rest.

"Let's just hope nothing else heard it," said Jess in a cold, flat voice.

A shrill call echoed in the distance.

Alex raised her arm, pointing past the pub and across the river. As the only things moving, the dark figures were easy to spot; the small crowd leaping to the air every so often gave us no doubt they were what we dreaded the most.

# 74

"They won't be able to make it across the river." Alex's voice cut through my thoughts.

Letting my stare fall down to the dirty brown water, I gazed at its alien motion.

"The mud flats either side of the river will swallow them up if they're stupid enough to try."

I nodded, but any sense of relief fell away when the high-pitched calls cut through the air at our back from the place I knew there was no such natural defence to keep them at bay.

"We have to take a fucking chance," I said, as I struggled to hold back my rising panic. "Open the gates." I turned inward to the circle, glancing at each of their faces whilst searching for a sign someone saw sense in my words.

We each turned to Cassie at the sound of another distant call, so much closer than the last. Cassie looked back, stony-faced, as if she hadn't heard the noise or didn't care. Instead, she took the three steps to the wheelhouse and peered forward.

After a moment she turned to Gibson with the pole still in his hands and nodded. "It's hard to tell how far it's risen, but I guess we have little choice."

Gibson didn't wait, leaning out with the pole to push away from the hotel side of the bank. As we drifted, water splashed up to the sound of hands slapping at the hull.

Nearing the edge, Gibson used the pole to drag us closer, but the bodies in the water stopped us from getting right up to the concrete, their squirming motion pushing against the boat as we squeezed them against the bank.

Cassie jumped the gap and I followed, the soldiers coming too, pointing their weapons across the striped grass toward the line of trees blocking our extended view.

Cassie and I stood at the far lock, staring to the water lapping gently at the lock gates.

"Is it enough?" I asked, despite seeing the level only halfway to the tidemark on the dark wood.

"I don't think so," Cassie said as she drew a deep breath.

I glanced over to Jess lingering on the deck, staring across the estuary to the columns of smoke, her face almost a mirror of Cassie's blank expression.

I shuddered at the comparison.

"How much more? How much longer?" I said, not able to hold back.

"I don't know. I don't know how low she sits down in the water," Cassie replied.

"Can't we just open both sets of gates and let the rush of water carry us along?" I asked at the first idea jumping to my head.

Thompson spoke and I turned to see him standing a few steps behind me.

"It's impossible," he said. "It's what they're designed to stop. The weight of the water on the other side means you'd need a lorry or something bigger to pull them open."

"There must be a way?" I asked, looking between them.

They shook their heads.

"Unless you have explosives," Thompson added, but continued to shake his head when he knew what my next question would be.

A shrill call came from the other side of the river and I turned its way, twisting back when an equally high-pitched sound replied at our backs. We had to do something.

Sprinting along the gates and across the water, without looking to the others, I ran back to where the key sat in the slot of the rear gates before grabbing it and running back to the front pair.

To my surprise, Thompson called out orders, shouting for Gibson and Sherlock to head to the trees and find out what they could see.

"Wait, no," I called out. "Shouldn't we stay together?"

"Yeah," Alex added.

When Thompson ignored our words, I wound the key in the mechanism and I glanced up, watching as Thompson threw the rifle to Sherlock. Neither Sherlock nor Gibson questioned the order; instead, they ran toward the treeline, spreading out as they raced to get a better view.

"We need to know what we're dealing with," Thompson said, not turning my way. "Stay out of this."

Pushing hard with each turn, I shook away the dread we wouldn't see either of them again and that with every turn we were closer to abandoning them as we washed down the river. Instead, I concentrated on working through the ache in my arm as the key went around to the sound of the cogs clunking together and water rushing out of the gate to splash to the river the other side.

High calls came again, one after the other, but no shots were fired. Looking down, I urged the level of water between gates to drop quicker as Cassie jumped back to the boat, the engine soon coming back to life.

"Shit," I called, as the receding water revealed the dank hair of too many heads to count. Thompson followed my look, his eyes widening at the sight of the water running down their foreheads. Only Jess and Cassie didn't look as the vanishing water revealed more sodden features of the creatures still standing in the water.

I couldn't stop looking at the sight of the water lowering, knowing if it dropped too low, they would easily overwhelm the boat.

With the sluice gates fully open, the handle stopped and glancing back to the river side of the lock gate, I saw we were so close, the levels nearly the same.

Arms were out of the water, grappling and clawing at the hull. Fingers held at the edge as more made their way to the boat in the ever-lowering waters.

We couldn't wait much longer. Alex rested the shotgun to the deck to grab at the pole and jab at the fingers and heads of the creatures as their hands came over the edge. They couldn't feel pain and didn't care how hard the wood struck them, continuing to grasp for purchase to pull themselves up to the feast in waiting.

I looked to Cassie and without words she calmly nodded, hoping it meant it hadn't grounded yet.

Pushing my weight into the gate, with surprise I felt it move against my pressure, sending water rushing in between as Thompson heaved the other side. With the water dropping at such a rate, our efforts were rewarded as the gates stood open, resting against the concrete.

Arms reached over the edge with Alex, Jess and Shadow standing dead centre of the rear deck. Jess looked on impassively, as if biding her time. Alex held the pole like a spear, ready to attack the first creature to climb.

The boat moved forward, the hull scraping against the bottom of the canal, but with the engine note rising, she pushed past the friction.

Thompson jabbed his fingers into his mouth and issued an ear-splitting whistle whilst Alex walked around the deck, sweeping off the remaining fingers clinging to the edge.

Rushing along the side, I realised with the boat so low I had only moments before it slipped into the estuary and I would have to swim to join her once it cleared the concrete marking the end of the lock. Thompson leapt from the bank, landing on the deck with a great scrape echoing from the hull with the extra weight.

It was now or never. I took a running leap and pushed off to the side. As I leapt, I made the mistake of looking down to the murky water and the bodies standing with their arms flailing as if trying to grab me from below.

Landing, Alex wrapped her arms around me, stopping my fall off the opposite side and I stood, legs like jelly, trying to push away the thoughts of what could have happened if I hadn't made it.

Each of the grasping creatures fell from the edge and the waters must have deepened as Cassie lowered the throttle to keep us from slipping along into the estuary. We had two passengers to wait for.

All but Cassie stared out at the treeline. The air filled with the splash of water as a hand or appendage rose above the surface, the slow current drawing the creatures from the lock, passing our hull and out to the river.

A chorus of short, excited squeals called out from the trees; the sound of something enjoying a chase. A chill raced down my spine as I peered to the treeline, searching for anything that could be the two dark-clothed soldiers running towards us.

When the soldiers weren't apparent, I knew we couldn't wait forever. We were too close to the bank for the distance to protect us from the bounds of those creatures.

If they overran the soldiers, we were next on the menu. We had to make the terrible call. We couldn't just wait and see what fate would fall upon us.

Thompson decided.

"Take us into the estuary," he said in a quiet voice. The rise of the engine note replied as our speed increased.

"No," I called. "You can't leave them here. Just a few moments more," I said, not able to leave them to their death when there could still be hope.

"We're going. They knew the risks," Thompson said, shaking his head, but I still looked past him at the treeline.

"Look," I shouted, pointing to movement I hoped wasn't in my imagination. When I saw the two distinct black shapes, my lips pulled into a smile I couldn't hold back and I waved furiously like an excited child.

"Hold," Thompson snapped, and the engine noise dropped back to an idle as he followed my outstretched finger and held his palm out to Cassie.

Looking up as a collective gasp rose in the air, at first I couldn't see what had prompted the reaction. Then I saw the figures leaping to the air as they chased Sherlock and Gibson, their number too many to count. It was then I remembered what Alex had said in the restaurant; I didn't want to believe they could multiply, that they could make more of their own, but the sight told me she must have been right.

I expected Thompson to call out an order for us to leave. I expected Cassie to push the levers up, forcing us to watch the running men perish. There would be no chance of outrunning the frenzy chasing at their backs.

I hadn't expected the movement across my front. I hadn't expected, like an Olympic gymnast, Jess to leap in a great arc from the boat to the bank, running in a blur towards the soldiers.

The soldiers were soon close enough I saw their expressions, their wide eyes at the sight of Jess running towards them, their faces contorting and giving her a wide berth as she ran between them.

"Hey." The call from Alex pulled me away and I turned to see an arm reaching over the edge of the boat, a pale hand gripping to the base of a metal rail.

Alex stood to the edge, looking down, jabbing the pole at the figure. I rushed to her back, peering over to see an old man clinging to a handrail, with two more grabbing around his neck as they tried to use him as a ladder.

Gripping the shotgun up from the deck, I flinched at the terrible sounds from where Jess had run to and saw Sherlock and Gibson had made it to the manicured grass.

"Get ready," Thompson called, and I turned away, rushing to Alex's aid as she jabbed the pole over the side of the boat to the sound of sucking flesh and the strike of bone.

When two heavy thumps hit the deck, Thompson gave the order and with the engine revving high, I didn't need to look to know the two soldiers were on board and Jess was the one we were leaving behind.

"Jess," Alex called, as a creature's hand wrapped around the pole with the bodies slipping away in our trail to sink below the surface whilst still grasping out towards us.

Her head rose, pale and wide-eyed when we turned to see the receding woods. Staring out, I watched a figure at the head of a group, a pack of creatures running and bounding toward us. It was Jess, but we were slipping down the canal to where it swept into the river at our right to become the estuary and lead us to the sea with the sticky mud flats either side at the edges of the water.

There was no way she would make it in time, even if the creatures chasing didn't catch up to take her life.

# 75

## JESSICA

There were too many. Their number so great. I could have stayed and fought but I knew it would be my last and I wasn't ready.

With their thick blood dripping from my hands, I turned from the fight, watching the boat move, my gaze catching on Alex's desperate expression as she stared from the deck.

They'd made the right decision. The needs of the many and all that. Still, I couldn't help my regret as Alex screamed, her voice so desperate in my direction. I kept running for the fear she might do something stupid.

I kept running, somehow ahead of the charging pack. I knew they were only interested in me because of my attack, my battle to save those soldiers and take away their prey.

I thought I would pay for my stupid act. I thought I would pay for saving their lives with mine. I was in no doubt these creatures, who were only one step removed from me, would rip me to shreds when they caught up and I'd no longer be able to save the children, or find the answers to my questions.

Somehow my speed increased. Somehow, to the calls from the boat, a chorus shouting from the small vessel for me to rush and with hands reaching out across the water, I jumped, leaping into the air with gunshots cracking, not checking where the weapons aimed.

I landed, the boat almost tipping, my weight almost too much for it to cope with in the shallow waters. The engine sound rose and I pushed down the surprise that Cassie hadn't already powered away at full speed. I put the rifle shots out of my mind whilst staring to the shoreline, barely panting, watching and waiting to see if any of the monsters followed.

Four figures took to the air, but none could match my power, each falling long before they even got to where the boat had waited. Each creature landed in the mud, its depth taking them to their shoulders with water lapping at their necks as their mouths snapped open and shut whilst staring at our vessel shrinking into the distance.

The rest followed, rushing along the bank, but getting smaller with each moment.

Alex took my hand, her skin so warm, despite the sticky blood. I'd never felt so alive as in that moment.

With her other hand, Alex passed a rag so I could clean my face.

I looked to the other shore when high screams called out, my gaze following another crowd of creatures unable to keep up, but trying as they ran along the bank. I knew then our only hope would be to take the vessel out to sea, unless the soldiers had something more substantial waiting in the estuary's mouth.

# 76

## LOGAN

There was no other plan, at least no one spoke of one. All that was left was to head out to sea in the tiny boat. The figures racing along the banks of the widening estuary were a clear enough answer to any question we could ask, compounded by the columns of smoke rising from the lost town at the mouth.

Winding our way through the quickly deepening waters, the movement on the banks kept pace like shadows on either side. Although the creatures travelled slower than we did, new numbers joined with every mile travelled, soon too many to count. Their leaping frenzy and the speed at which they raced painted a terrifying picture for the future of humanity.

Peering out across the estuary, I looked to the calm waters ahead. Squinting, I could almost block out the rising smoke in my peripheral vision. Salt in the air became the new perfume, giving an overwhelming relief. I couldn't remember the last time the terrible combination of bodies decaying and foul sewerage didn't surround us.

I could almost kid myself we were on a daytrip; a pleasure cruise on the river before heading back to a comfy bed in a house with a roaring fire.

As we wound around a long bend, the vision shattered at the sight of a ship in the middle of the wide water with the deep orange of its hull turned towards us, leaning away at a sharp angle out to sea to hide most of its battleship grey.

Water lapped at its edge as desperate expletives launched from the soldier's lips.

"Tyne," said Sherlock at my back, as murmurs spread across the boat.

Cassie couldn't steer a wide gap; the narrow channel

either side forced the detail into view, the sharp, rust-free lines of the ship's hull adding to the deepening sense of despair.

"How's the fuel?" Thompson asked, bringing me back to the next leg of the journey.

Cassie peered down to the controls and replied without looking up. "Three quarters of a tank. Is it enough?"

Thompson replied, "I'd say we need three or four hours if it's not too choppy."

"There's no way of telling how big the tank is," she replied, her voice still flat.

With Thompson's nod, I knew we were committing to a wing and prayer we'd have enough fuel to get to the Isle of Wight.

Although the sky had darkened, as we passed the great hulk of steel looming over us there was still enough light falling on the ship's steep angled deck to see the bodies caught up in its abandoned equipment.

The stench of fuel caught in my nostrils; the rainbow shimmer slick on the water's surface looked so beautiful in the last of the light.

I turned away as something in the distance fell to the water, but no shouts for help came after. No one wanted to rescue what had fallen.

With our view clear, I looked out to the water and the vast expanse of the English Channel stretching as far as I could see. With the sun almost gone over the horizon, I rocked with the gentle motion of the boat as we cut through the low waves.

Thompson climbed the steps to the wheelhouse, speaking with Cassie loud enough so we could all hear. "Keep land to the left and don't drift out until you see the coast of Weymouth jutting out. Then we'll head straight for it. We can navigate by the land and if we get low on fuel, we won't have far to go."

I turned away as Cassie gave a shallow nod. With the light almost gone, I sat on the deck, looking to the coast to the left. Watching the glowing lights, I tried to pretend flames weren't climbing high as I relaxed with the rise and fall of the waves.

With a nudge at my side I turned, surprised to see Gibson's smile in the last of the light, then glanced to the bright moon high in the sky. Looking back, he offered half of a small bar of chocolate.

Nodding a thank you, I savoured the sweet milky taste coating my mouth as the treat slowly melted, watching the others in the sitting circle do the same. Except for Cassie and Jess, who'd refused.

Turning from the coast, I stared to the dark horizon ahead, the white of the shallow waves catching the moonlight and the fuzzy mirror image of the great ball in the water.

Our battle was not with the cold cutting through our still damp seams; we could have taken it in turns to wait in the cabin. It wasn't the constant motion of the waves or the darkness which made the sea so alien, or the quiet, the only noise coming from the rhythm of the engine.

The battle came from the time we had to think. A fight against the calm after so many days of constant fear, of constant racing from death, not knowing what would come next. At least here I knew the worst would be for the sea to turn us over. We would drown, but it would be the end. Or I could just fall over the edge and slip beneath the surface and it would be done.

I looked to Cassie, watching her back with her staring out along our path. Unerring. Not looking away. Not seeing me.

But had the shared moment when she'd spoken about her childhood been a glimmer of a future together? Or once we'd saved the children would I have to move on and find safety for myself?

I looked to the water with its inviting darkness.

Turning to Jess with Alex sat at her side, I glanced at Alex's hand resting on top of Jess's. Perhaps all was not lost.

Shaking away the thoughts, I peered out to the coastline our journey tracked. The land was still so dark. I couldn't help but think of where the other escaping boats had gone. Were they lost like the ship beached in the estuary? Or had they, some of them, made it to the land further along and found somewhere not overrun? I had to hope for their sake and for ours.

"I haven't seen any airplanes."

The words came from Alex and I turned to her looking to the sky, Jess's head following at her words. I didn't want to imagine what those two were going through.

I looked up, taken aback by the brightness of the stars in the cloudless night, the view unbroken by vapour trails lining the sky. Was this a sign that our country was not the only infected?

I looked to Alex staring my way and as our eyes met, she nodded in my direction as if I had something on my face. Wiping the back of my hand to my eyes, I looked away.

## 77

# JESSICA

Alex's words were the last for hours, Thompson's voice the first to point out the approaching land and the emerging light from the coast. "The Solent."

"What happens when we get to the island?" Logan asked after a few moments when we saw the white Needles jutting from the sea.

Thompson didn't meet his gaze; instead, he looked to Gibson before turning to frown in Sherlock's direction.

"We land at Fort Albert and take you in," he eventually said, twisting to catch my eye as he spoke.

Logan looked to Sherlock for his reaction and Sherlock frowned back, not bothering to hide his contempt.

"But..." Logan said, turning to me and then to Thompson. It was my turn to speak.

"You've seen what they've done to me," I said, peering to Thompson, then the other soldiers. "What they've turned me into. You want to hand over that kind of power?" I tried to keep my words calm and considered, watching as Logan looked over to Cassie, but she still had her back to us.

"It's not right," Gibson said, leaning forward towards Thompson before looking at Sherlock as he spoke. "If everywhere is as bad as the South West, can you think of anything..." He held his words, pausing for a moment. "Anyone who can take those things on?"

"You'd give them the power to make more like me, to condemn more to the life I face? Is your life worth more than mine?"

"Superhuman strength and to run and leap like that. You could be a superhero. The saviour of the world." Sherlock's words dripped with sarcasm.

I couldn't help but chuckle and looked briefly to Alex.

"I don't wear my underwear on the outside. Have you ever heard of a hero who goes home with the need to devour human flesh?"

Alex swallowed hard and I looked to Logan, but he turned away as our eyes met.

"And did you know they can reproduce by themselves?" Alex said, not looking at me.

"And heal broken bones in hours," Logan added, this time catching my eye as I looked his way.

Alex spoke again. "To kill the monsters, we have to make something so much worse." She leaned toward me and I felt her warmth radiating through my clothes. She took my hands and wrapped hers around mine. "But what happens when all the monsters are dead? What happens when we're left with just what we've created? Are they going to lie down and let us kill them after they are of no use? Do you think they'll let us control them?"

I looked at each of the soldiers in turn, nodding as Alex spoke.

Sherlock was the first to reply. "Do you want us to put you out of your misery?"

"No," I said without pause and Logan looked at me as if I could jump up at any moment and attack. Instead, I kept my calm. "I want to end this. Let me off at the Fort. Alone."

Only the sound of the engine and the water lapping at the hull replied.

"And what do you expect us to do?" Sherlock finally asked.

"Sail off and find somewhere safe," I said. "Or join with us and make sure my message gets out to the people."

"What message?" Thompson cut in.

I looked to him and spoke again. "We have to tell everyone to prepare. We have to tell them what's coming. There must still be people who have a chance. I need to make a live broadcast to the people. It's all set up with my editor."

"Huh?" Logan said, and both he and Thompson turned

my way.

"When I went to get the satellite phone, I made a call. Stan said the BBC is under military control." Thompson nodded in the corner of my view. "He has to be so careful or they'll put him back under arrest. They've locked me out. We know that already. We have one chance to make one last broadcast. All I have to do is call him on the sat phone and he'll get me in, but we have to make the broadcast great. One shot only. He's willing to sacrifice his position, and possibly his life. So am I."

Alex nodded, and after a moment Logan did too. Gibson tipped his head without pause.

"I don't know about all this," Thompson finally said after taking his gaze from Gibson's resolute expression.

"Do you have families?" Cassie asked from the wheelhouse and we looked her way, watching as she stared out across to the dark coastline with her back to us. "Wives. Children. Parents. Friends?"

"Yes," Sherlock said, nodding. The others kept quiet.

"Do you want them dying in fear, rushing down the street to help an injured old man only for him to turn on them? Are you prepared to go home and put a bullet in their heads?"

A murmur came from under Sherlock's breath and he looked at Thompson, squinting slightly as if he was trying to say something without speaking. He looked away when Cassie spoke again.

"Well, most of my family are dead because we weren't prepared. The rest are with that woman, helpless to stop her testing like they did on Jess and ready to make more of these creatures we'll never defeat. So I know what I'm doing."

I had nothing else to add; between us we'd said it all. Logan then spoke to break the silence that followed.

"You see," he said to the group, looking at each of the soldiers, glancing to the weapons on the deck or holstered at their side, and then to me. "We all have our reasons to go to that place and end the plans of those two psycho-doctors and we can't have anyone getting in our way." He tensed, readying for the fight as Cassie glanced over her shoulder and despite knowing some of us would lose our lives, we knew it was a battle we couldn't prevent.

I stood and stared at each of the soldiers for a moment before I spoke.

"So are you with us or against us?"

# 78

## LOGAN

Thompson turned away, moving his gaze to Gibson and then to Sherlock, and with it our attention followed, but theirs stayed fixed on his moonlit features.

"That's a brave thing for someone in your position to say," Thompson said, his words slow and considered as he turned back to glance down to the pistol strapped in his holster before looking Jess in the eye.

My muscles tensed, readying for the fight and the engine note slowed as Cassie let down the throttle.

Thompson didn't flinch. "But this is something we have to decide as individuals."

"I'm with you," Gibson said without delay, and I looked his way, tipping a nod. All heads turned to Sherlock as he stared at Jess.

"But what if you're the answer?" he asked, his brow furrowed. "You came after us. You put yourself in danger, at massive risk to save us. Who's saying those that come after wouldn't do the same?"

Water lapped at the hull as Jess stared back to Sherlock.

"I live on a knife edge. Your scent is so powerful I'm picturing you naked on a platter with an apple stuffed in your mouth. Do you know you'll taste somewhere between chicken and pork? The dark meat is the best," she said, licking her lips and taking a deep swallow as her face bunched to highlight the dried blood around her hairline and in the creases around her nose.

I swallowed hard. I had no idea if what she'd said was true, but turning to Sherlock, his hardened expression remained unmoved. Jess spoke again.

"During your training, were there people who were

great at getting the job done? Those that could summon so much aggression they were amazing at doing all the physical stuff, but come the dinner bell they just couldn't turn it off?"

Thompson looked to me, and then to Sherlock, his eyes narrowing. Sherlock caught his gaze, then turned back to Jess with a slow nod.

"Do you want to take the chance that the monsters you help to create will have enough self-control to stop themselves splitting you in half and eating your organs whilst the blood still pumps around your body? If you do, then I suggest you start swimming now."

Silence hung for a long while as we drifted towards the shore.

"Okay. I get it," he finally said. "I'm with you."

"And so am I," Thompson added, but I could tell by his expression he'd made his mind up long ago.

Without delay the engine note rose, and we picked up speed as Jess sat back down.

"So what's the new plan?" I asked, looking back at Thompson. I expected a thoughtful delay as he considered the options, but I soon realised he'd not been sitting idle all this time.

"The main objective is to find your family," he said, turning to Cassie's back. As he spoke, she twisted to acknowledge his words.

"And the other children," I added, as he continued to speak.

"Yes. Then Jess sends the message and we shut the place down. Do you have everything you need?" he said to Jess.

Alex replied, nodding as she twisted around to show the small pack she'd been lugging around all this time.

"Good," Thompson said, before looking to his bulky watch. "It'll be dark for a long while once we've landed, but this moon won't help us. They'll be watching the water, probably for survivors, but it was always an option for us to arrive by water. We'll have to land down the coast. I know a place."

"I thought you'd never been there," I said, biting down a sudden suspicion.

"I haven't, but it's what we do. We prepare for anything." He held my gaze as he spoke.

I nodded, looking away from the intensity of his expression as he continued to speak. "I don't know the state of the island. If the population has evacuated, or lost, or perhaps the trouble hasn't got here yet. Either way, we can count on patrols. We must stick together and see what we find."

Nods repeated across the deck.

"How about we use the Death Star approach?" I asked, turning to raised brows.

"The Death Star approach?" Gibson was the first to ask what the rest seemed desperate to answer, but Sherlock burst out laughing.

"Are you a fucking child? Do you think this is a fucking game?" he said, shaking his head as the laughter slowed.

"Can it," Thompson said, as Sherlock stared my way. "It's not a bad idea."

I turned to Alex as she spoke. "No one's tying me up, pretending or not."

I watched Thompson almost deflate at her words and Gibson glanced over to Sherlock with scorn until he saw me looking his way. He gave a shallow nod and then turned away.

"Listen, whatever. We'll get in. There's a back route. The place is only half built and with patrols out it's not going to be heavily guarded," Thompson said. After clearing his throat, he spoke again. "If we go that way then we won't need anything elaborate to get you in."

Sherlock raised a brow and shook his head.

Thompson stood, taking the steps up to the wheelhouse and we changed course to the right, moments after he spoke with Cassie.

Before Thompson could retake his seat, Sherlock met him at the bottom of the steps. I couldn't quite hear what he said, but Thompson screwed up his eyes as he cut Sherlock off, clearly not liking it.

I tried to listen in harder but Gibson called my name and as he pulled my attention away, I looked to Sherlock glaring back. They were just playing along; it became so clear. They were going along with our idea, but either Sherlock couldn't bring himself to act, or he was too dumb to realise he was giving the game away by being an asshole.

Rubbing the back of my neck as I turned to Gibson, I couldn't pay attention to what he said, instead trying to think what we could do next.

"Are you okay?" Gibson's repeated words finally came into focus.

I couldn't reply; instead I turned to Jess. She was looking my way, her eyes narrowed and slowly nodding.

We both knew it, but I had no idea what we could do.

# 79

## JESSICA

Now, I mouthed in Logan's direction. He stayed still with just his eyes widening in the pause. We had to do this at the same time; it was the only chance we could have to make it work. Then he moved; as if in sudden realisation Logan jumped up, bending over as he launched himself at Gibson sitting on the edge of the boat, watching as he rose to his feet.

I didn't see the soldier's reaction; I had my focus ahead on the other pair and I was up, time slowing as energy surged outward as if pulsing from my bones. With it came the need to tear into their flesh, but I fought the strain of want, the gaping hole in my gut that came with the power radiating out from my fingers as I ran, touching them with a hand on each.

They'd seen me, but a blink of an eye later they were travelling sideways, pushed out in front and away from my bared teeth desperate to rend their flesh. They had no time to speak, only to call out in surprise before they were gone, the water rushing up from over the edge, the spray catching my face as I stopped myself just in time so I wouldn't join them.

Panting, I turned to the flurry of movement in the corner of my vision.

# 80

# LOGAN

Gibson was like a brick wall as I hit him, with my hands pushed out in front and my full body weight behind. He barely moved backwards; his biggest reaction was his smile dropping as he heard the splash I could only hope wasn't Jess falling into the water.

A call went up, Alex swearing as if taken by surprise, Shadow's bark absorbed into the night. Then Alex was by my side with both her hands on Gibson's left as she tried to stop his reaching for the rifle by his feet.

With his grip so hard, he had hold of my wrist, twisting and turning as he did the same to Alex, then dragging us both forward having given up on the gun, now intent to pull us over the edge. And he was succeeding.

But then it stopped, his grip released, at first for no apparent reason. I looked up just as he fell backwards with his neck at a right-angle and Jess pulling back her fist.

He slipped slowly into the water as I regained my breath.

I turned around, not sure what I'd see, but there we were. The five of us on the deck. Alex regaining her breath. Jess gritting her teeth as she stared between us. Shadow with his tail wagging and Cassie in the wheelhouse with her hands covering her eyes as if she'd not wanted to see.

"So this is who we are now," Alex said between breaths.

I looked around and no one replied. No one corrected her as Cassie turned back to grab the wheel.

I didn't look in our wake. I didn't want to see the bodies slip under the water even though I knew they'd be long out of sight. Instead, I stared at the shoreline getting closer with each moment and a building sat on the edge, marked out by three rows of lights to our left. With more lights scattered across our view, I couldn't help but think it was a positive sign, whilst knowing the opposite could also be true.

"That must be the place," I said. No one disagreed.

As the darkness of the land built, I licked my dry lips, regretting the salty taste and last drink of water I couldn't remember taking.

It wasn't long before we were just off the coast and Cassie slowed the engine and made another turn. No one spoke as I stroked the length of Shadow's back, pretending it was for his reassurance.

We aimed for a sandy beach and I shuddered as I realised we were going to get wet again.

Soon we heard the familiar scrape of the keel on the sand below and we lurched to a stop, despite the engine noise rising as Cassie tried to get us as close to shore as possible. The engine soon silenced after a last-minute flurry and we were left with just the waves slapping gently against the hull and washing to the shore.

"Come on," Jess said, waving her hand to the water as Cassie threw the anchor over the side with a splash.

I peered along the edge of the beach, scouring in the white moonlight for any movement. Beyond the sand, light glowed from over the dunes but when no one called the alarm I watched Jess, then Cassie, lower themselves backwards over the edge and slip near-silent into the water, which came just below the knee.

Grateful for the water's height, I handed over the rifles as they beckoned us to join them.

Alex lowered herself down next, gliding with as much grace as the pair had, then she stood at the edge of the boat as I corralled Shadow to let Alex take him.

Slipping as my foot touched the edge, I landed heavily in the freezing water, sending out a great bow wave. Flashing a silent apology all around, no one seemed to care as we strode with wide steps to the beach and I wondered if they too could feel their legs already going numb.

Revelling at the solid ground, and with the freezing cold coursing down my ankles as we rose out of the water and on to the beach, I wasn't able to stop their sway even though the motion of the waves was only a memory.

Lowering Shadow to the beach, Alex wrapped her arms around her from the cold as she rushed to catch up with Jess and Cassie. She caught up as they stopped with their heads rising just above the level of the dunes and I soon joined at their side, Jess handing over the rifle.

I looked at the gun in the dark, trying to make out how it differed to the one I'd used before, but it was too dark to tell.

"Anything?" I asked, leaning into the group and looking out across the thin grass rising up on a bank.

"No," someone whispered in the background of the lapping waves, but I couldn't tell who and I followed as they each moved to the left, rising up the dune and heading towards a coastal wall where Shadow rushed off, sniffing the sand.

Halting by the wall, I stamped my feet against the cold, but stopped as Jess turned around.

"I'm going ahead," she said, her voice low. "It's your best chance."

"Bad idea," I said, leaning in. We gathered up and Cassie spoke.

"But what if she can free the children without getting you into danger?"

"Exactly," Jess replied, looking to Alex.

"No," Alex and I said almost at the same time.

"We go together," I added.

Without a chance of discussion, Alex moved off at pace and we followed in a cautious line behind. Rising up the beach whilst keeping the sea wall to our left, I peered along a well-lit static caravan park coming into view to our right.

Passed the deserted park, I focused on a spaced-out line of figures, stopping as the others did.

"They're a long way off," I said.

"But if we can see them..." Cassie added.

I nodded, edging closer to the wall.

We waited, each of us gazing at the distant line. As the minutes passed by, I was sure I saw long rifles held out, reminding me to have hope because we hadn't already been picked off by snipers or charged by a hoard of the undead when we rushed up the beach.

Perhaps the chaos had been contained in the South West and the rest of the country could be saved?

Chancing a move, and with great care, I walked along our line, stopping where Alex still peered out to the horizon.

I glanced across at the dark foliage clinging to the wall as it snaked out in front, then realised someone was missing.

"Where's Jess?"

# 81

## JESSICA

Slipping away along the path as they stared out at the line of soldiers, I knew going it alone was the right thing to do. What Toni had given me was a curse, but with it came the ability to help them and to stop the others from getting hurt. I'd be foolish, selfish, not to take advantage, despite their unwillingness to consider the options. What could they do? They were only human.

Surprising myself at my new perspective, I didn't let it delay my progress when out of their sight I rushed along the foliage with the blocky fort soon coming into view.

The plan was simple enough. I'd make myself known, let them take me. I would be safe; they didn't stand a chance against me. I could break any bonds they'd care to tie and they'd take me straight to her. I'd play nice until I was ready to finish this once and for all.

I'd do it for myself. I'd do it for my crew, for Jordain, but most of all I'd do it for everyone they'd hurt in the future.

# 82

## LOGAN

Turning back, I looked in the opposite direction for any sign of Jess, but with a rustle of the bushes just ahead, we each turned to the sound coming at a low level. For a moment I thought it would be Jess crawling out on her hands and knees, but instead, Shadow emerged, walking past us and heading along the line we'd been following.

"Shit," Alex exclaimed and I pushed my arm out, grabbing at her jacket as she made to run along the bushes after her.

"Didn't you see her go?" I asked in a hurried whisper.

"Jess," Alex called out, but the sound was so quiet against the lapping of the waves the other side of the wall.

Spinning around, I followed Cassie's look toward the distant line of soldiers, seeking any reaction. When we saw their dogged march along the road, Alex moved off and this time I didn't try to hold her back.

Following behind, we hugged the foliage and Cassie sped past me. I glanced to the soldiers in the distance. With my eyes widening, I concentrated on the view, hoping our speed wouldn't point us out, but they were out of sight, disappearing somewhere between us and the long row of static caravans.

Our speed picked up and ahead came the orange glow of streetlights. We slowed, forming up behind Alex as she stopped.

Leaning tight to the hedge, I realised Shadow was at my side and I stroked down his back, staring past Alex down the hill to the edge of the fort we'd seen at a distance from the boat.

Resembling a brick box designed by someone used to

building utilitarian prisons, it looked nothing like the castle or medieval construction the name conjured. With small, arched windows stacked on top of each other, it sat right to the edge of the water, surrounded by a deserted concrete platform.

Cassie called our attention with a click from her lips. I followed her outstretched hand and she pointed to the right, up the rising hill and a collection of construction vehicles; JCBs and tippers parked amongst cargo containers with a mobile crane folded up at the edge of a fenced-off compound.

"That must be the construction site Thompson mentioned," I said.

A muffled intake of air made me look back down to the fort and I saw movement, Jess, strolling to a door in the middle of the wall.

Alex stifled her call with her hand, watching the door open and a rifle point out.

I expected chaos to ensue, a bloodbath, but to the shouted commands, Jess turned her back to the door and let a soldier drag her through the opening.

"She's given up."

The words fell from my mouth and I turned to Alex, getting ready to grab her.

## 83

"We're screwed," I said, letting the words slip with too much volume.

"No," Alex replied, standing tall whilst backing up closer to the hedge line.

"She's sold us out." It was Cassie's flat voice which came next.

"No. Jess will have a plan. She's not just going to walk in there and give herself up after all this time," Alex said, peering around the hedge and clasping her hands under her chin.

I took a moment to calm my breath. Despite appearances, I also struggled to believe Jess could hand herself over, but I'd known her only a few days less than Cassie. "What good can she do locked inside? That's where they wanted her in the first place," I said, moving to stand beside Alex.

Shaking her head, her eyes narrowed as she spoke with the moon lighting her face. "You've seen what she's capable of. Do you think they can hold her back?"

I had, and Alex was right; unless they had some very big guns, there was no chance of standing in her way. "I hope she destroys that place from the inside."

"Ellie," Cassie said with a gasp as she rapidly blinked.

I opened my arms in hope she'd let me comfort her, but Cassie walked past me, taking a wide step out of my path as she walked toward the construction compound.

"Cassie, wait," I said, and she stopped, turning my way, glaring with such rage and anger as if about to explode at any moment.

I couldn't help but think it was the moment the monster inside her would reveal itself and prove my worst fear.

But she turned and spoke, her voice soft. "That's where we get in."

Taking a deep breath, I pushed down my selfish thoughts and my need to comfort her and my want to take control so I could make everything okay again. She no longer asked for my opinion, so all I could do was be there and help any way I could.

Running up the grass, bending at the waist to keep low, I followed Cassie, then after a moment I looked over my shoulder, relieved to see Alex had followed. As I turned back, I couldn't help the feeling that I'd seen something in the distance, right where we'd walked from.

I stopped, Alex running past me, asking if I was okay as I concentrated on the darkness.

"Fine," I said and turned, having dismissed the movement as only in my imagination.

Shadow ran alongside Cassie and we rose up the hill, soon out of the glow of the caravan park and despite still glancing in the direction of the long road, I couldn't see the soldiers who'd been heading towards this place.

Hearing a metallic rattle and cringing at its volume, I turned the way we headed to the temporary fencing around the construction compound. Tall lamps climbed into the air from generators at their base, but they lay silent, producing no power to glow through the lights at the top and leaving us only with the eerie white illumination from the moon.

Cassie slipped the chain wrapped around the gates, sliding them open.

Shrugging off why there was no lock, I pushed away the nagging feeling it was too easy to get inside the compound. Taking a step, my foot knocked against something in the mud and I turned down to see the brass bullet casings scattered across the ground.

Rushing past Alex, I joined at Cassie's side just as Shadow came level and I scanned the rifle around the view. In amongst the yellow construction vehicles and shipping containers were grey temporary buildings, which we ignored, instead staring at the raised ring of concrete in the centre of the site surrounded by another fence.

Creeping forward, the ring with a dark centre was as wide as the length of a long van. Slowing our pace, we edged towards the strange structure and what seemed to be the focus of the construction.

With a break in the inner fence line, not barred with a gate, it led to scaffolding, the only object taking up space inside the concrete ring. As we edged closer, I saw scaffolding steps at the side, leading down through the shaft.

Sharing a look with Cassie and Alex, I was surprised when Cassie leaned over the edge before turning back towards us.

"There's light coming from down there," she said, raising an eyebrow.

It seemed obvious enough from Thompson's short words; this was where we needed to go. Cassie must have thought the same, as without pause she hurried on down the steps and I followed her lead, as did Alex behind.

Taking hold of the cold metal uprights, I stopped to lean over the edge and peer at the soft glowing light above two arched openings opposite each other, around ten storeys down the shaft.

We lingered for a moment, still taking in the view, but when Shadow pushed past my legs, we followed his way down, turning around level after level. I glanced up as we descended, but saw no one peering over the edge.

Shadow arrived at the lowest level first. With his nose in the air and his tongue lolling out of his mouth, he stood on the fresh concrete floor, not looking to us or waiting for anyone to arrive by his side before he headed through the archway to the left and out of sight.

I called his name in a stage whisper, but he'd gone before the echo died.

Cassie arrived at the concrete soon after with Alex and I at her back.

The archways were formed into the shaft wall, one roughly facing the direction of the fort and the other opposite way. Turning back to the arch to our left, I saw

Cassie heading in Shadow's wake.

"Wait," I called, keeping my voice light and, with surprise, she stopped before entering the tunnel, turning back with her eyes wide and face as pale as the moon as if scared and excited at the same time.

With Alex at my side, I pointed the rifle down each of the doorways.

"Which way?" I whispered.

"This way," Cassie said, pointing the way she'd been about to head. "It takes us closer to the fort, I guess."

It was as good a reason as any and I nodded.

"Why are there no soldiers here?" Alex asked.

I stood tall. She was right. We knew from what Thompson had said that this was at least in part a military complex, or would be when they'd finished building it. We'd seen the soldiers out on patrol, just as Thompson had said. So why hadn't we seen any guarding this place? Could it be this lightly guarded, or were the scattered bullet casings above a sign of what had happened?

Perhaps there were none of them left. Maybe they'd all been bitten. Had they all turned and left their posts?

"We haven't got time to think about that," Cassie said, but from her look and Alex's too, I guessed they'd come to the same conclusion.

The sound of metal hitting against metal echoed from the corridor ahead and before we could question what to do next, Cassie moved off and we followed.

"We need to find Shadow," I whispered at Cassie's back, and looked to Alex nodding at my side as I tried to keep my footsteps light to dampen their echo.

The smell of fresh paint and concrete dust filled the air as the tunnel headed on with building materials and tools lining the rounded walls. Evenly spaced lights glowed from the ceiling and the tunnel soon split with routes going left, right and straight on to the sound of Shadow's claws echoing on the concrete.

At the junction, I looked left and right, despite Cassie

not pausing and heading straight on. With what I thought was the sound of Shadow's claws on the concrete floor, I looked again to the left, now certain I'd seen his tail disappear around a corner.

"Stay with her," I said, looking to Alex for a moment before jogging down the left corridor.

Arriving at the bend where I thought I'd seen Shadow, the corridor continued on after the slow turn, with doorways to the right; none of which had doors, but metal frames and fittings as if they were yet to be installed.

I heard voices, two men in light conversation. I edged forward and looked through the shallow angle to cardboard boxes stacked high. Past the last box, a guy stood in army fatigues and I stepped back as he moved, hoping he hadn't seen me.

With the voices receding as I retraced my steps, I arrived back at the junction and cringed at the sound of footsteps coming from all around, hoping they were from Cassie and Alex and not the patrol returned from the duties.

Instead of following in their footsteps, I took off to the right, the tunnel much the same as the previous.

Reaching the turn at the end, a mirror image of the last, I found, instead of another corridor with rooms off to the side, a white plastic sheet blocked the route.

I slowed at the sound of voices, two women this time, one of which had Jess's unmistakable tone.

Taking care as I stepped closer, I approached the sheet, stopping when I heard her words.

"I can bring Cassie to you."

Despite being stunned by what she'd said, I turned at the sound of steps at my back to see Thompson soaked through and pointing a pistol in my direction.

"Drop your weapon," he said, as water dripped to the floor from his clothes.

# 84

## JESSICA

"Where is she?" I said, but Doctor Lytham just stared back from a few paces across the room. In the bright light of the workman's lamps pointing to the white walls in place of the dark strip lights high in the ceiling, she looked to my wrists bound with the manacles screwed tight to the fresh concrete walls. Turning to my face, she seemed to examine every detail as if looking for differences manifested since we'd last met.

I tried to relax against the tension in the straps, but with my mouth the only part of me not secured with thick leather bounds, I found it hard to fight the rising helplessness despite knowing at any time I could call the hunger from the pit of my stomach and snap the leather like they were made of paper.

I had to bide my time.

I had to wait until she was here and gave the answers I needed.

So I let the doctor linger her examination on my face, peering as I stared back in search of similarities with her daughter. Despite having seen Toni on the roof through the camera, I was desperate to see her with my own eyes.

"Where are the children?" I asked with growing impatience at her examination, but when she continued to stare, squinting as if to take in more detail, I turned my attention to the room.

A great round space with raw unfinished walls, the room was split in two with curtains forming four cubicles along the far wall. All but one at the end had the mint green fabric pulled across, but I guessed each would have the same bed and medical equipment inside. Only the thick leather straps fixed to the bed wouldn't be at home in an emergency department.

Splitting the room in two were tall stainless-steel tables, the type found in commercial kitchens. In addition, two more stood at the left wall with the edges taped with packing foam.

Great beakers and twisting glass tubes stood on the two tables in the centre, along with small microwave-sized machines, their power cords running off to sockets hanging from the ceiling. Two large fume cupboards sat against the near wall with protective packaging across the glass and nothing connected to the stubby end of the ducting rising from the top.

Stacks of tall stools lined the wall as if the place would soon be home for many people, but the speed of infection had caught them by surprise.

Spread out equally along the walls were four doorways, each with a plastic sheet only in part covering the great steel banding around the edges, as if heavy metal doors you'd expect to see on a warship or submarine were waiting to be fitted.

"Is this where the cure came to life?" I asked as I finished looking around the room.

The doctor's stern smile faltered. "What do you know of the cure?" she said, squinting.

I tipped my head to the side as a weary smile rose back to her lips.

"Cassie's alive," I said, forcing myself not to take joy in knowing something the doctor was interested in.

"Who?" she said, and I repeated the name.

Doctor Lytham pulled out a notepad from the white pocket of her coat and flicked through the pages.

"You can have her if you let the children go," I replied, watching the doctor's expression with care.

Her smile rose as she lingered on a page. "Ah, B23A," she said.

"I can bring her to you."

Her eyes rushed wide and she looked to the curtained bays before turning back, her smile absent. "Where is she?"

My reply dried up to the sound of scuffling feet and the

figure pushing through the plastic sheet.

# 85

## LOGAN

"How the hell...?" I said, stumbling forward with a jab of the rifle's muzzle as I fell through the plastic sheet. "She saved your life."

"Yes. And that's why they need to make more of her," Thompson replied in a low voice.

Clear of the plastic confines, I was about to ask Thompson how the hell he'd managed to survive and if he'd listened to anything we'd said on the boat, but on seeing the round room and the figure strapped to the wall in the heavy leather straps, I was stunned into inaction.

Only as I gawked at the eyes of the figure held could I tell it was Jess. A great knot bunched in my stomach at how she'd been taken so easily and that our journey had come to such an abrupt end.

The thought dropped as I spotted the other figure in the room. With her grey hair flowing down her white coat, I realised it was Doctor Lytham standing just in front of Jess before she turned so casually to me. The spiralling glass tubes and lab equipment arranged on the centre table took me back to the view from the hospital's glass cell and the desperation I felt when I stood alone, sick with worry at what was happening to the people I loved.

I could only watch, helpless as the doctor raised her brow and looked past me as if I wasn't there, then double taking at the state of the person behind me.

"What took you so long, Major Thompson?"

I heard the start of his reply but she cut him off, the flourish of her hand dismissing whatever he would say.

About to turn and check if Thompson's betrayal was real, a rustle of the plastic on the other side of the room turned my attention to the woman who'd given Cassie the drink. Wearing no make-up this time, the yellowing bruises were easy to make out, even in the eerie light.

Her open-mouthed excitement turned to a bunched-cheek smile, and I knew she must have been Toni. Jess tried to hide any show of emotion, but I saw the reaction in her eyes and the twitch of her mouth, despite her obvious effort.

As they stared at each other, I noticed for the first time the second set of restraints on the wall next to Jess, the space vacant with steel clasps open and the leather hanging limp down the wall. A rustle of the plastic sheeting to my left turned me away.

Alex stumbled through the sheet much like I had, grasping for air as she fell forward. For a moment I thought it was Gibson risen from the dead and following stone-faced, but instead, another soldier stepped through.

My legs went weak and it was all I could do to hold my weight as hope drained away.

Alex wouldn't meet my gaze as I stared on open-mouthed.

Footsteps echoed from the doorway behind them and for a moment I expected to see Cassie falling through the doorway with a soaked Sherlock stepping out.

"Jess," Alex called, the sound so pained as she stared at Jess strung to the wall. The soldier grabbed at her arm to stop her rushing forward. She didn't fight his grip, instead peering around the room, pausing at the sight of Thompson, then meeting my eyes. Her eyebrows raised and I couldn't help but shrug, regretting the weakness of my expression.

At the soldier's back, the plastic sheet fell from the door and settled to the floor.

Despite not being able to move her head, Jess stared to Alex and then to me.

I felt as if her thoughts mirrored mine. All of our effort and struggle to stay alive; all the people, the friends we'd lost for it to come to this ending.

We'd done exactly what they wanted all along.

I wished I could punish myself for my stupidity. It wasn't enough just to curse at how I could have been so naïve. How else could this have gone down?

Movement echoed from the corridor at the soldier's back and I expected Cassie to emerge, forced forward, but two soldiers, dressed as the others, came through the doorway carrying the same type of rifle as their colleagues.

With black helmets and black bandanas covering their mouths, all I saw were their eyes set in a squint as they looked around the room before the lead guy spoke.

"One unaccounted for," he said in a deep voice.

"Cassie," Doctor Lytham said, looking at first to Jess; when she didn't respond, she turned past me to Thompson, nodding at his silent reply. She turned to Toni who had followed her. "We administered B23A and Jessica here tells me it was successful. You did it, well done."

I watched as Toni's breath caught and her face filled with delight and she twisted away from the older woman to Jess.

"We've done it," Toni said, then moved back around, unsure who to look at. She settled in my direction then turned away, back to the older woman. "We found it."

The older woman nodded. "Yes," she said, but her voice and expression lacked any emotion.

"You know what that means?" Toni said.

"Of course," Doctor Lytham replied.

"We have the cure," Toni said, her voice rising. "The last piece of the system."

That was the moment I realised the implication of her words.

The cure. They had cured Cassie. She wouldn't turn into what Jess had become, and I felt a great weight lift from my shoulders, sending an urge for me to scream for Cassie to run, to get away and go live her life. A normal life.

But I knew she wouldn't. She wouldn't go anywhere until she found the children. Until she found Ellie and could take her to safety.

"So that's it. We're saved," I shouted. "You've saved humanity."

Toni and Doctor Lytham span around to face me, lingering for a fraction of a second before they burst into laughter.

# 86

A sharp pain at my shoulder forced me forward and I stumbled, dropping to my knees. Looking up, both the doctors had already turned away and their laughter halted. Toni stepped towards Jess and I watched, rubbing my shoulder to ease the ache.

Jess tried to flinch away from Toni's touch and Doctor Lytham took a step forward, grabbing at Toni's shoulder to hold her back.

"You came," Toni said, still leaning out to Jess despite her mother's pull.

"And you survived," Jess replied, her voice deadpan.

"It was touch and go," Doctor Lytham said with venom as she let go of Toni's shoulder.

"It can't have been that bad. You were up the next day," Jess said.

"Luck," Doctor Lytham replied. "If your aim was better, she'd be dead."

"If my aim was any good, you'd be dead," Jess said, for the first time taking her gaze from Toni.

Toni's posture inflated, and she looked back to Jess with her head tilted to the side. "You didn't mean to shoot me?" Toni asked, her voice rising.

"No," Jess replied. "Despite what you've done."

Silence hung in the air and I tried to clear my mind and figure out why they laughed at my words, whilst listening to the stilted conversation.

"It worked," Toni said.

Then I saw Jess look back to Doctor Lytham and with the slight rise in the corner of her mouth, I got it. Everything became clear and I realised I'd been so blind to what was going on around me.

She'd called the cure the last piece of the system.

Jess spoke, pulling me away from the thought. "If you meant to turn me into a cold-blooded killer with superhuman strength and a thirst for human flesh, then yes it worked."

"But you have control?" Toni asked, looking back to Thompson for a second time.

I went to turn, but I held still with the jab of the muzzle in my back.

The rise in the corner of Toni's mouth confirmed she'd got the answer she wanted.

"Yes. I've turned into your soldier. I can control it at will," Jess replied, still with a vicious edge to her voice.

Doctor Lytham turned my way, to Thompson at least, and I chanced a twist and saw him nod as if corroborating her story. I twisted back, hoping he hadn't noticed.

"I just need you to show me how I can live without doing those terrible things," Jess added, and the room's attention came her way.

"Cassie," I said, barely able to make the word come out.

"We still have some things to work out, but with what you've just told us about B23A, I think we have what we need to finish the work," Toni said, her words calm and soft as if she was explaining what she'd be cooking for breakfast. She glanced to the curtains pulled across the bays.

"Like not needing to feed on human flesh?" Jess asked, and her expression hardened, but when Toni slowly nodded, I saw a tear falling down Jess's cheek to glint in the orange light.

Jess nodded. "If that's the way it needs to be, then you've got me and you can let the children go."

Toni looked to Doctor Lytham and the old woman replied with a shake of her head.

"Where are they?" Jess asked, looking at the curtains on the other side of the room.

"That doesn't matter," Doctor Lytham replied. "What matters for you is if that woman is cured, then we've got what you need. She is what will stop you from needing to do those things." She looked to Toni, but Toni turned away.

"Well done, Major, for thinking on your feet. Now where is B23A?"

Doctor Lytham stared at Jess, then to Alex and my way when no one replied.

"Do you want to stop the hunger? Where is Cassie?"

Jess blinked just as Shadow's bark echoed from the outside of the room, resounding as if it came from each of the entrances at the same time.

Doctor Lytham raised a brow as if remembering the one kindness I'd seen her show. A loud gunshot ripped through the air, but Alex and I were the only ones to flinch.

Realising the sound wasn't loud enough to have come from inside the room, I listened, eager to hear Shadow's call again. Only silence replied.

"Quick now," Doctor Lytham said, and Toni hurried to the nearest table, pulling up a paper towel resting on the side to reveal a syringe in a kidney bowl. She picked it up, but the doctor called out.

"Antonia," she said, nodding back to the table.

Toni glanced her way and then to Jess. Placing the bowl back to the stainless-steel table, she pulled up a surgical mask before wrapping its mint-green material around her mouth and hooking the elastic over each ear.

Jess did her best to shake her head, and I thought about doing something rather than just standing by useless. Feeling the pressure of the muzzle in my back, it was as if Thompson guessed my thoughts. Still, I considered rushing forward.

I didn't move; instead, I watched as Toni stepped up to Jess who barely flinched when Toni pushed the needle into her forearm to draw blood. My gaze fixed to the bright red liquid, marvelling at how normal it looked.

"Cassie," Doctor Lytham called. "You can come out now," she said in a sing-song call.

For a disconcerting moment I thought Cassie would come through the doorway with a smile as if she'd been involved all along. But she didn't.

"Cassie," the doctor's call snapped again.

Like Alex said on the boat, they couldn't have soldiers rampaging on the enemy and not be able to turn them off when they'd completed their objectives. They had to have a cure for their hunger for the concept to work.

"You need her, don't you," I shouted. "You need her to complete your plan. You need her to make this work."

I looked to Jess, then twisted away, turning instead to Alex. "Cassie is the cure. Cassie is the way they can fix the problem of the hunger." I watched as Alex's brows raised, then she turned to Jess as if longing for it to be true. "When they have her, that's it. They've finished and there's nothing that will stop them."

"And no reason to keep us alive," Alex added, shaking her head as she looked up at Jess.

I couldn't look at her bound to the wall; instead, I called out. "Run, Cassie. Stay away. You're the answer to their problems." I didn't get any more words out before pain flashed across the back of my head to the sound of gasps from around the room as I fell to my knees.

"Keep him quiet," I heard Doctor Lytham say as the darkness at the edge of my vision faded.

Pushing through the pain, I struggled up from the floor with Thompson gripping my arm.

"Well, if she won't come voluntarily..." Toni said, and I watched through the crack of my eyelids as she nodded to Doctor Lytham.

Doctor Lytham smiled, raising a brow. "This is it, Antonia. This is the culmination of all our work."

Without pause, Toni nodded to the two other soldiers. They shouldered their rifles before heading to the door where Toni had entered, whilst she stepped across the room to the first bay and pulled the curtains wide.

The three pale children lay under thin sheets. They were bound to the beds and weren't moving. If they were breathing then it was shallow at best. Each of them looked nothing like they had when we last saw them; Ellie so old. Tish so young, so small in the bed. Memories surged of Jack, old before his time, and the moment I met Shadow, waking to find him licking my face and the two children were just there.

I tried to push away thoughts of how I'd almost shot Ellie when we'd first met.

Beside them were monitors. For a fleeting moment I questioned why I couldn't see their heart traces, panicking they much be dead, but then I saw the cables and tubes wrapped in bundles hanging down. A thin metal IV stand stood at each of their sides and a bag of clear liquid hung upside down with a tube flowing to each of children's arms, giving me the first sign they weren't dead.

Toni strode to Ellie, pulling back the cover to grab at her wrist. Cassie's sister didn't react when Toni held her arm high, not even when she let it fall back to the bed. Toni reached to a cardboard box by the side and unfolded a square of absorbent pad before placing it under Ellie's forearm.

I turned to movement from where the soldiers had left and I saw the dark back of a soldier with his outstretched hand hidden from view. My mind raced over what he could hold out in front, but the question soon dropped at the terrible stench I hadn't smelt since we'd left the mainland.

# 87

## JESSICA

With a stilted pace, the soldier stepped sideways into the room with a catchpole, like those used to control feral dogs, held out in both his hands. The noose gripped tight around the neck of a girl, but with her face dark and bruised, her skin slack with decay; it had been a long while since anyone could call her human.

Pulling through the doorway, her mouth snapped closed and open as it stared, locking its gaze to the soldier. I half expected it to grapple with the pole, until I saw the straight jacket with the semi-circle of dried blood at the front, binding its arms at its sides.

A second noose dug into its neck and I followed the second pole heading through the door, gripped by the other soldier gritting his teeth as they held the tension between them to guide its travel into the room.

The soldier walking backwards chanced a glance to his side and the bed where Ellie lay unconscious.

"No," Logan and Alex called out.

This was it. This was the moment; I couldn't let this go on any longer.

"Stop," Logan shouted.

Thompson swung his rifle down on Logan's back again and he went quiet before collapsing to the floor. With Alex's furious shouts echoing across the room, I stared at Toni, whose gaze fixed on the teenager between the soldiers. The hunger rose as I watched, holding my breath.

With her head tilted slightly up, Toni looked on, squinting with interest at what was about to happen. I looked to Doctor Lytham to see her wearing the same detached intrigue and the energy surged from inside me.

Holding my breath, I tensed against the bounds and the room grew silent. Out of the corner of my vision, Logan rose to all fours and looked my way as if he knew what I'd planned all along.

This was it; this was the moment. I felt so alive. So full of energy, the power coursing through my veins as I fixed on the flesh at Doctor Lytham's neck and I pulled my muscles tight, straining with everything I had.

But it wasn't enough.

# 88

# LOGAN

I watched her effort fade, leaving her panting with the leather holding her tight. Toni turned, catching my eye as she followed my look to Jess where she lingered for a moment. When Jess puffed out a second breath, tears flowed down her face and I knew it was all over. The last hope lost.

Turning back to Ellie, I could barely watch as the soldiers guided the dead creature to the bed. Bile rose and I gritting my teeth.

"No," Alex screamed, but her cry cut off with the thump of something heavy.

Rising to my feet and finding enough energy, I twisted around, holding my breath for the pain. I surged up and took Thompson by surprise as I caught his eye with my balled fist. He barely moved, instead raising the rifle, teeth bared and glaring back, but he didn't pull the trigger.

We'd lost and clutching my pounding fist, I closed my eyes, opening them again when I felt another presence in the room. Cassie stood at the doorway behind Alex with her arms held out to the bed, her mouth hanging wide but silent as she looked towards Ellie.

Renewed with rage, I brought my arm back and punched out towards Thompson, but the rifle butt swept across my face, sending me spiralling to the floor, my vision blackening as I slumped to the side of a metal cabinet.

"Stay the fuck down," he shouted, sending spit my way.

As my view cleared, I looked up to see Thompson turning his rifle away and looking back across to where Cassie stood.

From my low position I could still see across to the beds, but trying to rise, my legs were like jelly.

"Ellie," Cassie called, her voice high and pained and I knew she must have been held back or she would be across the room fighting with all that she had.

Ellie flinched, but her eyes remain closed.

I called out her name when I saw the pain bunch in her face with the soldiers angling the creature's head to her exposed forearm, its teeth grinding into her young flesh.

The room fell silent but for the effort of the soldiers pulling the creature from Ellie's arm to leave a ragged mess with blood flowing to the absorbent sheet underneath. Tears streamed down my face to mix with the blood and sweat already coursing. Others sobbed around the room but I dared not stand again.

Time seemed to slow and I felt numb, unable to make out the words spoken, barely flinching when a gunshot burst out and the girl creature slumped to the floor. I wasn't insulated from the smell, which seemed so much worse as they dragged the body down the corridor.

On my knees, all I could do was shake my head, overcome with grief as I watched, waiting for the doctors to rush over and bandage Ellie's wound. But neither moved. Instead, Toni turned her attention to Jess whilst Doctor Lytham bent to a cupboard built into the table, pulling up an aerosol and spraying plumes of white mist in a circle as her face contorted at the stench.

"Help her," Cassie's angry call came out, but dull as if my ears were stuffed with cotton wool.

Still on my hands and knees, I made to stand and rising a little I watched as Cassie fought against her hands held at her back by another soldier. As she struggled, she stared to the bed where Ellie lay with her blood spilling to the floor.

Doctor Lytham raised her hand at Cassie.

Cassie stopped moving, her face contorted with rage.

"Ah, Cassie. That's not how you save her," Doctor Lytham said in a voice like they were talking over dinner. "Thank you for joining us."

"You're an animal," Cassie shouted with her face

contorted. Then her expression changed as she forced herself to relax. "Help her, please. Help her," she called out, looking to the doctor as if she was the only person in the room. "Fucking help her."

I tensed to move, but felt the slap of the rifle across my shoulders and I collapsed to the floor again.

Doctor Lytham smiled as if Cassie had asked her to check a mole. "There is a way to save her," she said. "You hold the key. Your blood can help her. Do you understand?"

Rising up from my hands, my vision blurred when Cassie looked to me, her eyes darting between myself and Doctor Lytham.

"Cured?" she seemed to say but with no volume.

The soldiers strode back through the door, holding their rifles again. Cassie turned to the doctor and nodded.

Doctor Lytham smiled and Toni moved around to a cupboard, pulling bandages before working on wrapping Ellie's arm.

To the snap of zip-ties, I watched through blurred vision as Cassie wept, but didn't put up a fight when the soldiers pushed her further into the room with her hands behind her back.

After hurriedly wrapping the bandages tight against Ellie's arm, Toni rushed past the metal table in the centre, grabbing another syringe as she passed. Pulling a rubber tourniquet from her lab coat pocket, she moved around Cassie's back and wrapped the rubber around her arm. I watched Cassie wince through gritted teeth as the needle plunged, her gaze fixed on Ellie.

With beaming wide eyes, Toni came from around Cassie's back, heading to the second table and opening up a round machine which looked like a pressure cooker. She removed the lid and decanted half the blood from the syringe, splitting it between two glass vials. Pulling up a second syringe and the blood from Jess, she did the same, writing their initials on each of the glasses. I watched, transfixed as she took one of each of the vials and put them inside the machine before pressing a button on the side.

The machine whirred, and I felt a slight vibration through the floor. The timer pinged after a brief moment and she pulled both glass vials out. The blood had separated to a yellow and red liquid sharing the vial equally. Toni drew out the yellow from the top of each, before pouring the remaining deep red contents into another which was already half full and changing the settings on the machine and replacing the vials. The rumble it made was a little different to the last.

With another ping and rather than take the vial out, she grabbed a new syringe, drawing up the deep red.

"No," I called again, but my voice came out so feeble. "No," I shouted. "They're not making a cure, they're mixing the two together. Save Ellie, you fucking bastards."

Doctor Lytham looked over her shoulder at Ellie, but waved her hand in the air.

I rose again, fighting against the pains across my head and back.

As Toni headed to Jess with the syringe pointed out, I looked to Alex, then Cassie, my heart melting at her despair. I turned away to Jess who barely reacted as the needle jabbed into her arm and Toni pushed down the plunger.

"No," Cassie called as she tried to pull her arms out from the binds and grip of the soldier standing unmoved by the situation. "Save Ellie. You said you would."

Jess closed her eyes, screwing up as if in pain, then shook, her body convulsing against the bounds as Toni pulled the syringe from her arm. Twisting around with her brow furrowed, Toni looked towards Doctor Lytham, who raised her eyebrows as if in surprise at the way Jess's body reacted.

"Interesting," Toni called out.

Doctor Lytham nodded as Toni turned away, setting the syringe to the side before looking back again.

With pink foam pouring from her mouth, Jess contorted with her eyes sealed shut, then as if at the flick of a switch, she opened her eyes and stared at the wall across the room.

"Jess?" Toni said, furrowing her brow as we all waited for the answer.

"I told you it wouldn't work." Doctor Lytham's voice was almost sing-song. "We need someone fresh."

Toni's hands dropped from her face and she shook her head. "That is bloody annoying," she said, as if having already moved on from whatever relationship they'd had in the past. Toni's mouth bunched and she glanced back to Jess and for a moment I thought she would stride over and release her from her binds, but she turned away, pointing toward Jack and Tish still laid in bed.

"What about those two?" she asked with renewed interest.

"They have natural immunity," Doctor Lytham said and Toni nodded. Then she turned my way. "Him?"

"She made him take the drink, remember?" Toni replied, then turned to Alex with narrowed eyes. "Her then," she said. "What's your name?"

"Alex," she replied, and I looked to Jess without moving my head when I thought I saw the first sign of movement since she'd been out cold.

Toni raised a smile, showing off her white teeth, beaming at Alex as if she'd spotted her across a bar and wanted to talk. As she walked in Alex's direction, she grabbed the syringe left on the table.

"No," I called out, but I didn't know where to look when this time I was sure Jess moved. Her whole body had tensed against the bounds.

The soldier gripped Alex tight with her arms around her back as Cassie stared on at Ellie, shaking her head with tears rolling down her cheeks. I heard the distant continuous tap of something echoing in the background.

One of the unnamed soldiers strode across the room, overtaking Toni and took an arm from the other at Alex's back to keep her still. Toni pulled up Alex's sleeve to expose her pale flesh as the soldiers let go of Alex from behind to instead grip the top of her exposed arm and around her wrist.

Toni stepped closer, raising the syringe, tapping it with a finger then lowering it needle first. Just as the needle was about to puncture the skin, a darkness flashed across the view.

Shadow bounded high in the air, gripping tight with Toni's hand in his mouth, sending the syringe shattering to the floor and spilling the scarlet liquid. With a great crack of bone as he pulled her to the floor, he shook his head as if her flesh were a toy with a primal look that was anything but playful.

Shouts filled the room and the soldiers rushed from their posts; Thompson left my back and rushed to Toni on the floor, still grappling with Shadow. His rifle swayed with the motion of the dog's head.

I knew this was just the last flurry of rebellion before the pain of defeat came back.

But instead of gunfire, there was a great snap from somewhere in the room and looking up to Jess, she wasn't there. The leather restraints hung loose from their mounts.

A great blur filled my view and I closed my eyes, hoping to clear the effect of so many blows. In the hurry of noise that followed, I heard the rush of boots resounding from the corridors all around us.

Opening my eyes, I looked to Jess in the centre of the room with blood dripping from her mouth and Toni at her feet, her neck ripped out. Thompson and the other soldiers were down too, slumped to the floor, their blood leaking to the concrete.

I followed her blood-soaked stare to behind where Alex stood with her mouth agape and to Sherlock, soaking wet like Thompson had been, poised with his rifle out in front and more soldiers at his back.

Turning around, I stared at the death and destruction in the room; Doctor Lytham lying face down and Shadow with a red dripping mouth, standing over a pool of blood with one front paw raised off the floor. I waited for when Jess would pounce and destroy the rest of us.

When nothing happened, I looked back to the corridor

as Sherlock nodded, letting the rifle drop and raising his hand to the air.

"Stand down," he said, and looked to me as the soldiers behind him lowered their aims. "I'm sorry, Logan. I have to hope you're right. I have three kids and a wife."

"We tried to kill you," I said, regretting the words as if he might change his mind.

"You got balls and you clearly believe what you're saying," he replied.

Before I could say anything else, Alex jumped up, rushing towards Jess.

"No," I called, but she took no notice. "Stay away from her," I said. "She's changed. What they gave her, she's not Jess anymore," I shouted, but as she closed the gap, Jess relaxed her bloodied glare, her clawed hands flattening and her arms opening to take the hug as her eyes closed.

Cassie bounded to Ellie, despite her hands being tied to her back, slipping and sliding in the blood in her path.

I rushed over, grabbing a knife from the table and freed her from the plastic ties, then took the syringe of her blood from the side and handed it to her open hands.

## 89

Standing on the roof of the fort, I peered out across the horizon as the sun peeked over the rolling land. With Jess along the way, cleaned and changed into army fatigues, the only clothes available, she told all to the camera Alex pointed her way whilst I contemplated the look on Sherlock's face as he arrived in the room.

It was obvious from his attitude right from the start; he'd rallied against the idea of bringing Jess to the doctors, despite his orders. Unlike the others, who I now knew had been acting on the journey from Exeter, when we explained the doctor's plan it should have been clear he was the one who could help us to stop them.

I still couldn't get over how they'd swum ashore, a feat of strength like I'd never witnessed in anyone still living.

In such a short space of time he'd rallied the remaining soldiers to our idea, along with their detachment doctor to take care of the injured. Only Ellie, Jack and Tish needed their help; the others were past saving after Jess had finished in those few moments.

I'd left the round room, leaving the doctor to tend to Ellie with Cassie watching as they injected her with what we all hoped would be the cure. Once I was told Jack and Tish were okay, I didn't want to be a spare part as Cassie leaned to the bed and held Ellie's hand tight.

Staring off into the distance, the crowd filling my view answered my question of hope as I only half listened to Jess's well-pronounced words while she told the truth to the nation so they might prepare for what would come their way, if it wasn't too late already.

With footsteps climbing the steps, I turned to a fresh light brightening Cassie's face as she raised her brow in my direction. Shadow followed behind with his tongue hanging out, panting.

Taking slow steps, she walked toward me and I couldn't

tell by her expression if she would hit me or deliver terrible news about Ellie. Perhaps she'd push me over the edge to the concrete below for giving the children to that awful woman. Could I let her have the moment and dish out the punishment she saw fit?

As she drew closer, her mouth turned to a smile, and she opened her arms, beckoning me into a hug. Despite the confusion, I took the step and ignored the ache across my body as I gripped her tight with my arms around her back.

After a long moment she relaxed her embrace so I could breathe again.

"Ellie?" I said, and felt her nod as she spoke.

"She's doing well, so far at least."

"So you're the cure?" I said, but she didn't reply; instead, I heard her sniff as she spoke.

"I thought I would turn. Every time I felt my emotions rise, I thought I'd burst open and lose control, taking you with me. That's why.... That's why..."

"You've been so withdrawn," I said, finishing the sentence she couldn't. As I struggled to stop the rise of my emotion, she spoke again.

"I thought I would turn and so I stayed back. I was ready to leave when I felt any urges. Like Jess."

She pulled me in tight again.

"I'm so sorry," I said. "It's all my fault. I don't know how you can stand to be near me."

Cassie let go, pulling back and looking me in the eye. "What do you mean?"

"I brought the kids to her. It was my decision."

She shook her head. "No," she said. "I was in that room, too. She'd given us hope. We didn't know what she could have meant to do. I urged you on, but it's not either of our faults."

She grabbed me again and pulled me in close. Then when I could no longer hear Jess speaking to the camera, we separated, turning across the roof to see Alex and Jess holding hands and walking towards us.

Drawing closer, Alex spoke.

"Is this the end?" she asked, looking to me, then Cassie before turning back to Jess.

I twisted around, gazing across the grass to the horizon. I didn't speak, instead lingering on the massing crowd in army fatigues who were jumping high into the air, the others stumbling our way as a waft of that foul stench blew across from their direction. Our future was inevitable.

"Of sorts," I said. "But not in the way we would want."

Jess spoke. "It is for me. Logan, you were right. What Toni put in my arm changed me and although it gave me the strength to break free, I can't... I won't live as one of her experiments for the rest of my life."

Turning back to face the three of them, I expected to see Alex complain and fight for her to see the life she could have. Instead, I watched tears roll down her cheeks, and she nodded in my direction.

"But I can give you each a chance," Jess said, pulling Alex in close before taking Cassie in an embrace.

Patting Shadow on the head, Jess opened her arms and as I drew near she spoke again. "Thank you all."

"What for?" I asked as she let go.

"For making me feel human again," she said, walking to the edge of the roof and peering down to the ground below.

"No," I shouted, not hiding my alarm as I realised she would jump to stop herself from attacking us if she lost control.

Before I could reach out, she stepped over the edge and disappeared. I closed my eyes, pushing my hands to my face at the thump of flesh hitting the concrete.

Despite knowing what we would see, pulling my hands from my face, I stepped with the others to peer over the edge. Rather than seeing a crumpled heap of flesh, Jess stood looking up with a solemn smile.

"Get to the boat," she called up, then didn't linger before turning away and rushing to a blur toward the massing crowds heading our way.

"I can't believe she'd do that for us," Cassie said. "It's suicide."

I shook my head, and Alex did the same as I spoke.

"Don't be so sure. Now let's get the kids and run."


The End.

For now, at least...

# Liked what you read?

Please leave a review on Amazon and **Goodreads.com**. Honest reviews are difficult to come by and are so important to indie authors like me.

For new of new releases, special offers and free content from time to time, visit:

# gjstevens.com

Printed in Great Britain
by Amazon